FIEND

FIEND

A NOVEL

PETER STENSON

CROWN PUBLISHERS

NEW YORK

Copyright © 2013 by Peter Stenson

Published in the United States by Crown Publishers, an imprint of the Crown Publishing Group, a division of Random House, Inc., New York.

www.crownpublishing.com

CROWN and the Crown colophon are registered trademarks of Random House, Inc.

Library of Congress Cataloging-in-Publication Data

Stenson, Peter.
Fiend : a novel / Peter Stenson. — 1st ed.
p. cm.
1. Methamphetamine abuse—Fiction.   2. End of the world—Fiction.
3. Zombies—Fiction.   I. Title.
PS3619.T4764777F54 2013
813'.6—dc23   2012025546

ISBN 978-0-7704-3631-5

eISBN 978-0-7704-3632-2

Printed in the United States of America

Book design by Maria Elias

Jacket design by Christopher Brand

1   3   5   7   9   10   8   6   4   2

First Edition

To anybody who has helped me with anything

FIEND

MONDAY

So Typewriter John and I have spent the last hour lying to each other, faking concern, panic, and desperation, all the while helping the other look for the last hit. The thing is, we each know the other is holding on to an eraser-sized shard. It's like a standoff, both of us wanting to be left the fuck alone for five minutes. Finally Typewriter caves, says he's going to take a shit, which I know isn't true because we haven't eaten in close to three days.

I pull out the tiny bit of glass. Burn it. And it's barely two hits and I'm spun bad, like from our weeklong bender, but this one really does it, because when I peek through the G.I. Joe

1

sheets we've draped over the windows, I see a little girl playing with a dog. I'm thinking this is kind of sweet—this blond child crouching on all fours, inching closer to the dog, like maybe she's playing a game of make-believe where she's a dog too. But then I notice the dog is shaking. And it's a big dog, a rottweiler, and he's shaking, his head down, his tail covering his nuts.

What the fuck?

I'm about to return back to our cave of a world because the sun is ungodly bright, but I see the dog take a snap at the little girl. She dodges him just in time. I think about pounding on the glass. I need to warn this kid. I need to do *something*.

But I don't.

I stand there. The little girl creeps back to the dog, and once she gets close enough to touch it, she does, only her touch isn't a pat but a lunge for the rottweiler's throat. It reminds me of this time I saw an elderly woman crossing the street, she almost made it across when a black Hummer turned right and came straight at her not slowing, and the old woman looked up in time to see her fate as an extravagant flaunting of male testosterone, and she crumpled, lost underneath tons of metal.

The little blond girl rips open the dog's throat.

I rub my eyes.

Blood spouting like Old Faithful. Her white dress now tie-dyed, swatches of brilliant red on cotton.

I close the G.I. Joe sheets. I sit down.

I'm telling myself that it's gone too far this time, this latest run, smoking half an ounce of scante, that I need to chill the fuck out, like KK said. I tell myself that this is it. That I will leave this house on the outskirts of St. Paul, go find something to eat, take a handful of Advil PMs, and call it a day. Call it a career in smoking speed. Never have I experienced such vivid hallucinations. Sure, tracers and voices and shit like that, but not seeing carnage on this scale. I laugh to myself. I try to analyze my hallucination—the little girl represents innocence, and it's probably significant that she's blond, because KK's blond, and that ties into innocence, because we were close to that, her and I, at least in the beginning. And the dog, maybe that's man's best friend, maybe it's the natural world, maybe primal nature. And the subversion of the natural order, the child killing the dog, that's pretty simple— innocence wins out.

EVERY fucking epiphany and realization and coded message all tell me the same thing: I need to get clean.

I'm rubbing my hair. It's greasy like a motherfucker. I smell my breath. It's like abortions. Then I look around Typewriter's house and it's disgusting, that eerie shade of manufactured darkness, the sun doing its damnedest against the strung-up sheets to tell us the world is still going about its boring-ass business. I'm on the one couch left over from his mother, the only thing he hasn't pawned. I hate my life. I think about Typewriter smoking shit in the bathroom. Maybe he has more than a shard? I stand up because I could really go for one last hit, a nightcap.

Something tells me to take one more peek outside. I'm

nearly positive the blond apparition will be gone, a fire hydrant standing in her place. I peek. She's still there and her dress isn't a Jackson Pollock anymore, just red. So's her hair.

Typewriter, I yell.

Innocence has her face buried in the dog's stomach. She pulls at the intestines like saltwater taffy.

Type, I yell again.

Shitting, bro, he calls back.

I'm practically chewing on my overworked heart when the girl turns. She stares right at me, her face nothing but canine blood, a piece of matted fur dangling from her jaw.

Need you right fucking now, I say.

I close my eyes, rub them, breathe, just breathe—one one thousand, two one thousand—and when I look back out, the little girl's standing, dripping guts, still staring at me.

Shit, man, I yell at the bathroom door, I found half an eight ball.

This gets his attention. I hear him rushing through the house. He comes jogging into the TV room (minus the TV, sold six months before). I stare at his fat Italian face, his eyebrows a launch ramp over his nose. He says, Fucking A, bro, let's get it.

I've smoked enough meth in my life to know the power of suggestion among the tweaked is realer than AIDS, so I don't tell him about what may or may not be going on outside. I pull the curtain back.

Bro, the dope, let's see it.

I step to the side. I motion with my head.

Typewriter John stares at me, his chubby body all sorts of impatient.

I nod again at the window.

He looks outside. He screams. He drops to the floor. He's saying *fuck, fuck, fuck*. I take one final peek, and Innocence is standing two feet from the window, bloody like the First World War, and before I can scream and close the drapes, I take one solid look, like really study her. Pieces of her flesh peel off her face like thin slices of gyro meat.

I'm on the floor.

Typewriter continues his refrain of *fuck*s and I still am not one hundred percent sure of the situation so I say, What did you see?

What the fuck?

Type, I need to know what—

Blood. Girl. Monster.

He's crying. I wonder why I'm not. I tell him to follow me, that we need to get the fuck away from the window. I lead on my stomach. We make our way to the staircase, my heart is sixteenth notes, I'm still telling myself it's a lack of sleep and bowl upon bowl of meth, and I look over my shoulder past the whimpering snot that is Typewriter to the window, and I can see a three-foot silhouette through the thin bedsheet. Then I hear a crash, and the sheet moves, and this isn't fucking happening.

Go, go, go, I yell.

He's on his feet and running up the stairs and I watch the blond girl climb through the window and sit on the sofa like nothing happened, maybe she's just returning from eating a handful of potato chips off the coffee table. I can see bone underneath the peeling flesh. It's whiter than I would have guessed.

Chase, Chase.

I turn to see Typewriter at the top of the stairs and then look back to the girl sitting there like a used tampon. She smiles at me, starts to giggle. I sprint upstairs.

We get into Typewriter's room and lock the door. He bends over a stack of spread vaginas in glossy pages, and I want to be like, What the fuck are you doing, but he starts to vomit. I tell him we're fine. That the dope must have been bad. That it was nothing.

We hear footsteps, slow and methodical.

I say that we need some benzos or opiates or barbiturates, something to come the fuck down.

He's expelling bile with the force of a capped volcano.

And I say that these things happen, audio and visual hallucinations, that the shit from the Albino was always strongest, and we've been at it hard, and we're probably dehydrated, and starving, yeah, starving. The footsteps seem to be getting closer, and I'm staring at the chrome door handle, and I'm telling Type that we just need to think about something else, anything else, something happy. Okay, Type, think about something happy, peaceful, and shit. And it's more vomit from him and I'm shaking and the door handle starts to jiggle and I'm like, Happy thoughts, man. Then for some reason I remember one of KK and my first dates two years before, how we'd gone to see *Spider-Man 2*, how we'd waited for the

16 bus, neither of us having cars because we'd fucked up our lives smoking shit, but we were getting better, together, living in sober houses and going to meetings, and how she was the first girl I'd ever thought of in terms other than a means to an orgasm, how we'd just sat there, throwing rocks from the faux garden in front of KFC at a metal trash can, how that was the only thing I wanted to be doing at that very moment.

The little girl starts pounding on the door. I know it won't take long. The door's not actual wood, this being a prefabricated suburban house and all. The next tiny fist splinters the frame. I wish we were the kind of drug addicts from movies, the kind with guns. I keep telling myself I'm spun. Her one hand becomes two. And it's me and KK sitting along Ford Parkway, waiting for the 16, debating the merits of *Spider-Man* vs. *Spider-Man 2*, our pinkies touching, grazing.

The middle of the door cracks open and I'm screaming at this hallucination, screaming because I'm going to be dead at twenty-five, dead without having accomplished one fucking thing in my life, having burnt every fucking bridge worth having, my primary relationship now being with a junkie called Typewriter, and I think how everyone who'd ever said they loved me had told me this would be my fate—drugs would eventually kill me.

The door's off its hinges and this little girl is smiling at us with blood and flesh and dog fur. All I can do is close my eyes and listen to her labored breathing and giggles, her cute fucking giggles. Then I hear the bedsprings to my right. I look over. Typewriter jumps off the bed with something raised above his head and by the time I realize it's his actual fucking typewriter, by the time I scream *no*, it's too late. He's brought it down onto the little girl's head. She falls limp on the floor. I'm covered in bits of skull.

Typewriter looks at me. He says, I did it.

No, fuck, no, Jesus.

I did it, he says again.

Fuck me, Jesus, what the fuck?

Typewriter spits, then rubs his tongue like he's trying to snag a pubic hair.

I'm picturing the headlines—JUNKIES BRUTALLY MURDER PRETEEN IN DRUG-INDUCED PARANOIA. I'm picturing the press and TruTV and *True Crime* reenactments and then an MSNBC *Lockup* special edition and then prison and getting my young ass blown the fuck apart and this is the last image because this will be my life.

I did it, he says again.

I look at the little girl. She's wearing black shoes with tiny silver clasps. Her socks have printed umbrellas and raindrops on them.

Think, think, think.

I'll flip. I'll tell the authorities it was Typewriter. He was the one who killed the little girl. They'll make me some sort of deal for my cooperation. And I can give them the Albino, the biggest cook in Minnesota. Yeah. They'll put me in witness protection and move me to Spokane or somewhere, someplace I can get a job pouring foundations or flipping burgers, and it'll be okay.

I take a step back from the girl. Type kicks the actual

typewriter off the kid's face. There's nothing left. It's my turn
to vomit.

I think about all the things I've touched in the house, my
DNA or whatever on every surface. I think about no jury believing me. I think about terms I've heard on TV, *conspir-
acy* and *accomplice*. There's no way I'll get a fucking deal.
They'll want to make a case out of both of us. They'll use this
murder to champion their antimeth campaign, and instead
of the commercials of kids with picked faces it'll be a black
and white of this little girl, maybe one from her third-grade
class, then a picture of the crime scene, then my mug shot. I'm
fucked. I'm going to die in prison.

What do we do now? Typewriter asks.

You fucking killed her, I say.

Yeah, somebody had to.

I grab his T-shirt around the armpits. I shove him hard
against the wall. She was a little girl, I yell.

No.

Look.

She was going to kill us.

A hallucination. A fucking hallucination.

Typewriter looks at the mess on the floor. He's shaking
his head and I push him again and then his shaking changes
direction. He crumples onto his bed. He says, But the door?

Part of the trip.

We're silent. What is there really to say? *Shit, my bad?* I
think about calling the cops, maybe the volunteering of information might look good. I pull out my phone.

What are you doing? Typewriter asks.

I don't know, I say.

No, no, stop.

I stop. My phone's dead anyway.

We can take care of this. Like, we can fix this, he says.

We can't.

Yes, bro, like we'll clean it up . . . and . . . and . . . like leave town, you know, like Mexico. We'll go to Mexico. Live on the beach. Fake names and shit.

I quit listening. I'm remembering terms like *temporary insanity* and *unfit for trial.*

Typewriter keeps telling me there's no fucking way he's going back to prison.

I need to think. To clear my head. To not be high. The room is starting to smell like my father's halitosis. All I see is blood. And her socks. I'm picturing the little girl's mother coming into her room, maybe suggesting a different pair because it's so sunny, the little girl sticking out her tongue, telling her no, these are my favorite. By now the mother is probably wondering where her daughter is. Maybe it's time for lunch? Maybe she's out on the driveway, in front of a two-car garage, her hand shielding the sun, calling her name, her tone playful at first, now becoming frantic.

I smell booze. Typewriter is pouring a liter of vodka onto his sheets.

What the fuck are you—I start to say. I realize what he's doing before I finish. I want to tell him no, this is a horrible idea. The cops aren't fucking stupid and they'll catch us and this is only going to make things worse. But then I think that it doesn't matter if we tell them or not, we'll be guilty as Arabs at airports. The rest of my life will be spent getting one in the stink, one in the mouth, on a rotating basis.

And part of me knows this is one of those moments after which nothing will ever be the same. Like out-of-body or whatever-the-fuck. Like when you can see yourself crystal fucking clear. When you know one choice will result in hooded sweatshirts and downcast eyes and running from every set of flashing cherries and how your habit will take on astronomical fury because it needs to kill out the memory of who you were. The other choice will mean being turned into a monster, having every person in America hate you, think you're evil, and death by anal fissure in prison.

I've had this feeling once before—the watching-yourself-fuck-up-your-life moment. It was with KK. We'd decided enough was enough with powerlessness and unmanageability and prayers to a god we knew didn't exist. We bought a teener. We somehow waited until we got back to our apartment. We sat on our bed. Her pale legs looked blotchy against our blue down comforter, one we'd bought together at Target. We told each other it would only be this once. We said it was a special occasion. We said we'd only smoke it. We said I love you, smoke slipping from our lips.

You have a lighter? Typewriter asks.

I watch myself reach into the pocket of my jeans. I watch myself hand over the red Bic and then study the flames along the soiled sheets, amazed at how quickly they grow.

I wonder if this—the murder, the burning of the house— isn't just a continuation of my relapse with KK.

The posters of DJs catch on fire. Then the mattress. Smoke rises. Typewriter motions for the door, or where it used to be. We jog down the stairs, and then into the basement. I climb in his ancient Civic. He opens the garage door. The sun is absolutely fucking blinding and we pull out into a neighborhood that doesn't know we exist. I'm looking for the girl's mom and praying I don't see her. I glance back at the house. The faintest plumes of smoke slip out from the upstairs window. As we're driving away, something in the front yard catches my eye. I press my face against the window. It's the carcass of a rottweiler.

10:15 AM

We drive down Summit Avenue. The houses are nice and then they're not. I tell Typewriter to go five under the whole way. He tells me there aren't any cars anyway. I haven't noticed. But then I do. I look around Summit. It's just Victorian mansions with rows of evergreens like please stay the fuck away, cars parked in driveways, empty streets.

I'm so spun.

I look at the dashboard clock. It's a quarter past ten. Maybe everyone's already at work? We're down Summit Hill and onto West Seventh. This is my stomping ground. Has been for a year. Strip malls with laundromats and apartments above Chinese takeouts and narrow barrooms filled with smoke and televisions, none of them flat screens. I know what this area's supposed to look like. Busy with people standing at bus stops and girls standing on corners and brothers spitting balloons of dope out of their mouths. But it's not. It's empty.

I ask Typewriter if it's a holiday or something. He doesn't know. I check my shirt to see if it's still covered in blood. It is. I flick off a nugget of skull. It sticks to the dash. Nothing makes sense. I keep telling myself I've spent the last hundred and sixty-eight hours smoking meth, that I'm beyond delusional, beyond sane, one more awake hour away from completely breaking the fuck down.

We turn onto Marshall. I see my boy Tibbs walking down Seventh. This makes me feel better. Like things are normal, okay. Type says, Bet Tibbs is holding, could hook it up with a teener for the road.

Not trying to flee yet, I say.

Huh?

Get to my apartment. Got a few Klonopin. I need to sleep, man, like my head is bad.

Feel you, Typewriter says.

We pull over at my sublet. I get out. Stretch. I wonder where the hell everyone is. Nobody's waiting for the bus, nobody's driving or honking, there's no foot traffic over at the Groveland Tap. Typewriter scans the streets too. He looks at me. I shrug.

We go around back of the split-level and it's nothing but red chipped paint and cracked sidewalks but Rebecca gave me the tiny-ass apartment for three fifty a month, so whatever. I open the door. The house splits inside the tiny foyer, one door to the two upstairs units, one door to my dungeon of an efficiency basement. The mildew stench from the walls is at an all-time bad. I think about complaining to Rebecca but decide against it, having smoked July's rent.

It's a strange feeling inside my apartment—part relief, part dread—and I wonder if that's what everyone feels coming home. Like, yeah, I see the one piece of furniture I own, my mattress covered in unwashed navy blue sheets, and I'm like, motherfucker, I missed you. But I see nothing but dust bunnies on the scratched wooden floors—and I'm like, motherfucker, this is it. This is my life.

What's up with those benzos? Typewriter asks.

I walk to the bathroom next to the efficiency kitchen. It doesn't have a door. I open the tiny medicine cabinet. A toothbrush that has gone unused for weeks sits next to an Advil bottle. I pour out its contents—four beautiful Klonopin. I think about swallowing them all, the four of them spreading through me like the warmest of quilts on a January night. I run the faucet. I want to sleep and forget what happened with the umbrella-socked demon. I glance up. Something is staring back at me. I nearly scream. It's me. My eyes are the deepest of oceanic trenches.

Give it here, Type says.

I hand him two pills and swallow mine.

I think about how much time I spend trying to find a balance between artificial moods, the equilibrium of acceleration and deceleration.

I plug my cell phone into the charger. Typewriter lies on my bed.

Get the fuck out, I say.

Bro, where am I—

Not on my bed.

But there's no other furniture.

Sorry, not all of us have a house from our mom.

Typewriter looks at me like I've spit in his mouth. I feel like a dick. I say, Listen, man, I'm sorry. We need to sleep and figure out what the fuck happened, you know, like what's real, what isn't.

He starts to get off the mattress. I tell him it's fine, just don't try any faggy shit. He calls me a faggot. I tell him that was a good comeback. I lie there and my heart still thunders and I'm willing the soluble shell of the Klonopin to break open and spill its contents into my bloodstream, for my eyes to become heavy. Typewriter curls at the foot of the bed like a wary dog. This reminds me of the rottweiler. The little girl. The giggles. The little fist coming through the door. The typewriter. The flames. I picture the police there, the fire department too, Typewriter's childhood house alive in its death, flames reaching toward the telephone poles, the electric wires connecting everything. I should call KK. Tell her I might be going away for a while. How long until they come looking for Typewriter here? I strain my ears to hear Rebecca's TV through the floorboards. I can't hear anything. This is odd. That fat bitch has that thing blaring at all hours of the day. I yawn, and this makes me smile. They're working, the Klonopin. I know that when I wake up, I'll be terrified, either because of what we've done, or because of what drugs are turning me into.

7:51 PM

I wake up, not ready to. Typewriter slaps at my feet.

What?

It was real, he says.

Huh?

He points to his shirt. It's still covered in blood. I look down at myself and see the same thing and I'm thinking, fuck my ass, what did we do? I rip off my T-shirt and throw it on the floor. I look at my pants. Smears of the little girl stain the denim.

Bro, Type says.

We need to get out of the bloody clothes. Burn 'em or some shit, I say.

He understands then, stripping down.

There's a pile of clothes in the corner, all dirty. I pull out a white T-shirt and a pair of green sweatpants and toss them to Typewriter. I dress in jeans and a navy blue shirt, musty with cooled sweat.

Then I'm packing what little I have in a trash bag. I stuff in some clothes, my phone charger, a jacket. I'm thinking about passports, about money, about Mexico or Canada, my parents, KK, about not using the one credit card I still have because they can track those things, about maybe ditching Typewriter because one person disappearing is easier than two. I pack my toothbrush, my unopened mail. Typewriter stands at the one excuse for a window, looking up through the basement metal grate. I feel a slight craving, just a hit to get my head straight. I wonder if Typewriter still has a shard. I ask. He doesn't respond.

Yes or no?

He shakes his head.

What the fuck does that mean?

Still nothing and I want to bash his head in because he can be such an idiot. So helpless. So desperate. Playing the whole poor-fucking-me-my-mom-died-of-cancer junkie thing. And he's shady as hell. Always stealing people's scraps, shorting bags. And here he is, facing murder, staring out my piss slit of a window like he can't get enough of the sunset.

You gonna help? I ask.

Something's not right.

I laugh. You kidding me right now?

Look, he says.

I decide right then and there to leave him. I'll be better off without his constant bitching, his tendency to destroy everything he touches.

Help me pack up the bloody clothes.

Chase, look.

I'll humor him until we get out of the city, until we stop for gas. I'll leave him while he's paying.

I walk over to the window and look up to the street level. There's nothing. I ask him what he's talking about. He points. I say, Yeah, so?

Nothing, he says.

That's a good thing.

Not one person. Nobody. When's the last time you saw Seventh empty?

We don't have time for this, I say.

Serious. When? Never, bro.

I look back out. I half expect to see the little girl with umbrella socks and flakes of missing face. He's right. There's nobody walking around and I want to tell him that it's probably because people are at work or maybe the Twins are playing, but even as I formulate these objections, I'm countering them—nobody works banker hours on West Seventh, not one pregnant teen is waiting at the bus stop, I can't hear the motor of a single car—and I realize that something *is* wrong.

I tell Type to go check it out.

Not going out there.

Then pack this shit up while I do it.

He tells me no. He picks at the constant scab on the left side of his jaw. He whispers something. All I catch is *apocalypse*.

Just stay here, okay? Pack up those bloody clothes so we can get the fuck gone.

Chase.

Do it.

He nods. I walk outside. At this point, I'm still hoping it's the drugs, maybe the Albino's latest batch was cut with a PCP derivative, that we're spun. I stand on the sidewalk and see not one person on the street. The Groveland Tap is empty. No cars. I walk around to the front of Seventh. I'm starting to shiver because it's like that dream when you're walking alone and you finally realize it—your solitary venture through this life—and skyscrapers are covered in vines and the road is buckled open like a whore's gap and it's just you and your stupid footsteps, the sound of your rubber soles dragging on aged asphalt.

I'm thinking about a conversation with KK, back when we were sober, in love with second chances and each other's naked flesh. She'd asked, if I was offered the gift of immortality, would I take it? I'd kissed her German triangle of a nose, said something cheesy about *only with you*. She'd said, No, that's not what I mean. Everyone you know will be dead but you. Would you do it? I'd thought about it, KK straddling me, my dick starting to harden, my lips brushing against her self-proclaimed biggest embarrassment, her nose, wondering if my breath was foul. I'd said, Yeah, I would.

I stand there, feeling my sanity stretch to its limits, thinking about KK fucking that scumbag Jared, that stupid fucking prick.

I take another look toward downtown St. Paul. Lights are on in the modest skyscrapers. I hear birds. The sun shines but just a little. There's a slight wind coming from the Mississippi. Are Tibbs, Type, and myself the only people to survive Armageddon? I laugh. I realize it makes more sense that I'm really sitting on Typewriter's couch, the glass pipe in my lap, my heart having finally quit.

I walk back to the apartment. Typewriter's still standing by the window. I tell him I'm going to go see if fat Rebecca can tell me what's going on. He says he'll come too and I want to tell him that isn't smart, but he's practically crying so I say, Let's go.

At the top of the landing I knock on her door. I wet my lips and try to do something with my hair. No answer. I knock again.

Everyone's gone, Typewriter says behind me.

She never leaves. Even gets her groceries delivered, I say.

I press my ear to the door, expecting to hear the shuffling of slippers.

Fuckin' stinks, Typewriter says.

The mildew in the walls, I say.

I knock one more time. Then I test the handle. It turns. I open the door a foot and call her. I step in and the smell is horrific, like rotting pot roast. I pull my shirt over my mouth and nose. Her apartment looks just like always—a couch and recliner centered on a TV, the kitchen full of take-out Chinese boxes, everything dirty as fuck.

We should go, Typewriter says.

I walk into the main room and feel the TV. It's cold. She has that thing running twenty-four–seven. I push Power. The screen fills with static that bathes the evening room with white light.

Something crashes in the bedroom.

I stiffen. Typewriter runs for the door and I flash on what the little girl did to the dog and think about whatever is in the next room doing that to me. I see a streak of black. A cat freezes in the doorway, staring at us. It runs back to the bedroom. I follow. I'm cautious, I know whatever I see will be bad, and Typewriter is behind me, which I'm glad about.

The bedroom door is open a slit.

I nod to Typewriter. He nods back. I push open the door.

All three hundred pounds of Rebecca is splayed out on her bed. Her slew of cats look over at me, their mouths covered in blood and flesh.

Jesus Christ, I say. I turn back to the hallway.

What? Typewriter says. He looks inside. He says, Fucking shit, man, they're eating her. The cats are fucking eating her.

I want to cry. To throw up. To go back to Typewriter's house and have my only concern be trying to find a minute alone to smoke a dime piece.

Let's get gone, Typewriter says.

I follow him to the door. One of the cats stares at us like we'd just interrupted something sacred. It keeps licking its bloodied whiskers. I'm beginning to grasp the reality of our situation and I just need some sort of confirmation. I need somebody to tell me this is real. That everyone I've ever known has died or disappeared somehow. That we did, in fact, crush the skull of some possessed child. That it was okay because we had no choice.

I knock on the door to Svetlana's, the Russian tenant.

Bro, let's get ghost, Type says.

She's got Internet. Just need to see what the fuck is going on.

She's gonna be dead.

The door is locked. I kick the shit out of it. The wood splinters on the first kick. We go in. It's the same smell and we both pull our shirts over our faces and I walk over to her computer. An old Soviet flag hangs on the wall. I sit on a ratty brown couch, right next to about seven dildos, a bottle of lube, and a butt plug thicker than a baseball bat.

Typewriter gives a chuckle. He says, Bitch be loving dick, huh?

Did those webcam shows, I say.

He's holding the black butt plug. He gives it a tentative sniff. I think about telling him to grow up. He's smiling though. I sit and get the computer going. The shit takes forever to get warmed up.

You ever hit it? Typewriter asks.

I shake my head.

Bullshit, some Russian debutante sitting up here all day fiddling her pussy, and you never hit it?

Windows loads. I don't tell Typewriter I can't remember the last time I'd been sober enough to get a hard dick. I click on Internet Explorer. He's on to the dildos now, holding them up to one another, maybe mentally comparing where he would stack up in the equation.

Finally, the Internet is up and I'm at her home page, 18to play.com, and I see my face streaming on the screen. I really do look like hell, nothing but scruff and scabs and eyes sunken like the *Titanic*.

You streaming? Typewriter asks.

Yeah, guess so.

I move the cursor to click to a news site.

Hold on, he says. He sits next to me, giving me a shove. His face streams online. He's the only fat meth addict ever. His cheeks take up the whole screen.

He says, Is anybody out there? Anyone? Is there any single motherfucker left alive in this world?

Stop, I say.

Type keeps going, overenunciating like he's talking to a retarded kid, We are in St. Paul, Minnesota. There is nobody left. Maybe some little girl but she was—

Fucking stop, I yell. I push him out of the way. You stupid?

Typewriter balls a fist. Part of me hopes he swings, hopes this can be the logical end to our relationship. He relaxes his hand. He says, There's got to be somebody out—

A chime comes from the computer. I look at the screen.

BIGHRYBALLS: wtf u do w Russiandoll69?

Another chime.

BIGHRYBALLS: she ok?

Typewriter yells, Hello, hello?

BIGHRYBALLS: don't tell me she's gone.

I say, Can you hear me?

BIGHRYBALLS: did she turn?

Can't hear you, write something, Type says.
I peck on the keyboard. It chimes.

RUSSIANDOLL69: Who is this?

BIGHRYBALLS: is she walking?

Typewriter says, What is this guy talking about?

RUSSIANDOLL69: What is happening?

BIGHRYBALLS: you kill her—y or n?

I'm hoping this guy is fucking with me. Maybe he's some narc trying to uncover the murder of that little girl. At least this is what I'm telling myself. Like it's so much better to be wanted for murder than for . . . shit, I don't know, whatever the fuck the alternative is.

RUSSIANDOLL69: Of course didn't kill anyone.

BIGHRYBALLS: she didn't reanimate?

Ask him where everyone is, Typewriter says.

RUSSIANDOLL69: Please tell me what is happening. Where is everybody?

BIGHRYBALLS: dead

My stomach drops out of my ass with this chime. Typewriter is saying he fucking knew it. I'm thinking about the little girl and about this guy's comments about *walking* and

I tell myself that it's only in movies and comics where people can come back and eat flesh. I'm thinking about every show I've ever seen, every film, about arms outstretched, moans, and decaying flesh, and ghouls and living dead.

I'm muttering *no, no.*

BIGHRYBALLS: u kill her?

RUSSIANDOLL69: I said no.

BIGHRYBALLS: why not?

I hear something resembling a two-pack-a-day fit of laughter. I scream. Standing maybe ten feet away is a naked Svetlana. Her blond hair is matted to the side of her face, which is half dark, like her blood has pooled there and there alone. She just keeps laughing. Typewriter and I run to a corner of the room. He's holding on to a giant black dildo like a sword.

She takes a step forward.

The computer chimes and chimes and chimes.

She rolls her head and we hear a cracking of vertebrae and she's smiling, laughing, walking toward us. I've envisioned my death countless ways, none of them at the hands of some walking dead Russian whore. She's getting closer. I need to do something. I'm looking for weapons. Typewriter throws the dildo. It bounces off her chest. This really gets her going. This is my chance; she's distracted, thinking how that rubber dong would do anything but annoy her. I reach for the coffee table and shove it with everything I've got. It bumps into her knees, sending her back a few steps. Then in one motion, she kicks it to shit, shattering the glass across the floor. A jagged piece shaped like a slice of pizza clatters at my feet. I grab it.

Fucking run, Typewriter says.

I try to grab him before he sprints for the door. It's too late and he's running and she turns and claws at his back and there's blood and I'm not thinking, just acting, *reacting*. She's got one hand on his shoulder and she's clawing and scratching and he's flailing and crying, begging for God to save him, for his mother, and I'm behind Svetlana, and I don't know the first fucking thing about arteries or jugulars but that doesn't matter. I stab the shit out of her neck. She seems to go limp for a second. I do it again. Thick, oil-like fluid oozes out of her. Then she's on the ground and I'm screaming and still stabbing. I feel something break and I think it's the glass but no, it's still in one piece in my sliced hand. I look down. The end of her spine juts out from the top of her neck. Her severed head rolls in a semicircle.

The computer keeps chiming.

Her naked body gives soft jerks. I think of KK falling asleep, how her path to sleep was violent.

I'm holding on to Typewriter's arm and we're running down the stairs. We're outside and the sun is about to set behind the small river valley of St. Paul and we're not alone anymore—the streets have started to fill with what looks like the usual haggard motherfuckers of tame midwestern ghettos—and we get in Typewriter's Civic and they are coming toward us, these people, these walking dead motherfuckers, all of them probably having reanimated and broken down their doors, and we're driving away from them all.

I tell Typewriter to give me what he's holding.

He starts with some shit about not knowing what I'm talking about. I pound the dash. I say, Give me your shit.

He reaches into his pocket.

It's a decent-sized thirty rock.

I pull the pipe from my pocket. I put the whole piece in the bowl. My hands shake. They're stained black from Svetlana's blood or maybe that's mine and the lighter won't catch. I just want a hit, that's all I want, like everything—survival and death and being one of the few still alive—doesn't matter, not really, the stem shaking in my mouth, my breath held. Finally the flame stays. I drag. It's the smell of burning plastic and chemicals, of being sixteen and wanting to be rad like the kids I skated with, of wanting to fit in behind the dumpster at Burger King, of fear, of not knowing what I was smoking, of my lungs rebelling against poison, and then the release, clear smoke expelled with a sigh like pissing in a pool.

My head becomes lighter, my shoulders released from the vise grip of being me sober.

It's okay then, everything.

9:29 PM

Sometimes when I smoke shit, I reach the perfect balance of motivation and concentration. This is one of those times. I create a list as we drive north. A list of things we need to do, and of things we know or think we know. I'm writing on the back of an El Sombrero single-slice box.

1. We have killed two ~~people~~ things today (self-defense).
2. These things are zombielike.
3. Zombies don't exist.
4. There are at least two other people (perv on 18toplay, and Tibbs) who aren't dead.

I stop making the list and pull out my cell phone for the first time. Why the fuck haven't I tried to call anyone? I hit speed dial one, KK. It goes straight to voice mail. I think about her being Svetlana, naked and skinny and laughing a demonic laugh. I picture her as Rebecca, alone and dead, being eaten by greedy cats. Then I picture her as me, trying to make sense out of everything, terrified. I call again. I tell the machine I love her, it will be okay, to call and let me know she's alive.

Then I call my parents. It's been at least a year since I've talked to them. The phone rings and I'm picturing them sitting around the kitchen table, my dad with his graying hair, his readers resting on the bridge of his nose, holding my mother's hand, maybe brushing her dehydrated-piss-yellow hair away from her eyes. They're sitting there worrying, waiting for the call that tells them their son is dead.

It goes to voice mail.

Guns and shit, Typewriter says.

Huh?

Supplies. Weapons. The list. Cabela's is 'bout twenty miles away.

I write:

5. Weapons. Food and water.

And dope, Type says.
You fucking serious?
As hepatitis, he says.

6. Meth

I look over the list. My fleeting sense of accomplishment fades. The list is retarded. It gets me no closer to understanding what's happening. I light a cigarette. Typewriter asks for one. He tells me to put cigarettes on the list.

Fuck the list, I say.

I look out the window and it's dark now, like really dark, an hour and a half north of the Twin Cities, nothing but an abandoned two-lane highway. Where is everyone? Like, if things really were the way they seemed—people were either dead or walking dead—then where was the panic? Movies showed that shit all the time. Some dude getting bit in a shit box of a country, then flying back to the US, chewing up his family, and from there the plague shit spreading with the speed of herpes on an Ivy League squash team. But people panic on TV. They break into stores. They board up houses. They run out of gas. And here we are, driving eighty, not a single car in the way. I mention this to Typewriter.

He looks over, a Newport dangling from his swollen lips. He says, How the fuck do they know?

Who?

Hollywood and shit.

What do—

Like there's rules to the fucking apocalypse? Bro, this shit here, whatever is going on, you can bet your ass it's never happened before. Not in some movie. Not in a book. It's some dinosaur shit, you know?

I tell him I have no idea what he's talking about.

Extinction, man. The end. Finished. Us. Humans. Thanks for playing. Better luck next—

Yeah, got it, I say.

Typewriter starts to chuckle—like real live chuckles, like he's playing a part in a B movie. I think about those scratches on his back, if something could be transmitted that way. I think about him turning, his face even paler, him ready to tear my throat like the little girl did the rottweiler. I don't write it down, but I put it at the top of the list in my head: Typewriter might become one of *them*.

He finally quits with the staged laugh. He says, Just kind of weird that we're the motherfuckers chosen to last.

We're quiet after that and I'm chewing on his word *chosen*. I've already peaked and am coming down and we're out of shit and I can't stand the silence, so I turn on the radio. Static. Typewriter pushes in a CD. It's techno. I hate the shit, like it's so stereotypical that baseheads listen to trance, but at least it's a distraction. I call KK. My parents. Nothing. I picture them all dead. I know my parents would be lying in bed together, both of them in *Christmas Carol* flannel nightgowns. I wonder if Jared is next to KK.

Typewriter pulls off Interstate 35E. Cabela's, a giant Lego-shaped hunting and fishing store, sits in the middle of a sea of asphalt. I can't see any cars in the parking lot. Typewriter turns down the music. The energy in the car shifts, and neither of us says anything. This world shouldn't fucking exist.

We park right in front of the entrance. Through the glass windows we see the store is pitch black. Typewriter takes the keys out of the ignition but I stop him. I say, Maybe we should leave them in the car.

Why?

Then he understands. He says, I'm not trying to get left in—

Neither am I.

We get out. We're nothing but swiveling heads, spooked by every gust of wind. I try the door. Locked. I give the plate glass a kick. It hurts like shit. Typewriter slams into it with his shoulder. He yells, Fuck.

Shut up, I say.

We look around for what could have heard us. Somewhere an owl cries and I think this is about the worst omen the world could possibly give us. Typewriter kicks the door again. The glass won't budge. This makes sense, a store housing guns having fortified security. I keep kicking. I feel useless, my efforts, my inability to break into a fucking store.

And it's with this refrain of failure that my idea to smash the car through the door is born. I tell Typewriter.

Not smart, he says.

We need the guns, I say.

And the car.

How else are we going to break—

Not with the *one* car we have.

I tell him I'm not talking about the *whole* car. Just enough to crack the glass. That it will be a little damage to the front bumper. That's it, I say, I promise.

He shakes his head.

I get into the car and back it up, maybe fifty feet from the entrance. Fifteen miles per hour is all I need. I give it some gas. I'm closing in on the entrance and it's a brilliant idea and I hit the curb and bounce and then I'm at the door and there's a solid thud. My head hits the wheel. My ears ring. I look up. The glass is smashed, the door cracked. Perfect.

I get out and the ringing's even louder and Typewriter's yelling something I can't make out and I realize the ringing isn't inside of my ears, it's a siren. I've set off an alarm system. Red lights flash inside the store.

Type's practically shouting into my mouth. He points to my head. I wipe my forehead and feel it's wet with blood but I tell him I'm fine. I point to the doors and we climb over the hood and into the store. I don't know what the fuck alerts the walking dead to their victims—light or sound or smell—but I know that flashing strobes and piercing alarms can't be helping us. The cut on my forehead fills back up. I wonder if it's maybe the smell of blood that attracts these motherfuckers.

In and out, I shout.

Typewriter nods.

The scene alternates between sheer darkness and flashes of emergency red—a rack of raincoats, sleeping bags, camping stoves—pulsing every second, maybe quicker, and I'm just waiting to see decapitated Svetlana naked and ready to tear into my jugular.

We're making our way to the back-left corner and I barely notice that my hand is holding on to Typewriter's T-shirt and we're inching forward during our milliseconds of red, still and flexed during our breaths of blackness.

The strobes remind me of my short time being a club kid, all about watered-down Minnesota raves, abandoned warehouses along the Mississippi, grams of ecstasy, techno, filthy red couches, and reach-arounds from random girls/maybe guys—basically my nineteenth year on this earth. I'm remembering one night in particular, Halloween, me dressed as a slut in fishnets with a run up my inner thigh, having smoked more scante than I'd ever done before. I'd stumbled through that warehouse, knowing I was going to die. I could feel it at the base of my throat, death. I knew that my only chance at redemption was fresh air. The strobe lights and my heart pounding and my dick practically hanging out of my mini-skirt costume and everyone I saw some gross perversion of people who had once said they loved me.

The sirens are so fucking loud.

Both then and now.

I'm swallowing spittle thicker than come.

That night, inch by inch, I'd made my way to a steel door, the flashing Exit sign like pure love. I'd pushed with all of my might. It wouldn't budge. I crumpled there in my miniskirt and pumps. My left stuffed tit had fallen out. I cried because this was the end and I was dressed like a slut and I felt better than I'd ever felt before.

Typewriter says, Right there, the guns.

I can barely make out the glass cases of guns. I'm hoping for machine guns and grenades like Call of Duty and I just want the siren to stop and the lights to pick a side, red or black, and I'm still holding Typewriter's fat arm like a life preserver. He hands me a canoe paddle. I ask if he sees something. He doesn't respond. I'm about to cry because this isn't my life and there has got to be something so bad coming our way and I tell myself in and out, then back to the car, back to the deserted highway, but then where?

Typewriter smashes the case full of handguns. He shouts for me to do the same with the shotguns. I run behind the counter. The first display holds shotguns, that much I know, mostly because the barrels are fatter than the butt plug from Svetlana's arsenal. I swing the oar into the glass and it shatters, bits raining down on my hair. I reach in and grab the first shotgun, some *Terminator 2* short-barrel number. It's heavy like a motherfucker, but I love it, the weight. It's the first gun I've ever held. I scan the store, giving it a pump. I'm almost hoping for some walking dead piece of shit to charge me.

Something lands at my feet and I scream like hell, jumping toward the wall. It's a giant green duffle bag. Typewriter already has one full of the pistols. He walks to the other case, presumably full of rifles.

I take the shotguns out one by one. I wonder why we could possibly need this many guns. I've loaded ten into the bag, with six or seven still to go. A bag of pistols. Another bag of rifles. Like what are we expecting? Then I think about us being the only ones left. Just us—Typewriter and his B cups, me and my forehead tic—driving around, breaking into stores, killing fictional characters. How long can this really go on? A week? A month? A year? And then I'm thinking about that Halloween again. About wondering how long the shit I'd smoked would last. About how long it would be until the rave was over and I could get out of my whore getup, how long until everything got back to normal. How fucking badly I'd wanted things to go back to normal. It's funny, you go through your whole life thinking everything sucks, that if only you had this, said that, then things would be better. But when shit happens, like real shit, say smoking enough scante to kill a village or choosing drugs over KK or the world dying and reanimating, it's only then that you pray for the rewind, when you realize your life had been just fucking peachy before.

I have no idea about ammo. I just take boxes of everything. My duffle bag is ungodly heavy and I struggle to put it over my shoulder. Typewriter waddles over, a bag in each hand. He yells something about camping gear. I tell him we need to get out of here. I hear *sleeping bags* and *tents*. I say, Right fucking now.

We get back to the car and throw the duffles in the back. The parking lot is still vacant. Typewriter takes the wheel and throws the gearshift into reverse. I'm breathing a little steadier now, not quite believing that we accomplished what we set out to. The back tires go over the curb, then the front. I think I hear a hiss. It feels like my side is sagging. I keep quiet because I'm not going to change a tire in the middle of all this noise.

Fucking flat, Type says.

Just go, I say.

s driving. I look out of my window, half expecting
shooting out.

No spare, anyway, Typewriter says.

You serious?

You know that.

Shit, I say. I think about the space in the bottom of the
trunk where a spare normally sits, the space we fill with the
ounces of shit we get from the Albino and transport back to
the city. But part of me is glad that at least we won't be fucking
around changing the tire. I ask how long we'll be able to ride
on it. He shrugs. I ask again. He says, Just pretend the shit isn't
happening. I like this line of reasoning. It's been my motto before I even knew what a motto was. None of this is happening.

We drive thirty-five on the highway.

I ask where we're going.

Again with the shrug. I'm not sure why I even asked, because we both know damn well we're going to see if the Albino is still alive. That's the only reason we've been driving
north. Maybe we didn't *say* anything, but it's one of those
things that is understood.

You think he's still alive? I ask.

Typewriter tells me it doesn't matter.

How not?

A week's gone by since we last paid him a visit.

I smile. He's right. It's Monday, our normal pickup day.
And I think about our ounce of methamphetamines waiting
there like an ice pack for a sore knee. Normally, it's us having
to sell at least enough shit to smoke for free, which is hard as
hell, breaking it down into teeners, Typewriter taking the bars

along West Seventh, me spending a weekend at the clubs over in Minneapolis. And this selling isn't to make money, since neither of us owns a TV, a computer, even a headboard. It's selling twenty-dollar bags, each one a felony possession, our pockets accumulating to felony intent to distribute, in order to support our habits. I laugh. We can't call this shit a *habit* anymore. That stopped years before, back when crystal was for special occasions or to fuck all night.

What's funny? Typewriter asks.

Kind of messed up, I say.

What's up?

Like the world's ending or whatever, and here we are . . .

Tryin' to get our heads straight, Typewriter says.

Yeah.

He pulls his fat lips in on themselves. The fuck we supposed to be doing?

I have no idea. Driving to our cook's house with a flat tire and thirty guns in our backseat is about as logical a reaction to being attacked by a little girl with umbrella socks as anything else.

No, really, he says, I'm asking you, what would anyone else be doing?

I don't answer. Instead I pull out my phone and try KK and my parents again. Nothing.

Probably fine, Typewriter says.

I'm quiet for a second. For some reason, I know my parents are dead. *Know* might be a bit strong, but I just have this feeling, an image, them together, not breathing. I tell Typewriter I doubt it.

Typewriter tells me to keep the faith. I wonder what faith he ever kept. Maybe he's heard somebody say that in a movie. I say, Yeah, I guess.

He reaches over my legs to the glove compartment. I notice the tears in his shirt, the bloody scratches from Svetlana. I need to keep an eye on him, need to get a loaded gun in my possession. Typewriter rifles around in the glove box and I tell him I've got the pipe and it's cashed anyway. He pulls something out, turns on the dome light. It's a photo. He hands it to me. Typewriter as a pudgy grade-schooler. He's standing next to an Italian-looking woman, short and dark, her hand resting on his shoulder. Both he and the woman are smiling.

I don't know what to say or how long I'm supposed to look at the picture. I don't know what the fuck he's showing this to me for. Then I realize he thinks my parents are dead and this is his silent vigil, his burning candle, his feeble attempt at keeping the memory of his mother alive. Miss her, man, Typewriter says.

I hand the picture back. Typewriter studies it. I don't have a picture of my parents. He puts it back in the glove compartment. I find this whole thing uncomfortably touching, this sharing and opening up. I need to get high.

11:21 PM

We pull into a Shell station. I tell Typewriter to keep the car running. He reaches behind the front seat and pulls out two pistols from the duffle bag, then digs around for ammo. He tells me they're Glock nines, like this means something to me. I watch as he loads the clip. I try to do the same to the one he hands me. My fingers work like I have cerebral palsy. Bullets keep slipping out onto the floor. Typewriter tells me to leave them, that dirt can jam up the gun.

Safety, he says. He flips a little switch. Orange means you're live. Two hands. Always.

How the fuck—

Not all of us are little trust-fund junkies.

You're from the fucking suburbs, I say.

He laughs and says, My uncle taught me when I was like fifteen. Shot his pistol at his place in Wisco.

More than I know, I say.

Then it's on to the shotguns. I'm kind of hoping for the short one, for some reason I really want it to be mine. He finds the shells and slips them in one at a time. Maybe Typewriter senses my preference, because he hands me the mini gun. He nods for me to pump it. I do. The *chu-chunk* feels like I'm jerking off God. I still can't believe what is going on—walking dead, death, guns—but the disbelief and the need to figure out my stupid life have morphed into something else, something one notch below on my brain function map. Now it's acceptance and survival and a fucking short-barrel twelve gauge in my hands, a Glock nine in my waistband.

The first thing I notice when we step out of the Civic is the temperature, probably ten degrees colder than in the city, with a strong breeze. We stand under the overhead lights of a four-car station. One of the lights keeps flickering. This kind of freaks me out. I scan the squat gray brick building.

Advertisements for Marlboros and Red Bull cover the window. Just past the building, I see the dumpster, and next to that a rack of tires. Typewriter must see them too because he says, Fuck yeah.

Being in semirural Minnesota, the gas isn't prepay, which I'm stoked about. I start filling the car and Typewriter stands at my side, gun pointing at an invisible enemy, at darkness, at nothing. They have to be out there and maybe they're devising strategy, like how to flank us, how to attack from all sides, from above. I look at the top of the gas station and see nothing and I tell myself to calm the fuck down, that it's only us, that we're safe.

We make our way over to the rack of tires. I feel like having explosive diarrhea. Typewriter slips a step behind me. The tires are secured with a crappy Master Lock. I act without thinking and smash the lock with the butt of my shotgun. It falls to the ground. I feel about as cool as I ever have.

We roll a Bridgestone back to the car. The wind has picked up even more. Why didn't we steal some warm clothes at Cabela's? Typewriter starts working on the tire. In thirty minutes, we should be at the Albino's place, and if he's alive, great, if not, oh well, because he's a fucking dick anyway, but what's important is that I'll be high. I'll burn grams of shit, my head a fucking balloon, my body preorgasmic thuds of blood, and from there, once my head is taken care of, we can figure out what to do. I hope KK is okay. I think about my parents decomposing, their skin falling off sturdy bone.

Then I see two giant headlights coming toward us.

Type, I say.

He doesn't respond.

Someone's coming, I yell.

I point my gun at the blinding lights. I'm about to unload whatever I've got when the semi stops. Typewriter stands by me. He's pointing his shotgun at the truck too. I can't see what's getting out of the truck, but I hear the door open.

Hello, I yell.

I'm expecting a giggle, a groan.

Friendly, a man's voice calls back.

Kill the lights, Typewriter yells.

My finger presses against the trigger. I have no idea how hard I actually have to pull for it to discharge, but I suspect I'm close.

The fucking lights, Typewriter says again.

Ain't here for trouble, the man says.

I can see his shape now. His hands are raised to about head level. He keeps coming toward us. I glance over at Typewriter, who has his shotgun in the crook of his shoulder. The man finally gets close enough for me to make him out. He's an ugly motherfucker, skinny like the third world, with maybe two weeks' worth of pubes covering his taut face.

Guns down, guys, not one of them, he says.

We keep them trained on him.

What do you want? I say.

Who are you? asks Typewriter.

Saw your lights, figured I'd stop and see—

Who the fuck are you? Typewriter repeats.

Shh, he hisses.

He extends his hand in the direction of Typewriter and

this seems like an aggressive move and I'm about to shoot because what the fuck do I know about this man and his intentions and how the world now stands?

Noise, man, noise.

Back away from me, Typewriter says.

Okay, okay, just keep your voice down. They'll be swarming if you keep with the shouting.

Who's *they*? I ask.

The man looks at me. It's then I notice his eyes, deep like mine, sunken, like they've seen everything they possibly could and now are on the retreat. He's either starving or smokes scante.

Everyone, let's just keep it down. How long you all been here?

We don't say anything.

Cuz I've found any longer than twenty minutes and one of 'em catches wind.

Typewriter's eyes dart from swaying branches to a Doritos bag blowing along the pavement. My finger tightens even more. Typewriter asks if he's the dude from the porn site.

The guy gives a snort. Tells him no. He grinds his jaw like he's chewing a Starburst. He's spun. He asks where we're staying. Type keeps asking who he is. The guy is getting nervous, I can tell, how quickly his gaze shifts from me to Typewriter to our guns to the dark behind the gas station, and he keeps saying *shh* and he doesn't like it one bit when Typewriter pokes him with the barrel of his shotgun.

Stop, I yell.

Both of them give me their attention.

I say, Please, tell me what the fuck is happening. We were holed away for a week, and we come out to this.

He stares at me like he thinks I'm full of shit. I raise my gun. He says, End of days. Apocalypse. Whatever you want to call it. Talked to a few truckers still left but you're the first live guys I've seen in a week.

I can tell he's scared, maybe not of us, but of everything. The speed coursing through his veins must be making shit worse. I ask if it's just in Minnesota or America, if it's terrorism.

He shrugs. He says, People just didn't wake up last Saturday. Died in their sleep. Everyone, far as I can tell.

What about the . . . Typewriter stops, maybe feels stupid to say *zombies*.

Started two days after, the man says.

How? I say.

Whatever it was, virus or something that killed everyone, obviously turned 'em. But only the healthy ones, I think, the young, the able. Haven't seen any old walkers.

Zombies?

The guy shrugs again. He says, Yeah, I guess. Call 'em Chucklers. Chucks for short.

It's obvious this motherfucker thinks he's clever.

How we know you're not one of them? Typewriter asks.

Am I giggling?

Jesus Christ, I say.

He ain't about to help you, he says.

Type lowers his gun. I don't. I'm thinking about the twenty minutes of grace time the guy told us about. We're probably right at the mark. We need to get the tire finished, get away from this guy, and head to the Albino's. Then I realize the trucker has got to be holding, and a taste would be about the best thing I could imagine.

I whisper to Typewriter that he's spun.

The guy is telling us that we should team up, that three against however many is better, that we can cruise in his rig, and then Typewriter raises his gun again. You holding?

The man narrows his eyebrows. He shakes his head like he's not following. Typewriter pumps the shotgun. He asks again—You holding?—and the guy puts his hands up in mock confusion. I'm thinking that it's so fucked up, us junkies, our inability to get honest with anyone, how we keep pleading ignorance, innocence, even in the face of two loaded shotguns and worldwide death. This guy standing there like he has no idea what *holding* even refers to, this guy with eyes like train tunnels and a jaw like a gearshift, he will continue this act until he has no alternative. It's a form of survival. I get it. I do it.

I tell him that we're just looking for a teener to get back on the road.

He realizes he's at the point where coming clean is the better tactic. He says, Can't give you that much. 'Bout all I have myself. Can give you a ride for a trade, maybe for one of those there guns.

Not sure you're in any position to be bartering, Typewriter says.

Come on, not with all this, the guy says, sweeping an open palm to the engulfing darkness. His tone has become more singsongy, and he's saying things about sticking together and only having a pistol himself and if we thought tweak was hard to get before, and I feel for this guy for some reason. Here he is driving the interstates alone in a semi, smoking meth and hoping to see another human, anyone. He might have a family, maybe a little boy and a wife back in Kansas or someplace, and they are either dead or undead and he's just trying to connect. And here we are stealing the only thing he has left.

Okay, I say.

He grins at me.

No, not okay, Typewriter says.

Dude needs to be able to protect—

Motherfucker doesn't need shit.

We're fine. We're set. Just get him a piece.

Typewriter takes a step closer to me and leans into my face and his breath is all sorts of sour. He whispers things about being smart and conserving. I say, Think about somebody besides yourself. Typewriter backs away, shaking his fat jowls.

We good? the guy asks.

I tell him to get his shit and we'll get him a gun. He jogs back to the semi and Typewriter is giving me fuck-you eyes and I tell him to finish up with the tire. I reach into the shotgun duffle bag and take out a lighter one. I grab a handful of shells. The guy is back by the time I'm done and he's holding on to a cellophane cigarette wrapper with a single shard. I know he's just transferred it from a larger stash but I don't say anything because we'll be at the Albino's in no time.

Travis, the guy says.

Chase, I say.

We shake hands in the form of him giving me the baggie. I can tell it's decent glass when I place it in my pipe, the color a little chalky, but clearer than most. I use the torch lighter. I give myself the honor of first hit. I inhale and wonder if any part of my decision to trade had to do with being a good person, helping out a stranger and all that shit, or if I simply couldn't wait thirty minutes until we got to the Albino's.

Type and I pass the pipe. We don't talk. Travis loads his gun. The overhead light flickers and the wind picks up even more. It's coming from the north because with each exhale, the smoke slips past my face, back toward the Twin Cities and my dead parents and KK.

But for a brief moment, I'm not thinking about all that. I'm feeling the closest thing I can think of to God and he's playing the samba inside of my body, his fingers gentle as they press on the backs of my retinas, my spine, the tendons along my hip flexors. I'm thinking that I love drugs more than anything. That they are the one and only constant in my life. Yeah, they demand a lot of attention and effort, but their love is legendary, their compassion endless. I hold each hit for hours, exhale for decades. The determination that comes with the onset of a high rushes back and I'm all about conquering the world and making money and finding happiness in the form of a loving woman who knows when it's time to spread her legs and when it's time to brush the backs of her nails across my cheek and then I'm thinking about this being the same thing as what God is doing to me now.

I love it when my heart rattles against my uvula.

I love it when my vision is a camera shutter.

I love it when I know that someday, I will do great things.

I love it when methamphetamines make things okay.

But I don't love it when I start to hallucinate because the line between knowing it's only the drugs and knowing your psyche is about to snap the fuck apart like a high wire is oh so delicate. The giggles. I hear them. I close my eyes and try to remember how I felt half a second before—glorious, about to take over the world—but it's too late, I've switched. I've gone from high to completely fucked. I hear more giggles.

The guy, Travis, spins around, shotgun raised. Maybe he's fucked too. But then Typewriter drops the pipe and I know the giggles must be real because he's not the kind of guy to ever drop the pipe.

Travis says, We got to go, and Typewriter keeps repeating *fuck*. I point my shotgun in the direction of the giggles, the dumpster, the tire rack, but there's just darkness and I realize we're under the lights with open space on all sides. I have no idea how to hold the gun. Then demonic laughs come from behind us and we all spin in that direction and then to our right and I see these things coming out of the shadows, a hand here, a face there, giggles all around us. They're closing in. There must be ten of them, kids and women and men, most of them naked or in pajamas and it's not God inside my body anymore, but their giggles, loud like sick little kids burning ants, amazed at their power over another living thing.

They don't shuffle like the ones in the movies. They walk in careful steps, spines straight, arms at their sides. Some laugh with their mouths closed, some open. I don't know how long I'm supposed to wait, how far my short barrel can fire, if the sound will attract more, and I'm thinking of these things, along with visceral images of their fingers and nails—ones that a week ago were braiding their daughter's hair and ringing up packs of cigarettes at SuperAmerica—tearing into me, gouging out my eyes.

I want Travis to tell me what to do. Even Typewriter. Somebody to give me direction, tell me where to aim, when to fire, but my voice's gone dry with fear.

We can see these walking dead motherfuckers clearly now under the overhead lights. I've locked onto one guy and it's like his upper lip has disintegrated, the space between his nose and mouth gone, just flashes of white bone and tooth. He's staring right at me and for a second it seems like there's a person inside there, maybe still able to think and feel. Maybe he can't help the giggles and missing flesh, maybe it's something beyond his control, some outside force. But then he laughs really fucking loud and I don't think I mean to, but I press a touch harder on the trigger.

The kick is worse than I would have thought. I take a step back and look at the guy. I've blown my load into his left shoulder. I have a clear view of his ball joint. He laughs. I fire again.

And then it's nothing but the drumming of shotgun shells and I'm Rambo—fire, pump, fire, pump—I'm shooting more by feel than sight, more by instinct than logic. I can hear Travis and Type doing the same and I might be screaming or maybe that's one of them but we just keep shooting and they keep coming, their laughs taunting us like our efforts are futile and we'll never live to see the sun and they will prevail because they don't give a fuck if they live or die.

My shotgun runs out of ammo. I panic for a second, then remember the pistol tucked in my waistband. I pull it out and fire. I don't come close to hitting anything. These motherfuckers are less than ten feet away and I glance at Travis, who swings the butt of his shotgun like a baseball bat. I steady my aim on a woman of about thirty, completely naked, pale like moonlit lakes. She's a few feet away and I tell her I'm sorry. She swipes at me. I pull the trigger. The edge of her forehead explodes. She drops.

I do this again.

And again.

I hear a different kind of scream and turn around. One of these things is locked up with Travis and he's writhing and crying for help and I take two steps over and know my shot could easily miss the Chuck and kill Travis but he can't stop yelling and I figure he'll be dead either way. I fire and the re-animate stumbles for a second. I fire again and it drops to the ground.

Let's go, let's go, let's go, Typewriter yells.

I spin around and can't see anything but I still hear the laughs. All the noise must have attracted more and I picture them coming, throngs of the motherfuckers. All around us are the bodies we shot, some twitching, some crawling, and blood, thick, so fucking thick.

Typewriter grabs me and shoves me toward the car. I climb in and Type slides in the driver's side. Just outside my window, I see Travis sitting on his ass, knees up, his head between them. Then he glances up. Blood runs down his face. It's beautiful in a way, the bite of flesh missing above his eye like an Amazonian waterfall.

We need to get—

Fuck him, Typewriter says.

He turns the ignition. The piece of shit Civic sputters, doesn't catch.

Travis seems to understand he's being left. He reaches out. He mouths something. The engine turns again and I look ahead and see more coming, a steady stream of people who went to bed one night, probably annoyed at the thought of getting up and having to go to work or feed the kids or deal with a complaining wife, only to never wake up again, at least not as a human. Typewriter bashes the steering wheel. I hear something bump the side of the car. Travis has one bloodied hand pressed against the back window. He's yelling for help. His eyes are so fucking sunken. More sputtering from the engine. I'm thinking I should unlock the door and get Travis in here. But could he already be one of them from that bite? How do I know if a bite really changes somebody? I see more of them coming now, close enough to be fully lit. I reach for the door handle to get out and grab Travis. But then I notice that the gash above his eye isn't bleeding anymore. It's already coagulated, crusty and purple. He's yelling, Help, open, but now I know he's going to turn, that his wound is not normal and whatever the fuck has caused this is already changing him into one of them.

The engine finally catches.

Type guns it. We hit a hillbilly Chuck and then he's nothing but two bumps under our tires. In the side mirror, I watch Travis try to stand. He's circled. He's dead. And at that moment, I understand that certain people are meant to make it, others aren't. I'm not sure why. But I've spent my entire adult life walking that thin line between suicide and preservation, everything I do is to get more dope, to keep going, to survive. I've done bad things in my life, things I'm not proud of and things that won't let me sleep sober. I remember the first time I saw somebody overdose, Frank, my best friend I'd gotten sober with, my roommate at the halfway house. We'd gone out together, relapsed, and we sat in a restroom at Starbucks and I smoked my speed and he shot his heroin. I knew he was going to die, the way his body went both rigid and limp. I stared at his freckles, ones that made him seem years younger than he was. I knew that in order to survive, to keep my habit, I had to leave him, pretend I was never there. I did. I left him propped up on the toilet, the sleeve of his puffy down coat still rolled up.

I do what I need to, just so I can get up and do it again.

TUESDAY

Typewriter tells me to make a wish. His voice startles me, our drive nothing but silence after the gas station.

Huh?

He points to the clock. He says, All the same digits.

How can he be making idle talk after what just happened? Make a wish, he says again. I look out of the car and it's so dark and I think about a TV show I saw about what will happen to our world after man dies. How the shrines we've built to money and security and happiness and love will be reduced to rubble in the blink of a geological eye. I know I'm

53

at the precipice of the most important moment of mankind's history—fuck the invention of the wheel, the happy accident of penicillin, the fungus over Hiroshima, the Internet—because what's happening right now, it's biblical in scope, the end of fucking days.

I glance at Typewriter. His lips are moving but I can't hear him. Maybe he's making a wish, or praying, same thing really. That the Albino is still alive? That this is all a dream? He mouths the words with a sincerity I haven't seen in him before. And then I think of him as John, not Typewriter, a person, a son, and that's probably it, he's focused on his mother, because that was his moment, her passing, the moment he can't recover from, the moment that puts his lips to glass stem.

Pretty soon 1:11 is going to become 1:12 and it feels important that I make a wish because I'm pretty much out of other options. What comes to mind is KK—her being alive, holed up in a fortress, with enough food to last years and books to pass the days.

The first time I ever saw her was in the psych ward in the Somali neighborhood of the South Minneapolis ghetto. I wound up in the ward because I'd dropped out of college to smoke scante and finally my parents came to the apartment they paid for after I'd quit answering their calls. They knocked and knocked while I sat in my room with all the shades drawn, trying not to breathe. They called the cops, who didn't think an arrest was in order, just a nice trip to the nuthouse. So there I sat in my scrubs and socks with little treads. I doodled during arts and crafts. That's when KK walked in. Just a wisp of a girl, nothing but sharp angles and a big nose and chopped blond hair, her arms pulled in tight across what little chest she had.

I'm not sure if I believe in love at first sight or any of that shit. But I know that sitting there in a room with half-retarded motherfuckers drooling from their lithium and trazodone, whatever I felt, it was close. Like I had this need to hold her, protect her bones from her parents or drugs or whatever wouldn't let her sleep at night, and I wanted her to think I was funny and sexy and smart and beautiful, just fucking beautiful. Sitting there while the tech introduced us to her, I wanted to be better than I was, not just to fuck this girl, but to be better for her. Guess that's a good enough definition of love.

Her waving really did me in. She kind of brought up her right hand all timid like. Her fingers didn't even move. She looked around the room and then brought her face back down, her bangs shielding her from our predatory stares. But she still looked at me—two dots of topaz, not precious, but semiprecious.

That night, I started doing pushups. I quit masturbating to visions of the sluts from my recent past. I wanted to be better and I would be for her.

We hit it off, at least as well as any two people connecting in the psych ward can. We laughed sometimes. We rolled our eyes at stupid people. She told me she loved shooting speed and I felt like a fucking loser because I just smoked mine.

Then one day, toward the end of my stay, we stood at the garbage can scraping off our untouched beef Stroganoff, and she told me to meet her in the janitor's closet in ten minutes.

I walked down the hall, excited because things were going

to work out. I thought about rhyme and reason and about the universe putting me in the position to get to her, KK, my savior, the girl made of birdlike bones with swathes of gauze along her wrists.

I knocked.

She opened the door and there she was among the trash bags and wet mops and bottles of industrial cleaning supplies. She smiled a genuine smile, little kid and bashful. It was hard to do sober, bridge the gap between indecision and decision, but she met me halfway, our lips touching.

I made love until she told me to fuck her.

Afterward, she sat between my legs, her head resting on my raised knee. I was thinking about us working out in the long run. She could go into treatment and we could be sober and together. I was also thinking about my sperm finding a suitable home in her tiny tubes and about the different guys she'd fucked and I told myself to stop, that every dick she'd sucked was only to get her to me.

I buried my face in her hair. It was grapefruit and sleep. My hand was around her arm and she moved it to her wrist. I felt the thick gauze. I wanted to protest, to tell her this made me feel weird inside. She wrapped her fingers around my index finger. My face was buried in her hair and I was huffing her, greedily wanting to remember this moment, and she guided my finger under her gauze bandage. It was the strangest feeling, how tender and moist her fresh wound still was, how much it was raised above the rest of her forearm, and I thought about telling her no, that I could get it dirty, infect it. Then she moaned a little, maybe a gasp, and the warmth and intimacy of touching her most vulnerable moment are what books are written about.

I didn't mean to tell her I loved her.

My finger was still touching her gash when she said, I love you too.

So with the digital clock still reading 1:11, I wish for KK to be safe. But that's not all. I wish for her to be thinking of me, praying that *I* am safe, needing me, wanting me. I wish that KK and I can live the rest of our lives together, whatever that might mean, just together, to feel the tickle of her nose against my neck.

1:38 AM

We park at the end of the dirt drive. I rush out to open up the gate. There's nothing but pine trees. I sprint back to the car and we drive into the Albino's compound. The little log cabin is pitch black inside. This doesn't necessarily mean anything. The Albino is a sort of minimalist, no phone, a woodstove, that kind of thing. But still, I'm not trying to fight his reanimated corpse.

Just hope he cooked a big ol' batch, Typewriter says.

For real, I say.

Neither of us cares if he's dead or alive, just that our ounce is there, shrink-wrapped like a package of ground beef.

We get out of the car and I already have my shotgun pumped and I hear Typewriter's and it's weird because it all feels so natural, the cocking of guns, the killing of shit that shouldn't exist. We're at the front door of his little shack, and I call out that it's Chase and Typewriter.

The house stays dark.

I know there's no way to get through the door—reinforced steel, double base rods (also steel)—and after we call out a few more times we say fuck it and head toward the prefab Lowe's shack farther down the trail.

I see the faintest light coming from the baseboard of the shack, and I ask Typewriter if he thinks the Albino's in there cooking.

Who the fuck he cooking for?

Himself?

Typewriter shrugs and puts his gun to his shoulder. We're outside of the gray shed and there definitely is a band of light at the base of the door. Typewriter looks over. I nod. I knock.

It creaks open a few inches. This isn't normal because the Albino is nothing but paranoia, both because he traffics in life sentences and he shoots shit on a four-hour rotation, and I squeeze the gun, using the barrel to open the door.

I'm about to step inside when a blast of noise fills my ears. I drop to the ground, crawling on my stomach to the side of the shed. Another blast and I realize it's a gun and I'm screaming that it's me, Chase, Albino, it's Chase here. This is met by another shot.

I'm covered in sweat, or maybe that's piss, and I don't know if I should run into the woods or fire back or just keep calling out my name. I go with shouting. I say, It's me, Albino, Chase from the Twin Cities. You know us. We're cool.

Then I think that maybe it's not the Albino in there.

Maybe he's dead, and this is some tweaked motherfucker who had the same thought as us. Maybe it's somebody who just stumbled across the shack and a gun. Maybe it's one of *them*, maybe they know how to use weapons.

Type's to my right and he's on his stomach too. The light from the shed lets me see his back. I notice the scratches from Svetlana. They look healed, just like the gouge on that trucker's face.

I don't know any Chase, the Albino's voice calls out.

Typewriter smirks at me.

I roll my eyes. I tell him it's Crooked Cock—the name he's dubbed me so he doesn't have to know my real name.

Crooked Cock, that really you?

Yeah, and Typewriter.

You one of them?

No, man, we're all good.

Bullshit.

You hear any giggling? I say.

Here to steal my shit? Figured I'd be dead?

Just had to get out of the cities.

Figured the Albino be a walking dead piece of shit, huh? Cuz I already lookin' like one of them. That it?

Nowhere else to go, Typewriter says.

Figured the Albino was ready for this end-of-days shit, huh?

Maybe, I say.

I hear his laugh, followed by his cough, both unmistakable, both somehow reminding me of cement mixers.

Fucking Albino livin' alone in the woods, *he'll* know what to do, he says from inside.

Can we come in? I ask.

Fuck no, he says.

His laugh, his cough.

Is that a yes? I say.

I hear the pumping of a shotgun.

You been shooting your profits? Typewriter asks.

I kick him.

Fucking old Albino, all alone in them woods, cookin' and ready for the apocalypse. That's what you was thinking, huh?

Just didn't know where else to—

Come here to rob me, that it?

No, we thought that maybe you—

Was either dead or would protect you. Either way, don't look too good.

Maybe this is a giant waste of fucking time. The Albino is nearly impossible to deal with on a good day, one where he'd been cooking and shooting, but with this, the world completely fucked, it's pointless. I decide to switch tactics. I say, We brought guns for you, to trade.

Sure as shit you did, Crooked Cock. Don't come to the Rapture with a knife fight.

This doesn't really make sense but I get where he's going with it.

Rifles, shotguns, and pistols. Can take your pick.

Type, your faggot friend tellin' the truth?

Yup.

Y'all fucking with me?

No, straight up, got guns, go ahead and take your pick. Just a simple trade.

Didn't care if I was dead, huh?

What? Typewriter says.

Just here to get shit. That's all I am to you.

I think about chiming in about him only wanting that role, our whole relationship predicated on us giving him money for crystal, that's the way he wanted it.

Can we just come in? Typewriter says.

If you want a shell through the chest.

I whisper to Type that the Albino is so far past the point of spun that he'd probably see us with decaying flesh, hallucinate our giggles, and blast us full of shotgun BBs. Maybe we should just wait him out, go back to the car, lock the weapons up, take turns trying to sleep. Typewriter isn't feeling this. I know his reasoning—he wants to get high.

Albino, Typewriter says.

The, he calls back.

The Albino, Typewriter says, we will trade you a shotgun and—

Got one of those.

Then a rifle and a pistol.

Got one of those too.

Then a pistol with a shit ton of ammo.

For what? To watch you suck Crooked Cock's crooked cock?

He thinks this is funny.

Just to let us in, I say.

We wait in the darkness on our stomachs and I know we're talking more to a drug than to a person. It was always hard to tell the difference with the Albino, but it's worse now, everything heightened. Methamphetamines can be a nasty old cunt, greedy in their possessiveness over reality. I tell Type *no sudden movements*, and I call out, Sliding in a pistol now, okay?

We'll see, the Albino says.

I'm not sure what this means. I inch forward and push open the shredded door and I'm trying to keep my head out of his sights. I take the nine out of my pants. I say, Here it is. I put it on the linoleum floor of the shed. Pushing it toward you, I say, giving it a little shove. I roll back to the side of the building.

Now where's those shotguns? he yells.

Thought you didn't want any, Typewriter says.

Oh, yeah, sure do. Can't never have too many friends.

So we give you one, then you let us in? I ask.

Silence.

I motion for Typewriter to crawl forward on his fat stomach. He shakes his head. I kick him. He does it, shoving his gun into the shed. We can hear the Albino sweet-talking something, and it's probably closer to porn talk, the suck-that-shit-you-filthy-fucking-whore monologue, and I can hear movement in there, then the sturdy sound of oiled metal, the loading and unloading of a clip.

We all good? I say.

Your cock crooked?

The answer is no, not really, but the Albino thinks it is, so I'm taking his comment as a *yes*.

So we're coming in, I say.

With your motherfucking hands ticklin' God's feet.

I crouch on my knees. I tell myself that the Albino's just a little jumpy. I stand, bracing myself against the shed's corrugated siding. I'm trying not to remember the moments in my life when I knew I was dealing with people completely swallowed by chemicals, moments when I looked at friends or acquaintances and they stared back without a single morsel of recognition, not just of me but of anything or even their own fucking hands, themselves. At those times it wasn't Typewriter or KK or whoever sitting by my side, but shit, pure fucking shit coursing through capillaries, clogging overworked synapses with come-shots of dopamine.

Coming in, I say.

I give a tentative push on the door. I'm expecting a shotgun blast to the face. The Albino is talking, guttural whispers followed by squeals, and I hope he's lost in the promise of the new guns, forgetting about us and the threat he thinks we pose. I peer inside and see the skeleton that is the Albino— all elbows and kneecaps, his skin dirty-snow white, baby blue contrails of veins swirling down his neck, a supernova of bruised veins exploding from the crook of his left arm, his balding head and ratty ponytail, his chapped lips, his red eyes—and he's cradling two shotguns, petting the one Type just handed over. I glance around his lab. It's still immaculate, the burners and Erlenmeyer flasks and beakers and the five-hundred-milliliter round bottom and burets and funnels and evaporation dishes, and this makes me almost as happy as not being shot dead.

Hey, man, how you doing? I say.

Old Albino, just minding his own business. Been waiting for this since I was born.

For us to show up? Type says. He smiles, looking down at our cook.

They always do, he says.

So where you hiding the—

It's good to see you, I say, interrupting Typewriter.

The Albino looks up at me. He points the shotgun right at my dick. I'm trying to laugh and move out of the way, but really I'm thinking about getting buckshot in the pecker. The Albino says, Crooked Cock, tell me why you're here.

See how you're holding up.

I know you've been eyein' my dick for long as I know you.

Just here because we didn't know where else to go. Less people.

Less them walking dead, the Albino says.

You've seen 'em? Typewriter says.

The Albino points the gun at Typewriter. He jams the barrel into his pooch. He says, Killed one.

So they're out here, the Chucks, like in the woods and shit?

In town. Headed that way when none of y'all bitches showed up. Figured somebody got popped, rolled. That's what you'd think, huh?

Nobody got pop—

No shit, Crooked Cock. Saw what's out there. Killed one woman with no face. Run her over in the Jimmy.

The Albino starts laughing and ends up coughing.

So what's up with the trade? Trying to get some of that Albino shit, Typewriter says.

Ain't shit left, the Albino says.

You're fucking me?

Want me to?

Bro, come on.

Got this here, he says. He holds up a fistful of needles, none of them packaged.

Typewriter walks over to the main cooking station. He lifts a few beakers, a baking tray.

Touch my shit again, gonna get your fucking spine blasted, the Albino says.

Stop, I whisper to Typewriter. But it doesn't matter, I can tell he's about to freak the fuck out. One of his meaty hands pulls at his greasy Italian hair. He's shaking his head, scratching the pink film of congealed ephedrine from the inside of a beaker. I worry that he'll smash something. Even in the best of times, the Albino would kill you for fucking with his equipment. I tell Typewriter it's cool. He's not hearing me. He's at that point of expected payoff. Like he's killed a soccer team's worth of walking dead; driven away from Travis the trucker, sealing his fate with the acceleration of his shitty Civic; he's nearly been blown to bits by a tweaked cook and sacrificed his shotgun—and now he expects to get high in return. I get it. There's no task too big, as long as the trade-off is crystalline Tina's plump lips wrapped around your cock. It's the only way we're able to do what we do, the thank-you, the love, the smoke telling us she understands, motherfuckers just don't get it, it's all good, you're okay.

And if that isn't there, the reward? Then you're stuck with yourself and every stupid and horrible thing you've ever done.

What about our ounce, fucking Monday, Typewriter says.

Expecting the Albino to be cooking during the apocalypse?

Fuck, Type screams.

Stop, I say.

The Albino points his gun at Typewriter. He says, Ungrateful piece of shit.

He didn't mean anything, I say.

Comin' up here, to *my* place, trying to smoke *my* shit, raising your voice in *my* lab.

Just put the gun down, I tell him.

I grab Typewriter. His eyes are seconds away from tears and I know it's not because of fear, but because he needs dope. I feel him on this, like really I do, because the majority of me is screaming for more, but I tell him to chill the fuck out.

My Sudafed guy didn't come down from Canada. Probably turned, all gigglin' now, huh? the Albino says.

Typewriter keeps saying shit and fuck and I'm still holding on to his shirt, telling him it's cool, we'll figure out a way.

The Albino holds out his hand. It's a bouquet of single-use syringes. He says, Pick a card, any card. He laughs. Ain't got time to load 'em while I cook, so do it beforehand.

The Albino is a disgusting man and he's fingering an open sore smack-dab in the center of his forehead. I want to tell him to shut the fuck up, that the last thing we need is to cross the irreversible line between smoking and shooting up. I'm remembering the people I knew who started putting holes in their veins. How they're dead, in state pens, or state asylums. But then I'm thinking about KK, how she'd had the sexiest eye shadow of discoloration on the back of her hand from where she shot shit, how she'd stumbled, to be sure, that year with me, but she'd gotten her shit back together, chosen sobriety over the mess I was again becoming.

Typewriter goes over to the Albino. He asks if they've been used. The Albino tells him they're clean. And just like that it's a done fucking deal.

Typewriter sits next to the Albino. His stomach bulges over his sweats. They start talking but I'm not really listening because I've always been scared of needles and I know this isn't good, my best and only friend starting down this path. The Albino is tying a rubber hose around Type's arm, and I'm trying not to watch, I want to go outside, and I think of the darkness and the wind and the walking dead. This isn't even what fucks me up, but rather, the thought of KK dead, of my parents dead, of never being able to tell them all that I'm sorry.

Typewriter looks like he's been waiting his entire life to be called up to the majors. He finds a vein on his second try. I watch him thumb the plunger and then that magic moment of pupil dilation. The change is instant, and I'm jealous because I know his night just got a lot better. I'm thinking about how long it will be until I can get high. Like having to track down Sudafed, which means having to go into town and dealing with whatever the fuck there is to deal with, the two hours to cook, like fuck, it'll be so long. I'm thinking about all the drugs I've done, how they've always fallen the tiniest bit short, how this shortcoming was because I smoked, chewed, or snorted them. The refrain gets louder and louder in my head: nothing matters and you'll be dead soon anyway and nobody who loves you is still alive.

I sit next to Typewriter, who's smiling.

I prepare as I've seen KK do.

I use the back of my hand. I find a vein and push the plunger and the liquid hits my heart and explodes dopamine and love and God and I think *everyone still alive is addicted to methamphetamines.*

5:08 AM

We're in the Albino's main cabin. The left side of my tongue is bleeding because I've been chewing it. We're not allowed any lights but I'm fine with that because my eyes are like an eagle's, my hearing like an elephant's, my mind like Einstein's. I've named my shotgun Buster. Typewriter alternates between war stories and bouts of silence. He's on the stories right now, talking about the gas station, how it was a fucking videogame, a movie, how he just kept unloading into Satan's children.

The Albino gets excited at this, saying, Fucking right, Satan's children.

We've each shot another tenth.

I call KK.

It rings.

I try to remember if it rang before or went straight to voice mail and it keeps ringing and I'm traveling upward and I give a high five to a satellite and then fly back down to St. Paul and into her apartment and burst through her cell phone and I interrupt Typewriter, asking him if it went straight to voice mail before.

The Albino screams at me, tells me no calls on his property.

I hang up.

I tell him the world is dead.

This makes us laugh.

I whisper to Buster that she's alive, that we'll find her.

7:19 AM

Typewriter slams on the brakes in the Walgreens parking lot. We're going fast, or at least it feels like we are. We're all sorts of prepared, the battle plan hatched as we blasted our third tenth thirty minutes ago. It's Operation Get Sudafed. We're out of the car and jogging to Walgreens' glass doors. I'm carrying Buster and Typewriter's shotgun and we each have a spare rifle tied to our backs like ninjas. Typewriter holds the duffle bags and two bowling balls, both engraved with THE ALBINO in the space between thumb and finger holes.

Objective One—Break doors.

We've learned from Cabela's. Typewriter is a fucking maniac charging the door. He lets one of the balls soar from five feet away. The glass spiders. He sends the other one. It spiders more. He kicks the glass inward and it caves still in one sheet and the alarm sounds but the lights are no big deal because the sun is shining.

I toss Typewriter his gun.

We walk through the smashed door.

Objective Two—Get into pharmacy.

We're running down the aisles and I can't feel my feet hitting the floor or really anything other than my breathing, heavy in my chest. I'm at the closed pharmacy window way before Typewriter because I don't weigh two thirty-five. I aim Buster at the glass, close my eyes, and fire. The glass shatters. I use Buster's butt to knock out the loose shards and I crawl onto the counter and through the window. Typewriter hands me one of the empty duffles.

Objective Three—Fill bag with Sudafed.

Ever since the government started keeping tabs on ephedrine sales, stores keep it right by the counter because it's annoying for the pharmacists to have to go dig it out for every motherfucker with a cold. I see boxes and boxes on the shelf and I empty them into the bag. There's got to be more and I tear through the shelves tossing bottles into the bag without reading labels, not knowing if I'm getting opiates or something for bladder infections, thinking that the Albino can turn anything into drugs. Toward the back I find the mother lode of Sudafed, hundreds of wax boxes of red and white packages and I'm grabbing them all, giddy at how kick-ass our plan is, giddy at the thought of the Albino cooking this all into pure dope.

I hear a gunshot.

Then another.

Typewriter, I yell. I grab the duffle bag and rush to the window. Type's standing over a guy in a uniform.

What the fuck?

Typewriter's jaw is clenching and unclenching. He wipes blood from his brow.

Fucking rent-a-cop must have turned, he says.

Any more?

Let's go, let's go, he says. I hand the duffle bag over and then crawl through the pharmacy window. I'm worried about the sound attracting more of them or maybe the security guard having a partner and we're almost at the exit when I stop dead in my tracks and scream. Typewriter rams into me. I feel his front teeth on the back of my skull.

There's a Chuck a few feet away. It's a burly man, thick and squat, rocking a pair of stained yellow undies. I unload into his sternum. He stumbles forward, his arms outstretched, and I pull the trigger again. His head explodes and I'm covered in him, little chunks of his two-inch beard all over my arms, a piece in my mouth.

Suddenly a teenage boy is in the doorway taking swipes at me and I fire again, catching him square on the jaw, and then there's a woman behind him. I start screaming because they just keep coming, an endless parade of motherfuckers trying to eat our flesh, and it's more rounds into their giggling faces, me and Type firing, brown blood, pump, shot, giggle, and then Buster is out of shells and Typewriter is yanking at my arm and screaming that we should run.

I turn and sprint down the tampon aisle. I'm still holding on to the duffle bag and we're at the back of the store, panting, being followed by a steady stream of giggling pieces of shit, and I point to the cubbyhole that is the pharmacy window.

Typewriter crawls onto the counter and they're getting closer, at least five of them now in the store, and Typewriter is taking all fucking day so I shove his ass and he tumbles inside. I throw the duffle bag in because if we somehow survive this, I'm not about to return to the Albino empty-handed.

As I scamper through I can feel clawing at my feet.

I fall to the floor. Typewriter stands with his pistol raised firing shot after shot after shot. The sound is deafening.

I check my legs for cuts or claw marks. I'm fine. I stand up and see a pile of twitching bodies at the window. More are behind them. They can't seem to figure out how to get inside and Typewriter is about to move onto his shotgun, but I tell him, No, wait to see if they can climb through.

We watch their reaching hands and listen to their shrill laughs so fucking loud I can't hear the alarm. They swing at the open space of the window but can't figure out how to raise a fucking knee and climb in.

Typewriter decapitates one with a shotgun blast.

Stop, need to conserve ammo, I say.

Fucking everywhere.

It's cool, they can't get in.

We look at these abominations a few feet away. They smell like period sex. Bits of flesh are missing and grins expose missing teeth, and there has to be at least fifteen. This wasn't part of Operation Get Sudafed, getting cornered by tides of the motherfuckers.

The shelf, I say.

Typewriter helps me knock over one of the metal racks of meds. We smash it against the window opening, pills spilling everywhere. The giggles don't stop, but at least we don't have to see the Chucks.

Jesus, Type says. We're fucked. Completely fucked. Like there's no way out and—

Stop, I say. We're safe. They can't get through.

For now.

That's all we've got.

Fuck your day-at-a-time AA shit, he says.

It's not—

How the fuck are we going to get out? Serious, this is it. Fucking done.

You need to calm down.

Typewriter fires his gun into the shelf. I grab his arm and think about smacking him across the face. I say, We need to stay calm. Figure this out. This is when the tears start. Typewriter's chubby cheeks redden and he's full-on crying, so I drop my tone, tell him I'll get us out, I promise.

I guide him down to the floor and take the shotgun out of his grasp. He just keeps saying, I don't want to die, I don't want to die.

I know I need to calm him down. Yeah, we are pretty close to being fucked. God knows how many Chucks are feet away, they'll figure out a way to get through the pharmacy window. And then I realize I need to calm down too. That I'm crying. Both of us crying and holding on to the other's shirt. I stand up. I need to find something to take the edge off.

Where are you going? Don't leave—

I'm not, I say.

I'm not sure if pharmacies alphabetize their drugs or

organize them by type. I'm looking for anything that will re-
tard my mind—benzos or barbiturates or opiates—and I'm
throwing bottles on the floor, scanning for anything resembling a name I know. Finally, I find a bottle of grape cough
syrup with codeine. It's not great, but it will do. I rip off the
top and take two long pulls.

The hell?

Drink this.

We're going to die and all you care about—

Fucking drink this.

Typewriter takes the bottle in his shaking hands and
brings it to his lips. Like a mother I tell him, Good, there you
go, and he drinks and some dribbles down his chin. It feels
kind of queer but I use my finger to dab it.

I take another drink. So does Type.

The giggles are getting louder. Hands reach through the
shelf.

Give me that, I say. Back to me. Back to him. We kill the
bottle and it might not have been the smartest thing to do,
drinking the *entire* bottle, but whatever. I can already feel my
world slowing. I'm not sure if this is a placebo or a chemical
reaction but I guess it doesn't matter.

We're going to die, Typewriter says.

I don't know if this is a statement or a question so I say
nothing. I tell myself to think. I picture our situation like a
middle school riddle—if two men are trapped in a pharmacy
with limited resources and a horde of flesh-eating parasites at
the window, what do they do? The answer comes to me. Look
for another exit. The fuck is wrong with me that I hadn't

thought of that before? I stand and tell Type to stay put. I see a metal door at the far end of the room. I'm about to open it to see where it leads, when I hear clawing and scratching and giggling from just outside.

Fuck, I yell.

I hear a gunshot and I'm afraid Typewriter has just put the barrel in his mouth but I turn and he's just shooting at the flailing hands at the window.

Stop wasting ammo.

I search the rest of the death box we're locked in. There's no other window, no other door. Maybe this is it, the one corner I won't be able to escape from. And maybe it's fitting, me dying locked inside a pharmacy. I sit next to Typewriter. I can tell the cough syrup is working its magic because his pupils are shrinking.

I don't know, man, I say.

Don't tell me that.

I just don't know.

The door?

Is surrounded. Can hear them.

So this is how it ends?

Dude . . .

He fires his shotgun again.

I can feel things shutting down—my reflexes, my verbal opposition to Type's shotgun blasts, my God-given adrenaline at the very real possibility of death—and I think about how long it's been since I've slept, like *really* slept, and I'm counting on my fingers and I lose track but I'm guessing it's got to be somewhere in the range of eight hours in the last week.

It takes me a second to realize Typewriter is kicking my foot with his. I struggle to pay attention. He says, Rip Van Winkle motherfucker.

I tell him that I like girls who wear those velour sweat suits.

He laughs.

Serious, man. Gives me a boner.

Let me guess, KK wore them?

I try to remember if this is true and I can't for some reason, KK's image being cut off at the shoulders and it's those trenches of her collarbones and that skinny neck and that sharp chin and that nose like a half of a sandwich and her bangs just barely past her hairline and I wonder why I said this in the first place. Then it's the grainiest eight-millimeter clip of a memory. I'm following KK in a department store. I have the feeling of being a dog on a leash. I like it. She's touching the fabric of racks of clothes. We're sober, that much I remember, and she's complaining about getting a fat fucking ass because of this very fact. I keep telling her no. You're perfect. I make a grab at her ass. She says, Don't touch that flabby piece of shit. I tell her *shitter*. She gives me that look—one like I'm complete fucking scum, but a loveable piece of scum. She tells me that a sweat suit will be the only thing she can fit into. She picks out a few. We sneak into the dressing room. A thirtysomething tries on business clothes. She looks nervous that I'm sitting there watching. I knock on the dressing room door. KK's standing there topless with her boy-flat chest and puffy nipples and she's wearing a pair of black velour sweatpants and I need to have her and maybe she needs to have me because she greets me with a forceful kiss and that's how it is, force, passion, too much, us not knowing how to deal with the world and our bodies and jobs and parents and rent and brushing our teeth and making our beds and us not knowing how to deal with a fucking thing without the aid of scante, and I feel the soft promise of those pants against my hand and then my dick and then it's KK's loud moans and I think about the thirty-something hearing this, if she'd be smiling or calling the cops.

I'm thinking this shit with Type a foot away. It feels kind of gay. I fumble around in my pocket for a cigarette. We're quiet. I find my pack and the first drag tastes like heaven. Type asks me what I wanted to be when I grew up.

I stare at the cherry of the cigarette. I watch the smoke rise in vertical plumes. I think this is weird. Then I'm thinking about his question and it was a professional soccer player when I was a kid and then it was an astronaut for a short while and then I think about high school and loving music and me not being horrible on the drums and our band that played a few local shows, places like the record shop and a school bonfire, and then in college how I took a philosophy class and was all about that and then it was a human geography course and I knew I'd be good at the interplay between humans and the environment and then I think about smoking shit and how I didn't have to worry about a future because for those moments, I could be anything I ever fucking wanted to, and it wasn't just a fantasy, but a reality, me able to conquer the world, to matter, to make a fucking difference. And I'm watching the smoke and I'm thinking about his question about what I wanted to be and the answer comes quick and it isn't sexy or amazing and it startles me because I'd never allowed myself to think it before—my dad.

Typewriter doesn't laugh. He says, I feel you there.

I'm not sure if I'm sleeping or awake and I'm seeing my father's face decompose and I'm seeing maggots crawling from his parted lips and I'm imagining his readers now resting on the cartilage of his nose and then I'm seeing him one Christmas Eve and it must have been close to three in the morning and I'd snuck downstairs to see if I could get a glimpse of Santa and there he was, my father, sitting on the Persian rug, a G.I. Joe base erected between his legs, a penlight in his mouth, an instruction sheet spread open to his right, and I understood at that very moment that there was no Santa. I'd snuck back to bed, resentful and hurt. It'd taken me years to realize that my father would do anything for me. That he would go the entire night without sleeping just to set up my toys. That everything he did was for the family, to keep up the illusion that magic happened, that he wasn't the person who made it all stick together.

They're all gone.

I don't realize I've said it until Typewriter agrees. He says, Each and every one of them.

I let my eyes close. I don't fucking care anymore. I'm not sure if it's the drugs or the sleep or acceptance. This almost makes me chuckle, *acceptance*, the cornerstone of everything they taught us in AA. I think of my counselors telling me I was withholding something. How I wasn't fully *letting go*. I wasn't fully *accepting*. They told me I'd be back, beaten down even more because the disease of addiction had a way of making believers out of everyone.

So this is it, I think. This is me accepting my fate. To die at twenty-five. To die with the only person who might still be considered a friend.

The inch-long stack of ash falls from my cigarette. I take a drag.

It will all be over soon.

Some pleasurable sensation starts radiating through my thigh. Maybe this is death? I let the vibrating continue and I'm like maybe God or my father or whoever is taking me away, sparing me the suffering of however long it is until real death, and I'm smiling, ready for this, ready to be done with this fucked-up trip through life, but the vibrating continues. It's a familiar sensation. I fight my way back to consciousness. My fucking phone!

I rip out my phone and it's ringing and ringing and the caller says KK and I'm like, No fucking way, and I flip it open and I'm all, Hello, hello?

Chase!

Fucking god, you're okay.

You're alive.

I thought you were—

Me too.

I'm pressing the phone to my ear and yelling into the receiver and Typewriter wakes up and I'm crying for real now, bawling and shit, and we keep saying I thought you were dead and this goes on forever and things will be okay because she's alive.

I ask her where she is.

She pauses. It's a pause I know well, one that is the precursor to bad news, and I ask her if she's okay, where is she? She tells me Jared's apartment.

This stings.

I know it shouldn't. That I should just be happy that the only girl I've ever cared about isn't dead or reanimated and that there's a chance for some hand-in-hand-happily-ever-after shit, but I'm not. I'm thinking about that dickhead Jared. Jared with his slicked Jersey hair, all reciting the Seventh Step Prayer, stalking the meetings for all the wrong reasons, fronting like he gave a fuck about sobriety, all the while just trying to pound newly sober girls' pussies.

Jared's? I say.

Yeah. On Summit.

At Jared's?

Jesus, I knew it was a mistake to call.

No, stop, stop. KK?

Yeah.

Are you safe? I mean away from *them*?

She pauses the same pause. Finally, she says, I can hear them in the hall.

But the door's locked? They haven't broken through or anything?

Yet.

What?

Haven't broken through *yet*.

I'm standing and my world is making more sense because

I have a purpose and that's all I've ever really wanted. I'll save her, that much is certain. I'll be the motherfucker who rides in on a white Civic and my sword will be Buster the shotgun and that shit will be a fairy tale, me the hero.

I ask about Jared having any weapons. A gun or something?

KK stammers and I want to tell her to spit it out. I picture the apartment door being ripped apart, the little girl with umbrella socks giggling at the easy prey.

What?

He's not . . . I think he's . . .

What?

He won't wake up.

She's crying and I want those tears to be for me and I think that maybe he's dying and this isn't the worst thing ever. I can hear mucus in her throat. She's not talking, just crying. I want to tell her it will be okay. I want to tell her not to worry. But then I think about Jared maybe turning. Maybe his not breathing is the precursor, just like that trucker Travis said about people going to bed and not waking up unless they were Chucks. I ask KK if he's breathing. She says yes. I'm not sure if this is a good thing or bad thing and I ask if he'd been bitten and she tells me no, they'd been locked in his apartment shooting shi—

She stops.

It takes a second for me to realize: she'd been using. I ask her what the fuck and she tells me she can't do this right now, that she's scared, that she didn't know who else to call. I want to yell at her because she's such a fucking hypocrite, breaking up with me because I couldn't stop, and there she is blasting her veins full of meth with that cocksucker Jared.

I'm sorry, she says.

If Jared starts to giggle, cut his throat, I say.

She's crying. I tell her to barricade the door. To remain silent. That I'll be there in a few hours.

I tell her I love her.

She says, Please.

I don't want to hang up. She does. My phone goes black. Typewriter asks if she's okay. I tell him yes. I tell him no. I say, We need to get the fuck out of here. She needs me.

And this is different from a minute ago *how*?

I don't respond. I look at one of our two exits. There are at least six hands swiping through the metal shelf in front of the window. I jog over to the door and I hear more of the same. I'm telling myself to think. This is your one fucking shot, Chase, think, goddamn it, use your fucking brain. I do jumping jacks to rid the cough syrup fog. I'm telling myself that I'm a problem solver. I figure shit out. I make it happen. I'm thinking about being unemployed over the last two years. How I was able to keep a roof over my head. Able to smoke hundreds and hundreds of dollars' worth of dope a week. These are the marks of a *problem solver*. And maybe all of us drug addicts are? Give a motherfucker a carrot at the end of a string and we'll do whatever it takes to nibble its end. I'm seeing the love of my life sitting with her back to the wall and a butcher knife in hand waiting either for the door to break down or for Jared to reanimate. I know she needs me. I know this is my shot. I walk back to where Type sits. He's smoking a cigarette. The smoke travels straight up. I follow the smoke and it's being pulled into a metal AC duct and I scream because it was right there the whole time.

Fucking got it.

Huh?

The vent, man, the fucking vent.

Typewriter looks at the ceiling. It takes him a second to understand. Then smiling, he struggles to his feet. Fucking shit, he says.

Fucking shit is right. Help me push this shelf over.

We move the rack so it's directly under the vent. I tell him I'll go first, that it'll be easier for me to maneuver and clear the way. I gather Buster and climb up the shelves. I push the vent upward and slide it out of the way. I look down at Typewriter. He's holding the duffle bag full of Sudafed. I guess it's stupid to go to all this trouble and walk away empty-handed. I take the bag, shoving it ahead of me into the rectangular air duct. I slither in. It's tight as hell and there's barely room to crawl, both width- and heightwise.

I yell back for him to come up.

I hear him climbing. He curses when he pokes his head in.

There's no way I can fit, he says.

No other option.

Bro . . .

I can't see him but I hear the whole thing—labored breathing, gasps, *fuck*s, thin metal meant to transport air being dented and pounded. He grabs on to my ankle. He yanks like hell. I start to slide back so I jam my elbows and knees against the confining walls. The duct sags and makes a groaning sound. I know it won't hold us for long so I start crawling. Typewriter keeps telling me he's stuck and I tell him to shut the fuck up and hurry.

After about fifty feet, I come across another vent. I can see through the cracks. There are hordes of them. Everywhere, naked, decaying flesh, and giggling.

Don't look down there, I say.

I make my way across the vent and I can feel the fragile metal give under my hundred and fifty pounds. I try not to think about what will happen when Typewriter crosses. He's like, Jesus, there's got to be hundreds, and I tell him not to look, that we're getting close. Typewriter can't stop saying, Holy shit. I'm thinking about rescuing KK, about blasting the Chucks outside her door, about blood dripping from my brow, maybe my shirt's off, and she comes running, throwing herself at my feet and I pull her up by the chin, tell her she's the best thing to ever happen to me, that all is forgiven.

I'm at another vent and I can see fewer Chucks down below so we must be getting close to the exit. I haven't really thought this through. Like what if the vent doesn't go all the way outside and I have to drop down into the store? No way out and shit? My forearms sting. They're getting wet. I dab the wetness with my finger then bring it to my mouth. Blood. I can't imagine what Typewriter's body will look like after he squeezes through this shit. Just behind me, he keeps calling out that he's stuck and I keep saying shut the fuck up. I can see light at the end of the tunnel—literally. The light's coming in from a dead end. I reach it. It's a metal vent leading outside.

I feel around and it's pretty sturdy. I pound it with my fist. It doesn't move. Type is right behind me now. He says to use my gun and I tell him the sound would be deafening, that it would attract all the walking dead outside. And it's me searching for a screw or nut and there isn't anything, just solid metal.

Sometimes life is a cruel joke.

And sometimes, life is a real motherfucker, because now I feel something start to give, like the earth is dropping out from under me and I realize it's the duct we're in ripping from the ceiling. I hear Typewriter screaming, not like before, but like he's about to die. I crane my neck just in time to see him sliding down the vent, which is gaping open behind him.

Fuck!

Only his upper torso and head and arms remain inside the vent. The rest of him must be dangling from the ceiling and I think about the walking dead standing under him trying to tear into his legs and I'm about to lose my only friend. I grab Buster and I fire into the metal vent leading outside. My eardrums explode and it's nothing but a high-pitched wail. I fire again and again. The vent falls off. I yell for Typewriter to grab my leg. He does. I feel his nails digging into my calves. I grab the square where the vent was and pull with everything I've got and I flex and maybe I'm shitting my pants and blowing out my asshole and maybe I'm an Olympic squatter and maybe I'm making up ground and pulling us to safety.

Keep going, keep going, Typewriter yells.

I think about KK. Back to us first meeting each other and back to us in the closet in the psych ward, knowing right then and there that we'd be together and I'm pulling, I'm close, my head's out of the vent, I see trees and sky and the sun, like the world's still normal, and Type keeps yelling *go, go, go*.

Suddenly I fly through the hole and onto the pavement. The duffle bag lands on my head. I'm disoriented. I grab my gun. The Chucks haven't figured out where we are yet but I know it's a matter of seconds. I stare at the vent opening. I've never been so happy to see Typewriter's fat face. He pulls himself through. I grab his arm and we run toward the car. When I look back I see them coming now, their mouths open, giggling.

4:06 PM

We're pulled over a few minutes from downtown St. Paul. There's still nobody around, no sign of struggles, no abandoned cars or broken windshields or anything that would indicate survivors. We see a few reanimated. They walk around looking bored as hell. We're splitting one of two loaded rigs from the Albino. It's not to get high, just to get straight, kill off the remains of the opiates. We need to be in tip-top shape for this rescue shit. Type gives himself half a plunge and I think about possible diseases. A motherfucker like that at least has to have some letter of hepatitis but I tell myself it's for a greater cause.

I find my vein on the first try.

Fuck, that's good.

We start the car back up. KK texted me the address and told me Jared was still hanging on but has a terrible fever. I call her and she picks up before one full ring. She asks if we're here. I tell her a block away. She's crying. I tell her not to. She says, He's not going to make it. I want to tell her that's the point. I tell her that we're almost there, that we can take care of whatever is waiting for us in the hallway, and then she says it again—*he's* not going to make it—and I realize her tears are for Jared.

Just be ready, I say.

She tells me to be careful.

Typewriter parks. His face is scratched from the vent. Blood collars his shirt. I don't even notice his one pick spot. It blends in.

Keep this shit quick, I say. In and out. Shoot anything that moves, long as it's in our way.

He nods, staring at his shotgun.

I wonder if he's had too much. Like just today, he's faced certain death twice, and here I am asking him to do it again, for KK, for myself, and I tell him he doesn't have to come.

Bro, saved my life. He pumps the shotgun.

We get out. I lead the way. I run, holding on to Buster. I'm remembering her directions as I near the squat brownstone— two stories up, turn left, first door on the right—and I stop at the door and give it a jiggle. It's locked. I blast the handle with my shotgun and kick the splintered wood. The door creaks open. Typewriter is at my side with his gun raised. He kind of looks like a badass, all blood and guns. We take the red-carpeted stairs three at a time. I'm straining my eyes for movement, my ears for giggles. KK had told me there were at least three of them outside her door. She'd been able to differentiate them by laugh pitch. I run up those stairs and I'm feeling good, like life is a videogame, and there are so many chemicals coursing through my food- and sleep-starved body that the paisley carpeting is slithering, the streaks of gold growing vines, and the walls pulsating to each breath.

Up another flight.

Then I hear one. Judging by the cackle, it's a woman pushing middle age. I see her before she sees me. She's wearing a long black T-shirt over bare legs. There's blood all over her thighs and I think maybe she died giving birth or forgetting a tampon. I take the stairs like I'm a god skipping over planets, and she turns just in time to see Buster feet from her face and then it's that familiar explosion—both sound and sight—and I don't even stop, just keep running, spitting out what might be a bit of her earlobe.

This is everything I've ever wanted.

Maybe not the exact circumstances, but the situation—me saving KK, me proving that my inability to quit smoking shit a year before doesn't mean I'm useless. The vines on the carpet try to ensnare my feet. Like everything always has—drugs and jobs and friends and family, all holding me back, and I see that now, me running to save the only thing I still care about. I'm Chase Daniels the motherfucking hero, and I'm on the third floor and there's a group of them trying to break into *my* girl's place, trying to claim *my* girl as one of their own.

Pump, shot, pump, shot.

Typewriter is doing the same. We're both screaming. I wonder if he's having the same trip—a two-person shooter arcade game versus the entire world.

They're stumbling and I'm yelling, Who's giggling now?

I see my first fully exposed ribcage. The boy can't be but ten. He's just white ribs and Scooby-Doo underwear and a twitching left foot.

Typewriter and I stand over four bodies.

I am Tarzan.

The door opens before I can knock and there she is, KK, my Jane, KK, the most perfectly imperfect woman I've ever seen. She's standing there with a chopping knife. She's wearing a white cami, tighter than hell, and her breasts make the smallest of bumps. She runs toward me. Or maybe I run toward her. We're hugging, crying, telling each other, I'm so glad you're alive. Her perfume has changed to something murkier but when I press my face to her neck, it's still KK—her breath, her skin, her sweat, all of it sweetly grounded in an earthy base—and I don't know if I've ever been this happy.

Maybe I'm telling her I love her.

Maybe I'm kissing her neck.

KK backs away and points to Jared on the couch. He looks horrible, pale and sick, girl-jean skinny, his black hair shielding half of his face.

I tell KK we need to go.

Help me get him to the car, she says.

Typewriter steps into the apartment. He's jamming shells into his shotgun. He's telling me we need to go, he can hear more coming.

I grab KK's wrist. I could wrap my fingers around it twice. She must have been shooting shit for a goodly while.

Now, let's go.

Jared.

We can't. They're coming.

I yell to Typewriter to guard the door.

KK's nothing but snot and shaking bangs. I tell her we need to go right fucking now.

Help me get Jared into—

He's turning. He's done, baby. He's fucking turning.

Two more, Typewriter yells.

Three shots fill the efficiency.

I yank on KK's wrist.

Stop, she yells.

I stare at KK. Her face is the same as it was when she told me that she was finished, that she couldn't stand by and watch me kill myself. I'm replaying that morning, even though I don't want to. KK stood at the end of our couch in nothing but a pair of kitten-print panties and a baby blue tank top. I'd skipped bed that night, told her I couldn't sleep, and spent the early-dawn hours smoking speed, not even getting high, just right, just adjusted. She told me she couldn't do it anymore. That she was leaving. Going back to treatment. I laughed. I told her she couldn't quit. She'd gotten on her knees then and rested her face on the side of our couch cushion, like the simple act of keeping her head upright was too draining. She begged me. She said, Chase, I'm on my fucking knees begging you to come with me, to get clean. We can do this. We have to do this. And I sat there with my stupid stem in my hand and a blister on my lip from the hot glass, a dick rubbed raw, and a life I'd once again suffocated the fuck out of. I sat there staring at the only person I'd ever really loved, and told her I wouldn't stop using.

I know now, standing in her apartment, that it's the same thing. I either choose the path I always do, the one that leads me to being alone wanting to straight-up kill myself, or the one where I do something for somebody else.

I go to the couch and drape one of Jared's lanky arms over my neck. He's got a sloppy track mark from his greedy haste to get high. He can barely stand. KK is at his other side, telling him things like *you can do this, come on, baby, use your feet.* Typewriter fires another shot into the hallway.

Clear? I yell.

Go, go, he says.

He leads the way. Jared's head keeps smacking into my ear. It hurts. We take the stairs as fast as we can. I hear giggles, then a gunshot, then silence. I want to drop Jared and pretend it was an accident. We keep going. We're on the first floor and then at the door and there's a twenty-something guy guarding the way and Type flips his gun around and swings the butt at the guy's face. It cracks. He giggles. He takes a swipe at Typewriter and I maneuver Buster one-handed and fire from the hip. The Chuck slumps against the wall. Then we're outside and now they seem to be coming from every direction. I'm practically carrying all of Jared and running as hard as I can, knowing I'm a good person, a decent person, a person at least trying to do something differently than I have for the previous twenty-five years.

KK opens the back door.

I throw Jared in. Jump in myself.

Type starts the car and fists crash on the glass as we pull away, and we're driving, bodies visible, thud, then not.

5:11 PM

I've made KK climb up to the front seat next to Type. She protested, saying that Jared needs her. I've told her that on the off chance he does change, I don't want her back there, that I can take care of it.

We've been driving for an hour and we've exhausted the range of conversation. KK's given me lots of one-word answers. Type plays techno. We'll need gas before we make it back to the Albino's. I sit in the tiny backseat staring at Jared. The dude's about to die, that much is certain. He licks his lips and there's no moisture there, just thick spittle, already having moved past foam, now on to stages of crust. He's nothing but shivers. I wrap him in the bloody spare clothes we'd jammed into a garbage bag at my apartment. KK breaks her silence with a sudden outburst: He's going to die. I wonder if this isn't all of our fates once we get farther north. The Albino isn't too fond of strangers.

I keep trying to figure out what happened with KK and her sobriety. I drop hints, say things like *maybe he's got a collapsed vein* or *maybe your batch wasn't good*. These are met by silence or her telling me to stop. As good as it is to see KK, she's being kind of a bitch. She's spoken all of ten words to me, was pretty light on the thank-yous, and doesn't seem to give two fucks about Typewriter. I'm staring at the back of her neck. I can see the tail end of what must be a new tattoo. It looks like writing, numbers maybe. I move the ends of her blond hair out of the way. KK jerks forward.

What the fuck, Chase?

Jesus, just seeing the tattoo.

KK covers her neck with her hand.

Sorry, I say.

Fine.

We listen to synthesizer and bass and Jared's soft groans.

It's fucking stupid, anyway, KK says.

This is good. She's talking. I say, What is?

The tattoo.

What is it?

A date I thought meant something.

Then I understand she'd put in her sobriety date, stamped the shit right onto her neck. And I get it, I do. The need to make something impermanent permanent. To tell yourself that this time it's for real. That you are done. Forever. And what better way to mark that decision, the finality of it, than scar it onto your body? I understand it's one more block between you and the next shot. But I also understand the perverse pleasure of relapsing with this permanent marker there to remind you that you're a piece of shit, always will be, that this is what you deserve, addiction, sucking dick and robbing and spreading your sickness to teenagers with too much money.

I know the date tattooed on her neck. The day after she left our apartment and checked herself into rehab.

And then I'm looking at Jared. I move the sweatshirt I've

draped over his body. He barely registers this with a fluttering of his eyes. I look at his arm. He's got one vein beat to shit, bruised an inch in either direction of his injection site. A vein like this must have been at least a couple months of using. And I'm looking between his arm and KK's neck and Typewriter who's thumping the dash to the beat and then I think about seeing Tibbs walking around West Seventh the other morning and about the trucker Travis and about the Albino—all of us speed freaks, all of us the dregs of fucking society—and how we'd joked about us being the ones who'd survived, but it's *true*. Everyone I know who shoots scante is okay. All of us. We're the only ones who haven't turned into the walking dead. I wonder if there's something in the drug, some chemical that counteracts whatever the fuck caused the mass epidemic. This makes about as much sense as the rest of my life. I put my index and middle fingers to Jared's wrist. He's rocking a downbeat sober pulse. Then it hits me—the reason he's dying is that he needs more. His body is succumbing to whatever the fuck is in the air. He needs shit. I'm about to tell this to Typewriter and KK but I stop. I know under no circumstance will she see my logic of injecting our last rig into her dying boyfriend's arm.

I reach forward to the middle console and pretend to be digging around for a lighter. I palm the rig. I light a cigarette to cover my tracks. Then I move the coat over Jared's hand and my lap. I feel the back of his hand for his middle knuckle. From there, I press my finger along his skin until it hits the largest vein. I slip the cap off the needle and pinch the vein and am pretty sure I hit it and I tell myself I'm doing the right thing and saving his life and KK moves her hand off the back of her neck. I was right, the date is the first day of my life without her.

This breaks my heart even though I know it shouldn't.

She'd just wanted a better life. One that kept her out of psych wards and strange men's beds. But I can't help but take it personally.

Jared's eyes are smog. I think about the one second methamphetamines take to travel the length of a vein and hit the heart and then the brain. How long will it take to counteract the pathogen causing the epidemic? Did I just kill this motherfucker? He's still licking his lips, still trying to ease the pain of swallowing. I imagine Hoover Dam–sized floodgates opening and dopamine spilling out. Norepinephrine. Serotonin. Maybe whatever the fuck has almost caused the extinction of the species, maybe it binds to these sites. Maybe we meth addicts are immune because every spare receptor site is clogged the fuck up with extra neurotransmitters. Jared's leg starts to twitch. Then it starts to bounce. I don't want KK to turn around and see her man looking like an epileptic. I smoke my cigarette. I'll feel bad if I have just killed Jared but then I tell myself he was gone anyway. It was a last-ditch effort, maybe even heroic, and KK will never have to know. Then I think about starting the rest of our lives under this weight—my silent burden of having killed off the competition.

Water, Jared says.

This is the first word he's spoken. KK doesn't hear. He says it again. I look around for something. All I can find is a two liter of Mountain Dew. It's got to be better than nothing.

I unscrew the cap. It doesn't fizz, not even a little bit. I lean over and splash some into his mouth. He's able to swallow.

What the fuck are you—

Baby, Jared says. He reaches a sickly hand in her direction. It's the same one I just blasted full of dope. There's a pin drop of blood on its back. KK screams, clasps his hand, crying, saying, You're okay, you're okay, and she's climbing to the back and her flat ass is in my face and then she's sitting in my lap, lavishing her affection on another man.

Typewriter holds his pistol. He asks if he's turned.

No, I say. He's all good.

Jared's coming back. His leg twitches and he's able to mutter simple phrases. Mostly he says, I'm so thirsty.

KK kisses his eyes. His nose. She even kisses his come-crusted mouth and I know right then, it's serious, them, their love. I remind myself that this was all I had wanted. Simply for her to be safe. I'd told myself and God and my father and Typewriter this and I'd gotten my wish.

I tap KK on the side, tell her I'll slide up front. It's awkward and I might have a chub and I'm only a little careful that it doesn't brush against her hand.

It doesn't take long for Jared to become more coherent. He asks questions about what happened and if it was real, the death, the reanimated. KK fills him in. Then he sees me and I tell him what's up. I feel like Einstein. I've figured out our limiting variable. Nobel Prizes should be coming my way. I'm Mother Teresa and Gandhi. So fucking selfless, saving the guy who fucks the love of my life. I hear KK tell Jared that his heart is racing.

That's because he's spun, I say.

Typewriter laughs.

Jesus, can you just stop with that. Like I know I fucked up, KK says.

I figure I have to share my knowledge. It's life or death. I say, No, I'm serious, your boy's spun.

Feel like it, Jared says.

KK asks what he means. She touches his forehead.

I gave him a booster.

You stupid fuck, KK says. She hits the back of my head. Typewriter continues laughing, tapping the steering wheel.

I turn toward Jared and KK. I say, Listen, it was a gamble, but I realized that all of us have been using. I mean like every one of us still alive is on shit.

So fucking selfish, KK says.

So I gave him a hit, and he's fine now. How the fuck does that make me selfish?

Because you could have killed him.

He was about to die anyway.

Can't believe—

And it worked, right? I fucking saved him. He's talking, sitting upright. Am I right, Jared?

Jared puts his arm around KK. He whispers something. Then he looks at me and I hate his long stupid face. He says, Thank you.

Are you serious? KK says.

He saved my life. What the hell more do you want from him?

Bro, Typewriter says, you realize what this means?

I do, but I don't say anything.

He says, We're in this shit for life.

8:46 PM

The Albino sits Indian-style on the one couch in his cabin. He's only wearing underwear. He looks like one of the Chucks. He's let us in, and now just stares at us like we're the stupidest motherfuckers he's ever seen. I'm telling him that it's better, having more people, safety in numbers, that we can fortify his compound, that everyone can be of use, that we need to pull together.

He clears his throat. He points to KK. He says, That a boy or girl?

It's kind of funny so I laugh. He's taking it better than I would have guessed. His skin is Christmas morning snow.

This is KK, I say.

She steps forward.

The Albino makes no move to shake her hand.

And this is Jared, I say.

Jared says hello.

The Albino sits like a sage, some gatekeeper, some protector of this shitty life we're trying to build. He finally says, The blond thing can stay, but fuck horse face.

I'm liking where this is headed.

KK sniffles.

I toss the duffle bag of Sudafed and other pills on the floor. I say, We all stay.

What we got here?

The Albino gets up. His dick swings a little in his under-wear. He rifles through the bag, his face going from solemn to ecstatic as he pulls out box after box of ingredients.

You's done good, Crooked Cock. Done real good.

So they can stay? All of us?

Not promising shit.

For now, though?

For now, need to get cookin'. I'm not stopping for shit.

Fuck yeah, Type says.

Okay, so, what about us? What do you need us to do?

Fiddle yourselves, kill yourselves, don't make shit differ-ence to me, the Albino says.

But we're good to stay in here?

For now, yeah. Just don't make a fucking sound. They're out there, believe you me, out there waiting.

The Albino grabs the duffle and heads out the door. I lock the deadbolt and floor bar. KK says, This is the *safe* place you were talking about?

Far as I know, yeah.

With Casper tweaked out of his gourd? That's your idea of safe?

Jared tells her to stop, to keep her voice down.

And I'm supposed to feel good about sleeping in the same filthy room with *him*? asks KK. May not eat me, but sure as shit won't think twice before raping me. God, it's *Deliverance* up here. Nice.

I don't understand KK. I'm thinking this as I stare at her massive nose—I don't understand one thing about you—

because I not only saved your life, but that of your lover, and then I bring you away from the city, that is to say, away from large groupings of walking dead, to the fucking riverhead of the finest crystal in Minnesota, which we already determined was the one thing keeping us alive, and this is how you treat me? With disdain? With resentment? Like what the fuck?

You have a better idea? I ask.

Just stop, baby, Jared says.

I hate Jared because his arm's around KK and she seems to be calming and because he has that power now. He's me. He's who I was, who I want to still be.

They sit on the couch. She makes a disgusted face examining the cushions. Typewriter stands by the single-burner stove. He's drinking a longneck. I tell him to toss me one. It tastes amazing. I haven't had shit to drink or eat for what seems like days. I offer the rest to KK. She takes the bottle and our fingers touch. I glance at Jared, who sees the whole thing.

So what's the plan, yo? KK says.

I'm not sure who she's talking to. It's just more bitching.

She says, Stay up here in the woods and shoot Tina? Is that as far as we've gotten?

What the fuck is your problem? Typewriter says.

This takes us all by surprise. The lumbering giant has a voice.

Serious, man, like what do you want from him? He saved your life. Get it? Your fucking life. And yours. And mine. Fuck, Chase like a regular old Forrest Gump.

Jared laughs and KK's giving daggers with her eyes and

then they soften and the smallest hint of a dimple grows on her cheek.

Fuck me, she says.

I'm about to agree but I catch myself.

Fucking Rambo over there, she says.

We laugh.

We pass two bottles of beer.

Jared says, Funny, if you think about it. I mean, how many times did you pray that this was what life was reduced to? A group of friends holed away, enough crystal to pass the time?

For real, Type says.

Am I right? Pretty much heaven, if you ask me.

With an entire species trying to kill you, KK says.

Well yeah, it's not *ideal*, per se. But there's a bright side.

No prison, Type says.

No having to get money, Jared says.

No AA, KK says.

Fuck AA, Type responds.

We grin and laugh and light cigarettes and maybe Jared isn't a complete dick.

He says, In a way, it's our chance to create the kind of world we want. From scratch. However we want it, we can sculpt it. Utopia, you know?

With the walking dead.

Half full, baby, always. We've talked about this.

I know this is a mistake on his part. KK does her snort-head-jerk-eye-roll thing. She says, Not hearing that shit right now.

Yeah, I know. I'm sorry. Just trying to say we can make this work. That's it. That's all I'm saying.

He's right, I say. It can work. Has to.

Straight up, Typewriter says.

I say, We have enough weapons to survive anything. Albino cooks like a motherfucker. We have shelter. Can make the grounds all strong and shit tomorrow, fortify them with fences. Set traps. You know Albino has canned goods to last months.

Exactly, Jared says.

And it will work.

Has to.

Has to what?

Has to work, KK says. She peels the paper label from the beer bottle. Has to work, she says again.

WEDNESDAY

I'm not sure if any of us are really asleep. I'm curled into a fetus in the corner of what passes for the kitchen. The Albino is still out in his shack. Type tosses on the couch. I hear the deadbolt unhinge. I sit up. I'm pretty sure I see KK's silhouette slip out the door.

Shit, she's bolting.

She's had enough, seeing her future as one of five people trapped in a one-room cabin and the rapid descent into a full-on shooting gallery, the walls splattered with the last squirt of our used rigs, us covered in scabs, grinding our molars down to nothing.

I get up, grab my pistol, and head outside. KK turns. Her face is a tired shade of fuck-my-life. She's sitting on the one wooden step. I motion with my head and she nods. The wood is wet, slippery almost.

Probably shouldn't be out here alone, middle of the night, you know?

Yeah.

She stares straight ahead. She wears an oversized University of Kentucky shirt pulled over her bunched-up knees. I tell her she's got some big old titties.

She looks down at her kneecaps bulging against her shirt and laughs and it's nice, the softness of it, genuine. Wind blows. The air is the mixture of pine and damp earth and ammonia from the Albino's cooking. I tell her it smells good.

For reals.

I look at my wrist like I'm wearing a watch. I say, Should be done in about an hour.

He a good cook?

I cock my head. You for real? Guarantee you've had it. Clear as ice, shards bigger than golf balls.

Talking shit now.

Bigger than . . . I don't know, pretty big though.

Word.

Yeah.

It's fucked up talking about dope with KK. It feels like some violation, the colliding of two worlds that were never supposed to intersect, us and drugs, us together using, and that's what had fucked us up, us trying to make them merge, us trying to have it all.

Maybe she senses this because she says, How you been?

I laugh. I say, Other than everyone who isn't a junkie being dead, nearly dying myself, and now being stuck here?

Fucked up, right?

So fucked up. Like for the longest time, thought I was done for. Dead. That this was some sort of fucked-up trip that wouldn't end. Like that shit people talk about when you die and your brain floods with chemicals.

Have no idea what you're talking about.

You know, like white light?

I guess.

She hands me a butt. I light it. I think about the Chucks seeing two floating cherries.

Pretty shitty, I say.

What is?

Me. How I've been.

Word.

You a gangster now?

Sho' nuff.

Just the same old shit. Selling and smoking. Selling and smoking. Day after day, I say.

The life and times of Chase Daniels.

Pretty exciting, huh?

Beats the alternative, KK says, sometimes, at least.

You really believe that?

Not even a little bit.

Then what the hell happened? I mean, Jesus, thought you were all about sobriety.

Don't have to be a dick.

No, no, I say. I put my hand on her knee. This feels weird because it's kind of like her boob. I put my hand back in my lap. I tell her I just meant how serious she was about it.

I know.

I'm waiting for more but it doesn't come. Finally, she says, The same thing that always happens. You know how shit goes.

Yeah.

Life. You're going about your day, maybe six months into the *new* you, and then one day you look around and you're stocking shelves at Target, wearing that stupid fucking outfit of khakis and red polo, and people are just walking by, you know, like you're invisible? Just some girl working for fifty cents over minimum wage. And all you're thinking about is getting off work, but then you think about what you'll do, like really, and you know you'll drive home, cook macaroni and cheese, go to a seven o'clock meeting, listen to the same bitches complain about the same shit—I'm fat, my dad abused me, my job sucks, resentments are the number-one offender— and then you'll go home and watch *Laguna Beach* and a rerun of *Everybody Loves Raymond* before going to bed by ten thirty. All to get up and do it again.

Suicide, I say.

That's what I'm saying. But that shit always comes. Always. You know?

Don't have to tell me.

KK says, And the thing I get to thinking is that maybe it's not that great either way. Like I take one look at you, no offense, and know you're fucking dying, like inside. And then I think about the alternative like I was just talking about, that moment when you realize that the best you can do, I mean the absolute fucking best, is to be a less successful version of our parents. Like what the fuck? Seriously?

She's speaking pure fucking gospel. The truest things I've ever heard and I want to believe there's something else but I'm not sure.

Guess that's not a problem anymore, I say.

How so?

Sobriety isn't much of an option.

KK laughs. It's not as gentle as the one earlier. She flicks her cigarette. She says, Full-on guiltless using, yo.

We smile. I want to kiss her.

Guess we'll figure out the answer to that question, KK says.

What question?

If shit still sucks when you get what you wish for.

10:17 AM

We're staring at a Tupperware bin of scante. We're giddy. It's like the moment when the first pair of spread legs says *come on in.* I put the blue cover back on the bin. I say, We need to be smart about this. A schedule. Yeah, we need to make a schedule.

Bro, Typewriter says.

Yeah, for real, KK says.

No, he's got a point, Jared says. We need to do this responsibly.

Yeah, that's what I'm talking about. Okay, KK, how long did it take for Jared to start getting all fucked up?

What do you mean?

In the apartment. How long was it between the last use and when he started getting a fever?

They look at each other. Jared shrugs. KK thinks it was maybe two days. Jared agrees, then adds, Probably closer to a day and a half.

Okay, good. So we know we can't go more than a day without dope, give or take a handful of hours.

Not going to be a problem, Typewriter says.

Stop, man. This is serious. So we should be smart about this. Maybe each of us is rationed a teener a day. This can be consumed however you want. But that's it.

Dude, KK says.

Let me get my teener then, Type says.

In a minute, Jesus. We've got to get organized first. Have to make this place livable, safe.

That's what I was talking about, Jared says.

So we each have responsibilities—

KK says, You serious? We're going to have chores? Checklists?

Not chores, just . . . *responsibilities*, like I said. Let's not forget what's waiting out in those woods.

Can we get our heads first?

KK, Jared says. He touches her forearm. He says, We need to make this place as secure as possible.

Fine, KK says.

Type?

Yeah, fine.

Okay, good. So the fence needs to be inspected, make sure it's sturdy all over. And we need to do something about the sleeping arrangements. Get bedding or something.

And food, Jared says.

And food, yeah.

The Albino's got plenty. Dude stocked up for this, knew it was comin', Typewriter says.

Right, but we need to organize it. Make sure there's nothing we need.

Weapons, Jared says.

Good, yeah. We've got plenty, but need to teach KK how to use them.

And Jared, she says.

Good, this is good, I say. I'm feeling better about everything. I'm holding hundreds of thousands of dollars' worth of meth. I'm thinking about handing out the rations. I'm wondering if I'll smoke mine or shoot it. And I'm thinking about us getting this rural shithole White House secure, us doing our *chores*, as KK called them, us sweating in the sun and working together and then us sitting around at night telling funny stories and it being good, a dinner party, friends catching up after years estranged.

So I can start with the fence, I say. Could use another hand, though.

I look at Typewriter. He stares into the dense forest. He says, Fuck that.

I'll go, Jared says.

I'm still staring at Typewriter and his eyes jump between the trees and the bin of dope, never meeting mine. Okay, I say.

KK says, So that puts me in the house, making beds?

Unless you have another idea?

Could teach her how to load a gun, Type says.

Fine. That's fine. But then you guys get the house ready, check on the food.

And what about your BFF? Casper the Friendly Ghost over there, KK says.

Not really trying to fuck around with him. Just let him be, I say.

Smart enough, Jared says.

Okay, so we're good?

They all nod, staring at the bin. I crack the top. KK starts forward and I tell her I'll dole out the rations and she tells me I'm a controlling motherfucker and I say, We need to be smart about this.

Got needles? she asks.

This breaks my heart. I tell her inside.

I hand a hardy shard to each of them. I take one for myself, palm an extra little guy. I tell them this needs to last the day. To not do it all. None of them respond. They're already heading back inside. I think about following and distilling my dope on a spoon. It was better, shooting it, and I know it's a quick hop, skip, and jump to completely fucked when needles become oxygen, so I head to the Civic. I hide the bin under the trash bag in the backseat. I take out the glass stem from the glove compartment. I place the smaller of the two chunks into the bowl. I take out my torch. I burn and the chamber fills with the acidic aroma of meth, of pure fucking love, of any person I want to be, of any mood I want to claim as my own, and I take a slow pull, release the chamber, and my mouth is being suffocated and poisoned and ass-fucked and then my throat and lungs and I hold my breath, hold on to Buster, hold on to the pipe, hold on to my vision of us being some new colony, harmonious, all of us.

11:22 AM

It's obvious Jared is one of those annoying tweakers who can't stop his stupid mouth from flapping when he's spun. He also pulls out his pistol at every swaying branch. I tell him to shut the fuck up.

He doesn't. He's all, I'm extremely excited about all of this. It's not unlike make-believe. Cops and robbers. Indians and cowboys. Marines and aliens. God, that's totally what it is. Am I right or am I right?

I try to ignore him.

Jared drops his voice all movie trailer–like. He says, They survived the apocalypse, and awoke to a foreign world. Five of them total. The Albino, Typewriter, KK, the Ex, and . . .

He stops, probably realizing he'd just typecast me as the ex.

Sorry, he says, then continues with his fake voice, The only thing that kept them alive was Tina, her touch sometimes loving, sometimes gentle. . . .

I run my hand along the chain-link fence enclosing the

Albino's compound. We've been walking for a half hour and there's still a third to go. I've marked one section so far that's in need of repair. I hope the Albino has some extra fencing. I figure he probably does, because he's *that* guy, the one who's thought people were coming to slit his throat since he was old enough to crawl.

Jared's still blabbering: And lurking behind every tree, the Chucks crouched giggling and licking their lips, waiting for night to fall. . . .

I wonder if the fence will do a damn thing. Probably not. It's about five feet tall, staked every few yards. I remember the little girl with the umbrella socks. How easily she bashed through Typewriter's door. But what else are we going to do? Sit in the shack and wait for them to beat their decaying fists through century-old cedar? Maybe it's just the feeling of movement, the illusion of productivity that I'm craving, that I think we all are. To feel like we have options and actions we can take. To feel like we can do something other than wait to die.

Jared's like, But the walking dead weren't planning on crossing paths with one young man with a deadeye shot. With this, Jared lunges into a wide stance, his gun held like a gangster from a rap video. I tell him that's enough.

Huh?

Noise, man.

Then he's whispering. He says, Roger that. I feel what you're putting down.

I can't stand this motherfucker. If this is what it's going

to be—daily role-play-Jared-as-adolescent-hero—then count me out. I'll take my chances elsewhere. I wonder how KK was able to deal with it. She was so deadly serious when she used. Everything doom and gloom, and if she didn't have blond hair you'd think she was goth queen of America. Then I'm remembering us using together. How it was fun at first. How this changed, like it always does. I'm remembering one night when she locked herself in the bathroom. I was annoyed and then worried and then frantic, knowing I'd see her ninety-pound body in a crimson bath, one wrist hanging over the porcelain, the tile stained with blood. So I broke through the door. The lock crumbled. She sat on the toilet, wearing an ugly pair of cream panties. We made eyes, then I followed her gaze to her abdomen. It was covered in raised circular bumps. I was like, What the fuck? She didn't say anything. Just took the cigarette dangling from her thin lips and pressed its burning end into her stomach. I rushed over, knocked the cigarette onto the floor, and I was on my knees, my hands on her thighs, yelling, demanding she tell me what she was doing, and her stomach was like a fly's eye—countless raised circles, each one staring at me like I'd let her down.

She petted my hair. She said, Can do bad all by myself.

J-Bone, Jared says.

Huh?

J-Bone. You like it?

What?

A nickname. J-Bone. I think it has a nice ring to it.

I shake my head and keep walking.

C-Money, Jared says.

No.

No?

No.

Hmm. Thought I was onto something with that. You sure? C-Money? J-Bone and C-Money out patrolling the grounds?

No.

We keep walking.

J-Bizzle and C-Maker.

You need to stop with that shit. I can't deal with it right now. You feel me?

Roger.

I wish we had cameras set up around the property. That each square foot was covered with an eye in the sky and we had a control station set up and we'd take turns watching these grainy feeds, take turns making sure of our relative safety. Then I'm wondering how long the power grid will stay up. Nobody's left to do whatever they do to keep power going. I think about total blackness and about having to go out and loot generator after generator and gasoline and how much this is going to suck.

J-Snizzle and—

I turn and grab the front of Jared's T-shirt. His eyes widen. I'm about to hit him because he's so fucking annoying and because he's somehow found his way into the pants and heart of KK. He looks scared, surprised, his eyebrows all sorts of arched. I let go of his shirt. I say, Stop talking.

The hell, man?

I blame it on the need for silence, that we don't know what's out here.

He seems only somewhat satisfied with this explanation. He starts walking. I can see him straighten out the creases I've caused in his shirt. We're quiet. I run my fingers along the chain link. I like the way it feels. It reminds me of driving on roads under construction, the smoothness between bumps.

Jared starts talking, his back to me. He says, I know this is hard for you. Would be for me too.

I don't want to have this conversation with Jared. The proverbial husband and ex-husband moment of forced connection. It feels trite. I don't respond.

But I appreciate it, he says. I really do. I know it would have been easier to leave me in that apartment. Nobody could have blamed you for that.

You would have done the same for me.

He shakes his head. He says, Not sure about that.

I laugh because this takes me by surprise, this comment, its honesty.

Seriously, Jared says. If the situation was reversed. . . . Shit, even if it *wasn't* reversed, even it was still me with KK and I had to save you while putting my life in danger . . . might have been on your own.

Bullshit, I say.

Maybe. I don't know.

The fence turns right, not quite at ninety degrees. We're a good distance behind the shack. I'm glad to see he's calmed down with the JLo comments and the aiming of his pistol.

The reason is simple, he says.

What is?

The difficulty I would have saving you.

Kind of a dick, I say.

I see the way she still looks at you.

I ask him what he's talking about and play it off like he's crazy, that I'm not following, but really I'm thinking that he might be right, that I wasn't delusional, that we still share a connection, and maybe that's just the reality of any two people coming together under the most fucked up of circumstances, us meeting in a round-cornered psych ward, and then us doing it together, sobriety, meetings, the moments when one of us was the lifeboat to the other's ship sinking under the weight of self-hatred, and then us succumbing together to that sinking, convincing ourselves and each other that it was a good idea, scante, that we could weather any storm as long as we did it together. And then the end, us realizing we couldn't. Maybe having gone through that, we shared something deeper than vows? Maybe there's still a chance?

I'm about to try to change the subject because I don't want Jared to see my full hand, but I hear something. I grab Jared. He flinches, thinking I'm going to get all aggro again. I whisper *listen*. It sounds like a motor, maybe the beaten motor of a pickup coming from somewhere deeper in the woods. My heart pounds in my ears. Then the engine noise fades.

You hear that?

Jared nods. He says, A car.

That's what I thought.

Are there even roads back there?

Not sure.

They can't drive, can they?

The walking dead? No, man. No fucking way. But somebody is.

Should we go check—

No.

You sure?

I run through the possibilities—some local guy trying to flee, some high school kid waking up from a bender, somebody who knows we're here—and whoever it is, they are junkies, have to be, if my theory is correct. This person or persons must realize this too. They must know about the Albino. I think about meth being the one limiting variable to survival, and we have it, at least a week's worth, and I hold Buster a little tighter.

What do we do? Jared asks.

I think about going out to investigate. Maybe it's just a kid wanting a fix. I think about the walking dead roaming through the forest. I should warn the others that we heard a truck, that we might be expecting trouble. Or I could just tell the Albino. Other people know he's here because that's what he did, cook shit, ounces a week, and Typewriter and I weren't the only ones he sold to. There are others. He'd know what to do. But then I think that maybe alerting him isn't such a good idea. He's already fucked up about us being here, and the thought of more coming might be too much.

Keep quiet about it, I say.

You serious? I'm really not sure what good that will—

Because it's probably nothing. We don't need the others

more paranoid than they already are. Have enough to worry about. And we're taking the precautions to shore up this bitch.

I hardly think that's fair.

You want to know what's not fair? This, man, fucking *this*. I span my arms to either side. I tell him it's not fair that everyone's dead, that shit will never be the same. I want to keep going—tell him it's not fair that he, the AA predator of newly sober girls, is the one with KK. That I have to pretend like shit's all good. That I have to play the mentally together leader, that all I want to do is lock myself in the fucking car with the bin and shoot enough Tina to make my heart explode. I tell him to trust me. That the noise we just heard was nothing, at least nothing the others need to know about yet.

4:15 PM

We take a group consensus—one teener isn't enough per day. We settle on two.

5:33 PM

We're bored and spun and the Albino won't put on clothes, outright refusing, telling us we're lucky he's letting us stay here at all, and then he smiles, his irises outlined in red, and says, When them sons a bitches come, they won't know I'm not one of them.

I can tell KK's drifting off into the dark cocoon of her

sped mind. Typewriter's back to working his pick spot. His fingers are covered in skin and blood. Jared's rocking in the other corner. I feel like masturbating. Each of us is having a completely different experience not five feet from one another. We need to get out of the shack. I smell my breath or maybe my crotch and it's awful, stale butter popcorn covered in yeast. I think about the small pond Jared and I had passed on our walkabout. I ask the Albino if he dumps any chems in there.

Stupid fucking Crooked Cock, that's my drinking water.

I feel like my mother when I suggest to the group we take a swim. I'm trying to raise morale, to lift spirits, and I *am* my mom. When I was growing up, she was coated in an exterior of pep, of good cheer. She'd been the first one to suggest activities. Bowling night. Game night. Picnic night. Everything with a title, everything trying to bring the family together. My father and I would trudge out of our own little worlds—me in my room playing Nintendo, him in his office doing bank work—and we'd climb into the family Suburban. We'd piss and moan. My mom would talk it up, how fun the science museum would be, how picking apples at Pine Tree would be perfect. But then something would happen. We'd start to have fun. My dad would forget about deals that didn't go through. I'd forget about dying on the last boss of Mega Man. We'd be together doing something seemingly stupid but we'd make it fun, my mom the smiling family mascot. So this is what I'm thinking. I need to get us doing something other than shooting dope and caressing the barrels of our guns.

You guys want to go swimming?

Nobody responds.

Swimming? Anyone?

Typewriter mutters something to himself. He keeps touching the sore on his face, then examining his fingers, then back to digging.

I stand up. This gets their attention. I say, Let's go. Everyone. We need to go swimming.

Busy, KK says.

Not acceptable. Everyone. Pond just behind the house. Will do everyone some good, get the stink off us, refreshing and shit.

I pull Typewriter's hand away from his face. I tell him there's nothing on or underneath his skin. He asks if I'm sure. I tell him I'm sure. I look over at catatonic Jared and I say, J-Bone, let's go, man.

He gives me the widest shit-eating grin.

J-Bone, he says.

That's right. Time to take a dip, J-Bizzle.

I could do that.

Fuck yeah, you can do that.

KK's jaw is working overtime. She looks at me. I wonder what kind of shit is turning over in her head and then she gives a hint of a smile, at least her eyes do, softening from their cold-ass glare.

So we're good? I say.

She nods.

Albino?

The, he says.

The Albino, you down?

Pass up a chance to see that fucking miraculous curving cock?

It's not . . . I stop. What the fuck does it matter? We're gathered at the door and I'm back to being my mom and I'm handing out after-school treats in the form of shotguns and then we're all walking out of the house, into the woods, us a family, dysfunctional to the fucking core.

We head past the meth lab. I trail behind the group by a few paces. I like us—five motherfuckers who would steal a retarded kid's helmet to pawn for a buck fifty—and we're making this work. We're beating the odds. We're sticking to our new rations. We're loaded and dangerous and there aren't any walking dead and I tell myself not to think about the truck I heard earlier, that it was nothing, that it was somebody just trying to get by.

This is it? KK asks.

Yeah, not bad, right?

Scum all over the shit, yo.

Better than Chuck blood. Am I right?

Hey, Crooked Cock, take a look at perfection, the Albino says. I turn. He's stretching out his cock. He's completely shaved. I laugh. He says, Straight as a motherfucker. Jealous?

Jesus Christ, KK says.

The Albino lets go of his dick and gives a few hip gyrations, sending it in a helicopter, and he says, Ready for takeoff, and then he laughs like this is the funniest thing ever and we do too and he sprints in his gimpy gait to the pond, jumping, his legs pulled to a cannonball. He lands in about a foot of water. He curses. I toss off my shirt. Typewriter already has his off and his B cups jiggle as he kicks off his sweats. I see his back, the scratches from the reanimated two days before. They're still scabbing. I figure this is a good thing, remembering the trucker's eye, how it healed itself in seconds.

Jared mumbles about J-Bone taking a skinny-dip. I give him a quick once-over. He's in decent shape, his abs visible, his cock a tad on the tree-stump side of the spectrum. I try not to imagine KK loving it and sucking it and spreading her malnourished legs, but I'm fucked because there it is and she's laughing, telling him to keep on his fucking clothes, and I make sure I'm rocking a decent chub before I drop my shorts and boxers. I start toward the pond. Typewriter, the Albino, and Jared are just bobbing heads farther out.

You coming? I yell to KK.

Some fucking privacy, yo.

My bad, my bad.

I pretend to shield my eyes as I walk by. I hope she notices my dick is bigger than Jared's. I'm really watching her and she's got her shirt off and her tits are like a prepubescent boy's and her stomach is nothing but ribs littered with pink circular scars and I'm taking my sweet time pretending to acclimate to the water, my feet then my shins then my knees then my dick, and I'm watching KK pull off her Daisy Dukes and she's not wearing panties and it's bald and I'm making sure I'm fully submerged because I'm getting all sorts of excited.

I swim twenty yards out to the middle of the pond. Type tells me to come a little bit closer. He says, Totally pissed, bro. Feels like heaven.

I splash his face.

The Albino tells me I can't hide that bent beast forever. Jared spits arcs of algae water. Then we hear a shriek. My heart nearly fucking stops. KK comes splashing into the water, her arms above her head, her body starving, broken, the most beautiful thing I've ever seen with the sun behind her head and the water nothing but reflected diamonds and I relax because we're kids in a simple time when there's no better joy than escaping an afternoon of chores in the coolness of fresh water.

She swims out to us.

I want her hand to brush any part of my body.

She finds refuge in Jared's arms. They face each other. I know she has her legs wrapped around his waist and that's as far as I'll let my mind go. I think of anything else. Anything. I think about the fence we shored up with a ribbed sheet-metal panel. About the small shard of scante I'd pocketed in the morning. That I can go smoke it after the swim. But it's not really working, the distractions. I'm picturing Jared's dick pressing against KK's vertical smile. About it knocking on her door, maybe poking its head in for a quick visit.

Marco, Typewriter says.

He has his eyes closed. It's not hard to see him as ten years old, always Marco, never Polo.

Marco.

The Albino whispers *Polo*.

Typewriter turns in his direction, waving his fat arms at the sound.

Polo, I say.

Typewriter spins again.

Marco.

Polo.

I duck under the water and swim a few feet.

Marco.

Polo, KK says. She's out of Jared's arms, off his stupid dick, now swimming away from a thrashing Typewriter.

Fish out of water, he says.

Fuck you, I say.

Typewriter lunges for me. I think I'm out of his reach but his Italian sausage fingers hit my face and I say, Fuck my life, and he says, Yeah boy.

Marco.

I hear *Polo*s all around me. I hold my eyes tight. I'm calling out *Marco* and I'm moving a few feet this way, then a few feet that way, and really, I'm tracking KK's voice, her soft calls of *Polo*, her voice playful, inviting. Marco. Polo. The Albino's telling me that Polo's got a nice straight dick for Marco's pleasure. I'm pretty sure Typewriter isn't responding, probably terrified of once again being *it*. I hear KK's *Polo*. I know I'm close. I tell myself that a simple peek would speed the whole thing up, but this is cheating, a betrayal for a game meant for lazy summer afternoons, maybe a betrayal against innocence, and then I'm seeing the little girl playing with the rottweiler, the little girl ripping out its throat, how I thought this had been something to do with innocence, and it's *Polo*s all around me, Marco, me as Marco, and I'm exploring the world of an algae-filled pond, the world of postapocalypse, the world where nothing matters besides keeping enough shit in our system to not end up dead. I block out everything besides KK's calls. I swim in slow motion. I'm a moth to her voice. I've got to be close. I want to look. To see her smile. To see the triangulation of dimples between cheeks and chin, to have these be directed at me.

Marco.

Polo.

Marco.

Polo.

I'm close. I've got to be a few feet away. I reach out with my hands. I think about being one of them, the walking dead, because I'm laughing with my arms outstretched. I'm trying to find another human being, something living. I'm so close but she's stopped calling Polo and I wait, my flexed toes just long enough to touch the baby-shit-soft flooring of the pond.

I feel something close behind me. Then I feel skin pressing against my back. Then there's pressure against my neck and KK whispers, Polo. Her hand wraps around my stomach and I can't move because this is the most amazing touch I've ever received and I'm praying her skeleton fingers never finish their journey, that they stay there on my stomach, dip lower, that we share this touch underneath the surface of everyone else's vision.

I reach my hand behind me. It makes contact with what I'm guessing is her ass. It's nothing but a compact curving of body. I want everything to stop. For this moment to be my happily ever after. For me to reach lower.

But that doesn't happen. She says, Shit. Got me. Marco.

Then she swims away.

I'm left there with a raging hard-on. I'm left there wondering what the fuck just happened. Was this her telling me that I love you, always will, you and you alone? Was this her being completely spun, nothing more than a physical pleasure response to the brushing of skin against skin? My mind is a keno wheel. I am Marco Polo. I am my mother. I am Chase Motherfucking Daniels.

And life is perfect.

A moment painted in watercolors.

Maybe Jared is right about our creation of utopia. That this here—five people swimming, splashing, laughing, forgetting about everything other than a simple game—is as good as anything can get. This is what Thomas More had been trying to describe. And here we are, the outcasts, the people America wants to pretend aren't walking the streets, living an impossible dream.

Something catches my eye in the trees. I peer harder. Some movement, a flashing of blue, an unnatural color to vegetation. I'm like, What the fuck, and I peer harder, straining my eyes for everything they're worth, but I don't see anything else. I tell myself that dope knows no sense of serenity and will crop up in paranoia at the worst times.

Marco.

Polo.

Just fucking relax, I tell myself. Everything's okay. You're okay. We're all okay.

Then I see it again, and this time I'm fucking sure of it, blue movement in a sea of green. It's a pair of jeans. I start swimming as hard as I can to the shore. I need to get to the guns because whatever it is in those woods can't be good and

I'm panting like hell and when I reach the shallows, I stand, looking over to the trees, and I don't see anything, and then I glance to our clothes and shotguns and two dudes are standing there, Buster in the hands of the taller one with a mesh cap, a trucker mud-flap silhouette of a naked girl on its front.

Well, fuckin' A, he says. Pretty precious out there.

The other one laughs. He's shorter, fatter, his bearded face a fifteen-pound bowling ball.

I stand in a few inches of water. I'm naked. I have no idea what to do, if these people are friends or motherfuckers who will slit our throats.

Must be cold, Mesh Cap says.

A little shrinkage, A?

What? Who are—

Friends of the Albino.

Albino, I yell. I turn around and he's staring at me. His face is a ghostly shade of fear or maybe that's how it always looks. I face the two guys again. The shorter one has a shotgun trained at my dick. I cover up with my hands. They start laughing then and yell for all of us to get the fuck out of the water.

I tell them we don't want any trouble.

Don't want any trouble?

Yeah, doesn't want any trouble, Fat Face says.

They laugh.

For real, guys, just drop the guns, man. Come on. We're all in this together.

I hear the others getting closer.

Mesh Cap says, Fuckin' A, look at that one there.

I turn. KK's standing there naked and exposed and she's not covering herself in the slightest and I love her and I can hear the fat one talking about her being a freak, that he can just tell, and I tell him to shut the fuck up.

Big talk for a guy standing there naked.

With a shrunken dick, the shorter one says.

Fucking A right.

Albino, I say. He's at my side now. He says, Fucking Canucks. Figured y'all be the first ones dead.

Little faith.

The fuck you want? the Albino says.

What do you think?

The Albino takes the lead. I wonder if he knows he's massaging the head of his dick. He says, So my shit ain't good enough for y'all before, but now it is?

Price has changed.

Fuck you.

Oh boy, now is that a way to talk to your neighbors from the north?

Ain't got any more. Shot the last bit last night.

The big motherfucker with the hat laughs. He pumps the shotgun, *my* shotgun. He says, We've been watching you for over a day now. Not covering the stink of cooking very well, know what I'm saying?

Shit, the Albino says, no more ammonia. Only able to get half an O.

We'll see about that. Got the boys checking out that rat's nest you call a house right now.

Oh no you don't.

Fucking A right we do.

So that's what this is?

A motherfucking jacking? You betcha. You really thought it would go any other way?

The big one motions with Buster for us to get the rest of the way out of the water. I take a few tentative steps. The fat one's eyes are all over KK's pussy and I tell him to watch his stare and he laughs and calls me an American hero. I am about to reach over and grab my clothes and the dude kicks my ribs and I cough, feel a little like puking, and he tells me to leave them, just keep walking.

So it's us walking on branches and pinecones and us shivering because of the drying pond water and us naked and exposed and Typewriter has that look in his eye like he's not about to give up his scante. The Albino isn't talking, just chewing his face, just rubbing his dick. We should just give up the shit. It's a big batch but it's not worth dying over. Yeah, we'll have to go rob a pharmacy again, which is pretty much a death sentence, but whatever. I wonder if the Albino is being serious about the ammonia, if we'll have to pillage farms for chemicals and whether it will take longer than two days to cook another batch. That seems to be the magic number, forty-eight hours, until our minds fill with the poison that wiped out the rest of our species.

There's a truck parked in front of the shack. I know I fucked up keeping that one to myself. I make eyes at Jared and he seems to be accusing me of the same thing. One lumberjack motherfucker leans against the hood. He's smoking. He laughs at our naked bodies. Then two more dudes filling the same bill come out of the cabin and one says, Empty, just a cashed dime.

Buried it? he asks the Albino.

Told y'all we blasted it.

Shot an entire batch? the big one says.

Yup.

Then he flips the shotgun around and smashes the butt into the Albino's face. KK screams. The Albino crawls to his knees. His nose seems to have moved over an inch or two. Blood streams down his face, over his mouth. The contrast of red on white is sublime. His pigment-lacking irises shine red.

Then Mesh Cap presses the barrel against the Albino's face. He circles his eyes, squishes the broken nose, and then inserts the tip into the Albino's mouth. He says, We're going to try this again. Where. Is. The. Dope?

I know I need to do something. To grab the gun off the little fucker and shoot until the ground is nothing but Canadian blood. I don't want to see the Albino killed. And it isn't because he's our cook, but because he's one of us, and he took us in, and because I'll be motherfucked if I let some other human make this shit any harder than it already is.

Mesh Cap slides the barrel out of the Albino's mouth. He says, What's that? I can't quite hear you.

If y'all kill me, ain't a motherfucker with you smart enough to keep cookin'.

Thought you were out of ammonia.

Can get more.

The fat one leans over to his boy. He whispers something.

The big guy shrugs like this might be a good idea. He kicks the Albino in the spine, then grabs KK's arm.

Fucking stop, I yell.

No, Jared screams.

The other three have circled us. They have their pistols drawn. Typewriter's trying to tell me something but I can't figure it out. I tell them to leave her the fuck alone.

Or what? the fat one says.

I'll kill you.

They laugh at this. I feel a pistol pressing on the back of my head.

Well, we'll just fuck around with this one until you tell us where the dope is.

I stare at KK. She isn't fighting, but has her head down, her wet bangs shielding her eyes. I wonder if she's crying.

Maybe get off on that sweet pussy first, one of them says.

I'll fucking kill—

The lumberjack cracks Jared in the face. He falls.

I tell myself it's only scante and we can get more and it's not even a question of what to do and maybe they'll kill us afterward but there's no other play.

It's in the car.

American Hero cracks, the big one says.

In the car, I say again.

Well, let's just see about that, he says.

He lets go of KK.

I yell for her to run.

She doesn't.

All of them laugh.

I need Type to do something, to get one of their guns, to get all Hulk like he did to the little girl with umbrella socks. I need a miracle. Mesh Cap pushes me over to Type's Civic and I'm thinking about running, just fucking taking off, and maybe I'd be able to make it into the woods and from there I could survive, find shelter, steal a car, get myself back to West Seventh, maybe find some baseheads still smoking, and it could be okay, me alone, me surviving. I'm at the car. He tells me to open the door. I tell him it's in the back. He tells me to open the back door then.

Keep your fucking hands up. See them drop for one second, I'll kill the girl, let you watch, then kill you.

I open the door.

I've stashed the bin on the far side of the backseat. I have my hands raised above my head. He tells me to get the shit. I crawl into the car. I push my hands against the ceiling. I'm sitting on something hard and then I realize it's the pipe.

Going to grab it, I say.

Grab it, then.

I lift the bin onto my lap. I'm about to start my way back out of the car when I think about the pipe that's practically wedged between my ass cheeks right now. I maneuver my weight so it's perfectly aligned. I squeeze with everything I've got. I'm praying that the pipe stays put and doesn't fall and it's not much, but a triple-blown stem could puncture a jugular and has to be better than nothing.

I drop the Tupperware at his feet.

I step out of the car, keeping my clenched ass out of his view.

He knocks off the lid with the barrel of the shotgun. He says, Holy fucking A.

He bends over, taking out a scoop. He lets the shards slip through his fingers.

I stare over at Typewriter. Then at the Albino. And then he's exploding out from his knees and has his hands on the fat guy's shotgun and then I see Type standing and I'm yelling no, no, because we could have found another way and I reach to my ass and grab the pipe and it's all so fast, me smashing its end on the door of the Civic, Mesh Cap realizing what the fuck is happening, me lunging at his neck, me making contact, the pipe plunging into flesh, and then I'm on top of him and I hear gunshots and I know it's KK and I know I can't live without her and I'm thrashing, the pipe just a nub sticking from the dude's trachea. I grab the gun and sprint over and it's a full-on gunfight. I'm yelling a primal fucking scream and firing rounds into the lumberjack. Then the short guy turns and points but I'm quicker, my slug ripping through his skull.

I'll kill every last one of them.

The motherfuckers who took her away.

I'm firing and firing and there's no more movement and somebody's calling my name and I'm standing over Bowling-Ball Face and I'm crying and there's a small gurgle of blood bubbling from his throat and I pull the trigger again. And again. And again.

Chase.

Chase.

Somebody touches my shoulder and I spin around with the shotgun and am about to shoot and it's KK and she's covered in blood and I stop, just fucking crumple at her feet. She's telling me it's okay. It's over. She rubs my hair. She tells me I did good. I can't breathe because I thought she was dead and because I'm a murderer of humans.

I hear Typewriter. This makes me cry even harder. Then I hear Jared and he says, He's gone. I look up from the dirt. KK pulls my face to her bare chest. She tells me not to look. I'm bawling. I fight against her hands. I see the body of the Albino. Brains spew from the back of his skull. She tells me we're safe—shh, we're safe, you done good, baby, you done good.

8:11 PM

KK's with me. It's just us in the cabin. She's wrapped me in a sleeping bag. I have no idea where my clothes are. Typewriter and Jared are out burning the bodies. They'd tried to shield me from this conversation, but I heard them argue about what to do. Somebody said burying them wasn't safe, they might come back. They talked about burning them and the smell and the sight and this maybe attracting the walking dead and finally they decided it was the lesser of two evils.

I guess I'm not doing well.

There's a pressure behind my eyes, kind of like I'm being skull-fucked.

I remember shooting enough scante to kill an elephant. They just sat there watching me.

People just keep patting me on the back. Telling me I've done good.

I sit on the couch covered in the Albino's down bag. KK cleans up the mess those stupid fucking Canucks made searching the place. I just keep seeing the neck of the tall one give way, keep feeling the glass stem going deeper and deeper.

You did what you had to do, KK says.

I guess I must be talking.

I've never been so spun.

I keep seeing the Albino's bloodied face. Then it exploding. And I'm standing over the short motherfucker unloading round after round.

I'm still crying.

KK's at my side. She shakes out a few pills from one of the bottles I stole from Walgreens. She tells me to open up. I do. They taste like aspirin. My mother is at my side and I have a fever and she's telling me to swallow them, not to chew them, but I can't, the little disks getting caught in my throat, me gagging, me crying, me just chewing them.

I mumble, Mommy, I can't.

Yes, you can. Take a drink now.

KK hands me a beer.

I want to tell her that I can't drink beer, that I'm a little boy.

I know you are, she says.

And it's confusing, me sitting there on my childhood couch, my mother nursing me back to health, and I tell her I thought she was dead. She rubs my buzzed head. She tells me that we're safe. I ask where Dad is. She tries to smile but her mouth quivers and I start crying again, and hide my face in the musty odor of the Albino. I hear KK tell me everything happens for a reason. I ask her if she's real. She promises me she is. I tell my mom I love her. She says she loves me too. I tell her I'm sorry. She says not to worry. I see my mom coming to visit me at juvie. She's sitting in a white room. Her boy-cut hair is the sun. She doesn't tell me I'm a fuckup. That she's disappointed. She doesn't ask where I went wrong. She just pats the metal bench beside her. I sit. I try to be stoic. She smells like Obsession and Sure. I curl into her lap. I tell her I'm sorry, I'm so fucking sorry. KK tells me it's one day at a time. I tell her to let go and let God. She tells me to accept the things I cannot change. My father is dead. My mom says that fevers are good, that we're still fighting. I ask her if she has one. She says she's fine. I tell her that she's not fighting anymore. She holds me. She holds me and it's KK and we're in the janitor's closet on the seventh floor of the psych ward and she's running my finger along her stitched gash and we're trying to put everything behind us, that's what they tell us, *put everything that got you here behind you*, and we're excited because we whisper how we'll change our lives, how we'll be better, how we can do this, together.

I ask her when she gets out.

She tells me to close my eyes.

She pulls the Albino's sleeping bag tighter around me. I'm naked. I'm crying. My heart is moments away from giving up. I'm thinking of killing another human being. How one second the tall guy with the mesh cap was living, the next second he wasn't. I can feel the texture of his throat. How I had to stab him harder than I would have guessed.

You did the right thing, KK says.

Is my fever gone?

No, honey, still there, my mom says.

I want her to feed me Sprite and Nilla Wafers. I want her to change the channel to the Ninja Turtles. I want her to take a wet cloth and dab it on my head and tell me again how this sickness is me fighting.

THURSDAY

6:36 AM

I smell scante all around me. I open my eyes and Typewriter is grinning his fat-boy grin and hands me a rectangle of aluminum foil with crushed shit lining its crease. He's holding a hollow pen. It's kind of an awful sight to wake up to. For the briefest of moments, I think I'm back at his mom's. That I'm sitting on the one couch. That I've just been on one motherfucker of a trip, spanning all of three seconds. Then I see the cedar logs. Jared and KK sleeping on the floor. Typewriter's face cut to shit.

You feelin' better, bro? A little base for old time's sake?

I don't respond, just sit upright. Type puts the Bic in my

mouth. He lights underneath the foil and it takes a second to start to smoke and I'm gentle with my inhales because a burning chunk down the throat is a horrible way to start a morning. The smoke fills my mouth. Then my throat. I lean back. I hold it until my lungs scream for oxygen. Then I hold it a second longer. I let go of everything at once.

And it's like magic.

How I'm better, not afraid of failure or dying or hell or that we're now down to four.

That's what I'm talking about, Typewriter says. He claps to some beat that only plays for him. He joins in with a little dancing. Just some bobbing of his knees, his torso jerking in opposition on the upbeats.

Uncle Typewriter fixes things, bro.

He lights the freebase again. I lean in and take another hit.

Yeah, that's what I'm talking about, he says.

Shut up, KK says.

Somebody needs a head adjuster.

What time is it?

The fuck cares?

Typewriter walks over to KK and Jared. They're covered in a blanket, lying on another one. They each take a hit. I can tell Typewriter hasn't slept. One, because he's dancing, and that only happens when he's spun real bad, and two, because he's getting us high, which again, he only does when he's completely tweaked.

KK turns onto her stomach. She rests her head in her hands, her elbows on the floor. She asks how I'm doing.

Good, I'm good.

FIEND

Yeah?

Yeah. Don't really know what happened—

Did what a motherfucking hero does, Typewriter says.

He's in front of me for another hit.

He says, Chase Daniels, everybody.

I take a hit and watch Jared get up and come over and he sticks out his knuckles for a bump and I think this is weird but I give one anyway. He tells me I'm the man. I must have been really fucked up last night. KK gets up and she's just in her panties and this gives me wood and I look down and my dick's just staring right back at me and I cover myself with the sleeping bag.

KK walks to the little kitchen area. Typewriter asks if she's cooking omelets and this makes him laugh and she says, Something like that. She grabs a spoon. She's holding a needle between her teeth.

Fucking onto some shit now, Typewriter says.

You get this ready, baby? KK says.

Jared tells her no problem.

And we sit there distilling meth into rigs and I'm a little high but then I think about the way blood gurgled through the stem in Mesh Cap's neck and I tell them to cook me one too. I don't need a belt. My veins are thick like ropes. I blast a tenth into my arm. My eyes are those of owls.

Morning coffee, huh? KK says.

For real, Type says.

Fuck, that's good, Jared says.

I feel like I have to say something so I do—there'll be more—and this is met by three sets of eyes turning. That and

141

silence. I don't mean to be captain fucking bring-down, but that's the way my mind works sometimes. Practicality. Worst-case scenario. Realism. I tell them about the other handful of dudes the Albino sold to.

Doubt it, Jared says.

What part of that do you doubt?

Just that there's anyone left. That they would come here, he says. He's shaking his head, massaging the crook of his arm. His vein looks bad, on the verge of collapsing.

Just a matter of time, I say.

Type's still dancing. He says, He's right. There'll be more. The whole Chicago crowd. Motherfuckers will do whatever it takes to get more dope. Y'all know that.

So what is it you're suggesting? Jared says. That we leave? Head back to St. Paul? Because I'm telling you that's a bad idea.

Real bad, KK says.

Not suggesting anything, I say.

We're quiet. We're feeling methamphetamines settle into our synapses, these pleasures pulsating against our fingers and toes and teeth. We're thinking about waiting in this shack, the walls closing and closing and closing, the outside world closing too, walking dead and addicts with guns facing death, their holy grail our little blue Tupperware.

There's another problem, I say.

Jesus Christ, Jared says.

KK shakes her head at him.

The Albino's dead.

You think I don't know that, Jared says. His voice is sharp. I haven't seen this side of him before. I miss his other half, the

J-Bone and C-Money side of his habit. He tells me he burned his body while I was inside crying.

Fuck you, I say.

Typewriter points a finger at him. He says, And who the fuck saved your life? You forget that?

Jared's face is long and tired and taut and he mumbles an apology. KK rubs his back. She did this to me just last night and it was more than a concerned friend, and her touch across my stomach while we swam was more than a flirtation and I want her to finally realize she loves me. Jared asks what I'm getting at.

We have no more shit. None. Just what's left in the bin.

Which is a hell of a lot, Jared says.

Which *isn't* a hell of a lot between four people. Like even if we're good, we're looking at a week.

Two, KK says.

One, Typewriter says.

Jared stands. I want to tell him to put on his fucking shirt. He rubs his head, pulls his hair, and I wonder if he's seen this on TV, the desperate-man-in-dire-straits scene, and he says, You guys know how to cook?

I shake my head. Typewriter tells him it's too dangerous, explosions and everything. KK says he knows she doesn't.

Fuck, he yells. He kicks the wall. KK tells him to calm down.

It just never ends, he says. He paces. I wonder how much of this is the dope and how much of this is him. I don't know who he's speaking to. He says, Never fucking ends.

That's what I'm saying, I say.

Give me that base, KK says. Typewriter hands her the aluminum foil. She gets a hit, maybe two, and I know this is her answer, all of our answers really—to sit and get high, pretending like life is nothing but endless opportunities.

We need to leave. Have no choice, I say.

Shit yeah, bro, Typewriter says.

Fuck, Jared responds.

I say, We can get back to St. Paul. I'm sure Frogtown is pumping out that Hmong-made crank. Can give my boy Cheng a visit. Shit's better than nothing.

KK exhales. Her jaw clenches and unclenches.

Jared kicks the wall.

I think about pumping rounds into the bowling-ball face of that guy. How each shot carved away more of his flesh until I saw the ground through where his nose once was.

12:21 PM

We're about a half hour from St. Paul driving down a deserted I-35E and maybe it's because we're scared, because we have no idea what we're doing, because we are driving to where we fled from, but we have each shot up twice more. Type blares techno. We're four nodding heads. We're talking over one another and laughing at our own jokes and I see the turnoff for Highway 96, for my parents' home.

Pull off.

What?

Pull off here.

Typewriter swerves onto the exit ramp.

What the fuck? KK says.

Need to see something.

Bro, Typewriter says.

What's going on? Jared asks.

I need to see something.

Jared leans forward, his face between the seats. He's telling me not to be stupid and then he's calling me selfish and I'm not responding and Typewriter keeps going down 96 past suburban strip malls and dry cleaners and gas stations and Subways.

Jared says, Why don't we just stick to your stupid fucking plan?

Shut the fuck up.

No, *you* shut the fuck up. He's in my face now. His eyes are nothing but pupil. He says, Turn this fucking car around.

Or else what?

You really want to know?

And I hate him at this moment. Him all up in my shit, flecks of his dry-ass mouth speckling my face, trying to assert his dominance and I don't owe him a fucking thing, the least of which is an explanation, but I say it anyway—my parents live here.

They're fucking dead.

My pistol is jammed against his eye socket before I realize I've moved. I'm thinking about having killed another human, how it's not new to me anymore, how this would be just one more notch on the fucked-up belt of the new me. I can hear Typewriter telling me to chill and KK is screaming. Jared has barely flinched and I wonder if he wants me to pull the trigger, to end his pathetic life so he can die a holy martyr in the eyes of KK.

I put the gun back in my lap.

Jared sits back down.

Bass and synthesizer rattle the Civic's windows.

I tell Typewriter to take a left at the light. We're the only car. We pass Pennzoil and Decoy's Bar and Grill and then downtown White Bear with its quant little shops on cobblestone streets and the bookstore and the 687 Saloon. When we drive past the gazebo with its wooden benches and a small fountain, I remember riding my bike down here, my deck strapped onto my backpack, and how excited I was when I landed my first kick flip off the set of three stairs, and hanging out with the other skaters, us in saggy pants and bare chests and backward hats. This was before we had armpit hair and we wanted to be older so fucking bad. We'd steal packs of Reds and smoke them behind the bank, and listen to boom boxes spit out Wu-Tang and Rage. Life was rad then, at twelve or thirteen, nothing but summer sun, skating, and feeling oppressed by our rich parents.

Turn right up here at McDonald's, I say.

Jared snorts. I want to put a bullet between his eyes.

I'm high as shit, my legs are bouncing and I'm smoking cigarette after cigarette. We're passing White Bear Lake now and I see movement along the highway. It's one of them, a reanimated teenager in tight boxers, and we all turn to watch, silent, him watching us too. I'm thinking about Fourth of Julys when we went to family parties on the lake. I was all about tubing and I would hold on to that motherfucker with astonishing force, and my parents would clap and cringe and maybe that's the role of a mother or father—simultaneous cheering and shielding of eyes.

I hear Jared whispering to KK and she tells him to be quiet.

Maybe she knows this is going to be impossible for me.

We pass the Maplewood Country Club with its three-tiered driving range and empty parking lot. I feel like vomiting. I tell Typewriter to take a right into the next driveway. I see the shed where we kept the riding lawn mower. We go down the little hill and the house is a giant white number with wood shingles. I remember the bats that would come out at five o'clock every night of the summer. We park facing the three-car garage. To my right is an area of grass where my father would set up a miniature soccer net and we practiced, him telling me to keep my ankle locked, strike with the laces.

I know they'll be dead.

I get out of the car. It's humid, hot. I leave the rifle and shotgun, slipping the pistol into my pants. The others get out too. Typewriter tells me I don't have to do this. KK says the same thing. She touches my back. I tell them I do.

I test the garage door. It's locked. I lead them around the garage to the side of the house into the fenced-in kennel for our long-dead retriever. I get down on all fours and push open the swinging dog door. I listen for movement, then climb through. I'm in a seldom-used storage room filled with

Christmas decorations and I hold the door for the other three and we're all there and I don't want to keep going, to see them dead, like maybe it's better not to venture inside, to pretend they're okay, making things work, in love and together.

The key is under the clay flowerpot. I put it in the lock. Then we're inside the mudroom, and there's a stale smell and I know it will only get worse with each foot traveled and I'm thinking about the nights I'd hide in the mudroom with the dog, sleep with her on her red pillow of a bed. Then we're in the hall and the smell is worse. My framed artwork lines the white walls—a still life in watercolor from the third grade, a castle in crayon from kindergarten—and I peek into the family room with its paisley couches and flat-screen TV and more of my artwork. I climb the stairs. Nobody talks. Upstairs it's rotting meat and family pictures: me as a toddler on a beach in Florida, a family Christmas card with my giant head in a red sweater, me as a baby in a diaper, an ice-cream cone in my hand, my chest streaked with gooey mess. KK's crying. I just keep walking. I stare at my parents' wedding photo. My mom has very short hair, the longest strands only a few inches, and her face is pressed into my father's, his seventies Afro, his nostrils wide. KK gasps, probably seeing the resemblance, and I'm walking down the red-carpeted hall and it's like I've never really seen these pictures, never understood they were the happiest moments of our lives, us at our best, our attempt to make our lives meaningful, before I was a fuckup, smoking speed, bouncing from psych ward to juvie to treatment center. Maybe these pictures were a reminder for my parents that I was still worth the fight.

The smell is horrific.

I'm crying. I turn left at the end of the hall and the carpet switches color to blue and I'm remembering every morning when I sprinted from my bed to theirs, how sometimes they'd be awake, other times asleep, and I'd jump into the middle of their queen-size bed, and they'd each wrap an arm around me, how safe I felt.

KK asks if I want her to go in and check. I shake my head.

Their dressing room is filled with light and outside the sun shines and birds chirp and all that shit. I have my T-shirt pulled over my nose and I would give anything to tell them I'm sorry.

Their bedroom door is open.

I can see the bookshelf of Dick Francis mysteries, the fireplace, the pink easy chair. I can see the right corner of their bed, the dark wooden bedpost. Then I'm in their room and I'm expecting a greeting—Jesus Christ, son, I've been so worried—and I don't want to do it, turn to my left, see them lying there decaying, but I do.

I want to vomit up everything inside of me.

I want to purge myself of who I am. My father lies there alone, his stomach ripped open, his ribs exposed, picked clean.

I turn around and stumble into their dressing room. Everything's spinning—the white dressers, the blue carpet, the green love seat—and I tell myself it's for the better, my father dead. But I know his body had been eaten and I'm wondering where my mom is, like maybe she escaped, maybe she's okay. Then I hear giggling, and I pinch my eyes and the giggling gets louder and this can't fucking be happening. I look up and there she is standing in the bathroom doorway, my mother, the woman who birthed me, who taught me to read, who told me she would never give up on me, that she knew I could beat this addiction. She's wearing a white slip covered in blood. Her face is the same but different, her right cheekbone poking through a patch of exposed skin. I look at her hands. They're covered in blood. I understand she's fed on my father.

Mom?

She takes a step toward me.

I hear the pumping of a shotgun. I yell at Typewriter to put his fucking gun down.

My mom giggles.

I remember ordering Domino's pizza on Friday nights, watching a rental movie, maybe *Uncle Buck*, us sitting together and laughing. Maybe her giggle is the same, my mom standing there like she's happy to see me, and maybe she is, maybe she knows who I am, her prodigal son finally returning.

She takes a step closer.

Chase, Typewriter says.

Mom.

Giggle.

It's me.

Another step.

And then we lock eyes, my mother and me, and I know she understands who I am. That she can change. That somebody will find a cure. That it will go back to how it was but I'll be better and I'll do what I couldn't before. She's coming closer and closer and she's going to hug me, and it's been over a year since I've seen her and I'm sorry, so fucking sorry. I hear

Typewriter yelling and so is Jared and my mom is almost in arm's reach now and her giggles are shrill. She sticks out one hand, covered in bits of my dad, and I just want it all to stop, the blinding pressure behind my eyes, for it to go back to how it was, for me to never have found meth, for me to never have been born. I know in my deepest core that she will kill me, that she's gone, that everything that made her Cheryl Daniels has been swallowed up by disease. I have my pistol raised, and I am bawling, telling her I'm sorry, I'm sorry. I pull the trigger. She drops instantly and doesn't move. I sit on the blue carpet. I am a little boy making snow angels on its freshly vacuumed surface, listening to my parents talk about their days.

1:02 PM

I'm given my first speedball ever. I'm sitting in the backseat. KK crushes up an Oxy and mixes in a tenth of Tina and she boils the whole thing on a charred spoon she'd taken from the Albino's. I'm not crying. I'm not talking. I'm not even thinking about killing my mother. I'm just watching KK work magic and thinking about all the things that led her to use her skills and deft hands for the mixing of drugs instead of transplanting kidneys. She tells me not to fight it. I give her my left arm. She slaps my skin. She puts in the needle. She presses the plunger down, stopping with an inch left. I can already feel it working and I tell her *the whole thing* and she gives me the last few milligrams.

I know I'm fragile, my psyche, my whatever the fuck you

want to call it, that thing that keeps me human, that keeps me as a person with a habit instead of a walking dead motherfucker just living for his next high. I can feel this fragility. I bob my head. I've been driving in cars getting high for half of my life. Everybody I know is dead. I killed my mother. My eyes are dry and I feel like I'm done shedding tears. My retinas feel like bungee cords. Something is breaking. Something has broken. And then it's opiates mixing with amphetamines and I know it won't be much longer for any of this, the snapping of my mind, putting up with Jared, wanting the impossible with KK. I'm looking at a handful of days before we're out of scante, until we fall asleep, not caring if we wake up.

1:33 PM

We're off the freeway and driving around behind the capitol. Its marble pillars are a pretentious joke. I wonder how Rome looked days after it fell. On Marshall the storefronts switch to Hmong lettering above small restaurants and clothing shops and we see a few squat gigglers, their naked flesh a copper bronze, their hair jet black.

I'm high as fuck, feeling like maybe junkies and their tar had it right the whole time. KK keeps asking if I'm good. I nod. Jared is talking, complaining, something about this being a stupid idea, an ill-conceived plan, and I mouth the word *conceived* and think of my mom.

Bro, what street does Cheng live on? Typewriter asks.

I think. I have no idea. I don't care, not really. Cheng was the one Hmong kid on scholarship at the academy. He was the shit on the soccer field. The ball stuck to his duck-toed feet. At the start of our senior year, he came back different. His clothes changed to incorporate red. He rocked Dickies with a handkerchief hanging out of the back pocket. He'd started selling crank. I'd seen him a handful of times since then. It was either him calling me or me calling him when we needed a ball for ourselves or because we shorted a bag and it was noticed.

Prince, I think.

Right?

Yeah, down University, right at the light.

So let me get this straight, Jared says, we're just driving around, hoping to find some kid *Cheng*, in the ghetto mind you, and what then? Say, *hey, I was wondering if you could cook us some shit?*

Something like that, I say.

Brilliant.

You have a better idea? KK says.

Let us not forget what happened when that was done to us, Jared says.

Different, Typewriter says.

We pass two walking dead teenage boys and their mouths open and I imagine laughs ricocheting against the Civic's windows.

We're not stealing anything, Type says.

No, we're just arriving with shotguns. They'll probably think kindly of four whites pulling up in this fashion. Good call, Chase.

Go fuck yourself.

I tap Typewriter on the shoulder. He flinches. I tell him up there on the left.

We pull over. We all stare at the yellow house, tiny, shutters long since broken, the front door rusted metal. I'm looking for movement. For light. There's nothing. I crane my neck and the two reanimated have stopped. They stare at us.

I tell them I'll go.

Be right here, Typewriter says, ready for anything.

I get out and hold my shotgun and it's heavy as hell and the sun is directly overhead. I jog to the front door. I glance at the two Chucks down the street. They've started in my direction. I give three knocks, wait, then give another two. Nothing. I pound my fist against the metal grate of the door. I yell for Cheng. I tell him it's me, Chase. They're walking faster now, maybe fifty yards away.

Cheng.

Cheng, open up.

I'm hoping for the door to crack open and to see the cautious eyes of Cheng and I'm gripping Buster's stock and yelling it's me, I need help, it's Chase Daniels, and I can hear the Chucks' giggles. They're different, the laughs, lighter, higher pitched. I wonder if this is due to their native tongue.

Chase, let's go, KK yells. She waves at me from the lowered window.

I pound and pound. Then I stop. He's not there. Why the fuck would he be? I'm not even sure he still lives here. And I'm looking at the two kids coming at me and I imagine one of them as Cheng and maybe he's turned, maybe the shit they cooked wasn't pure enough, and KK is yelling my name and I hear Typewriter's voice too.

I want to die.

The thought comes like an opened eyelid after sleeping off meth. When you wake up and know it's over, the high, the night or days or weeks that you've been running, and you know you're broke and you have no way to get more money and the rent's due and the TV's gone and the phone's shut off—your eyes open and you just want them to close again, to be asleep, for the blotting out never to end.

I want to die.

I lower my gun.

They seem to be smiling. The shorter one's missing his lower lip. I laugh at this. I'm laughing at the world for its perversion. I'm laughing at myself for the same reason. I'm laughing because I want to die.

I hear the rattling of metal. Cheng's at the door. He holds a Glock. He says, Stupid motherfucker.

And maybe that's all I need, a fucking option, something resembling hope.

I flip Buster up to my hands and I aim and they're close, the two walking dead, and I unload into one's throat, charge out the shell, and blow the other's nose clean off his face.

Stupid motherfucker, Cheng yells again.

I take a step closer and he's looking over my shoulder and I say, Please, and he says, Fuck no.

Cheng.

Fuck you.

Got nowhere else to go.

Shit ain't my doing.

Bro.

Not your fucking *bro*.

Dude, you've got to—

I ain't gotta do shit.

I stare at him. He points his gun at me, his black hair pulled into a ponytail, his red shants inches from his massive calves. Our area code, 651, is tattooed around his neck.

Cheng, all I'm asking is for one night.

He laughs.

Serious, one night. We can get your head, got some shit. Just need to find out who's still cooking.

So now our shit's good enough?

Trade you guns. Pistols, shotguns . . . I motion to Buster. I tell him we're out of options.

Cheng looks between me and the car and then down the street and I see a woman walking and I know she's one of them and I tell him it's for one night and we can get him high and we just need his fucking help.

One night, he says. He opens the door. I motion to the rest to get out and I yell to get the bin and the duffle bags. It's like we're an estranged family unloading our luggage. I grab one of the bags from KK and follow her inside.

It's dark in his house and it smells like pure fucking ammonia. Right there on his kitchen table, he's got a tiny lab set up, something portable, and he's distilling ephedrine and most of the poisonous smoke funnels into a tube that's connected to the base of the window.

Jesus, man. Trying to kill yourself?

What are the options? he says.

I nod. I set the duffle bag down and look around the room. It's red, the walls, the couch, the shag carpet, and there's a golden coffee table with curved legs. Some of the paint has peeled off and flakes lie on the floor. I wonder about the chemicals filling this room.

Cheng checks on his beaker. He flicks its side with his finger. He tucks a strand of his bangs behind his ear.

Thanks again, I say.

One night.

Yeah, yeah, for sure.

And give me a taste of that Albino shit. With this he smiles, his first, and his teeth are dark little nubs, crowded.

Now we're having fun, I say.

He sits in the red chair next to the couch. The arms are tattered. He rubs his hands together like he's cold. He looks at me and says, Knew you'd be one of the slippery motherfuckers left.

That's supposed to mean?

Shit ain't stick to you. Never. Not Chase Daniels.

I laugh.

He doesn't. He's staring at the bin. I open it up. We're not looking great, under an ounce left, and I'm thinking that maybe it makes sense that Cheng smoke his own shit, that we all smoke his shit because he's still cooking, still manufacturing our survival, but I don't say anything. I'm telling myself it's an investment.

I hand over a decent-sized shard.

Cheng holds it up to the light coming in through the

window. He turns it this way and that way like he's inspecting a diamond. Then it's his smile, awful, his teeth all sorts of rotten. He sets it on the table. He crushes it with a lighter. He covers one wide nostril and snorts the majority of it, then he leans back, one hand on the bridge of his nose, one hand tapping his thigh.

He rattles off something in Hmong.

I breathe. I glance over at the couch and Jared and KK and Typewriter seem to breathe too.

You got the recipe?

No.

Still tellin' me *no* with all this shit?

He's gone, man.

Little Chase popped him?

No.

Cheng laughs, rocks a little bit. He rubs some of the powder around his gums. He says, No, man, I can tell. Little Chase Daniels is a killer. Fucking rich kid learned to kill, huh?

I shake my head. Tell him something about doing what we need to do and he interrupts me by saying, Now you're gettin' it.

Getting what?

Just what you said. Doin' what you need to.

I nod.

I look up at KK and I start to introduce them and Cheng waves his small hand. I stop.

He says, Why you here?

Because—

Because you figured us Hmong trash know what to do when the world ended.

Dude, I just thought—

Your little game of pretend got bad, huh? Got bad. Got real. So you come running to the ghetto where we've been gettin' by the whole time.

No, like, all I was thinking was who smokes shit, you know? Like who might still be alive and we're—

And mommy and daddy are dead. Gone. Can't bail you out with rehab. Can't float you money.

Just trying to find people still alive.

Cheng grins. He leans back, his arms outstretched. He says, This is it.

This doesn't make sense. I wonder where his boys are, the guys he'd surrounded himself with since I knew him back in high school. I ask him about this.

He leans forward. He points a finger at me. He says, It's not a game for us. Get it? We don't traffic in this shit to get high. We do it to make *money*. To survive. We sell shit to stupid motherfuckers like you, the rich kids with daddy's checkbook.

His stubby finger waving in my face makes me feel like I pissed the bed.

My *boys*, they didn't fuck around with their own supply. I did. So it's just me.

I want to tell him that I didn't come here to exploit him and that we're not that different, that I was on my own, that my parents hadn't given me money in years, that I just put a bullet between my mom's eyes. But I get it, Cheng's anger. I know it's different. Growing up, I'd make the five-minute drive in my father's Camry across I-94 into Frogtown. I'd look for Hmong teenagers standing on corners. I'd slow down, money in hand, get my shit, and drive off to my seven acres, to my own room that locked and had a walk-in closet and connecting bathroom. I get it. I hand over another shard.

Atonement, Cheng says. He laughs. Snorts the whole thing. He sets his gun on the table. He looks over at the couch like it's the first time he's noticed there were other people besides me. He tells them to relax, that the big bad gangster isn't going to hurt them.

Jared lets out a nervous laugh.

Typewriter introduces himself. Cheng says, Remember you. Only fat guy who smokes crank I ever known.

I laugh at this. So does KK. Then it's what we know how to do. I dole out bits of shit and the three on the couch cook them up and I share a freebase with Cheng and we're better then, our energy veered away from confrontation and guilt, and we're just five people getting high.

I eventually ask Cheng if he knows anyone still cooking on a large scale.

He tells me everyone's dead.

We aren't.

Bullshit, he says.

Anyone?

He tells me that he'd heard a rumor, back when phones were still working, that a group of motherfuckers were staked out in Ramsey County lockup.

You for real?

What I heard.

Hmong?

Don't know. Heard it from Tou. Said he was going down. Haven't heard from him since.

Think it's legit?

Fuck if I know. But I know I'm set up here. Cookin' a dime a day, enough to keep me not dead.

Maybe Cheng sees the way I'm looking at him, the way it's a plea, a bartering, because he says, Enough for me. One day, motherfucker, one day.

FRIDAY

Cheng is a cartoon. Typewriter is his mother. KK's a demon. Jared's a horse. I'm peeking out of Cheng's windows and giving status updates about how many of *them* walk around. There's fifteen. I keep track, marking race, age, and gender. I think this is very important.

We all hold guns.

The paint on the walls is peeling.

Cartoon Cheng holds the bin. He's claimed responsibility for the dope, cutting everyone off. I'm glad that I'm relieved of this duty.

I see another one. A middle-aged man, squat, definitely

Hmong, and he wears the navy blue of a janitor's uniform. I mark him down on a sheet of paper.

Sixteen, I say or maybe think.

I can hear them all talking. Their voices get louder. I hear *just one more.* I can't be bothered because I'm on lookout and I'm important and I'm on the frontlines perched in a tree and our species' survival depends on my ability to catalog the enemy and I'm a researcher and these are my subjects and demon KK says, Fucking quit, and I need them to be quiet because my brain is beautiful, my mission of utmost importance, and I'm top secret and chemical weapons and I wish I had a battle-axe, razor sharp on both crescent arcs.

I'm not sure if I've already counted the woman in a fuzzy bathrobe. I jot her down anyway. Seventeen.

I taste the blood of my heart and it beats through my chest and my eardrums and the ooze drips down my throat and voices are raised and I need concentration, need secrecy. We're in a castle and our moat is Prince Street and dragons fly overhead and golems stalk the streets.

Movement in the yard across the street. Eighteen.

I open the blinds with the tip of my pistol. I think I see the Canadians, the motherfucker with the mesh cap, his throat, his sidekick, the concave dent of his face. I see my dad's rotting body. My mother's red Hindu dot of a bullet hole. I see them all and they're outside in a single-file line and Innocence in her little umbrella socks is in front and I'm only a little certain they can't see me. I mark them down—nineteen, twenty, twenty-one, twenty-two—and I report my findings to the group.

They don't respond.

I can't take my eyes off the street.

They know we're in here.

I tell them again—twenty-two.

I hear Cheng's accented English. He's saying something about pulling the trigger.

Twenty-two of them, I say again.

Jared, KK says.

Bro, Typewriter says.

I hear Jared's voice and it's waving in pitch and he's saying *just give me the fucking shit.*

For the briefest of moments, I understand what's going on—Jared has finally lost it, snapped—and I feel bad for him. But I can't turn to help because I'm Braveheart and I'm the only line of defense and what I'm doing is important.

Pull the fucking trigger, Cheng says.

Another one down by the stop sign. Twenty-three.

Give me the fucking shit!

Just chill, just fucking chill, Type says.

I'm not fucking around.

Pull the fucking trigger.

I hear KK's pleas, Cheng's threats, Typewriter's confusion. They need me. Everybody fucking needs me. I'm being pulled in so many directions and I'm a peacemaker and I'm a Boy Scout and it's painful to pull my stare away from the window but I do.

I'm like, What the fuck? Jared stands with a pistol pointed against Cheng's head. Cheng sits in the red chair, his arms around the blue bin.

Give it right fucking now, Jared screams.

You better fucking kill me. Because ain't nobody point a gun at me and live to tell about it.

Jared cocks the hammer.

Cheng smiles.

I understand everything and I see each of our auras—KK's is golden and withdrawing and Typewriter's is blue and stationary and Cheng's billows in red flames and Jared's is black and suffocating—and I see the future, somebody dying, and this doesn't make me sad, not like it should.

Everybody out, Jared yells.

Bro . . .

Everybody out. Right fucking now. Out.

Cheng says, You really going to do that? Be a fucking coward, send us out there, instead of killin' us yourself?

Put the gun down, KK says.

I was wrong. She isn't a demon. She's a princess. Her aura is too bright to be demonic. I love her. I think about how many Chucks I've missed counting. I say, Twenty-eight.

Get the fuck out!

Jared's pointing the gun at me now.

Drop the gun, and get out. All of you. You're all trying to kill me.

I want to tell him his aura is Satan.

He's screaming and waving his gun. KK and Typewriter make their way to the door but Cheng hasn't moved, still the king in his throne. KK's crying and begging. Jared screams at me to drop my gun. I do.

Open the door, Jared says.

Typewriter opens the wooden door but not the metal security door.

KK's on her knees. She's pulling at Jared's jeans. She's saying *please*.

You're waiting for me to fall asleep so you can slit my throat, he yells.

I see the twenty-eight walking dead outside. Some of them have started giggling.

Get the fuck out or I'll shoot. Jared looks down at KK. He shakes his leg. Tells her, You too.

Somebody is about to die.

I know it because I'm God or a fortune-teller and because I see our energies working things out before our earthly bodies have the chance and the red of Cheng darts toward the duffle bag and the black of Jared throws a thunderbolt into his back and the golden of KK reaches for the pistol. I see it explode, golden light blinding, and maybe angels sing and the black of Jared drops to the floor. It's a tire losing air and then it's just him, his horse face gasping, blood trickling, KK draped over his dying body.

4:30 AM

KK won't come out of the bathroom. I tell myself this is for the better. Typewriter and I have dumped Jared's body in the basement. Then Cheng's an hour later when he took his last breath. She's probably burning her stomach. It's probably worse, what she's doing. Slit wrists. Only part of me cares. We're all going to fucking die.

Bro, should probably go in there, don't you think?

She told me to leave her alone.

Dude . . .

What the fuck am I going to say? It's cool you killed your boyfriend? We're looking good, a few days' worth of dope left?

I'm just saying.

Fuck.

She was there for you, Typewriter says. He's digging his face. Blood drips down his chin. I don't have the energy to tell him the bugs aren't real.

I know he's right, that I need to try again. I think about how when she left me I'd called and called and waited outside her apartment, *our* apartment, and I'd bought gas station flowers and stalked her at meetings. I tried everything. I told her I loved her. I told her I'd kill myself. I told her she was the only thing I had and that I would do whatever it took.

But I didn't.

I smoked scante. Day in and day out.

And I think about the time I spotted her from the bus. She was sitting outside Starbucks on a black metal chair. My boy Frank from the halfway house had died in that very restroom a year before. She was with Jared and some other people I knew from my stint of sobriety. They were smoking and sipping from large white cups. They were laughing. They looked so fucking happy. And I was on the bus, taking it back to Summit Avenue, down, down, to the river flats of St. Paul, to West Seventh, to Rebecca and her loud-ass TV, to mysterious Svetlana, to the Groveland Tap, to Tibbs, to women working parking lots and brothers working corners, to my mattress on a dusty floor. I knew she was better off without me. Like not just some bullshit self-pity, but I legitimately knew it. I cried that night. I cried and dialed my parents' phone number. My mom answered on the first ring and this broke my fucking heart because it meant she waited there in fear. I didn't say anything. My mom was all *hello, hello* and then she was like *Chase, is that you* and I didn't know how to speak, to say I need help, to say everything I've ever tried has gotten me into this miserable little efficiency and alone, and she was like *honey, talk to me.* I was silent. She said *I love you so much.*

I knock on the bathroom door. I brace myself for what I know I'll see.

The softest of voices tells me it's open.

I push on the door.

She sits on the floor, her back against the side of the bathtub. I scan her wrists and thighs for blotches of red and then I look at the green tile for blood and there's nothing and she says, Remember last time we were here?

I sit on the toilet. It's covered in curly black hairs. I tell her I do.

She laughs and it's a defeated sound. She says, You were so fucking worried.

Yeah.

Still have them, she says, raising her shirt.

I'm not sure if I'm supposed to look so I study my fingers and she says, It's okay to look.

I do.

Her stomach is nothing but ribs and healed burns and she traces them with her fingers and it feels wrong. I pick a nail.

Thought I was gonzo, didn't you?

I don't know.

Crazy KK off slitting her wrists in the bathroom.

Stop.

KK reaches her hand toward me and flaps her fingers. This is an invitation to join her on the floor. I do. Our shoulders touch. I'm still looking at KK for an injury I missed, and she must see me doing this because she says, Didn't do anything.

I didn't—

Didn't have to.

She moves her foot on its heel. Her toes trace my shin. She asks me what the fuck happened. I tell her she did what she had to do.

Sounds familiar. That's what I was telling you just, fuck, yesterday, the day before?

Yeah.

I can feel each of her breaths against my side. Each one seems like so much work.

Is that enough? Reason, I mean.

It's all there is, I say.

You really believe that?

I think so.

Do what you have to.

Yeah, do what you have to.

I killed my fucking boyfriend.

I killed my mom.

KK laughs and it's real, her body clenching, leaning forward a few inches. When she settles back against the tub, she's closer. She rests her head on my shoulder. This is nice.

What if it's not? she asks.

What's not?

A good enough reason.

Then what the fuck do we tell ourselves? I say.

That we're fucked up.

That nothing matters.

That everything matters.

But what does that really do? I ask.

Fuels the fire.

Talking self-hatred?

Check.

I feel her hands on the outside of my thigh. They're moving up and down and remind me of a kneading cat.

She asks me if I really think Jared would have forced us out.

No doubt.

Fucked up, yo.

Scante takes over. You know that. Fucking snaps.

I killed him.

Then she has her right arm around me, her face buried in my armpit. Her leg ventures over. She's shaking. I put my arm around her and I tell her she's okay. I can hear her repeat *I killed him, I killed him.* She fumbles around at my zipper and I move my knee up and tell her to stop. She doesn't. She's bawling. She has my dick out and I'm telling her to stop, that I can get her some of the Oxys, that tomorrow she'll feel better, and she's stroking my dick and I feel wetness on my dickhead and realize it's tears and this is rape of some kind and I give a tentative pull of her waist but I don't do it hard and then she has her mouth around my dick and I'm a bad person because I close my eyes. She keeps going. My hips give an involuntary jerk. I'm trying not to think, to live in the moment, to be present and embrace this opportunity and to know that this was how it had to turn out, us, and I think about what we'd been talking about—doing what we had to do—and if this was good enough. This isn't something I have to do. Not even a little bit. And I can hear her crying and I'm a fucking pig and I wrap both arms around her. I pull her off my dick. She has snot running down her nose and over her thin upper lip.

Come here, I say.

She leans forward to kiss me and I pull her closer, past my mouth, my hand around the back of her head. She tells me to fuck her. I shake my head. She reaches her hand back down to my dick and I cross my legs and I hold her tight and she tells me to fuck her and I say *shh* and she's reaching for me, for anything that will distract her, and I know that shit matters even when it doesn't seem to and she's demanding that I fuck her and I tell her I love her and that it's okay and that I won't do that to her and she finally stops fighting and I feel her body relax all at once and she's a broken child in my arms and her eyes close and open, close and open.

Finally, they close.

I know she won't be able to sleep but I like to think of

her this way, asleep, dreaming of rainbows and lollipops and returned phone calls.

I hear the crashing of glass.

I hear Typewriter yelling fuck, and gunfire.

KK digs her chewed nails into my chest and I stand and yell, Are you okay?

Shot after shot. I sprint out of the bathroom and draw my pistol with my right and KK holds my left and I come to the main room and Chucks are climbing through the window and I don't hear their giggles because I'm unloading bullets into the opening. A few reanimated tumble against the windowpane. A crash from the left side of the house and I turn and there's another one, the janitor type, and I fire three shots, two of them hitting his neck, and he falls, his Hmong giggles fading.

There's the briefest of lulls and I ask Typewriter what the fuck happened. He says he doesn't know. KK says, They can smell death. I look at her and she's dropped my hand, picked up a shotgun, and I love her and know she's right. It's not just sound but smell and death and fear: that's how they find us. Another one appears at the window and she aims and fires.

Then a window in the kitchen explodes and I hear another noise in the back of the house.

Need to go, I say.

Type turns in circles, each sound a potential death sentence.

Get the shit, I say.

He grabs the bin and I step toward the door and I can

hear them out there, laughing. We'll never make it through the front door. KK screams and fires, this time at one coming from the back hallway. We're surrounded.

Go, I yell.

I grab her wrist and start running down the hall. A woman with short spiked hair comes toward me and I fire into her chest. She just stumbles so I pull the trigger again. It clicks. Fuck. She's still coming and I yell for somebody to shoot. The shadows behind her fill with movement. Typewriter's firing but in the other direction.

I reach to my right and hit a door handle. The basement. I fling it open and practically shove KK down the stairs and Typewriter follows and then me and I slam the door. I trip down the stairs, catching myself on the banister. A security light shines through the slit of a window. It casts its glow over KK. She's looking at Jared's and Cheng's bodies, one hand covering her mouth. Type pulls her away.

We hear fists on wood, fists breaking wood. They'll be down here in less than a minute. I'm looking around the basement, nothing but cinder blocks and empty bottles of HCl. The window is fucking small but KK could fit for sure and probably me and Typewriter will have to make do. I run over. The window's at head level. I bash it with my elbow. I don't give a fuck if the walking dead hear it. I don't give a fuck about anything besides getting KK out of this house. I rip the shards out with my hand. We hear the door splinter. I push the bin out of the window first, then grab KK and tell her to go. She says, What about—, but I squeeze her nonexistent bicep and yell, Go! I cup my hands and she steps in. I shove her up. She's saying fuck and shit and I push her legs through the small opening and blood leaks from the jagged glass down the cinder block. Giggles. Creaking stairs. I'm holding my hands for Typewriter and he says, Fucking go. I yell for him to hurry and he says, It's easier for you to pull me through. He knows and I know this isn't true, but I let myself believe it because I need to. I step on his thigh and squeeze through the opening. My stomach's cut to shit. I turn back. Typewriter reaches his hand up and I grab it with both of mine, bracing my feet against the foundation, and I pull like a motherfucker. His head comes through and then his upper body. I pull and pull and pull and blood seeps around his torso and I'm looking into his eyes and they are saying *fucking pull* and they're saying *leave me* and they're saying *you're my best friend* and *we tried*.

He screams.

It's the sound of knowing you're going to die.

The pitch is piercing.

It's the sound of knowing you're dead.

Something gives and I yank him through another foot. I drag his body the rest of the way out. I help him to his feet and I hear KK's shotgun. The only light comes from streetlamps and every shadow is a body and there's no way we're getting to the car. I grab the bin and yell for them to follow me.

I run between Cheng's house and another. There's a Chuck waiting. I don't have bullets so I flip the pistol in my hand and smash his head and I feel the cracking of bones. The motherfucker drops. We emerge into an alley. They're coming at us from both directions. Typewriter runs with a limp. KK grabs my hand and we keep running between houses to a chain-link fence, which we hop over. They seem to be everywhere. As we run, I'm trying to figure out what the fuck to do, where to find safety. Shelter. Cars. Dope. Guns. Then I scream *fuck*, because we left the duffle bag in Cheng's living room, so no more stockpile of weapons. KK and Typewriter still have guns but we're low as shit on ammo.

We're in a backyard. The intruder light flashes on. Three teenage Chucks look up like they've just been caught in a circle jerk. Their faces are covered in blood and the shit shines under the fluorescent light. Their hands are inside of a gutted corpse. I'm nothing but reaction, hurling a miniature Fisher-Price tea party table at all of them. I yell for KK to run and the three boys are laughing until Type blasts a hole through the tallest one's chest.

We keep running.

We cross Pike Avenue. Houses sit dim and uninhabited. Cars line the right-hand side. Past Baltimore, past Mason. The Chucks are starting to thin. I'm running, holding on to the world's last hit of scante. Holding on to KK. Past University, past Jefferson. It's just stragglers now. Everything is a blur. We're running and there's somebody watching, the creator of our world, somebody moving enemies into our view, moving them out, somebody watching over us with malice and love and I know no matter what we do, we're fucked, there will always be more of them than us.

KK tugs at my hand. She shakes herself free and runs back thirty feet to where Typewriter's curled on the grass. I follow. I can hardly breathe. I tell him to get up. He doesn't respond. I say, Get the fuck up, let's go, we need to go. KK kneels by his side. She's looking at the back of his calf.

Fuck me.

There's a mouthful of flesh missing. But it's not bleeding. It's already scabbed over. I remember the trucker's eye, how the bite healed almost instantly.

Fuck, I mutter.

I don't want to die, he says.

You're not going to . . .

Typewriter runs his index finger over the divot.

I look around. The Chucks are mostly gone, but I know that shit won't last. I tell him he's fine. I bend over and drape his arm around my shoulder. KK takes the other side. He's heavy as hell and can't put any weight on his right leg. We're right at the edge of Como Park. I remember there's a warming hut for winter skating down by the lake. I'd sat in it during some god-awful church field trip. We struggle in an awkward gait, Type mumbling into my ear. KK keeps looking over her shoulder. It's silence. Stars shine.

We finally see the building. It's a square of brick, ugly as fuck. KK tries the door. It's locked. She doesn't ask what to do, just points the shotgun at the handle and fires. She kicks the door in. Type tells me that he's dying. The inside smells like come and mildew and I lay Type down and his body's freezing cold. I tell him to flip over on his stomach. The bite isn't even crusty anymore, just purple. KK stacks benches and a trash can against the door. Typewriter whimpers. The only chance we have is to pump his body full of speed. I open the bin and motherfucker, there's not much left. I take out a shard.

I ask for a needle. KK pulls one out of her sock. I use my spit to break down the dope and it doesn't really work. I tear a piece of my T-shirt off. I use that as a filter, sucking spit and meth into the rig. I talk the whole time. I tell him it doesn't look that bad. I tell him all he needs is a little booster and he'll be fucking straight. There's blood all over my stomach and for the first time, I realize I'm cut pretty badly. I take the syringe and I'm not sure if it makes more sense to inject it into the wound or into a vein. I decide the bite's a better site. Type doesn't flinch, doesn't register there's a needle in his leg, and I push the plunger. I tap his leg. I tell him things are looking up.

Do it already, he says.

Just did.

Typewriter lays his face on the black spongy flooring. He says, I can't feel it.

I know. Doesn't matter. Just gave you a good shot and it's working its way through your body and it'll be fine.

I turn him around so he's lying on his back. He's shaking. I take off my T-shirt and place it under his head. He holds on to my hand. KK rubs his chest. His hand feels like frozen meat. I imagine the battle going on inside him. I picture evil-looking cells, maybe they look like Jared's aura, and they're coursing through his body, ripping chunks of healthy cells, and I will the speed to hurry up. To counteract. His fingers are stiff, then his arm, and part of him seizes, a partial seizure.

You're doing well, I say.

More, KK says.

Think?

She nods.

I pry Typewriter's hand from mine and load another shot. I find a vein in his arm and blast another tenth. His teeth chatter. His pupils dilate and I think this is good. That Tina is doing her damnedest. I hope it was quick enough. His eyes start to flutter. I slap his face and tell him to stay with me. His grip is ungodly strong.

John, John, KK says, tell me your favorite memory.

KK's rubbing his chest, her eyes trained on his, and I love her for this because she wants him to relive happiness when darkness descends.

What is it? she asks.

My family.

Good, that's good. What about them?

Little . . . three . . . summer.

Yeah? When you were three? The summer?

Typewriter nods. KK rests her hand on his forehead. She says, So what happened?

Watermelon.

She laughs. She says, So you had watermelon?

Typewriter gives the hint of a smile, only the left side of his face still able to move. His leg twitches.

Was it your first time?

Ye . . . yes.

I picture this scene—a chubby toddler sitting on a red blanket in the backyard, or shit, maybe here at Como Park, a picnic, the three of them, back when everyone was still alive, and he's in shorts, a Superman T-shirt stretched over his pudgy stomach, and he's stumbling around, probably amazed at seeing his first duck, throwing bits of bread his mother packed just for the occasion, and then she calls, Johnny, I have a treat for you, and he runs over, his arms wide for balance. His father swoops him off the ground and then he's flying, giggling, secure in his dad's steady grasp. They sit down, John between his mom and dad, and she opens a Tupperware and hands John a triangle of pulpy red fruit. He takes it in his little paws, surprised at its wetness, at how he can stick a finger into its surface and leave a dent. Maybe his mom takes a bite and says *mmm* and then John knows it's safe and bites down and the juice is an explosion, the best thing he's ever experienced, and it drips down his chin, down all of their chins, father and mother and son, the sun refusing to set.

That sounds amazing, KK says.

Wha . . . wha . . . yours?

KK smiles down at Type. She says, July twenty-fifth. I was five. Sister O'Hare pulled me into her office. I thought I was in trouble for breaking Claire's crayons during free time. She spit on her thumb and wiped the sleep out of my eyes. She brought me in and there were two strangers sitting in her office. They turned. I remember I'd never seen such white teeth, such fancy clothes. Sister O'Hare was like, Kristin, say hello to your new family.

Lo . . . ve.

Yeah, love, KK says.

I'm confused because KK never mentioned being adopted. She's biting her lip and I know she's being honest and maybe this makes sense because she hates herself with a ferocity that is completely fucked—KK the only one who can't see she's amazing. Part of me feels hurt she's kept this from me. I know it's petty. I keep my mouth shut. I squeeze Type-writer's seized hand.

Cha . . .

I don't want to play. To dredge up memories of times that will never be real again. I ask KK if I should give him another shot. She tells me to tell him. And I'm not trying to feel these things because it's back when life was good, when it was playing Transformers and believing in God and good-night kisses, and I can't go down that road now, seeing every one of my fuckups, how far I've fallen.

I'm going to give him one more, I say.

Please, Type says.

My best friend is dying. I finally realize it. More of his face has contorted and only one eye can blink. I know no amount of speed can reverse what's already taken over, so I tell them a story about the time my father and me stayed at a cabin up north. About bringing the tiny portable TV from our kitchen at home and setting it up on a chair. How we sat in sweat-pants and sweatshirts drinking hot cocoa. It was March Mad-ness and we watched basketball all weekend. My dad teaching me to wood carve, to use a knife, a gouge. My gnome carving looked nothing like his but he kept telling me how proud he was, how I had a natural ability, how this was the only place he wanted to be. I say, I don't know, maybe that was true of me too. Like the only place I wanted to be, you know?

KK places her hand over Type's and mine, already clasped.

His one functioning eye stares at the warming hut ceiling.

Our stories are all about childhood and family and we just want to be back there, life simple, life nothing but love and attention and not knowing what awaits, and I think about us wanting to be restored to innocence and about the little girl playing with the dog and me thinking this was cute and it really being the beginning of the end and her gashing the rottweiler's throat and maybe it was closer to the end of the end. Our favorite memories are Polaroids of ignorance.

Typewriter starts to choke. Spit dribbles from his mouth. I reach behind his head and lift him up. He doesn't bend at the waist. His body's a plank. I yell for KK to get another needle and I'm telling Typewriter to stay with me, Don't you fucking die on me. His body shudders in violent spasms. I pound his chest. I beat him because I can't face this without him and because I love him like a brother and because I'm mad that he isn't fighting harder and because it's easier than crying.

KK gives me the syringe.

I plunge it into his heart.

He's having a seizure and his tongue bleeds and his arm curls into a question mark. Then his grip loosens and his eyes blink. I'm telling him I knew he could do it and I'm cradling his head when I hear him giggle and it grows until his mouth is open and fills the moldy brick shelter with its heinous cackle. I stand and point a shotgun at his grinning mouth.

I'm about to pull the trigger when he starts shaking his head.

I pause. I yell for KK to get back. Typewriter's head moves back and forth and none of the other walking dead were aware of their dying but I tell myself it's a fucking head trip, imagining a life where Typewriter survives, and I fasten my grip.

He coughs.

He blinks both eyes. His face muscles relax. He starts to mutter.

John, KK says.

Fuck, he responds.

Then I'm back on my knees, the gun still pointed at his chest. I'm like, Are you okay? Type? Fuck? Are you okay?

He flexes his fingers. He runs his tongue over his teeth. He spits blood. He says, Bro, the fucking gun.

I set it down and I hug him and he calls me a faggot and KK laughs and so do I or maybe those are still tears.

SATURDAY

We've spent the last thirty minutes huddled against a red furnace that doesn't work, staring at the barricaded warming hut door with our guns drawn. Every barking dog and blowing elm branch makes me want to die. I'm a little nervous to use our one needle because it was inside of Typewriter but KK sterilizes it with a lighter and I guess I don't have an option. We don't have enough to fuck around snorting it. I shoot half a teener. So does KK. We pump Typewriter full because who knows how much he needs. He's feeling better, sitting upright, making jokes about his fat-ass calves finally losing some girth.

Me, I'm making mental lists:

1. Scante
2. Shelter
3. Food/water
4. Ammo

This list is pretty much the same one I made five days ago. Fuck, it's pretty much the same one I've made over the last five years.

Motherfuckers can't kill me, Typewriter says.

Pretty close, though, I say.

Close ain't good for shit, bro.

I'm counting rounds. We have two shotguns. Sixteen shells total. Typewriter has a pistol with a full clip and an extra mag. I tell them to empty their pockets.

KK dumps out a money clip with her ID and debit card. Two lighters. A pack of cigarettes with two broken smokes. The needle. Typewriter has a wallet and three pills that KK says are generic Klonopin. He has three wadded-up one-dollar traveler's checks he uses for fraud. I laugh at this. I'm pretty much empty. Just a wallet and a bloodied molar.

The fuck? KK says.

I shrug.

Some sick shit, yo.

I didn't—

Fucking with you, Chase.

Oh.

Then I open the blue bin. We're down to grams. We're down to a day and a half, maybe two. I think about nights where I've smoked that much in a matter of hours.

Survived just to die again, Typewriter says.

For reals, KK says.

I'm trying to remember what Cheng said about people cooking at the jail. I mention this and KK says, There's no fucking way we'll make it down there.

Don't have a choice.

Fuck me, Type says, you shoulda let this fat ass die.

KK says, Can't we just sit . . . She doesn't finish. She knows it's not an option.

I ask Typewriter if he can walk. He stands. He limps around a little. He says, Good enough.

Here, let me see those cigarettes.

KK hands over her smokes. I take the cellophane off the bottom of the pack. I pour the meth into the baggie. The fact that it all fits makes me cringe. I melt the plastic shut. I ask who wants to carry it.

All you, Typewriter says.

I look over at KK and she nods.

Guns?

I can't aim worth shit with the pistol, KK says.

Partial to the shotgun, myself, Typewriter says.

I take the Glock. The cuts on my stomach from crawling through the window have scabbed to my T-shirt. I peel them away with a wince. I say, It's our only chance, the jail.

They nod.

Figure Cheng's boys aren't fucking around, wouldn't lie to a guy like that. And we can get there, just have to be careful.

Wise shit, KK mocks. She meets my eyes and then says she's sorry.

I think traveling during the day is best, I say. Seem to be less of them around.

Worth a shot, Typewriter says.

County's just down Seventh, right there at Kellogg.

Never thought I'd be trying to get there, Type says.

Feel you.

No more than three miles, I say.

Need a car, yo, KK says.

Not trying to go back to Cheng's.

Then steal one, Typewriter says.

And you know how to hot-wire since when?

Motherfuckers all dead. Break in, take the keys on the kitchen table.

I nod. We fall silent, staring at the barricaded door. They're out there, the Chucks, somewhere. Maybe they're right outside the door and they've figured out silence is their best asset or maybe they're behind trees or maybe walking down streets under the artificial glow of lamps.

I know there's no other option. We have to leave.

We stand. I'm sore as a motherfucker. I take KK's hand. I want her to come into my arms but she raises her eyebrows and says, Get to it, yo. We hold guns. We move the benches and the trash can with a smiley face tagged on its side. I think about motherfuckers waiting on the other side and I think about my dead mother and I'm telling myself it will be fine, everything, and then it's that moment of predawn when shadows are long as fuck. We stare outside. It smells like duck shit. Buck up. My feet don't move. KK leads the way. It takes all my power to follow her, watching her flat back, her bony arms rigid at her side.

We walk through Como Park. There are houses up to the right, squat ramblers. It's us three spinning with every sound, guns pointed at trees and sometimes at each other. We get out of the wooded area and I see a Hmong Chuck who can't be more than five foot. She's just staring at a house and I wonder if somebody's alive on the other side. Maybe some teenager burning the last of his scante and he's scared and he knows he's going to die and for some reason I don't give a fuck. I just don't want to fight. Don't want to run. I want to be at the jail and for them to have a Mexico-sized operation and I want there to be food and unbreakable steel doors and I want KK to have my children and I want shit to work out. That's all we've ever wanted. It's the unsaid prayer each time we put a stem to our mouths or a needle in our veins—just work out.

We come up to some piece of shit Toyota Tacoma. It's probably not the best choice, but fuck it, it's the first car we come across. Our eyes go between the midget walking dead across the street and the truck and the house. It's a white rectangle. The wood around the windows is rotten.

I test the Toyota's door. It's locked.

Just break in? Typewriter asks.

The house, yeah, KK says.

I nod.

I'm not trying to make any noise. I don't want that cunt midget coming over and I don't know what's inside and I think about my mom feeding off the ribs of my father and we're at the door, jiggling the handle. Locked. Fuck. The window's our best bet. I tell this to KK and Typewriter and they agree. But they just sit there crouched, willing invisibility. The sun will be up in a few minutes. I'm not sure if this is a good or bad thing.

The duty falls on me.

I crouch down and scamper to the bay window. The glass feels cheap, wouldn't take more than a half swing of the pistol. KK motions for me to hurry up. I flip the gun around in my hand. I'm about to swing, but I stop. It's like a pure fear takes over, making me retarded. They're probably inside and they're probably coming, hordes of Chucks, and this shit will never end and it feels like too much, everything.

Hurry the fuck up, KK hisses.

I swing. The bottom corner of the glass shatters. I knock out enough space for my arm to reach through. I crank the handle. The window opens. I look back over my shoulder. The midget Chuck turns. She stares. She starts her steady walk across the street. I wonder how far the sound traveled, how many walking dead heard that single pane shatter. The window's open enough for me to fit through, and I do, whispering that I'll get the door.

I drop to the shag carpet.

I'm ready for demonic laughs and for my throat to be ripped open and I'm pointing a pistol at a La-Z-Boy and a TV and a framed Norman Rockwell print, the one with the little boy and girl staring at the sun, the one that makes you feel like true love is shit you know about from grade school.

I creep to the door.

KK and Type push in once it's open. The midget Chuck stands fifty feet behind them. Just as I'm closing the door, I see the sparkle of white, her teeth, her smile, then the start of a high-pitched giggle.

Typewriter deadbolts the door.

Get the keys, KK says.

We're in the kitchen looking on counters and tables. Typewriter stands some sort of guard or maybe he's scared too. Then we're in the family room and I can't stop staring at the print, like it's some cruel joke—life an idealized version of serenity—and KK throws cushions around and something tells me to turn around. The top two-thirds of the midget Chuck stare at me through the window. I scream a rich-bitch scream. Type blasts a hole into her face.

Fuck, I yell.

Bro?

The sound man, fuck.

She was . . .

Just help find the goddamn keys, KK yells.

She starts toward the stairs. I don't want to follow. I don't want to know what's up there. Outside, thick brown blood makes an amoeba on the trampled grass.

Typewriter nudges me, motions to follow KK up the stairs. He takes them two at a time. I lag behind. I'm slow in my ascent. I'm waiting to hear screams and gunshots and

I'm waiting for this shit to end. My body feels heavy, tired. I hear KK and Type in what is probably the master bedroom. KK calls out that they're both dead, didn't reanimate. They're rifling through drawers.

Some soft coo comes from my right. I'm at a door. I creak it open with the tip of my Glock. It's lighter in there, a single ray of sun coming through the back window. There's a crib. The walls are covered—I mean fucking covered, not a single inch of white space—with some sort of Rockwell wallpaper. What the fuck is with these people? I step into the nursery. The cooing gets louder. The wall is nothing but families sitting around Thanksgiving dinner, kids at baseball games, a pedophile doctor feeling a chest, the *Saturday Evening Post*, Rosie the Riveter, a cop at a diner—all of them staring down at me. The shit feels spooky. Otherworldly. So many sets of eyes.

I make my way to the crib.

I know what I'll see, but I tell myself I'm wrong. I'm not. It's a baby, maybe six months old. He's in a green one-piece with connected feet and that's what he's holding on to, his fucking feet, rocking just a little bit, a smile like he knows things will be okay.

I feel like vomiting.

I stare back at the door. They must still be looking for the keys. The baby reaches for me. His eyes are blue, the pretty kind that people notice. And I'm thinking about this baby and this family and they were probably the blue-collar type who grew up on stories from their grandparents about the happy misery of the Depression and the Greatest Generation, and for them, the people of this house, I'm sure there was nothing better than returning home to their family from a day of hanging Sheetrock and having a beer and grilling in the backyard, the wife adding a bit of garlic powder to the patties, sitting around listening to the Twins on the radio, just like their parents had done. A simpler time. That's what they wanted. That's what this baby would grow up to cherish.

His coos turn to giggles.

He has to be turned. There's no other explanation why he wouldn't have died of dehydration. His eyes are so fucking blue. His smile makes me think about Disney movies, the ones actually drawn, the ones from my childhood.

He will die.

He's already dead.

But maybe not.

Maybe he's survived because how much nourishment does a baby really need? Maybe these giggles and coos are real? The pressure behind my eyes feels like ice picks. I don't realize I'm talking to him, but I am. I'm using my singsongy baby voice. I'm saying things about him being so fucking cute, such blue eyes, such a nice pajama set. I'm telling him his parents are dead. I'm telling him those lies on your walls, those happy little moments from a dead generation, are bullshit. Your parents didn't believe in them. You wouldn't either. The baby wraps his chubby fingers around the nose of my gun. It's not a toy, I say. He laughs. I laugh. We laugh. We laugh because we don't know what's funny anymore, only that something has to be. I tell the baby I was wrong before about the little girl with the socks, she wasn't innocence, he is.

Yes, you are.

Such a chubby-wubby.

No, that's not a chew toy, that's a gun.

Oh, let me get your pillow a little more comfortable.

It's okay, just taking a nap. Just a little nap. Nap time. Shh, shh.

Look at your feet go. Kick-kick-kick.

What? Tired already?

My little boy is all tuckered out.

I straighten my back. I stare out of the window. Some stupid birds sit on the power line dissecting the alley. I say, Don't you fucking judge me.

I turn toward the door.

Typewriter stands a few feet inside the nursery. His fat face hangs slack, his mouth open. He fingers a scab with his hand not holding the shotgun.

What the fuck was that?

What?

He points to the crib.

Just putting the little guy to sleep, I say. I smile. KK yells that she found the keys, jacket pocket. She runs to the nursery. Everything about her is frantic. She says, Hurry the fuck up. She starts down the stairs. Typewriter's scab is bleeding. He puts two hands on the shotgun, his finger pressing against the trigger.

After you, I say.

Fuck that noise, he says. He steps aside.

Shit had to be done, I say.

He nods, Typewriter always fucking nodding.

I tell him there was no other choice. To lighten the fuck up.

I head downstairs. We stand at the door. A few stragglers are headed in our direction, but we'll be able to get to the truck with no problem. KK tells us she'll drive and I tell her fine and then we're outside and I'm climbing into the bitch position of the truck and it smells like feet. There's a small sticker on the dashboard. It's the same Rockwell from the living room. The boy and girl in love. I think about it being KK and me. The engine sputters and then turns. The Chucks are jogging now. KK puts it in reverse. I scratch at the sticker. Type stares out of the window. I use the nail on my index finger to blot out the little boy, then the little girl, then the sun. KK swerves to avoid a hysterical walking dead. The baby had turned. It was mercy. My head throbs. He had to have fucking turned.

6:54 AM

We drive through Frogtown. A few Hmong Chucks wander the streets, but we're able to stay clear. Past Midway it's more crowded, the skin color darkening, and it's weird to see the intersections clear, buses nowhere, shoppers nowhere. The teenagers who used to hang out smoking cigarettes in high-tops are either dead or lurching around giggling and I realize there's no real difference—people standing there bored either way. We pass Interstate 94. The houses get bigger and older. They're bastardized versions of Victorians in reds and blues

PETER STENSON

and slates. The skin color switches again and it's Caucasian
walking dead loitering around. And then we're at Grand, the
yuppie shopping district, and it's J. Crew and CorePower
Yoga and women sporting hundred-dollar haircuts atop their
decaying flesh. At Summit, the apex of our shitty little town,
stands the governor's mansion with its slabs of imported stone
and then the Summit Club, and I picture a young F. Scott sitting in there writing about Bernice bobbing her hair. From
this elevation we can see West Seventh, the flats of St. Paul,
where we see poor white Chucks shuffle around, tiny as ants,
each and every one of them unified in their singleness of mind.
Beyond them, across the Mississippi, not really visible, is the
south side, streets like Chavez and Independence, the skin
once again darkening. Our city: each neighborhood segre-
gated, first by economics, then by race. Each neighborhood
now hosting its own walking dead, its own hidden pockets of
shit-smoking motherfuckers trying to find their next hit.

We're quiet. KK because she's concentrating. Typewriter
because he just saw me kill that Chuck baby. Me because the
pressure behind my eyes is putting a yellow lens flare on everything. Or maybe it's because we're driving the speed limit
through an abandoned city, trying to pretend the naked people staring at us laughing are really friendly neighbors.

They're not going to be there, KK says. Nobody's gonna
fucking be there.

Can't think like that, I say.

But if they aren't? KK asks.

Eat a bullet, Type says.

Shut the fuck up, I say.

196

KK's like, He's right, last chance shit, yo.

Better than this, Typewriter says.

I say, They'll be there. Can't think like that, your mind will turn and shit.

Type snorts a laugh. I stare at him but he won't meet my eye. I ask why he's laughing and he just shakes his head.

They'll be there, I say again.

I think about County being locked and empty, not a single shit-smoking person on the premises, or worse, a bashed window as our entrance, our growing hope of a community with crank on tap, and us running in, giddy, our greeting committee thousands of giggles.

We descend Summit Hill. I grip my pistol, Type his shotgun. There's more of them. They're everywhere. They're standing in the Burger King parking lot and on the sidewalk in front of the dollar store. At least fifty in every shape and size. KK swerves to dodge a three-hundred pounder with tits for days. We go twenty miles per hour until a skinny black Chuck manages to smash his head into the passenger side window, and then we're gone, KK stomping the fuck out of pedal.

She skids through the intersection of Summit and Seventh. I'm worried about the car flipping and I yell to slow down and she's biting her bottom lip to the point of blood.

Oh God, Typewriter says.

Seventh is even more crowded. Like practically full of these bobbing and weaving pieces of shit. KK screams and I scream and Type whimpers and it's that moment when you realize all other options are gone, have been for some time, and you're unemployable and soon to be homeless and your parents won't return your phone calls and you're short on what you owe the dealer and you're out of scante and you'll do whatever it takes to get the next hit—rob a motherfucker, suck a dick. Only one option. Ours is to drive as fast as we can, hoping the Tacoma holds up to flattening a hundred Chucks.

Our heads bounce with each collision.

KK turns on the windshield wipers.

I'm thinking about Frogger and Mario Kart.

Some cunt woman flies up over the hood and crashes in through the windshield, headfirst. She's stuck and her neck is a postcoital dick, slow in its oozing of liquid.

Get her off, get her off, KK screams.

I'm frozen. I'm staring into this woman's eyes and they're black like the hallway to your parents' room after a childhood nightmare. She's still alive or dead or whatever the hell. She's chomping half a foot away from my crotch.

I can't fucking see, KK yells.

The thuds pick up in intensity. Glass trickles down on us. I'm thinking about the Whac-a-Mole game at arcades. The Chuck just keeps staring at my dick. KK starts swerving and she keeps yelling about not being able to see and our world is shards of glass and brown blood and violent collisions, each one like hitting Bambi.

Finally, I act. I lean back and kick the hell out of this Chuck's face. It makes a squishing sound.

Harder, Typewriter yells.

There's a wicked crash, this one metal on metal. KK's crashed into a parked car. The truck pulls to the right and we've lost air in at least two tires. I kick the face again. This finally does the trick, her dark eyes closing, her body rolling over the top of the Tacoma.

Typewriter yells to go faster and KK screams that she's got it floored and then I realize we're slowing, maybe down to fifteen miles per hour. But we're close. We're almost to Kellogg. County's a few hundred yards ahead. Ten miles per hour. KK tries to make the right turn, but the wheel won't react, probably because of the flats, and we spin out, slamming into a yellow traffic light. My head hits the dash, the fucking Rockwell I scratched out.

There's blood. I don't know whose it is.

Typewriter opens the door and I grab KK's wrist and drag her out my side and we have a few feet of clear and there's a guardrail leading down a grass hill. It's the wrong way, but we have no fucking choice. Type hurdles it. I try, but catch my foot on the railing. I roll head over heels for what seems like hours. This is going to be my death. Then the world stops spinning. I'm on the pavement and I can feel blood coming down my forehead and the first thing I do is check my pocket for my shit. I think it's a little light. Chucks come from around the parking lot on Seventh and from over the guardrail. Typewriter and KK scream for me to hurry. I'm on my hands and knees searching the pavement, picking up pebbles, throwing them, looking for a lost shard. Type grabs me by the back of the neck and shoves me and I stumble and regain my balance and then KK's pulling me by my hand and we're sprinting again.

We head under a bridge. I remember being down here in the back of a squad car. Me at sixteen, me a trust-fund hippie, arrested in front of SuperAmerica with a pocket full of Percs and a bag of mushrooms. I remember the cops apologizing that they didn't have any Grateful Dead to play, them thinking this was so fucking funny, the cuffs digging into my wrists, my pinky going numb. They drove me down here, under the bridge, and pulled into a garage just below where we are now, marched me up three sets of stairs into the juvenile detention center of Ramsey County, telling me not to trip, laughing at the play on words, telling me the walls aren't really melting, but you are really being arrested.

Straight ahead there's a tsunami of naked walking dead. Another group is gathering behind us.

Fuck.

I run with no thought but the need to find that garage. Then I see it—a shiny sheet of red metal that spans a story. I pound on the door. It wobbles. I pound and kick and KK and Typewriter are doing the same. The clanging sound of metal is almost loud enough to drown out the surrounding laughter.

I'm screaming to the metal garage door to open up and save us. I'm screaming to anyone behind it. I'm screaming to God.

KK fires into the door. It dents, rips a little. She does it again.

The Chucks come at us from both sides of the street. The closest one's a stone's throw away.

I'm pounding. I'm begging to be let in. I'm praying foxhole pleas about righting wrongs, getting sober, being a good person, giving money to the poor, never jerking off again, curing cancer.

KK unloads the rest of her gun and the hole grows to the size of a fist.

Typewriter faces the wave of demented motherfuckers. He hollers and shoots into the encroaching crowd. KK has both hands inside of the hole she's created. She tries to pry it open. It's futile. I pound with my fist and my head and scream.

And I start reciting the Serenity Prayer. I'm not sure where it comes from but I'm saying *God, grant me the serenity* as Typewriter fires and pumps and KK presses her bloodied hands in the hole; I'm chanting *to accept the things I cannot change*, and I quit slamming the wall and turn to aim my gun and it shakes like a motherfucker as I fire into the crowd screaming *the courage to change the things I can* and I put the barrel in my mouth and the final verse is inside my head—*and the wisdom to know the difference.*

I'm about to pull the trigger when I hear KK holler.

She's running toward an open door, yelling for us to come.

Some teenager with the worst meth-picked face I've ever seen holds the door.

Typewriter!

He turns, sees the door, and starts sprinting.

I aim over his shoulder and drop two Chucks a foot behind him. I run backward, firing into open mouths. Somebody grabs me and shoves me inside. Then the metal door slams shut and it's pitch black.

12:44 PM

The kid stands over me. He's skinny as fuck. His face is the unfortunate combination of severe acne and busy fingers. He points a snub-nosed revolver at me. Tells me to strip.

What the fuck? Typewriter says.

You too, he says. The gun swings in the other direction. All of you.

Dude . . .

Need to see if you're bit. If you're infected.

His hand trembles. I wonder if he's ever held a gun before last week. I tell him we're fine.

We've got rules here, he says.

We?

Yeah, we.

How many—

Stop. You need to strip.

You said *we*, how many?

Chase, KK says. She's taken off her shirt. Her nipples are Jolly Ranchers. She kicks off her shorts and I tell her she doesn't need to do this. The kid points the gun at me and it's shaking even more.

Jesus, Chase, just take off your fucking clothes, KK says.

She's naked. The kid stares at her, motions for her to spin around. She does. He seems to have a hard time studying her, glancing down at the cement, then at her, like he's embarrassed.

Okay, he says.

I strip. He asks what's on my stomach and I tell him cuts from glass and he seems satisfied with this answer.

Typewriter's next. His pasty body is blotched with cuts, scabs. The kid doesn't notice the healed scoop missing from the back of his leg.

The kid lowers his gun.

The Chucks howl from behind the metal garage door. A few hands poke through the hole KK made. He says, Sorry about the search, gotta, you know?

I have my pants back on and I stick out my hand and tell him Chase and he tells me Maddie. KK and Typewriter introduce themselves. I tell him thanks for saving us and he nods like it was nothing and motions for us to follow him up the stairs. It's weird being here. I'm remembering being sixteen, fuck, probably Maddie's age, handcuffed, arrested, being brought up this very staircase.

How many of you are there?

Three, including me.

How?

Maddie laughs. He says, I was here, locked up on some Mickey Mouse shit. Had court Monday. The others showed up together the next day.

How are you . . . I mean, for dope?

Cooking in here, he says.

Typewriter gives a *hell yeah* and I smile and so does KK and Maddie laughs and we walk up another flight. He says, Don't get too excited. It's pretty ratty crank. Plus, only one shot a day.

That's cool, that's totally cool, Typewriter says.

For sure, I say.

Maddie presses against a red door. It's the booking station—a small room with a few desks, some computers, interrogation rooms off to one side.

Still have power? I ask.

Yup.

I'm remembering pressing my fingers into ink, then sitting in the room and some detective in a short-sleeve button-down asking where I got the pills and mushrooms. Asking if I grew them, Got an operation in your basement, don't ya? Don't ya? I'd watched his mustache. It seemed to grow in audible slithers.

I hear laughter. My testicles shrink into my hip flexors.

The fuck? I say.

Maddie shakes his head, staring at a detention room. He's like, It's fine man, just a kid who turned, was handcuffed to the table in there.

Fuck that, KK says.

I'll kill the motherfucker right now, Type says.

I put my arm out and Type tells me to get the fuck off him and Maddie looks uncomfortable. I'm not trying to have our entrance be Type blasting Chucks, Maddie thinking we're psycho. Just let it be, I say.

KK gives me a look and I'm not sure if it's *fuck this* or *fuck you*. I interpret it as her saying she's not trying to be around a single laugh, so I ask Maddie if we're sleeping somewhere else.

He picks at his face and says, Yeah, yeah, for sure. Down the hall.

KK lets me take her hand.

Maddie leads us to a control room of sorts. It's nothing but monitors, all of them security-camera footage. Some artsy-type guy with thick black-rimmed glasses, probably late thirties, sits at a swiveling chair. When he turns to shake our hands, I notice he's missing his right ear, just a small river valley of scar tissue surrounding a tiny cavern.

He introduces himself as Randy. He speaks in a British accent. You were mighty lucky. Mighty lucky, he says.

I just keep telling them thanks. I figure this is all I'm good for. I look at one of the screens. It's a feed from just outside the garage. Hundreds of walking dead smash the door. I ask if he can rewind it, just to see how close we were to . . .

Stop, KK says.

Randy stands. The inside of his left arm's beat to shit, bruised to the point of black. I think one of his veins is abscessed. He says, Sorry, bud, no rewinding function, that must have happened somewhere else. Just live feeds.

I nod.

He slaps my back and says, Mighty lucky.

I smile. KK tries to. Typewriter holds his gun.

Shall we? Randy says.

They lead us back into the hallway. Things smell like industrial cleaner, something lemony, and ammonia. I'm dying to see the operation. I'm hoping it's big and sheets of crystal are being broken up right this second.

Can't believe anyone could make it this long out there, Randy says.

Can't either, KK responds.

We all laugh because we're nervous and relieved.

My prayers have been answered. Life inside secure walls. A controlled intake of dope. Electricity. Us being safe. Then I'm wondering about the third person—maybe it's Cheng's friend, the guy who said this was where he was headed. I realize when I showed up, Cheng got killed, just like the Albino, and everywhere I go, people die. I decide to keep this thought tabled.

We walk into a cafeteria. I smell shit being cooked. Rectangular tables with attached round seats span the large room. Metal mesh covers the line of windows separating wall and ceiling.

Maddie calls into the kitchen—Derrick.

I can hear the banging of pots.

Hey, mate, come out here for a second, Randy says.

I glance between KK and Typewriter and Maddie. A big motherfucker steps into view. He's got to be over six five and has a shaved head. It's obvious he's one of those speed freaks who shoots shit only to lift more weight. He's wearing a white apron over a bare chest and his arms are bigger than my thighs. He stares at us. There's some sort of tattoo on his neck, a set of praying hands maybe. The tension is palpable.

Chase, I say, and this is KK, this is Typewriter.

He crosses his arms over his impressive man tits. It's some Shark-Jet standoff and we're all waiting for an introduction, which I realize isn't coming.

Maddie looks at the floor.

Mr. Clean shakes his head and walks back into the kitchen.

That went well, Randy says.

Again, we give some uncomfortable laughs.

We leave the kitchen. Randy's telling us Derrick is the alpha type, survival of the fittest, paranoid about diminishing supplies, but a good guy once you get to know him.

Yeah, yeah, for sure, I say.

We head farther down the hall. A set of heavy-duty doors is propped open under a green painted C.

Welcome home, Maddie says.

It's a common room with round tables and a hanging TV and white linoleum. There're probably eight rooms—cells, I guess—built into the walls. It's juvie, the exact same setup I'd been in, only I was in block A. We're saying how nice it is, how perfect. We walk around like it's an open house. I peek into a cell and see a single thin mattress and an aluminum toilet. I ask if the water works and Maddie says, Thank fucking God.

KK studies a bookshelf. I join her. It's nothing but Bibles and AA Big Books. There's a stack of board games. KK turns to me. Her dimples show. She grabs my pinky and squeezes and I want it to be more.

Pick a room, Randy says.

Typewriter says, That far one taken?

Maddie shakes his head. Go ahead and shotgun that shit, he says.

I'm wondering where that big motherfucker Derrick sleeps. I'm not trying to be his neighbor. KK walks to the room next to Typewriter's and I follow. I'm not sure if we're sharing a room or where we actually stand. She pokes her head inside and says, Guess this one's me, and that answers that. I go into the cell next to her. I'm thinking about my cell as a teenager, how I was tripping and so scared, more of my parents than anything. My black roommate was in for stealing cars and complained how it wasn't fair because rich honkies were ignorant to park in his neighborhood—*fucking stupid, thinking their shit's safe*—and I'd agreed, embarrassed because he was describing me.

I sit on the mattress. There's even a sheet. I rub my temples. The pressure's still there. It's burrowing into my sinuses. I can't stop hearing that baby's coos. I need sleep or scante. I think about this room having been occupied a week before. Some kid had no doubt lay down in this locked cell to the chorus of shouts and cusses from his cell mates, tossed and turned, worried about his upcoming court date or maybe his sentence, thinking about everything unfair in the world—parents and race and money and drugs and the education system and getting caught just doing what he had to—and maybe sleep finally came, restful, all consuming, and, him being sober, unending.

Then I wonder what the fuck Maddie did when he woke up and nobody else did. How did he unlock his cell? Where were the kids who reanimated?

I may ask him but right now I don't care, not really. I'm tired and I lie down, kick off my shoes. I can't remember the last time I've slept. I yell that I'm closing my eyes for a minute. Typewriter yells that he's about to bomb out the bathroom. Our hosts laugh. KK shouts that she's taking a nap too. I take off my clothes. I have no boxers. I climb under the paper-thin sheet. It's cold, but good cold, a toe-in-summer-lake-water cold, relaxing.

6:39 PM

I'm rocking an orange jumpsuit with RAMSEY COUNTY J.D.C. stenciled in white across my shoulder blades. Type and KK are too. We're sitting in the common room with the others eating rice. It's the best food I've ever tasted. I eat what has to be close to a pound. We drink water. I can't get enough. Derrick's put on a shirt. I'm grateful for this. He doesn't talk and I want to be like, Give me a fucking break man, like sorry we crashed your private party, sorry the fucking world ended, sorry you were the last safe place in the city. But I don't. I spoon steaming rice into my mouth and it's thick in my throat and thicker in my stomach.

We finish.

KK thanks them again.

Thank Maddie here, British Randy says.

Right.

Serious, this bloke right here let us in. All of us.

I remember my questions about what he did the previous Monday. I ask what happened.

People's smiles fade. Derrick pushes his bowl to the center of the table. It's definitely praying hands tattooed on his neck.

Sorry, I didn't mean . . .

It's cool, Maddie says. He rubs his buzzed head.

KK stands and collects the cafeteria trays.

Maddie says, I was in the detox holding cell. I got out after a day.

I'm nodding, not really knowing what the fuck is so bad

about that. We've been through a hell of a lot worse, me, KK, and Typewriter—killed who knows how many Chucks, my mom, KK killed Jared, that cooing baby—and I'm waiting for more and then it comes.

I wasn't alone, he says.

Randy rubs Maddie's shoulder. Maddie starts picking at a scab on his forehead. I was arrested with my younger brother, he says.

Then I get it. I picture a smaller version of Maddie turning, giggling, him probably not having enough scante in his system to make it through the night. I picture Maddie having no idea what the hell was happening, an attack, a what the fuck, a punch, and then him realizing that it was for real, that little Danny or Johnny wasn't normal, wasn't human anymore and was going to kill him. I picture Maddie's hands around his younger brother's throat, and I know a kid like Maddie isn't a killer, just an addict, and I'm seeing him as me.

Had to deal with a few guards too, Maddie says.

Jesus, KK says. She's standing behind him. I can tell she wants to console him, to tell him she understands.

Cell block C was closed, something about the AC being broken. So that's where I went. Had an eight ball cornholed, got me through until these two showed up.

Randy nods. I stare into the hole on the side of his head. Randy says, Every other block is full.

Full?

Of them.

Bro, Typewriter says.

Not shit we can do, Derrick says.

Got earplugs, though, Maddie offers.

KK drops the trays and I'm up quick. I'm at her side, my hands on her shoulders. She bites the hell out of her lower lip.

It's completely safe, Randy says. If they haven't gotten out yet, they won't. They'll starve soon, anyway.

Fuck me, Typewriter says.

They're locked in here. With us, KK says.

I'm like, We're safe. We're good. I wrap my arms around her. She's rigid, everything flexed. Her big nose presses against my cheek.

Typewriter cleans up the dropped trays.

KK says that we need to go, that it's not safe here, that she can't fucking do it anymore.

Baby, we're good. I pull her tighter. I realize I called her *baby*. I tell her this is everything we've been searching for.

She whispers, This is a fucking death trap.

Who wants to get their asses kicked at Monopoly? Randy asks.

Fuck that, Derrick says. He stands and I'm shielding KK from him and we make eyes and there's nothing about this motherfucker I like and he says, Morning dose at seven.

I want KK to believe me, to return to how she was ten minutes before, grateful to have warm food and shelter. I tell her she can be on my team.

You good?

She nods.

We sit at the table and Randy sets up Monopoly. Maddie calls the top hat. Typewriter says to stay off the wheelbarrow. KK's the dog. I'm the iron. I haven't played this game since

I was a kid, but I remember the rules, the strategy, the idea
that you have to spend money early to make money later. I
pick up a railroad. We're rolling the dice, buying things with
fake money, building empires. We're barely talking; immers-
ing ourselves in the game is easier. Baltic Avenue, Atlantic Avenue, Electric Company, Community Chest. KK smiles when
she lands on Park Place and buys it. Things are better. Go
directly to jail, do not pass go. We can relate to that. Everyone
holds their money in their hands. I guess old habits die hard.
It's pleasant. Maybe we started playing because it seemed
ironic, but really we love it, the idea of taking over the world.
Everyone does. It's as American as cheerleaders and mission-
ary sex. Strangling the competition, the American way. Randy
catches me staring at his missing ear and I feel like a dick. His
hand goes up reflexively to shield it. I roll the dice. He says,
Few years back.

What's up?

My ear.

I'm not sure—

He laughs. He says, It was one of those moments.

I know what moments he's talking about.

Knew cleaving off the old ear was the only way to stop.

He tries to smile and KK takes his hand. He says, Obviously didn't work. Guess I should be thankful for that fact,
otherwise I'd be dead.

KK says, We've all been there.

Don't see you missing an ear, Randy says, like it's a joke.
We're silent. KK speaks the truth—each of us has had those
moments when all you want is your life before you took your

first hit, and you want this so badly you cut off your own ear, burn your stomach, or just keep upping and upping your intake, moving from snorting to smoking to shooting.

It's bad out there, huh? Maddie asks.

Typewriter shrugs. Tells him it's more of the same.

For reals, KK says.

Chase?

I look at Maddie. He's staring like I hold some answer he needs to hear. I say, Yeah, it's pretty fucking bad.

I move seven spaces to Oriental Avenue and buy it.

Is everyone turned?

No. Not everyone. I'd say the majority didn't make it through the first night.

Maddie fingers an infected cyst. He's probably wondering about his family and, like me, wishing them a peaceful death, together, sleeping.

And just like that, the mood's shit. That's how it always is among tweakers. Ecstatic to miserable in less than a second. Either too much scante or not enough or a thought that burrows into your brain and becomes an itch and then a fully colored panorama and then it's real, that vision like a DVD skipping, over and over and over again.

Need to find a cure and shit, Maddie says.

Randy smiles. He's missing the back two molars on his right side. I wonder if he can still hear out of his cleaved ear. He says, And I need a rim job from Queen Elizabeth.

We laugh. Type rolls the dice to see how much he owes for landing on Water Works. I'm thinking about the word *cure*. I'm thinking maybe I've already found it. Maybe it's copious amounts of scante. Shit worked for Typewriter. He was seconds away or maybe already turning and I saved him and maybe we just need to be able to produce tons of dope and our world would be restored. I mention my theory.

Bullshit, Randy says.

I'm like, What's bullshit? That scante starves this shit off? That we're alive because of meth?

So what are you suggesting? Randy asks. That we just find a Z—

Z? Typewriter says.

Walking dead.

Call 'em Chucks, like Chucklers, Type says.

Randy runs his index finger over the cavern on the side of his head. He's like, So, we find a *Chuck*, and just shoot him full of our limited supply of dope?

Worth a shot, Maddie says.

Type shakes his head and KK fiddles with her hotel on Park Place. Randy says things about the Chucks being oxygen starved, not to mention their thick blood and strips of missing flesh. That there's no way to reverse damage like that. I'm not really listening. I'm thinking this could all be over with, the fucking apocalypse, the Chucks, the need to carry guns and cry when we hear laughter. I'm thinking about inventing the cure, administering it, our numbers growing, me saving the fucking world. And then I think about the Hindu dot I put between my mother's eyes. The baby with Crayola blue eyes. If there is a cure, it came too late. I've already done shit I can't take back. The story of my fucking life.

Could use the Chuck in the interrogation room, I say.

Randy says, Bloke's looking for a Nobel Prize.

Dr. Kevorkian motherfucker, Type mutters.

Not trying to be part of this, yo, KK says.

Me neither, Type says.

Fuck it, Randy says, if your mate wants to play scientist, let him. I'll run it by Derrick in the morning.

I smile and then it fades and we're quiet. I hold play money in my sweaty hand.

Maddie stares at me. There's a light pus dripping out of his worst pick mark. He says, I just don't get how the hell . . . I mean, how'd you guys . . . you know?

I don't want to go into the whole thing—the little girl, Svetlana, the trucker, Walgreens, KK and Jared, the Albino and the Canadians, my mom, Cheng, that cooing baby. He doesn't need to hear this. I feel bad I asked him about his story, dredging up the killing of his younger brother.

I say, Junkies are about the most resourceful motherfuckers on the planet.

Cheers to that, mate, Randy says.

We raise our cups of water in a toast. KK says, To walking dead motherfuckers like us.

11:22 PM

The earplugs don't work worth shit so I've taken them out and lie on my cot listening to a symphony, an unbearable symphony, of giggles echoing from down the hall into our grouping of cells. The laughter penetrates my mind, my sleep, my consciousness. It reminds me there's no way out. No end. Nothing we can do to get away, and I hear the gales, am able to start to catalog the different sources, and I'm giving them names—Jerome, fourteen, second-degree felony for possession of a firearm; Andre, sixteen, first-degree felony for assault with a deadly weapon; and then me years before, Chase, sixteen, two counts of second-degree felonies, possession of narcotics, intent to distribute.

I hear bare feet on tile. I tense for a second until I see KK's skinny frame in my doorway.

You up?

Yeah.

Fuckin' awful.

I know.

I raise one arm as an invitation. She walks into my cell wearing a pair of panties and a wifebeater. I move my back against the wall and she crawls under the thin sheet. She smells like BO and yeast and she takes my left arm and wraps it around her waist and then brings my hand to her face. I breathe her in. I pull her tight. I'm naked and the head of my penis rubs just under the elastic of her underwear. I tell myself to stay calm. My dick isn't feeling it. I tell her I have earplugs if she wants. Maybe she feels my hardening dick because she pushes backward and I'm telling myself she just needs safety, she's scared, she isn't on board, and we hear giggles and roars and laughs and she raises her left leg an inch or two and my penis slides between her thighs.

You think it could work? she asks.

A cure?

Yeah.

Fucking hope so.

I kiss her vertebrae.

This is met by the softest of exhales.

What I've wanted is finally happening and I'm kissing her neck, telling myself to go slow, to cherish this moment, to not freak her the fuck out. She turns. We kiss. Her breath is rot and so is mine and it doesn't matter and we're kissing with tentative strokes of our tongues and it's years before, the psych ward, our apartment, and I ask if she really wants to do this and she tells me to be quiet. She's on top of me and she's wet and tight and I trace her nipples with my tongue and I tell her I love her and she has her eyes closed and goes faster and I tell her again and she leans forward and our noses touch and she tells me she loves me too. The slapping of our skin matches the howling giggles. She's going faster, faster, and I cup her head with both of my hands and she's gasping for air, biting the tip of my thumb, and her body tenses, the edge of her upper lip curling, and our rhythms match each other, everything the release of dopamine, our scarred synapses once again firing.

She rolls off me. She assumes the position of little spoon. I'm having trouble not smiling. She asks if I came inside her and I lie and she laughs and says, I can feel you drippin' out of me, yo.

Such loving pillow talk.

Speaking of, you're hogging it.

I move backward and she puts her whole head on the deflated pillow.

I'm a ball of fucked up. I think what we did was amazing and I imagine a baby growing in her belly and her giving birth with no doctors, nothing sterile, about her somehow surviving, and the three of us a family. Then I think about having to shoot my newborn up with drugs and this seems like the saddest fucking thought ever. Not so much abusing my baby. But that we're done as a species. There's no way to reproduce. No way to ensure our offspring make it out of the womb and no way to cultivate their minds and bodies. Even if there is some sort of cure, we'll still have to shoot crystal every day. A baby couldn't take that. So we're it. Pockets of motherfucking junkies around the state. Around the country. Probably other countries too. All of us hunkered down wondering how much longer until the next thing goes wrong. Until we're out of ephedrine to break down, or ammonia, or HCl. Until the power grid fails. Until we can't stand our lives and slit our fucking wrists. We're it. The six of us here multiplied by every major city and then rural areas like the Albino's farm. I bet altogether there are under a thousand of us. A thousand people who couldn't handle it when the world was normal, that's who's left to keep our species alive.

Haven't had my period in three months, anyway, KK says.

You're pregnant?

She laughs. I like the way her stomach feels against my hand. She says, No, my system gets all fucked up when I'm using.

Oh.

She places the bottoms of her feet on the fronts of mine. I pull her tighter. I never want to let go.

I knew this was going to happen, KK says.

Chucks?

No, us. I mean, fuck, not the way it happened, but I knew we weren't done.

Me too.

Figured you'd think that. Called me every day for six months straight after we broke up.

Can't blame a guy for trying.

Guess not.

I tell her I figured things were looking good during the Marco Polo game.

Get off it.

Just saying . . .

An accidental touch, KK says.

Bullshit.

I whisper *Polo* in her ear, running my hand over her pubic stubble.

In your fucking dreams, yo.

I know.

Cheese-ball motherfucker.

You fucking love it.

Kind of.

I rest my chin on her bony shoulder.

Breath is awful, she says.

I'm embarrassed but I can't help but laugh and I tell her I about vomited kissing her and she says, Fuck you, and makes a show of tossing my arm off and I grab her, spin her around, and pull her toward me. We kiss. I tell her I love it, her taste. She calls me a sick puppy and then rests her head on my chest.

I watch her rise and fall. We're kids. We're however old we were when we starting getting high. We insult to flirt. I love KK and I tell her this and she says, Do you remember the first thing you ever told me?

That you were sexy?

Serious.

I try to remember. I can't. The psych ward is a trazodone blur. I tell her I have no idea.

You said, and I quote, I just called my mom a cunt.

Her head bounces with my laughs.

Do you remember what I told you?

Yeah.

What?

That nothing's as bad as it seems, but nothing's as good either.

SUNDAY

Big cocksucker Derrick makes a production of doling out little cloudy rocks—shitty crank, impure as hell—and I know that Typewriter, KK, and I have been shorted but whatever, we're new, plus we have a little head stash of that Albino shit.

Derrick stares at me when he talks. He says, This is it for the day. Got it?

Roger that, I say.

He continues to stare and it makes me feel violated. I use KK's needle and blast the whole thing.

Shit's stronger than I would have guessed and it gives me a pulse in my asshole.

221

It's good, man, I say.

No shit it's good, Derrick says. He turns to leave, then pauses. He takes a few steps in my direction. He's holding on to a needle and I'm thinking he's either going to puncture my eye or offer me another booster and he's all, This is it, for your little fucking experiment. One shot. One motherfucking wasted dose because Maddie begged me.

I tell him thanks, but I'll probably be needing—

He cuts me off with a wet laugh in my face.

I think about the pain of having your Adam's apple tattooed. I tell myself to let his aggression slide. Really, I have no option. The dude's a fucking beast and would smash my skull with one clubbing fist. He tells me he'll hold on to it, to come find him when I want to play doctor. He walks out of the cell block and down the hall. Typewriter uses a new vein on the back of his foot. KK uses her darkened one. Randy and Maddie shoot theirs too. Our eyes get wider, our attention peaks.

So now what? KK asks.

Typewriter's standing on his tiptoes, hitting the Power button on the hanging TV.

Doesn't work, Maddie says.

I'm kind of dreading another game of Monopoly. I have the urge to retire to the cell with KK. I feel like I could fuck for hours. I try to give her bedroom eyes but she's dabbing her bleeding arm with her finger, then sucking the blood.

Go watch 'em, Maddie says.

Watch who?

Them.

Randy says, Don't have to. Might be a good idea to let it be, actually.

I'm confused, I say.

The monitors, Maddie says, that's how we saw you. We watch the Chucks.

Forget it, maybe another day, Randy says.

I'm down, Typewriter says, I think it'd be some shit to see them when I'm not running away. To study what they're like, you know?

It's wild, Randy says.

I know KK won't want to watch streams of walking dead, that it would probably be the worst thing for her, and I think about the brief moment last night when she actually fell asleep, how she talked in her sleep and woke up screaming.

You two are good? Randy asks.

All good, I say.

The three of them leave and part of me wants to go with and study these things, see how they move, see what the fuck they do when they're not laughing, but I know I should stay with KK.

You can go, she says.

No, that's cool.

Chase the chivalrous.

Not sure what I'm thinking is too chivalrous.

KK rolls her eyes, gets up. Her jumpsuit gives me a boner. She stops at her cell door and glances over her shoulder. I'm up and she's laughing and then we're doing our thing and I take her from behind and my dick's at the perfect sped level—

hard and lacking feeling—and she comes twice and then I do into her aluminum toilet.

We sit on her bed.

There's no sleep coming and there's nothing to do and KK must be thinking the same thing because she grabs her jean shorts from the floor and pulls out a shard of the Albino shit and we shoot each other up.

KK says, The hand of God, yo.

I'm leaning against the white wall. My forehead jumps in small spasms.

And sometimes it's all worth it, she says.

My heart is a snare drum.

Fucking love you, I say.

KK doesn't look, just gives me her hand. I stroke her long fingers.

10:45 AM

We're going over cartoons from our childhood. We're talking about the Gummi Bears. We're talking about Rugrats, trying to remember their names. KK swears the twins are Lil and Phil. I say they're Lilly and Billy. We lie on opposite ends of the bed, our legs intertwined. I ask if she remembers *Captain Planet*. She sings the song. She says, Fuck that noise, let's get spun.

11:06 AM

We're at the black bookshelf. We're debating between a game of War and cracking open the red Bible.

I'm feeling War.

Game is ridiculous, KK says.

Go Fish?

Fuck that.

KK takes a Big Book off the shelf. She doesn't open it. She says, Rarely have we seen a person fail who has thoroughly followed our paths. . . .

She's reciting "How It Works," the section read at the beginning of most meetings. She raises her eyebrows, wanting me to continue. I say, Those who do not recover are people who cannot or will not completely give themselves over to this simple program.

Remember, huh?

Kind of hard to forget.

Figured you'd blotted that shit out.

Tried, I say.

She says, Usually men and women who are constitutionally incapable of being honest with themselves.

There are such unfortunates.

We laugh and then we don't because it's sad. All of us, heads full of AA, veins full of dope. It's fucking sad because we'd bought into the whole thing—meetings and sponsors and prayers and steps and making coffee beforehand and cleaning up afterward and a life that involved working a real job and saving for small material comforts and because we'd been happier then, wanting a different life, believing we could have it.

KK puts the book back on the shelf.

Were you ever serious about it? she asks.

I don't want to have this conversation. To dredge up shit that has no resolution. I shrug.

You were, I know it.

Why are you bringing this up? Like what good does—

It was a question, Chase, that's it.

But why? So we can go through the whole thing again? How I was somehow responsible for us ending.

Not *somehow*.

That's great.

She stares at me. She has her cheeks sucked in like she always did when we fought. This is exactly why I didn't want her to bring it up in the first place, my *seriousness* for AA years ago. It would lead to the same fucking fight, our only fucking fight. Me ruining everything because I couldn't stop smoking shit. Her blaming me for fucking up her life, telling me that she'd have been clean the whole time if it wasn't for my pressure, my hints, my assurance that we could handle it, that it would be just this once.

No, Chase, it isn't *great*. I asked you a question, that's it.

What are you doing? I ask.

The tension in her cheeks releases. She blinks twice. She says, I don't know.

I take her in my arms. I kiss her forehead. She tells me she killed Jared. I ask her if she wants to get spun.

You're fucking with me?

Just something to do, I say.

You realize it's never going to end, don't you?

I talk to her about testing for the cure and about being safe and that Randy and Maddie seem rad and I tell her it'll work out.

KK's like, Not what I said, yo.

Stop doing this.

KK says, The cure, if there even is one, which there fucking isn't, is splice. It's more fucking dope.

I can't believe she's doing this. After everything, after finally being able to sleep for a few fitful hours, after being guarded by locks that keep hardened criminals tame, after finally reaching some sort of fucking destination and grasping on to some semblance of a future, she turns. Always the same thing. A tide pulling outward—her attitude and love and psyche—leaving nothing but cement-looking sand stretching for miles, desolate as fuck.

Just try not to fuck all this up for yourself, I say.

The look she gives me is disgust and hurt, her mouth slightly open. She pulls away and heads to her cell and I'm left standing there alone. I call out her name. She doesn't respond.

11:29 AM

I head out of cell block C. I can hear giggles down the hall. I reach the metal doors for the cafeteria and think about going in and seeing if Derrick needs help. Maybe it'll be a way to bridge the gulf between us. I push open the door. I'd eaten corndogs in this very cafeteria. I'm about to call his name but I don't. I'm not sure why. I make my steps light. I can't hear anything from the kitchen. Maybe he's with the others watching the security cameras? I walk around the stainless-steel serving stations. I know I should announce myself, Derrick just the type of motherfucker who takes being surprised as an act of war. I don't. I push open the swinging doors. There's nobody inside the kitchen. Beakers and tubes and Erlenmeyer flasks cover a stainless-steel rolling cart. It's the smell of poison, of better moods. What the hell is KK's problem? I take a few cautious steps into the kitchen. Derrick isn't there and neither is anybody else. There's a cookie sheet cooling on top of the oven and I'm a little kid sneaking to a tray of chocolate chip cookies my mother has made for her bridge group and I'm staring down at an eighth of an inch of chalky crystalline candy and who the fuck would notice if one cookie is missing? I can't shake the feeling of being watched. I give another spin around the room. I take the butt of my lighter, and as delicately as I can, strike it against the tiniest of corners. There's a soft crack. The half-inch shard is still a little warm. It's a pleasant feeling in my palm. I slip it into the pocket of my jumpsuit. Can't even tell it was ever there.

I make my way back out to the hallway. Giggles echo. I walk to the booking station. Type's sitting in the monitor room, doing the same thing he's done for the past five years: picking his face and watching screens. I stand in the doorway. He barely registers my presence.

Anything new? I ask.

No.

I stand there thinking of something to say. I watch a feed from outside the garage. There's an African-sized gazelle herd of Chucks. The door won't hold forever. I ask Typewriter if he and I are all good.

He sucks blood and scab from underneath his index nail. He still won't meet my eyes. I know he's been going over that scene in the Rockwell house for a day now, me with that baby, me losing my shit. I want to tell him the baby had turned. It was the only merciful thing to do. That my speaking to the baby was a momentary thing, scante and death and fear and that pressure behind my eyes and the sun coming through in a single spotlight on the baby's pajama-covered feet. To tell him that I've seen him do the same thing—the head of that little girl underneath his typewriter, the pawning of his dead mother's jewelry she kept in the hollow bottom of a Gillette bottle of shaving cream, the stuff he told me he'd hold on to until the day he died. I'll tell him we all get to that point. That I'm better now.

But instead, I say, What the fuck was I supposed to do?

He sits there staring at the monitors. I notice one-quarter of one screen is from the kitchen. Fuck. I wonder if he saw me and maybe I should offer him a little hit. I have the feeling of being a teenager and forgetting to clear the family computer's browsing history.

Finally, Typewriter says, It for sure turned? The baby?

For sure, man, hundred percent. Only explanation for it to still be making noise.

He turns to me. His fat jowls slide back into a reluctant

smile. I think about it being this easy, people willing to believe whatever they're told.

Should have seen the set of teeth on that little fucker.

Nasty, huh?

I slap my hand on his back. I tell him he has no idea.

The Chucks on the screen pry at the hole KK blasted in the garage door.

I ask where the others are.

Out divvying up the County guns.

Oh shit yeah. You're not trying to get one?

Type motions to the shotgun leaning against the wall.

Your loss, man, I say. I give Type another pat on the shoulder and tell him I'm going to check it out. He's a retriever, eager to forgive and be petted.

I hear voices from across the booking station. Derrick and Randy stand at a table. Six or seven shotguns lie there and I'm like hell yeah and they turn, Randy smiling, Derrick nothing but intimidating tits.

Randy asks how my skills are with a shotgun.

Survived a week out there, man.

Guess that settles that, he says.

I take hold of one of the guns, pump it, examine it like I know what I'm looking for.

Don't get too excited, Randy says, nonlethal rounds.

Huh?

The ammo. Rubber slugs.

I laugh like he's joking and Derrick looks like he's disgusted with me or the guns, I can't really tell.

So they're worthless?

'Bout to find out, Derrick says. He pumps one of the guns and starts toward the closed interrogation room. He fumbles with a set of keys and then it's laughter and I think about finding a cure and that Chuck being my test subject and about me saving the fucking world and I tell him to hold up, need to test my cure.

He laughs.

I stand next to Derrick's hulking body. I'm scared because the Chuck is handcuffed to a breakable table and because I'm holding on to stolen scante. Derrick's arm brushes against mine. His are like the thighs of midwestern milkmaids; mine are like little kid dicks.

Derrick says, Bet my experiment works better than yours.

Randy laughs. He says, Let him at least try.

I'm not really listening. I'm staring at this kid handcuffed to the table. He's missing a piece of flesh along his chin. It's like he had the tweak bugs so bad he struck bone. His freckles are so familiar. And then I'm feeling faint because it's coming back to me—the Starbucks restroom, Frank from the halfway house, us relapsing together, he with dope, me with crystal, the needle in his arm and the way he didn't close his eyes and how their little bit of green diluted into a shitty brown after ten minutes.

A rubber slug inside that mouth has got to do some damage, Derrick says.

I'm thinking about this somehow being my boy Frank. I'm telling myself it's not him, he's dead, saw the shit for myself, dead and I left him there with the belt still around his arm.

Mate, looks like you seen a ghost.

More like he's thinking *why the fuck would I want to cure that?* Derrick says.

I don't respond. I smell this kid's decay and I smell the pine-fresh cleaner of Starbucks years before and I'm not sure what to do, then or now, nothing but death and guilt and fear.

Having second thoughts? Derrick says. He waves the loaded rig in my face. He's laughing like this shit is so funny. The hands tattooed on his neck jiggle. He says, Plans always sound better sitting around shooting scante, don't they?

He raises the shotgun.

I take a step inside of the room. I reach back and he gives me the needle and Randy's telling me to be careful and I tell myself this isn't Frank and I had no other option back in that restroom than to leave him and the pressure behind my eyes is like a gouge on soft basswood. The freckles, that's the resemblance. I tap out air bubbles. Derrick says something about the Chuck not caring about air bubbles or cotton fever. Maybe the laughter is the same? I can't remember Frank's laugh, only that he did it a lot. But I'm hearing this little-kid giggle and it sounds innocent and I'm thinking about her, *Innocence* with her fucking umbrella socks. I inch closer. The Chuck snaps at me with his mouth. I jam the rig into his leg.

I step back.

The needle sticks out of the Chuck's leg.

I'm seeing the needle in Frank's arm, his North Face bunched up around his elbow.

Then I realize that it's not laughing, not even a giggle, dead silent, the Chuck just sitting there. Derrick and Randy step closer. They stare at this kid. They're probably praying for him to stay silent, telling whatever god they've abandoned that this is it, the one wish, please do this for me, please. They're probably thinking about production on a massive scale and maybe about an effective way to administer it, maybe some sort of dart gun loaded with Tina. I wish KK was here seeing the miracle. It'd fix everything. The best of both worlds—guilt-free using and safety.

We'll clear the jail one Chuck at a time. We'll start in the juvie wards and we'll select one, the five of us gagging him, handcuffs, demonic laughs, give him the remedy, watch his eyes become spun and feel his pulse kick and we'll know what he'll be feeling—a deluge of dopamine, a combination of orgasms and game-winning field goals and being tucked in by your mother, her hair tickling your nose when she bends over to kiss your forehead—and then the former Chuck will say, What the fuck happened? and we'll laugh, these ones real.

It starts low.

It's so low I don't know what it is and then Derrick steps back and they're louder now, this motherfucker's bellows. The kid fills the detention room with the sound of death. I picture KK hearing it all the way from her cell. Her first response will be lighting a cigarette and burning her stomach, her mind telling her she's a dumb cunt to believe in happily ever afters.

Goddamn it, Derrick says.

He whips the shotgun up and fires into the Chuck's chest. The kid flies backward, dragging the table with him. My ears ring. The Chuck's T-shirt is ripped and I wait for that thick blood to come dripping out, but it doesn't. He keeps laughing.

Derrick turns to leave and we bump shoulders and he says it again, this time a yell, Goddamn it.

Both experiments have failed.

Randy tries to be upbeat with his closed-lip smiles. He shakes his head, saying, Thought we had something. Thirty seconds of silence.

I don't respond.

Randy puts his hand on my shoulder, leading me out of the interrogation room. He shuts the door. There's a pane of Plexiglas. The Chuck stares. I think he knows me too. I can feel it, the recognition, the need to connect. Randy says something about trying again later. There's a stab of pain behind my left eye. The pressure will follow. And it's like this motherfucker is laughing right at me and everything I've ever done and it's like Frank is there, immortal in my guilt.

12:22 PM

I'm in the hallway. I'm not really feeling going back to KK yet, know she'll still be all you-ruined-my-life. I figure I'll duck off farther down the hall and blast a hit of the pocketed dope. I smile at this. The smile makes the pressure behind my eyes even worse.

I head toward cell block B.

The giggles grow louder.

Why the fuck won't these things die? There can't be any people left to eat. Maybe they don't need sustenance? Maybe they're more evolved? Some higher species, self-sustaining, not needing sleep or food or scante or love or daylight or shelter and maybe they're the perfect life-form to inhabit our stupid fucking planet. It's dark in the hallway. Their laughter gets louder. I'm not sure if this is because I'm nearer or if they hear me, smell me, sense me. I can't stop thinking about Frank. Maybe it's survival of the fittest. Maybe the world had had enough with *Homo sapiens*. Waved its white flag. Said fuck you, your turn is over. You ruined everything. You pissed in my water, polluted my skies, raped my mountains, built monuments to yourselves and the shit was shortsighted. So get the fuck off my tits. And boom. Armageddon. The apocalypse. It's the shit people have been fearing and having nightmares about since we crawled down from trees. An intuitive fear of extinction. That our turn would soon be over. And the next in line—fucking Chucks.

I'm standing a few feet away from cell block B.

The two white metal doors shake like they're holding back a flash flood. It's not just fists pounding, but whole bodies charging. I wonder if they have brains. If they can think. Maybe a little? Maybe that's the next step in evolution, humans losing our cognitive powers. Reverting to primitive animals. But maybe even lower, because the walking dead aren't trying to reproduce, as far as I can tell. I think about all the free time a male species would have without trying to get pussy. Without the fairy-tale notion of love, without any emotional connection to anybody. Motherfuckers would rule the world. Motherfuckers *are* ruling the world.

I see a set of fingers under the door. They wiggle. They're black. I inch closer. They flap and wave like a queen offering dick sucks for twenty a swallow. My retinas feel like they're suffering from a thousand simultaneous paper cuts. I smash the heel of my Nikes down on the four wiggling fingers. The sound is a shit plopping into a toilet. I giggle. The hand slips back under the door. The splattered concrete is like one of those Thanksgiving hand turkeys I made as a little kid.

I walk deeper into juvie.

It's darker.

KK should be over our little fight by the time I get back. She'll be spun bad, but she'll see me and she'll know it's love. She'll feel it, just like she always has. She'll drop the hardened exterior. She'll let me take her in my arms and tell her she's a good person.

I stop dead, looking at the doors of cell block A. There's a dent protruding maybe three inches. Giggles and laughs. I smell decaying flesh. It reminds me of worms left in the sun in a little white bait container. The force the Chucks slam into the wall with is scary. I can't stand it. I stare at the dent, wondering how long it took to create. Was it one charge? A week's worth of pounding? Either way, it's not good. It would take maybe three inches more for the metal to split open. For hands to stick through. For that hole to grow. For those giggles to become more than locked-away echoes.

I lean against the wall and watch the hands wiggle under the door and I think about that little girl who started this shit with the umbrella-and-raindrop socks and I'm picturing her jumping in puddles, splashing and laughing, happy. I'm seeing those puddles as Chuck blood, the source being the stomping of fingers. I laugh at this thought. I spit into a spoon. I use my lighter to crush a little of the stolen glass. I'm thinking about getting a knife, playing This Little Piggy with as many of their fingers as I can find. I load my syringe. The cackles are a chorus. I replay the idea that I'm still sitting on Type's couch. That my heart said fuck this and exploded and everything since is the release of death chemicals. The needle slipping into my vein is like the rehearsed sex life of a married couple and I push down and will the pressure in my sinuses to go away and I'm seeing Frank's body limp and I'm hearing his laughs through a piss slit of Plexiglas.

Hello?

It sounds like the voice is coming from behind the door.

Chase?

The voice comes from the opposite side of the hallway. I turn and see Maddie backlit, lanky and young and insecure.

I yank the needle out of my arm and slip it into my pocket.

What are you doing?

I don't know, man. Seeing what we're up against, I say.

Maddie stands ten feet away and stares at the door and then at me. I trace his vision straight to my arm, my bunched-up sleeve, my raised vein.

The hell you get more?

The fuck you talking about, man?

He points to my arm and I shake my head, shrug. I look at my arm like I'm just now realizing my sleeve's up. I make a big show of pretending to understand his confusion. I'm like, Oh, guess that's what it looks like, huh? Just checking to see how my vein's doing.

Oh.

I can tell he's not sold on my explanation. He won't come any closer. I put him on the defensive by asking what he's creeping around back here for.

He says, Checking on the dent.

I know, right? Was just looking at the cameras with Type. That hole's not looking good either.

Maddie's hand goes straight to his face, his forehead, his fingers finding a partially healed scab, picking. He's obviously quit thinking about me shooting a secret stash. But I'm not a dick, not trying to freak the kid out any more than need be, so I tell him it's fine, it'll hold.

Finally, he says, Like how big's the hole?

Watermelon.

Fuck. They aren't getting through, are they?

No. And there's the stairs and then the door, so I mean, we're all good. . . .

I'm not sure if I'm assuring him or myself. We watch the door to cell block A shake and we stand there for a while, not saying anything, waiting for it all to fall apart. Maddie's a mess, a scared, scab-covered fuckup. He picks zits and sores and he'll carry these scars his entire life and this amount of time probably won't be very long. This makes me sad because he's so clearly me. Maybe not exactly. Maybe different circumstance. Maybe his family lives on the south side and his descent into meth was more natural, wasn't a form of rebellion, but it doesn't matter. He's me. He's in juvie. He shoots scante because he can't handle a fucking thing. He shoots it because he thinks it's better than the alternative.

Let's get out of here, I say. I stand and put my arm around

his shoulder and I'm trying to be a big brother because I'm the motherfucking glue keeping the human species alive, but I feel like a fag so I bring my arm back to my side.

Think it will hold?

I say, Yeah, man, and like Randy said, they're bound to die sooner or later, you know? Can't survive on nothing. Probably start eating each other.

Yeah.

My mouth matches my pounding heart. I say, Might be onto something with the cure. About thirty seconds of silence after the shot.

Oh.

Then I'm on a roll, spun from the booster, telling him that we'll cook batches and batches, that we're planning on making tranq guns to shoot the remedy, from there it'll be bombs of scante, hand grenades of vaccination. We'll make the world safe and docile and we'll conquer this shit and it's going to start with my boy Frank in the detention room.

Frank?

What?

Who's Frank? Maddie asks.

Frank? Fuck man, don't know any *Frank*. I said *Chuck*.

I put my arm back around his shoulder and pull him in a mock embrace. He comes to me easily, so light. We walk toward our home in cell block C. I reach into my pocket and feel the little shard of stolen scante. I place it in his hand, tell him it was my morning dose, had a tiny bit left over from before. He grins. I'm not sure if this is me being nice or some sort of bribe. I glance at the Chuck blood pictograph from the stomped fingers as we pass block B. I'm smiling. I say, Gonna beat this thing, my boy, gonna beat it.

1:10 PM

I've made up with KK. It wasn't hard. Just as I figured, she'd blasted a little of the Albino Tina and our loose tongues rationalized and apologized—the stress, I know, God, so fucking scared, feel you, yo, we're safe, just want this shit to stop—and then we'd hugged and I pretended to be into her warm breath that smelled like yeast infections.

We're sitting around the table playing poker. It's all of us but Derrick, who's still working on a cook.

I'm holding on to a pair of jacks.

Typewriter's smiling his fat Italian grin, so I know he's got something. Randy fingers his disgusting ear nub. Maddie folds. KK's a little harder to figure out, the way she's staring at the name *CODY* scratched into the table. The pot is Monopoly money. I raise a hundred. Everybody checks.

The flop doesn't help me—a seven and a two and a king.

Type's grin widens and he's a little boy and simple and he tries to cough to cover up his tell. He raises a hundred.

Randy says, Bet anything this smirking bloke has three kings. He throws his cards into the middle.

I check.

KK does the same.

The turn is a jack of spades. I tell myself to show no emotion and to be medieval stoic and for some reason a memory of my father comes back. This was two years ago and I'd been smoking speed for maybe three weeks but it wasn't horrible yet, KK and I still keeping it to an every other day schedule. My parents invited me to a hockey game. I knew that not accepting would be a red flag and I wasn't trying to make them worried. I showed up a few minutes late. I saw my father all little and old standing there in front of the arena on Seventh. The tail of his jersey poked out from underneath his Columbia parka. I told myself to be calm and to make eye contact and he saw me and waved and smiled and this was pride—not for himself, but for me, his son coming up on six months clean, his son holding a job and a girlfriend and his son not dead—and I let myself believe that it was all real. I was a few feet away, ready for a fatherly embrace. Then everything about him changed. His mouth straightened. His cheeks loosened. His eyes became hooded. It was the crushing of his soul or psyche or hope or his vision of a future where phone calls didn't cause a sickening feeling in his chest. He said, Jesus Christ, son.

Typewriter gives a little frown. He checks. I put in my one golden five-hundred-dollar bill. KK does the same. Type leans back, stretches. He counts his money. He says, All in.

Oh, snap, Maddie says.

I have the feeling Type's got three kings but I'm not about to let him buy the pot and what does it matter anyway? I throw my money on the table. Everyone turns toward KK. She runs her finger over the etched name in the table. She says, Bet my morning booster.

We think she's joking and are all like *yeah right, good one.*

Wait, you're serious? Randy asks.

As pregnancy.

No, can't have you doing that, he says. Let's just be reasonable here.

Type looks uncomfortable, trying to figure out if KK's joking.

I make eyes with KK. Hers are flat and blue and remind me of the freezing tile of the psych ward floor. She's serious. She's willing to bet her survival on her cards, on a game. Randy keeps saying things about that not being allowed, about nobody knowing how long a person can survive without meth. Type folds. He says, Not getting in a pissing match with two conniving fucks like you.

I ask what that's supposed to mean.

Typewriter just shakes his head.

I block out the cautious pleas from Randy and the nervous shifts by Maddie. I stare at my pocket pair of jacks plus the one on the table. I'm trying to figure out what she has. With the two spades showing, it's probably a flush.

KK says, Shit's for keeps, yo. My shot against yours. And I'm not giving you a taste tomorrow. Swear to God I'm not.

I believe her.

Stop, both of you, this is ludicrous, Randy says.

In or out? KK says.

My father saying, Jesus Christ, son. The same deadpan face. Nothing more left to lose.

Crazy-ass bitch, I say. I fold. I lean over to kiss KK's cheek and she lets me. She talks shit, collecting the money. I pretend to gather the cards to start shuffling. I sneak a look at her hand—a ten of hearts, an ace of diamonds, a five of clubs. She had nothing. Absolutely nothing. Not even a hope for something.

Just then, Derrick's yell fills the entire common area: Who the fuck stole the dope?

He strides through the entrance with his bare chest leading the way, his orange jumpsuit tied around his waist. He holds the cookie sheet of scante. I wonder who would be that fucking selfish to steal our medicine. I realize it was me. I'm thinking he's going to bash my trachea into my spine and that it's not going to be the drugs or the Chucks that kill me, but a human, this skinhead motherfucker who can't take a joke.

Which one of you pieces of shit stole it?

My hands are up and I'm shaking my head, scanning the table.

Derrick, mate, just calm—

He drops the tray onto the middle of the table. Its whitish surface grows a hundred fissures. A few shards bounce out and land on top of KK's bluffed hand.

One of you did, know it. Stole a corner piece.

Now he's staring at me.

It's the same look Typewriter gave me at the Rockwell shrine, the same as KK's when she just called my hand, Maddie in the hallway, my father in front of the hockey arena—all of them like *you're a lying piece of shit. I'm onto you. You can't run forever. It's over.*

Don't know why you're staring at me, man, I say.

Bud, I don't think anybody would be that stupid, Randy says. He's standing, one hand stretched toward Derrick.

These three motherfuckers show up, and then we're short.

I feel KK's stare but I can't look because she'll see through me. I think about Typewriter maybe having seen me on the video feed. I thank God it can't be rewound. I stand. Derrick's a foot away, coming closer. I yell that it wasn't me. He doesn't care. I'm about to reach for my pistol in my left side pocket but I don't have time because Derrick's got his hand around my collar and his fist cocked and I'm yelling to check my pockets and his nostrils flare and I know he'll kill me because he's in charge of this fucked-up world and he's about to hit my face and I yell the first thing that comes to mind: I saw Maddie walking around alone.

Derrick holds back from crushing my face.

Yeah, man. Like I was here with KK and then with Type and then you, man, remember? Doing that experiment shit? But Maddie was walking around in the halls, the only one who wasn't accounted for.

Fuck you, Maddie says.

Derrick lets go of my jumpsuit.

Everybody turns toward Maddie. He's standing now, his finger pulling at a scab. He says, That's bullshit. You fucking know it.

Everybody stay calm, Randy says.

Where were you? Derrick asks.

Down by block A. This dude's lying. Framing me. Saw *him* down there with his sleeve rolled up.

And then Derrick's on my shit again and I think about putting a slug straight through the hands tattooed on his neck and then we'd be fucked, him being the cook, him being God, our limited survival dependant upon his ability to breathe.

I know Maddie still has the crystal I gave him. I know all I have to do is mention this fact. Derrick cocks his arm. I say, Check his pockets.

Fuck you, Maddie screams. He's crying. Snot starts down his face. He yells, You gave me this. *You* gave it to me. Said you had more of your own.

Type's face goes slack and he's staring at me and then at KK and he knows, he's got to fucking know I stole it, his eyes saying *how the fuck can you do this?*

Maddie's walking backward. He holds the shard of scante like it's some sort of shield. Derrick walks in gigantic steps. Maddie keeps saying, I didn't do anything, Chase gave it to me, I didn't fucking do anything.

We watch Derrick grab hold of Maddie and fists plummet down and we hear the yelp of a stepped-on tail and then it's bright red on white linoleum, Maddie's legs fighting to gain traction, smearing his blood like finger paint.

Derrick stands over the lump that is Maddie. His voice is even and low: If that ever happens again, I'll kill you. That's a promise.

1:46 PM

KK's gone to Maddie's cell. I told her not to, saying he'll just want to be alone, that he was probably ashamed and embarrassed. She's been in there for five minutes. I can see her clean his face with toilet paper, gentle motherly dabs. I know he's telling her lies about me giving him that piece of scante. But why the fuck would she believe him? Type disappeared down the hall, probably to the monitor room. Randy and I clean up. I'm collecting the spilled bits of crystal. I pretend to tie my shoe, slipping two slivers into my sock.

2:07 PM

We need to talk—words any guy knows are trouble. KK stands over me. I'm sitting on the toilet in my cell, pants on, not shitting or anything, just don't want to see or be seen by anybody else.

I'm only going to ask you this once, KK says.

I know what's coming. It's her taking Maddie's side and her not believing me and I just want people to cut me a break because who the fuck wouldn't take a teener of glass?

Look at me, she says.

I do.

Her face is all angles. She says, Did you steal the shit?

I laugh and shake my head and am like, Jesus Christ, I'm not doing this again. I stand. I say, I understand it from that Nazi motherfucker, but from you? Fucking hurts.

Yes or no?

I think about having to find Typewriter, having a come-to-Jesus talk, his loose fucking lips my greatest danger.

I say, I have done everything, fucking *everything*, for you. Risked my life to come back and get you, to save your prick boyfriend, to get you here, and it's still not good enough.

Yes. Or. No?

No. No. Fucking Christ. I didn't take anything. And fuck you for not believing me.

She starts nodding her head and it's subtle at first, her cheek growing a dimple, not her good kind, but the ones from biting the inside of her cheek, and then it's more, her nodding, her eyes the color of shitty crank, tears that she won't let herself shed drowning the blue of her irises. I take her hands. They feel like death. I squeeze because I want her to believe me and I want to believe myself. I say, Swear to fucking God, to our ability to find a cure, to get through this shit alive, to make it all end, that I didn't steal any tweak.

She's crying, coming into my arms, soft sobs, my arms around her, her shaking violent.

Swear on my life, I whisper. I kiss the line where her flat bangs meet her forehead. Then the ridge of her Germanic nose. I swear on everything.

2:30 PM

I'm in the booking station alone. I'm loading the test rig with some of my recently stolen dope. Randy told me it'd be pointless, any more experiments. Maybe he's right. He'd looked tired as fuck after Maddie's beating, like maybe he was seeing his safe haven crumbling like all dope houses eventually do.

The Chuck that reminds me of Frank laughs from the other side of the door.

I'm wondering if Frank is really Frank and if I'm coming undone and if Maddie's nose is broken and if KK believed me.

I unlock the door. The smell is like this one time I found a dead deer in the woods behind our house. It was so big, its stomach like a balloon. I put my shirt over my face and found a stick and poked its side. It was both firm and bouncy. Then I jammed the stick as hard as I could into the deer's white undercarriage. It made the softest of pops and sunk a few inches. A jet stream of warm air gushed across my ankles and the smell was so pungent I stumbled backward, dry heaving, wondering if my death would cause the same stink.

Chuck Frank stares at me. Frank's eyes seeing everything I've ever done. Frank's eyes knowing I left him for dead.

I jam the rig into his thigh. He snaps at my throat. I hold my breath. I watch his eyes for dilation. I pray for giggles to become words. Then it happens. Frank's pupils become saucers. He quits pulling against the handcuffs. He blinks.

I count in my head—One one thousand, two one thousand . . .

Frank's eyes lose their knowingness. Now they're just the eyes of a drug addict.

Seventeen one thousand, eighteen . . .

I pull out the chair opposite of Frank. I sit. It feels intimate, me studying him, us closed off from the rest of the world. It reminds me of a Fifth Step I did during my year of sobriety. I sat with my sponsor—some old sculptor with a Jesus beard—and I told him every single resentment I had, the cause, what part of me it affected, and what my role in the whole thing was. Then I shared my sexual inventory. Then my fears. The whole thing took close to four hours.

Afterward, we knelt on the concrete floor of his clay

studio. A single fan circled above us. We said a prayer that started, God, I am now willing that you should have all of me.

At thirty-one seconds, Frank starts to laugh.

Fuck you, Frank, I say.

I load another shot and tell him it isn't nice to laugh at other people. I think about Typewriter lying on the warming hut floor, how I blasted him until seizures came and he'd been right there at the cusp of death and I'd saved my best friend, just like I'm going to save the world.

In you go, I say.

Frank's quiet is the perfect high, the one that lets you feel like nothing you've ever done has hurt a soul.

He'll either die or he won't.

It's the same fate as every motherfucker.

I start loading one for myself with my own needle, taking a pocketed scrap out of my sock.

I watch Frank seize. I tell him to not make this about himself. I start with an impromptu Fifth Step. I tell him that I resent him. That he was my boy and he had to go off and shoot too much fucking dope and die on me. I say, How the fuck do you think that made me feel? My best friend in sobriety dying? And just leaving you like that? That shit did a number on me, man. Guilt like you wouldn't believe.

Frank's little bit of jaw tendon flaps like slurped spaghetti.

I know, I know, I say. *What was my part?* Fuck, man, you always cut straight to the core of it, huh?

I sigh, leaning back in the chair. I put my feet on the edge of the table. I say, I was the one who was in your ear for the two weeks leading up to the relapse. The one saying sobriety was gay and that I knew some sluts who wanted to party, and shit, think I even told you that you were getting fat. It was my money that bought your dope and my tweak. I was the one who told you to quit being a pussy.

Frank's seizure shakes the table. I have to really press my feet against it so they don't slip off.

As I'm watching this, something is happening to me, like the scante isn't working, isn't blocking out shit. I'm not trying to experience this moment of clarity. I'm working as fast as I can to boil more dope. I'm telling Frank that it's really about me, every resentment, every perceived injustice is really me having fucked up and hurt people or at least put myself in a situation to be hurt. I'm thinking about calling my mom a cunt in the psych ward and how she stumbled at the door, her hand shaking on the metal handle, and then about my father and his *Jesus Christ, son* and then about Type and the fucking picture of his mother in the glove box and him just wanting companionship and about seeing KK share at meetings, how she'd started being able to look people in the eye, how around six months clean she quit talking about how bad it'd been using, and started talking about good things in sobriety—I got a raise at work, I took my GED, I enrolled in an intro comp course at Metro—and then I'm seeing her in the bathroom with her stomach burned to shit and I'm seeing scared Maddie look to me for guidance and I'm feeling his bony shoulders under my arm and telling him it's all good, it'll work out, and then I'm seeing him back away from Derrick with that tiny piece of crystal like a cross to a demon. All this shit is on me and I'm crying.

I'm crying because there's no fucking cure—then or now or ever—and because the garage door isn't going to hold and because Frank's gone limp, his face pressed to the blue table, a halfhearted giggle bubbling from his lips.

I'm crying, on my knees, wishing I was with my sponsor, his stupid beard, his arm around me, him telling me we are not our actions, him saying repeat after me, and I'm doing it on the floor of the detention room, God, I am now willing that you should have all of me, both the good and the bad.

Frank's giggles fade. He's motionless. It's déjà vu.

I push my own needle into my arm.

It takes a few seconds, but it comes—Fuck Frank, it was his own motherfucking fault, both then and now.

7:33 PM

Typewriter seems to have disappeared. I need to find him because he's the last loose end to all this shit. I'll explain that I was really looking out for his best interest, just like always, trying to squirrel away an extra hit for him. I'll remind him of all the times I fronted him tweak, ask him who introduced him to the Albino, who saved your life three or four times this past week, who helped you through the death of your mother?

I'll tell him that me being alive is of paramount importance to his survival.

Motherfucker can't argue with that.

I just can't have him getting in the ear of anybody else, especially KK.

I finally see Type and Maddie in the kitchen and I'm like that cocksucker is stealing shit too, but then I see he's scooping rice onto plastic trays. I stand there on the other side of the swinging doors. It's just Typewriter and Maddie and they're talking, whispering, and I know that shit's conspiratory and Type sold me out. I can imagine him telling Maddie he saw the whole thing on the video feeds, me breaking in, scanning the kitchen like some two-bit thief, busting off a shard. I know Type's probably telling him about the baby. *Chase just suffocated a baby. Not even sure it was a Chuck. You should have heard him, the way he was talking to it, like a fucking bedtime story, bro. Dude's straight up lost his shit.*

Maybe Maddie's telling him they should go to KK. Maybe he's saying she's the key to me, as soon as she sees who the fuck I am, it'll be over. She'll get everybody to turn.

And maybe Typewriter is agreeing. He's saying, Should see how pathetic he is without her. For a year straight, all I heard was KK this, KK that. Such a fag.

I think I see them laughing.

My best friend's plotting against me.

7:46 PM

We're eating rice, everybody but Maddie. He's in his cell. We eat in silence and the weight is beyond heavy—the burden of utopia fallen. I catch Typewriter staring. He's obvious in his backstabbing. Derrick shovels rice into his mouth. Randy's good cheer is gone. He eats with his hands. A piece of rice hangs from his bottom lip. I reach under the table and give KK's leg a squeeze. She pulls away. It's like family meals when things first started to go bad, me at fifteen, suspensions and found joints, my parents not sure how to circle around the subject of my fuckups. We eat and pretend things are okay, wishing for everybody else at the table to choke.

The hole's huge now, Randy says.

Where? KK asks.

The garage. Gonna give, Type says.

The cure doesn't work, I say.

No shit, Derrick says.

Fucking kill me, KK says.

Randy's like, How about a little shot? He looks across the table at Derrick. Just something to take the edge off?

Derrick pulls a Ziploc out of his jumpsuit pocket. There's got to be close to two ounces in it. He says, Have at it.

We stare and salivate and we know it's his way of saying *see what the fuck happens*. Maybe it's the fact that I shot up a few hours before instead of at seven in the morning like Randy, but I have a little sense, a little perspective. I tell Derrick to put it away. I say, We've got a routine right now, let's not mess with that.

Easy for you to say, Typewriter says.

Derrick's like, The fuck is that supposed to mean?

Type shrugs.

I want to kick him under the table and to pin him in his cell and tell him it was for his own fucking good, everything

I've ever done, motherfucker would be dead without me. Instead, I say, The door's fine. Plus there's other doors, man, not like it's a free shot in.

Just because you pretend it isn't a problem, doesn't mean it's not, KK says.

It will hold.

Not for long, Derrick says.

And when the garage door gives? KK asks.

Then we go out another way. There's got to be some other exit.

Through general population, Derrick says. Big Chucks, hundreds, if not thousands.

I'm trying to figure out something that will appease their fears, some bit of excitement that will get Type the fuck off my jock, something that will give them a morsel of hope, because I know a junkie without hope is as good as dead. I picture the hole in the garage door. I'm remembering Maddie making us strip. I'm looking over his shoulder to the police cruiser. The fucking police car! It's perfect. If it gets bad, like really bad, the Chucks about to break through, we pack up the lab and get in the car and gun it over any walking dead stupid enough to get in our way.

I spit my plan out as it comes to me.

Derrick nods his head.

I tell them that we'll get out of the city, head north, way north, middle of Canada north, hitting every farm for ammonia and pharmacy for ephedrine along the way. I talk about reinventing ourselves in wooden huts and booby traps and eating berries and we'll reinvent the human species, some Garden of Eden shit.

Jesus, just shut the fuck up for once, Typewriter says.

I ignore him. He's just one person. But the others, I see it over each of their faces—the formulation of a thought, a kernel of hope.

Typewriter stands. He says, Can't listen to this bullshit. So fucking done with the Chase Daniels show.

And you've got a better idea? You want to step up for once in your fucking life and give a goddamn solution?

He says, So fucking done with you. He turns and heads toward Maddie's cell.

I look at those of us still at the table. I say, Fuck him if he can't get on board, because this shit here, this plan, it's as foolproof as anal sex is to preventing babies.

Those of us left at the table smile, even Derrick. KK's dimples are back, the good ones, her being happy.

9:11 PM

I'm lying in bed. KK's next door reading the fucking Big Book. Type's still with Maddie. I'm a little freaked out because the giggles from down the hall seem to be even louder than usual. Plus, I'm picturing the garage door caving like chain-link fences around South American soccer fields. I have our real guns spread out, the ones that can actually kill. There're two slugs in each shotgun. I have two shots left in the pistol.

Six deaths, if aim isn't an issue. Six *get out of jail free* cards. That's it. There's got to be at least seven Chucks in block A alone. Who knows how many in the mess hall. Hundreds or thousands outside of the garage. Six shots. Six rounds. Randy, Maddie, Derrick, Typewriter, KK, myself.

The lights cut. There's an instantaneous eruption of Chuck laughter.

My first thought is that Nazi Derrick is trying to conserve power.

I hold on to Buster and my pistol. Everything's pitch black. I hear Typewriter from across the common room say, What the fuck? I place the pistol in the pocket of my orange jumpsuit, grip Buster's stock.

Now I hear Derrick's voice, a bark: Who hit the lights?

I know nobody touched the lights. We're out of power. The grid has failed. We're now in the dark ages. I wonder about candles and flames to cook meth and about toilets that don't flush. I go out in the main room.

Six shots. Six deaths. It'd be that easy. Saving the last people alive from a death worse than death.

KK reaches out and takes my hand.

All I can hear is the echoes of laughter. Darkness and laughter. I know KK's imagination is the same thing—Chucks bashing down unlocked doors—because when we see a flicker of light, she screams.

Maddie holds a lighter in front of his face. It's the first time I've really taken a good look at him since the beating. His right eye is swollen shut, angry and blackening. He doesn't say anything, just stares at me. The flame dissects his face and he's scarier than any Chuck I've seen.

The power grid, I say.

Fuck me, Derrick says.

Typewriter flicks his lighter. He stands a few inches away from Maddie.

Need to go, Randy says, Christ, mates, we need to leave now.

Fuck, fuck, fuck, KK chants.

All gonna die, Maddie says.

Stop, everybody, Derrick shouts. Shut the fuck up with that. We planned for this. Chase's plan. It's fine.

Fine? Fine? Fuck, bud, half these locks are electronic, Randy says.

Got the keys right here, Derrick says. He jiggles a chain and it sounds like a toy poodle. He says, Not electronic, that's only in the pen.

We're quiet.

Finally, Derrick says, We're fine in juvie. Fine for the night.

Bullshit, Randy says.

Derrick's right, I say. There's nothing to do right now. We try to get out in this darkness, we're . . .

Dead, KK says.

Dead, Maddie says.

Derrick tells us to shut the fuck up. He says, We get up at dawn, take the cruiser, and get ghost.

We listen to giggles and I think about the backup plan of a slug in each of our sleeping mouths.

Derrick says, Get your personal shit together. We leave at five.

He's a shadow walking back to his cell. We stand there not knowing what to do. I feel a hand on the small of my back and it's KK and her nose is giant even in the dim light and I take my left hand off Buster and put it over her shoulder and she leans into me, my armpit, my shoulder, my girl.

All gonna die, Maddie says. He lets his lighter go to darkness. He says it again, All gonna die.

We stand there. None of us want to move away from the table, away from each other. Finally, KK and I walk to our side. She walks into my cell. I tell her I'll be back in a second. I go over to Typewriter's and he's sitting on his cot with his lighter casting shadows on the white walls. I know he hates the dark. Kid slept with a night-light his entire life, right up until the moment we burned his house down. I know he's scared. I know he needs me.

Need to talk, I whisper.

Don't.

I take a few steps into his cell and sit on the desk connected to the wall. I'm like, Dude, I'm not sure what you think I—

Just stop, he says. Just fucking stop, Chase, heard your shit for years.

Whatever you *think* you saw—

I don't *think* anything, bro. I saw you. I fucking saw you on the camera.

Here, is this what you want? I pull out a little bit of scante from my sock and throw it at Type and I'm like, Fucking take it. Is that what this is all about? You just mad I didn't give you a taste?

Fuck you.

Because I can remember a thousand times when you stole shit from me. From the Albino. How many bags you short in your life?

Not the same.

Bullshit.

Not the fucking same and you know it, he hisses. He tosses the cellophane back at me. He stands and I reach for my pistol inside of my jumpsuit and I wonder if I have what it'd take to kill my best friend and he's in my face now, the flame gone, just his hot breath and the whites of his eyes.

Fucking loved you, he says.

I know this is him saying he's done with me and I've fucked up things beyond repair and this is him saying he looked up to me like a brother from the very first moment he made *you holding?* eyes at me on the bus and that it's all gone now, everything changed, me, I've fucking changed, that's what he's saying—you're not the person I loved, you're not a person with a habit, you're a junkie, the motherfuckers we never wanted to become, the kind who rob welfare mothers for their EBT cards—and this is too much for me to handle. So I laugh. I laugh into his face. I call him a faggot. I say, I always knew you wanted to fuck me. His inhale has an audible catch. I tell him he's an ungrateful faggot, to have a nice sleep without his night-light.

KK's sitting on my bed when I get back to my cell.

She chars a spoon. I feel like slitting my wrists. I'm about to ask where she got more dope, but she beats me to it, asking if I want to get spun. I tell her yes. I sit. Our shoulders touch. Boiling splice, things are finally good again between us. She asks what that was all about. I tell her Typewriter's being a little bitch. She says, Fuck Type. I smile as she takes my arm and her fingers tickle as she strokes a vein and then it's the pleasant sting of a needle finding a home and then she kisses my ear and pushes the plunger.

Sucks, yo, KK says.

The words hang in the cell. I don't know if she's talking about Typewriter or the darkness or our lives. She takes my hand. We interlock fingers. Mine are short and nubby, hers long and slender.

Where are we going to go? KK asks.

I squeeze her hand, tell her, North.

North?

Canada. Northwest Territories. Alaska. Someplace where there's nobody. Where we don't have to worry about any of this.

Yeah, except some blubber-eating Eskimo.

Take that right now. Better than this.

Think it'll work? she asks.

Has to.

No it doesn't.

I cradle KK's head and kiss her lips. I take off her jumpsuit. Her skin is cold. I think about Typewriter. He'll get over it. He'll understand. He'll know that everything I do is for him. I take off my suit. We press our bodies against each other and our ribs rub together like a wooden instrument. I'm hearing Type's words, his saying he loved me, and I can't shake the feeling it was a good-bye. I'm hard. KK puts me inside her and I start to move my hips and she tells me no.

Huh?

Not tonight.

I think she's joking so I give another thrust but she shakes her head and says, I just want to feel you. She kisses me, then rests her head next to mine, her nose in my nook, her pussy lips tight, and she whispers, I loved you so fucking much. My hand is on the back of her head, her hair, then her neck, and I feel the different texture of the tattoo. I wonder if she meant to use the past tense. I tell her I love her more than anything, but these words feel somehow not enough, never enough.

MONDAY

There's noise from down the hall. KK and I are barely asleep because we're a little spun and scared. In four more hours we'll be out of this bitch into the great unknown. It sounds like something dropped, something metal. I grab the pistol from the floor and sit upright, tensed.

What is it?

You hear that?

You're tripping.

Listen.

We strain our ears.

Lie back down, baby.

263

But I'm thinking about the door to block A having caved, about the garage door being ripped apart, about block B, and the door to the mess hall. About it all caving and our cells filling with throngs of walking dead.

I'm going to look, I say.

Baby.

It's fine.

No, don't be fuckin' stupid.

Just stay here, be back in like two seconds. I lean forward, kiss the hump of her nose. I walk naked into the common room. It's pure darkness. I bang my knee on the corner of a table.

In the hallway, I keep my steps light and hold the pistol aimed at nothing.

Step, step, stop, wait, listen.

The giggles take over the silences. They occupy my rests.

I jump when I hear a door close.

I squint trying to make out shadows, movement, sound.

The block B door is still closed and I realize the sound came from the other end of the hallway, from the door to command central, the booking station, and the door to the garage. As soon as I trace this path in my head, I understand what the fuck is going on. Derrick's bolting. That's why he wanted to wait until morning. He's sneaking away like a little bitch motherfucker. This is as much a death sentence as putting slugs into our brains. I start to run. I throw open the door to central booking and then I'm trying to find my way in the darkness and I'm feeling desks and trying doors and groping the walls and I finally hit a metal push bar.

The stairway is dark and I take the stairs three at a time. I'll kill him.

I run and I'm out of breath and the concrete is cold on my feet. In the garage I see a shadow putting shit in the cruiser trunk. He's nothing but the vaguest of outlines. I'm about to yell, but part of me is like fuck that, this motherfucker's bolting, leaving us for dead, so I flip the Glock around. I charge. I jump into the air and I'm the Air Jordan silhouette, only I'm naked and my stupid dick swings and my basketball is a gun.

There's a scream.

There's the cracking of metal against temple.

He doesn't moan or anything, just slumps over. I peer down. It's not Derrick. It's Maddie. I crouch real close and touch his face and my hand comes away soaked.

The fuck?

Please.

Get up.

Maddie struggles to sit. It takes him at least five seconds and then he leans forward, his head between his legs. I hear the pitter-patter of blood dripping onto concrete. I'm speechless.

The fuck you expect me to do? he says.

I don't know what to say.

I sit. Lean my head against the bumper of the car. The cacophony of laughter is earsplitting. Maddie's blood on the concrete reaches my naked ass. The end of my sack dips in it. I replay every conversation I've had with Maddie over the last few days. The moments when I felt like some sort of connection was being made. My arm around his shoulder. Me thinking that he was just like I was. Me thinking that this kid looked up to me, was on my side. Me selling him out and the beating and him realizing I was just another piece of shit who would do whatever it took to save himself.

Just fucking kill me, he says.

It's a faucet, his wound. Maybe he'll die from this. Losing too much blood or an infection. I'd swung as hard as I could.

You did this, he whispers.

Maddie as me. That had been my whole fucked-up fascination with him. Maddie as a kid who didn't know his ass from his overcoat and a kid who was simply trying to not end up dead and he is me, both then and now, both of us doing what we can to survive. My eyes adjust a little. I see he has the lab broken down and put into the trunk. We'd have died without our ability to cook. He was leaving us to die. And then I'm remembering his creepy-ass voice in the darkened common room—*all going to die*—and it was premeditated, Maddie's idea to run, probably heard us talking about the cruiser earlier, and of course he knew how to hot-wire a car because he was in here for grand theft auto. This was his only play—take on the world alone, leave the family that betrayed him to go through withdrawals and then death.

I remember him backing away from Derrick, tears already starting, unable to comprehend my cruelty.

And I want to apologize. I want to tell him it was a moment of weakness and fear—I was just fucking scared, man. I'm scared of losing everything I have. I'm scared of not getting what I want. I'm scared I will amount to nothing and I'm scared the doors will cave and six shots won't be shit and I'm scared the baby hadn't really turned and that Typewriter will realize he's better off without me and I'm scared of KK because I know one day she'll kill herself and then I'll be alone, my real fear, all fucking alone.

I'm sorry, I say.

Maddie laughs. It's wet from the blood pooling in his mouth.

He doesn't owe me his forgiveness. I know this. Nobody does.

Get the shit over with, he says. He grabs my hand and pushes the pistol to his forehead.

A single shot, any fear of Maddie exposing the real me erased.

Fucking coward, he says.

I'm thinking about Frank, about it being my money and gusto for getting high that led to his death. But this shit with Maddie is different. He wouldn't be down here if I'd copped to stealing the splice. My direct actions forced his hand. I tell him I can't. I can't be that motherfucker. He says, You already are that motherfucker. I lower the gun. I stand. His blood runs down my nuts and onto my leg. I walk to the trunk of the police car and take out a canvas laundry bag full of lab equipment. Maddie clasps his hands together and starts begging between choking sobs. I tell him to come up when he's done crying.

I'm at the stairs. I hold the railing. Something white catches my eye. I tell myself it's nothing, but then it disappears for a split second, and I'm staring at these two white floating orbs and I realize they're eyes. Maddie yells that I'm a piece of shit coward. I drop the canvas bag, training my pistol on the blinking whites, blood dripping from the handle down my wrist to the floor.

It's a Chuck, has to be.

I inch forward. Maddie yells to kill him. The eyes keep blinking. My finger presses against the trigger, but I'm not some green motherfucker like a week ago—I know exactly how hard I have to squeeze to dole out death.

The floating eyes speak: Chase, Chase, I'm fucking sorry, bro.

It's Typewriter.

I can make him out now—a cowering mound of orange jumpsuit, his hands raised like I'm PD.

So fucking sorry, he says, please just don't shoot.

I stand there naked in the drafty garage covered in Maddie's blood. I'm realizing what the fuck is going on—the two of them teaming up, just like I thought they would. I want to blast a hole between Type's eyes.

Typewriter's bent forward like he's praying at my feet.

I was right thinking his comments were a good-bye. Motherfucker knew he was bolting. Knew he was killing us all.

He's nothing but tearful pleas and apologies.

Maddie keeps yelling that I'm a coward.

And the whole thing breaks my fucking heart. I lift Typewriter's face up with my hand and tell him to stand the fuck up and his whimpers become sobs and giggles from outside swirl around the concrete and I tell him the only thing that seems true at the moment: Any one of us is capable of anything.

So fucking sorry, I'm so fucking—

It's over, done with. Nobody needs to know, you feel me?

Please . . .

You came down with me, we saw Maddie, that's it.

Type's nods stop for a second as he's putting together what I'm saying and then he starts nodding faster and this is him understanding and agreeing, selling out a motherfucker who doesn't matter, becoming complicit, becoming my boy.

Maddie laughs.

He sits there in his own blood, his head leaning against the police car. Typewriter won't look in his direction. We take the stairs one at a time.

Fucking kill me, Maddie begs.

Step, step, step.

Kill me, you fucking pussies. Fucking kill me.

1:27 AM

I set all the lab gear down on a fingerprint station inside of booking. Typewriter keeps apologizing. I say, Shut the fuck up, didn't happen, feel me? Maddie was bolting. You came down to help. We made him see the errors of his ways. Simple as that.

Type nods. I hit him on the shoulder. He tries to smile. We're all just trying to smile. I hear giggles and I stare past Type's shoulder and my eyes have adjusted and I make out a shape through the Plexiglas. I inch closer. I stare at Frank. He has no idea what's going on. He won't die and he won't live and the cure didn't work for him years ago—God and power-lessness and service and turning our lives over—and it didn't work for him now.

I think about KK and about atonement and about not dying and the pressure behind my retinas is back and I just want to be out of this jail and someplace safe with the people I love and I wonder if they love me back.

We start running.

I'm sprinting back through the booking station and into the hallway and I see flames huddled together in block C and KK's voice is the first to reach me, her screaming about me being hurt, he's fucking hurt, and I grab her tight, tell her I'm fine.

Derrick has a pistol pointed at Type and me. He says, You're bit.

Maddie's blood, I say.

Maddie's bit? KK says.

No, no, it doesn't matter, it's fine—

Shut the fuck up and slow down, Derrick says. I know he's not messing around. I try to breathe and to tell them what happened, first about hearing something, that Type and I went down and found Maddie, about him being scared, thinking about bolting, but we talked and he apologizes, that he's coming back up.

I'll kill him, Derrick says.

He gets it. He's fine. Trust me. He'll never do something like that again, I say.

Jesus, Randy says.

So fucking dead, Derrick says.

I grab hold of Derrick's arm. It's not aggressive but it's confident and I tell him it's fucking done with, hundred percent, kid fucked up but gets it. I say, We need to leave right fucking now. Hole's big. We don't have time to wait until sunrise.

He stares at me for a solid three seconds before nodding.

We get our belongings.

KK won't leave my side. We're in my cell and she's crying and I tell her Maddie will be fine and we'll be fine and I'm giving her a shotgun, clasping her hands around the stock. I put my forehead to hers. She sniffles. Her bony shoulders shake. She says, Okay, even though I haven't said anything.

We start jogging down the hall and I'm holding on to KK with one hand, the pistol in the other. We reach the booking station. I'm expecting to see Maddie standing there all sheepish and begging for mercy, but he's not.

The fuck is he? Derrick yells.

I'm hearing pleas. I realize that we've accidentally locked Maddie down there in the garage. I run to the door and push it open and he stumbles down and crumples and KK screams or maybe that's Type and the giggles from the garage are deafening.

Randy flicks a lighter.

Derrick bends over Maddie's whimpering body. He puts his pistol to the back of his head and then our ears ring and I scream *no* and KK's body deflates at my side.

The fuck? I yell.

He was bit.

No, that was the blood from when I—

Derrick grabs my neck. He yanks my head so I'm looking at Maddie's back. It's covered in scratches and bite marks. Even just with a lighter to see, I can tell they're already scabbing.

He lets go and I cough and KK cries and I tell myself this isn't my fault, leaving him down there, my sealing of his death sentence by framing him with the stolen scante.

Typewriter's at the door to the garage, pulling it tight. He shoves a desk in front of it. It won't do a fucking thing. My ears still ring. Maddie's blood pools and I realize I'm naked and feel vulnerable and our exit strategy is fucked, the garage swarming with Chucks. We're silent in the dark amidst the smell of gunpowder.

I say, I need to get spun.

2:02 AM

We're passing out the guns. I make sure Type, KK, and myself have ones with real bullets. Randy volunteers to carry the canvas laundry bag full of our lab. We don't say much. Maddie's blood covers the floor. Right before we start off into the corridor toward general population, Derrick breaks out a big hunk of splice. We load our rigs from the same spoon. We get spun.

One hurried shot turns into two.

Typewriter says he wants to go to an island, St. Thomas maybe.

I wonder how the fuck he even knows there's a place called St. Thomas.

Randy says England would be good right about now.

KK pumps Buster.

I'm back to feeling and seeing auras. Each of ours is a dark cloud. I tell myself that no death is my fault.

2:17 AM

We go single file, pressed up against the cinder-block wall on our left. We're in some hallway or maybe it's a corridor. Derrick leads, then me, KK, Randy, and Typewriter brings up the rear. We creep past block A. The dent has become a hole. Hands reach through. We keep going. It's even darker. Shapes stop maybe two feet out from my face. I can't hear anything but demonic laughs. They're taunting us, damning us.

Derrick yells that it's a hundred feet to a set of doors separating juvie from County, then another fifty to the mess hall doors.

One foot in front of the other.

KK holds on to the back of my jumpsuit.

We don't have much time. The door leading to the stairs will give any second, if it hasn't already. The only thing worse than walking straight into a locked room full of criminal Chucks would be getting flanked by them on both sides.

We reach the first set of doors. I press my ear to the cold metal. There's no pounding, no giggling. Derrick fumbles around his key ring and he tries a key and says fuck and then another and I'm telling him to hurry up. Typewriter yells and it's the same scream he made while being bitten trying to climb out of Cheng's window and then Randy shouts, They're coming, they're fucking here!

The smell reaches me first and it's pure death. Then their cries of war.

I yell at Derrick to open the door and I'm watching his

fumbling hands insert a key and then I'm looking into pure fucking darkness and KK's nails dig into my back. I have no idea how close they are but the sound is growing louder and then the door opens, Derrick grabbing me, throwing me in, and KK tumbles on top of me and then Randy and Type and Derrick rushes inside, slamming the door shut. It's not but two seconds later that the metal erupts into a fit of pounding.

We stare at the door, unsure if that really just happened.

Let's go, Derrick says.

We start forward. We're not in a line anymore. We're close, touching, shuffling our feet, terrified with what's all around us. Somebody's crying. Maybe it's me. There's a strange calmness. Time standing still. Us wanting to. Derrick stops us. I squeeze the pistol, aiming it at blackness. He crouches down. I do too, not sure why. Then we all do.

See something?

He doesn't respond. He takes out the Ziploc full of crank. I'm like, Are you fucking kidding me? He doesn't respond, just dumps out a handful of chunks. He crushes one with his gun. He snorts it right off the floor. Mounds of it. I hear Typewriter say, Pass it, and I'm like there's no fucking way we're really doing this right now but I'm crushing dope too, snorting deep into my brain, and we all are because this is probably our last taste and because we want to feel invincible and then maybe we are, invincible that is, because I've just taken two teeners' worth and I'm licking my hand, pressing it to the residue, licking it again.

We stand.

I kiss KK hard on the lips.

One foot in front of the other.

I am a warrior.

I am not a coward.

I am God.

We're at the doors to the mess hall. There's noise on the other side but it's not as bad as block A. Maybe the metal is stronger inside the big-boy lockup? Maybe the Chucks are mostly still contained in cells? Maybe it's not as bad as we thought.

All live ammo up front, Derrick says. He has a single key separated from the ring. He says, I open the door, and you fire. They're right here. We unload and run.

I will lead us to the Promised Land.

Motherfuckers will talk about this for eternity.

KK's eyes are closed and her mouth moves and Typewriter's chewing his face off. I have two shots and that's it and my mind fills with music, with "Bullet in the Head," and it's building, the music, just about at the point when shit gets real and vocals scream and Derrick says, Ready? I nod and make sure I'm slightly in front of KK and I will not let her down and I will not let down the rest of them and I will not let down mankind or my parents and Derrick puts the key in the door and yanks it open.

A Chuck spills into the doorway and I am the first to fire—a shot through his gaping mouth.

Then it's three rapid shots, lightning striking trees.

Three more drop and Derrick holds up his fist like he's some Semper Fi motherfucker. We stop and there's ringing in my ears but no giggles. He motions forward. I hold on to

KK. We're not running like the plan. There isn't a need. The room's empty. That it? Four of them? All that fear for that? I whisper to Derrick if he knows where the fuck he's going and he tells me no.

I'm putting my trust in something greater than myself, just like they told me to do in AA. God. A higher power. I follow the hulking shape of Derrick.

I can sense there's a wall coming up. Derrick feels around for a door. Behind me there's a flick of orange. I spin around but it's Typewriter holding his lighter. This is his absolute worst nightmare—venturing into the dark, battling the monsters his mother insisted weren't real.

Derrick walks up to the wall and finds a door. He tests the handle. It's locked. I'm looking at the gray door—everything in jail either gray or white—and it doesn't have one dent. Not one fucking fist or head smashed from the other side. How the hell did the few Chucks get in? There's got to be some other entrance, maybe through the kitchen and I say this to Derrick and he says, Who the fuck cares? I nod, but something seems wrong. He's got the master key out ready to open the door when I tell him to stop.

What?

Maybe it's a trap.

What?

Yeah, like being quiet and wanting us to go through there.

They can't think.

He puts the key in the door. He turns it.

I'm expecting an ambush and I'm expecting shit to get

heavy but there's nothing, not a single laugh, not the rank stench of decay.

KK squeezes my hand. She says, Keep your shit together.

I'm trying to put it all together. The mess hall. The walking dead in there. The utter silence. My mind projects a map of County and it's in blueprint form and I'm picturing us in a hallway and maybe the mess hall is between cell blocks and this would make the most sense, not having inmates walk past other blocks to eat, so the kitchen is in the middle. I reach into my pocket and take out my lighter and flick it and it doesn't catch so I do it again and again. Finally there's light.

The fuck you doing? Derrick asks.

Mate, maybe the light isn't the best idea, Randy says.

I'm thinking that all I want is to be able to see. That's it. Life would be perfect if I could fucking see.

Baby, KK says.

I take my wallet out from the breast pocket of my jumpsuit and I take out all the paper—Subway punch cards, numbers to junkies wanting to buy scante—and I light them on fire. Derrick says, The hell you doing? I watch the paper catch. I hold flames in my hand and I am Hephaestus, god of fucking fire, and then I tell KK to give me anything she has—her jumpsuit she has tied around her waist—and Typewriter is like, Bro, let's move.

Fire.

Will you calm him the fuck down? Derrick says.

The fire alarm. It won't be on the main power grid. A generator. Get lights so we can actually see.

He's got a point, Randy says.

The burning paper starts to scorch my hand. I drop it.

Give him the suit, Derrick says.

KK unwraps the juvie uniform and I take its sleeve, holding it to the small pile of flames. I'm praying for it to catch. I just want light. Finally the sleeve catches. The flames leak up the stitches. More, I say. KK hands me what can only be described as a training bra. Randy gives me his socks. We need more. Derrick cusses and takes off his windbreaker and that shit catches right away. It's getting smoky and the flame is maybe a foot high. I'm waving the smoke upward toward the ceiling. I think I see something farther down the hall. I shout for more. Typewriter tosses me his T-shirt. I light it and ball it up and throw it down the hallway we've just stepped into.

The ball of fire lands on the floor and it's eyes, pairs and pairs of them, just like that fucking Rockwell nursery. They bob to uneven footsteps.

Oh, my, fucking, God, go, go, go, Randy yells.

We start running down the hallway in the opposite direction, but I know this is just as bad because there's another cell block down this way, meaning more Chucks and us being just as fucked. We need to get to the kitchen, the middle point, some place away from general population. An ear-piercing wail fills the concrete hallway and white strobe lights erupt in epileptic bursts. Sprinklers cover us in pre-come. Ahead, there's a wall of shuffling motherfuckers.

Randy's leading the way. He trips while trying to change directions. Every second there's a flash of light and we see eyes and open mouths and missing skin, the discotheque version of

Randy being torn apart. His cries are drowned by laughter. We turn once again, just needing to get back to the mess hall. I lead the way and KK's hand is my life preserver and I know it will be close, us getting to the mess hall door before the Chucks do, maybe three feet for us, five for them, but I get there first, throwing my shoulder against the door. It's still unlocked and somebody fires a shot and we tumble in and Typewriter slams the door.

He pushes against it and it's trembling from the Chucks bashing into it. He yells for Derrick to lock the fucking door. I slam my shoulder into it and so does KK. Derrick turns the key in the hole and yells that it's locked but I'm too scared to quit bracing.

Typewriter pulls at my arm, tells me, Let's go, it'll hold.

I hear KK's muffled cries. I could pick them out of any lineup, the way each one builds on the other, none of them allowed to escape the cavern of her mouth.

Derrick says, Door's secure. He has his massive hand around my bicep.

We need to go, KK says.

I ease up on the door and KK puts her arm around my waist. I press my forehead against hers. Our noses touch. She says, You need to keep your motherfucking mind.

3:11 AM

We can see a hell of a lot better with the emergency lighting. We cross the mess hall. Derrick reaches back and places something in my hand. It's a nub of dope. I eat it. The taste is crushed pills and ammonia. My teeth feel like they're coated in wool sweaters.

We are four.

Derrick and I push through the swinging doors into the kitchen. There's got to be another door leading out from here. My gun's eye level. The alarm shrieks. My breath is all sorts of heavy. My right arm is completely extended, my left bent, both holding the pistol.

I am Lara Croft. I am Spetsnaz. I am Chase Daniels.

The kitchen's a lot bigger than the one in juvie. We creep past metal prep stations and walk-in refrigerators and stove after stove and everything's the mix of pitch blackness and exploded stars. I have one shot left.

One foot in front of the other.

I'm hearing giggles matching the techno shrill of the alarm and Derrick says, Twelve o'clock. I wait, ready to dole out death with the flick of my finger. Shadows become forms, forms become shapes, shapes become bodies, bodies become tattered orange jumpsuits and exposed bones and open mouths.

I shoot.

Derrick shoots.

Type shoots.

I'm still aiming the gun when I realize I'm out of fucking ammo. I jam the pistol into my waistband. I search for a weapon, anything. I think about going back and getting Randy's rubber slug shotgun, but those bullets didn't do shit anyway. Typewriter must understand what I'm doing because he's rifling through drawers, and then KK says, Take the shot-gun. I won't do this to her, leave her defenseless.

Here, Derrick says. He reaches down to his leg, slides something out. He hands me a six-inch blade.

I tell him thanks and wonder why the fuck he hadn't given it to one of us before. Would Randy have been able to fend them off with this knife? I realize it's just another example of motherfuckers looking out for their own survival.

One of the bodies we dropped giggles from the floor. I'm about to step over his head when he makes a feeble attempt at clawing my leg. I bend over. He's white, maybe midtwenties. Gold teeth flash in the strobe light. I plunge the blade into his throat. I'm thinking of Mesh Cap. I pull out the knife and it's a small geyser of thick blood. I step over his body.

We make our way to the back of the kitchen to a single door, half caved, the two top hinges ripped from the wall. We have no idea where it'll lead but we walk through. Then we're in a tight hallway, not the double-wides from earlier. It only goes one way. We start walking, then we're jogging, and it's primal instinct, antelope fleeing a watering hole, one starts running, and they all run. The narrow concrete starts shaking with laughter and I'm fucking terrified and they're in my skull and behind my eyes playing bass on my retinas and I'm not sure what's real and what's an echo. We go maybe a hundred feet and come to a door along the wall. The hallway keeps going. Derrick's like, What do we do?

Open it, KK says.

He tries the handle and it's locked. I peer down the hall. The Chucks are grotesque in their costumes of death, their cocks flapping, and they're closing in fast. Derrick gets the door open and we go through. It's damp like the most humid summer night. The whole room is lit though, everything a ghastly glowing red. It's got to be some sort of mechanical room because the floor is grated metal and the ceiling is low, and it's humming with sound, and the walls are covered in thick piping on both sides.

A crawl space, Typewriter says.

Waterline or something, KK says.

We're moving again, ducking our heads to not hit the ceiling. This will lead us to some garage or power station or maybe to a sewer and it'll be outside of County and it'll maybe be off Kellogg and it will lead us to the river. Maybe the Chucks can't swim, and that's all it'll take and we'll be Huck fucking Finn with a raft and take the Mississippi down to New Orleans and then to the ocean. We'll be safe and happy and Mardi Gras will come and we'll smoke shit and KK will get pregnant and we'll raise a little boy, Portland, and he'll have KK's fair skin but my nose. We'll probably find another group of survivors living on an oil rig. We'll have a giant lab set up so running out will never be a problem. There'll be some motherly woman with kind eyes for Typewriter. We'll pass the time reading books we've stolen from the library and we'll celebrate Christmas with fresh fish and maybe a deer we killed back on land. One by one, we'll repopulate our world. Our reputation will be that of God, the creator of modern mankind.

We reach another door at the end of the waterline.

Fuck, KK says.

Maybe she was thinking the same thing.

I put my ear to the door and it sounds clear. Derrick nods at me and I nod back. We open it and it's dark again, then back to the flashing of white, and it's like we didn't even move, it looks like the same exact hallway we just came from. I try to calculate how far we just traveled. It had to have been at least a few hundred yards.

Which way? asks Derrick.

I go back to my imaginary blueprint. The same hallway. Different section. I see the architects thinking simplicity was best, most institutional, and I know left will lead us to a kitchen and then to a mess hall and then to a wide hallway with cell blocks on either end and I say, Go right.

One foot in front of the other.

I'm soaking wet from the overhead sprinklers. KK's bangs are matted to her forehead. I tell her I love her.

There's a T in the hallway. Derrick motions to the left and I nod because that's the way out. I'm sure of it. The other way just puts us farther into the bowels of lockup. I barely notice the alarm anymore.

Got to be gettin' close, Typewriter says.

For reals.

The fuck out of here, Derrick says.

Another door, our only option. Derrick opens it. Chlorine is the first thing I smell and the ceiling is much higher and I see a thin pool, a shimmering of blackness.

The fuck?

Pool, Type says.

No shit, but in County?

Privileges, yo, KK says. Good behavior and you get your recess in the pool.

We walk around the edge of the water. I'm picturing inmates playing Marco Polo. Criminals frolicking. I'm fucking thirsty. We start along the long side of the pool. It's eerily calm. Then the water breaks. We all scream as a dark figure rises from the water. It's a woman with long hair covering her face and water streaming from her in sheets. Typewriter's standing too near the edge, and he's staring at me for some reason with his stupid fucking confused lips, and nothing I do will ever make a difference and this Chuck reaches out with both hands and I'm screaming. My best friend gets his feet swept out from underneath him. He falls and slams his head against the concrete and then is gone, disappears, Typewriter nothing, dragged into the blackness of chlorinated water.

Derrick fires three rounds into the pool.

Still nothing.

I'm about to jump into the water but KK shrieks *no* and grabs me with both hands. I tell myself it's for her, me not going in after Type, that I'm doing the responsible thing, that he's already gone, that I'm doing it all out of love. I tell myself these things while my best friend's disemboweled.

I'm crying. On my knees fucking crying.

Stop, stop, KK says.

I think about the first time I ever met Typewriter. We were riding the 21 bus. His eyes met mine and I could tell he wanted to get spun. He came back to my seat and stuck out his hand and said, John, but my friends call me Typewriter. I laughed at this, and so did he. I liked this kid, and we ended

up getting off the bus together, going to his place in the suburbs, smoking shit and playing Grand Theft Auto all night. I
liked the way he laughed, the way he was so fucking innocent,
even as I led him into hell.

I can make out an even darker patch in the dark water
where he went under.

Derrick pulls me to my feet.

He holds the back of my head and meets my eyes and says,
Your girl needs you. *I* need you. You feel me?

I don't say anything.

KK and Derrick drag me away from the pool and my
knife feels pathetic and so does my life and I'm seeing Type's
face the moment before he was dragged under and I want to
apologize for feeding his addiction and about Maddie and I
hope he's happier. That he finds that shit he believed in. That
his mother is waiting, his father too. That they spread out a
blanket and he feeds the ducks and that his mom takes the
Tupperware out of a wicker basket and inside it's filled with
watermelon.

We reach the entrance to some sort of locker room. I
hear a single giggle and it's hers, I know, the cunt from the
pool. The locker room smells musty. We walk next to a set
of lockers. We are three. Everything's a possible threat, and
now we're running again, into a hallway and we've got to be
getting close because we reach a set of double doors. Derrick
finally gets them open. We glance behind us and they're coming, an advancing wall of female walking dead, naked and
vile, tits and chuckles.

We pass through a door, then a metal detector.

We're so fucking close.

The next door is slightly ajar but jammed and Derrick can't get it open. I yell to hurry the fuck up. I grab the edge and yank in desperate pries. Maybe this is the final door and then it's the exit and I'm pulling and pulling and Derrick keeps screaming, Fuck.

He lets go and turns around and they're right there at the door we just came through, the one right before the metal detector. Their angry fists crash through the double-pane glass.

Derrick looks around, then he runs over to an elevator. He's like Superman pulling the doors of the shaft apart, his elbows turned out, the muscles of Apollo.

Get in, he yells.

Derrick's whole body quivers under the strain and the door behind us is already breaking down. I peek into the elevator shaft. Red emergency lights flash. It's at least a two-story drop to the top of the elevator. He yells to grab the cable but I can't reach. Then I hear a screeching of metal, the security door breaks, and I crawl under Derrick's arms. I look back to KK and she yells to jump and I do.

I'm weightless. I'm a feather. I'm my first hit of methamphetamines.

I grab the cable and wrap my legs around it and start to slip, but I press my stomach against the cable and that slows me down. As I slide, slivers of metal burrow into my hands. I hit the bottom on my back with a loud thud. I see KK jump, grab the cable, and slide down screaming and I try to break her fall but she kicks me in the face. She's sprawled on top of me and I ask, Are you okay, are you okay?

Fine.

Sure?

Fine.

There's blood over both of us.

Then I look back up. Derrick inches his way between the doors. I see a foot. I see a leg.

Jump, I yell.

I see sets of hands and I know the Chucks have broken through and then he throws the canvas bag down and then it's his body tumbling. He makes for the cable and holds it for a split second, but his momentum is too much, his legs keep swinging, he loses his grip and falls.

He crashes onto the top of the elevator and the whole thing shakes and I'm at his side—Derrick? Derrick?—and his eyes open. They're leaking water and maybe blood. He struggles to sit. I put my hand under his head. He looks at his legs and I'm telling him he's good, that we're almost free, that shit will work out. His eyes go wide and then he relaxes and closes them. I look at his leg.

His jeans are torn. Three inches of thick bone poke through.

It's fine, it's fine, I lie.

He shakes his head.

We'll help get you out of here. One on each side. Can you sit up?

I help him get upright. The veins underneath the tattooed hands ripple.

Okay, good, good, now put your arm around me, one around KK.

I drape his arm around me and then I say, Good, now we're going to stand. Put all your weight on me.

It's like doing squats. He's heavy as fuck and I stand and he groans. KK's doing her best and we get him on his feet. Then he tries to put some weight on his left leg, and there's a snap, a pop, loud like the cracking of a frozen lake. He screams and drops.

The bone juts out another few inches. Derrick hyperventilates.

We're fucked. I'll need to put him on my back. I tell him this. His bald head is covered in sweat, his face is smeared with blood and snot and he says, Leave.

Not leaving you here.

I can't do it.

Shut the fuck up.

He's not listening anymore and he takes out a huge shard of meth and grinds it into his palm and snorts it.

KK rubs his back.

I'm like, Yeah, get yourself good and spun. It'll help. Need you, man, you can do this.

He snorts more dope.

I stare at his tattoo and I'm trying to get his mind off his fucked leg so I ask about it.

He says, Son of a preacher man.

This makes sense. A marring of flesh to remember where you came from. KK's tattoo of her sobriety date and her burned stomach. All of us trying to document our failures. But it's hope too. Hope that some part of us lives on. That kernel of humanity. The shit I'm going to save.

In his low voice, Derrick starts singing "Son of a Preacher Man."

I say, Okay, now you're ready. Let's do this.

He nods.

I search the top of the elevator for the opening. I find a panel. It flips open.

This shit's gonna hurt, I say. Have to drop you through. But that's it, then I'm carrying you. Good?

Derrick nods. He stares into space. He hums Aretha. Maybe he's pumping himself up. I let him have this moment.

He sets the bag of dope at my feet. There's a flash of metal as he puts the pistol to his head and KK shouts and it's over that fast, one deafening pop.

KK's on her knees, silent.

She's staring at Derrick's head, the puddle under it that grows with astonishing speed. I crouch behind her. I don't say anything, just wrap my arms around her—so thin, so delicate, so fragile, KK able to endure no matter what, KK the strongest woman I've ever known. We don't cry. I hold her as tight as I can. My heart beats through her back. My face is buried in her neck. A close-up of her tattoo—the day she left me—is all I can see.

3:39 AM

After a few minutes, KK leans forward and picks up the bag of dope. She hands it to me. She stands. She takes the pistol from Derrick's hand and gives me that too. She hands me the knife.

I take all of these things. KK's holding on to the short-barrel shotgun and she motions to the opening in the elevator's roof.

Her calmness disarms me. I'm not sure how to take it. I've seen this before in the bathroom of our apartment when she burned herself, cigarette after cigarette.

She kneels down and lowers her legs into the elevator and I take her hand, bracing myself, and lower her the rest of the way. I follow. I try my fingers in the elevator doors but can't get good leverage. I jam the knife between the doors. This gives me a few inches. I'm able to wedge my foot in, then a knee, then my body, and I'm sideways, and I get the sole of my shoe against one side, my back the other, and I open the doors. KK crawls through. Then I throw all my weight to my right and kind of roll out of the doors as they slam shut.

We're in a basement. The emergency lights are red, solid. The alarm is faint. The walls are unpainted cement and I touch KK's arm and she says, I'm good.

We walk. One foot in front of the other. Everything's quiet.

We walk hand in hand. We're bloodied and soaking wet, holding guns and a bag of dope and our fingers are inter-locked. Our footsteps echo. I'm having déjà vu. I've been here before. This very moment.

I remember being in the psych ward. They were letting me out but KK had to stay another week for observation and this was some shit because we'd been talking about doing this to-gether, sobriety. Meetings and living better lives. Never going back. I'd wanted to stay inside those locked walls because there was a girl who understood me and who *was* me, who saw my fuckups as humanity, who pressed my finger to her wound. My parents were coming to pick me up. KK and I skipped lunch. We walked down the white linoleum hallway. It was so fucking bright. We weren't allowed any physical contact, the staff Nazis about that shit, but she reached out and took my hand and our fingers were one and we were one and we walked toward the wall of windows. It was sunny. I wanted to spend my life with this woman. I wanted to be sober.

I was, I say now.

Was what?

Serious about it all. Wanted it more than anything.

KK squeezes my hand harder.

We walk.

She doesn't have to say anything and that's how we've always been and that's how we'll always be. I see a red door ahead. This is it, what we've been searching for.

Block letters are printed on its surface—EXIT.

I'm crying.

I'm crying because we'll be okay. I know we will. Just like standing at the window, us saying good-bye and unsure of our futures, us silent and touching, I now know we'll be okay.

I'm about to push open the door when KK stops me. Her head shakes. She won't meet my eyes.

Baby?

Her blond hair moving.

What? We're here. We're good, come on.

I pull at her arm. She lets go of my hand. She must be

scared about what's outside and maybe about what we'll do once our meth runs out. I say, It's fine, we'll figure it out, we always do.

I can't.

Can't what?

Do it anymore.

I laugh like she's being crazy and I tell her I'm scared too.

I'm not scared.

Then what the fuck?

That. I can't do *that* anymore. She points to the door.

KK . . .

I'm serious, Chase.

I stare at her nose because I know looking into her eyes will be too much.

She says, It will be the same. You realize that. The same fucking thing. The same shit.

No, we beat this shit. We'll go north and we'll find other—

That's not what I'm talking about.

The fuck is your—

Our.

Our?

Our fucking problem.

KK takes the scante out of my hand. It's like a mallet in her fist. She says, This. I can't fucking do *this*. Live this way. Live out there. I can't fucking do it anymore.

I try to take her in my arms and she says, It's not worth it. I tell her we'll be together. She's shaking her head and backing up and I tell her we'll control it, only one shot every other day, just so we don't turn. She keeps walking back and I'm getting angry because we're so fucking close. I say, We'll die in here, just like everyone else.

Already dead, Chase. Both of us.

Jesus Christ, we have to at least try.

We did.

Yeah, and we're right here. The fucking exit. We're good. Just come on—

I know you stole the shit, blamed it on Maddie, she says.

What? No—

Still fucking lying to me.

No, yeah, fuck. It's just like . . . We're so fucking close and I love you and, Jesus Christ, please.

I stop talking. I can't tell if she's laughing or crying.

Stole the shit too, KK says.

What?

Followed you into the kitchen, stole some after you left. Then just stood there and watched Maddie get killed.

He didn't get killed, he was the one—

We both did. We fucking killed the kid.

That's just the shit talking, like you're in one of your states—

I'm clear as day, Chase.

I can't fucking believe this, I say.

She stares at me.

I love you so much, I say. So fucking much. I'll do anything for you, you know that, you're all I care about. We'll get through this. We can make this *work*. We'll fucking change and this shit wasn't our fault, baby, just please, fuck, let's go.

KK bites her bottom lip. I think about just picking her up

and dragging her outside. I know this look from a year ago when I was sitting on the couch and she was begging me to stop and I was high and wanting to get higher and I couldn't fucking quit and she was giving me the same ultimatum as now.

KK says, You made this choice once already.

Jesus Christ, it's fucking different and you know it.

It's not.

This is the only way we can *survive*. Fucking *survive*, KK. It's not about getting high and it's not—

Not surviving.

KK.

Drugs or me?

Fucking ridiculous.

I start toward the door.

To die out there on the streets or die right here?

Enough. Let's go.

A simple question, Chase.

I close my eyes. I think about what awaits us outside of the door—the walking dead, the search for shelter and more dope, endless running, the hope that somehow shit gets better—and I know that life, I do, and it's not great, never was even before, but I can't stop. I can't give up. I can't sit here waiting to die.

I don't say anything.

She's crying now. She nods. She walks toward me. She says, That's what I thought. She rises to her tiptoes and kisses my lips. It's the softest of touches and it's everything that's been good in my life and it's the promise of new beginnings. Then she backs away and motions to the door. Maybe she just needed me to admit it. She's still holding her shotgun and we

ACKNOWLEDGMENTS

This book couldn't have been done without my editor at Crown, Julian Pavia, whose edits, criticism, and advice were always spot-on. Nor would it have gotten off the ground without my agent, James McGuinnes, a skilled editor, advocate, and handler of my crazy. I'm grateful as hell to both of you. I'd like to thank my mentor, Steven Schwartz, for urging me to write about my obsessions. And thanks to the rest of the MFA faculty at Colorado State University, especially Leslee Becker, John Caldorazo, and Stephanie G'Schwind. Thank you Merrill Shane Jones for being psyched on everything to do with fiction. And Matthew Batt for buying me lunch and saying I owed it to myself to give writing a serious shot. And to my brother who was the sole reader of my horrific first stab at a novel. And my mother and father who've been nothing but love and support. And lastly to my wife—thank you, you're fucking perfect, I love you.

will conquer the fucking world because that's what we tell ourselves and I press the exit push bar and, holding hands, we step into our futures. We're better versions of ourselves and I'm already looking around the street for motherfuckers who want to kill us when she squeezes my hand as hard as she can. This is her way of telling me she loves me and that we'll be okay and in that moment I love her more than anything. Then she lets go of my hand and we're on the seventh floor of the psych ward and we're exercising trust for the first time, trust we'll make it, that love is enough, and I turn to tell KK that we were right then about everything, but she's not at my side. She has caught the door and is slipping behind it and I glimpse the crucifixes of her collarbones and then her slender neck and her sharp chin and then her human nose and she says, I'm so fucking sorry.

The door closes. There's no handle on the outside. I pound on it. I'm smashing my fists and kicking my feet against it and I'm bellowing. I picture her on the other side crumpled into nothing and I see her at the end of the couch begging for me to quit and I'm on the ground now, yelling, pleading, and I can't breathe and I know they'll hear me and come walking and I don't want to die alone. I just keep saying, Please don't leave me, please don't leave me, and my hands work without me realizing it and I have the Ziploc open and I'm crushing shards and snorting and I don't know if I'm saying it anymore—please don't leave me—or if it's just a thought and then things are quieter, my mind loosens, methamphetamines fulfilling their promise, things okay then.

8 - 13

ML

Carmen, 1975

With Mady Mesplé and Michel Plasson, 1976

Cavalleria Rusticana, 1976

La Grande-Duchesse de Gérolstein, 1979

"The Cat Duet" with Leontyne Price, 1982

The Medium, 1985

The Queen of Spades, 1987

Dialogues des Carmélites, 1988

FOLLOWING PAGE *240*

In Marseille, 1930

First Communion Day, 1939

My mother, 1920

My father, 1940

With Mannolini, 1951

Edmond Carrière, 1953

With Lou Bruder, 1964

With Victor-José, 1969

With Philippe Rivier, 1979

With Isabelle Masset, 1980

With Gérard de Botton, 1984

With Henry Lewis, 1975

With Herbert Breslin, 1976

ILLUSTRATIONS

(x)

With Denise Dupleix and Philippe Bertrand, 1994

Mary Hanlon and Jean Capone, 1985

With Terry McEwen and Martina Arroyo, late 1970s

Summer 1977

With Gladys Bourdain, 1979

Pierre-Jean and Dany Bouché, 1989

With the Régine Crespin rose, 1990

Teaching in San Francisco, 1990s

With Jacques Chirac, 1990

With Maguy Molinari, 1943

With Maguy Molinari Lenain, 1990

I SAW Régine Crespin on a stage for the first time in 1965, when she gave a recital at Hunter College in New York City. I already knew her lush voice from recordings, and was happy to find that she measured up in person, offering elegance, warmth, sexiness, a profound commitment to expressing *meanings,* not just words, and diction that allowed the neophyte in French I was at the time to drop the printed lyrics and just listen.

In other words, the complete recitalist.

Although her opera interpretations are among my red-letter theatrical memories—the Marschallin in *Der Rosenkavalier,* Charlotte in *Werther,* Madame de Croissy in *Dialogues des Carmélites,* among others—a recital is the greatest test of an artist, and she is one of only two or three among the dozens I've heard in four decades who earned my personal rating of A-plus.

This book is remarkable in its revelation of the human being behind the artist, and in the fact that it was written with no help except from the author's ever-seeking, ever-assimilating intelligence. These are no ". . . and then I sang . . ." jottings from an engagement calendar. Rather, they are the personal recollections of a fascinating, multifaceted woman.

Régine Crespin and I have been friends since 1977. In those years she has become the sister I always longed for, and I can say sincerely that my translation was a labor of love. I hope I've done justice to her words.

G.S. BOURDAIN

Note: Part I of this book was published in France by Fayard in 1982, under the title *La Vie et l'Amour d'une Femme* (*A Woman's Life and Love*). It was revised for the expanded French edition published by Actes Sud in September 1997. I have taken the occasional slight liberty, with the author's permission, in translating the work into English. Unless otherwise noted, all translations of material quoted by the author are my own.

G.S.B.

Part One

Mannolini

*I love those who don't really know why they love;
they are the ones who love truly.* ANDRÉ GIDE

MANNOLINI!

It could be the name of a general under Garibaldi, a gondolier in vividly beribboned hat, an old Italian aristocrat—Il Conte Mannolini has a nice ring, doesn't it?—or a plump, merrily singing castrato of the Sistine Chapel.

Mannolini was my grandmother. And she sang—off-key as a soldering iron but at the top of her voice—all the time. She's the one who made me love singing.

I remember summer evenings when we settled down like the chickens at sunset in our high, wide bed. I felt so good curled up against her, but she would push me away, complaining, "It's too hot!" with the tender brusqueness that was her way. Among the people of the Midi, tenderness is something shown on special occasions: marriages, communions, burials, and such. People cry from joy or sorrow and shout a lot when friends arrive. But give a little kiss on the neck or take someone's hand?

Out of the question; too embarrassing. In any case, Mannolini was like that.

There we would be, at hardly eight-thirty, aboard the "big barque" that rocked with games, laughter, and songs, in the bedroom of the little house she rented for vacations at La Bourdonnière, a suburb of Marseille. The windows would be open on a distant symphony of color—red tile roofs, ochre walls, yellowed plane trees, green pines, dense pink mulberries, white and purple lilacs, delicate eucalyptus—under a cloudless sky of mauve.

My friends would be seated outdoors with their parents and pets, and things would begin with a timid "Mannolini, are you asleep?"

"Ehhh, no."

"And Régine?"

"Not yet."

"So, what if we sang for a while?"

And she would start it off. "O! Sole mio!" or "Funiculì! Funiculà!" or maybe:

> *Se vuoi venir con me alla marina*
> *Ti farò veder un pesce senza spina.*
> *O Marianna, va in capanna*
> *Quando il sole tramontera.*
> *Oilì! Oilà!*
> *Quando il sole tramontera.*
> *E bing, e bong, e bing, e bong.*

("If you come fishing with me, I'll show you a fish without bones. O Marianna, come to my hut when the sun goes down. . . .")

ON STAGE, OFF STAGE

The risqué lyrics sailed completely over my head.

Mannolini had a sort of rough, thundering bass voice. I took the high part, of course, and at the end, supported by the chorus below, I would push out one good, strong high note, which won my first applause. And my first flowers: on holiday evenings—July 14 or August 15—when the concert ended after several encores and bows and before Mannolini closed the window over the protestations, I would lower a cord and my first fans would attach a bouquet of flowers they had prepared. Mannolini took this for granted; a water-filled vase would already be in place. She was a bigger ham than I was, at least at the time.

Mannolini's pretty first name, Cesira (pronounced "chay-ZEE-ra"), became Césarine ("say-zah-REEN") in French, and I inherited it as my middle name. At the beginning, I called her Mémé—Grandma—but when she told me about her childhood in a little Italian village near Lucca, I was seduced by the lilting sound of her maiden name, and she became Mannolini, for me and everyone else.

She was a marvelous cook. Every so often a family friend would send a terse telegram: "Mannolini. Arriving Sunday. Ravioli for twelve. Love."

On Friday the whirlwind would begin. First, the shopping, all the way to the stores in the next village, and the return with the packages. As compensation for the heat, I had the right to a "romaine": a lot of cold water, a little sugar, and a drop of rum. Next, the preparation of a sort of daube for the filling, which perfumed the whole cabin. When it was almost cooked, I was allowed to dunk a piece of bread in the gravy; after the third or fourth piece, Mannolini would roll her eyes and yell, "Eh! The little one's going to eat up all my sauce!" and she would run me

Mannolini

out of the kitchen. But I always managed to sneak one more dunk.

Afterward she would prepare the dough. I would pester her: "Why do you do that, Mannolini? Why do you add water? Why? Why?" She would raise her arms toward the ceiling. "This child keeps asking questions!" I've never made ravioli in my life, but I'm sure I could remember exactly how to do it.

Only one part of the work was entrusted to me, the morning of the dinner. When the dough was ready—well kneaded, well rested for three or four hours under a dishtowel in a cool place, rolled out thin and transparent on the indispensable marble table, floured once more—Mannolini would arm me with the pastry wheel and set me to work cutting squares. Woe to me if they weren't geometrically correct! Her voice would fill the cabin:

"This little one can't even 'carculate' properly. Té, get out of here. *I'll* do it." And she would flick me out of the way.

I've never dared cook all the good dishes that Mannolini and my mother turned out so successfully: *soupe au pistou*, daube provençale, rice dumplings, polenta, sugared elephant ears, *pain perdu* (French toast), the fabulous vegetable soups so thick the spoon actually stood up in them, fritters with several jams, stuffed vegetables—tomato, squash, eggplant, onion—with their hats askew, fresh pasta with basil and no fewer than three kinds of cheese. My mouth still waters!

I must have been five or six years old when we started going to La Bourdonnière for the summer. From Nîmes, where my parents had settled, Mannolini and I would take the train to Marseille. We were always at the station an hour ahead of time because, "You never know; what if everybody gets there and the train leaves a little early?" We would be weighed down by suit-cases, packages, and the famous "just-in-case" wrapped in a napkin with a thermos of cold beverage. When I was little, this picnic was sheer joy; later it embarrassed me terribly, but she insisted. On trains, one had to be prepared.

At Marseille we would descend the enormous flight of stairs at St. Charles Station and walk, laden like pack mules, to the trolley stop. A taxi was unthinkable: we both had legs, after all. The habit of " 'conomizing," as she put it, was too deeply rooted.

The trolley trip lasted a good hour, on very hard wooden seats whose backs were ornamented with dark blue plaques that praised the qualities of Rivoire et Carret pasta. From them I learned to read lower-case letters, with Mannolini's help, as we crossed through charming little villages with musical names.

When we arrived, the entire Italian colony would be waiting, her childhood friends who had come to France to do the only thing they knew: work the earth, the grapevines. To them we were princesses, Mannolini because she had a few dollars and a trade, hatmaking; I because my father, a Frenchman, had a shoe store, and so far from there—sixty miles.

As soon as we arrived, Mannolini would revert to her first language, and after each sentence I would ask, "What did you say?" I would climb onto her lap and glue my cheek to hers; it didn't make me understand any better, but I think it was the reason that years later I spoke Italian without ever having stud-ied it.

Since it annoyed her to translate, she would eventually send me off to play with the other children. Games with the girls, races with the boys, in the pine forest full of chirring cicadas

Mannolini

(7)

and the odors of flowing resin and overheated wood. How many grapes I helped pick, back aching, drunk with sun and laughter.

They would tease me: "Hey princess, still lagging behind?" The nickname was due mostly to the fact that I wore shoes; what fool said that shoemakers are always badly shod? The others wore them only on Sundays to go to Mass, and put them on just at the church door.

Each year the three months passed like a dream, filled with games, parties, sun, warmth, songs, and stories Mannolini told that were so fascinating I would whine as soon as she finished, "Oh, tell it again!"

There were my parents' visits, of course, which filled me with pride because the two of them were so attractive. My father very tall, well built, with green eyes and eyebrows—it's true, the hairs were green; my mother short, stout, a beautiful brunette with wavy hair, superb black eyes, full of life and amusing stories. The men would watch her with gustatory looks, remarking, "La Margo, che bella robusta, che cicciona" (What a beautiful hunk of woman). Luckily, my father didn't understand Italian.

When they drove off in their black Citroën (I would tell everyone haughtily, "It's an eleven-horsepower"), our everyday life would resume. I was happy to stay behind with Mannolini. Surely it's obvious that she was the love of my life.

It may seem an exaggeration to say that my grandmother was extraordinary, but it's true. All my parents' friends thought so, and when I tell my friends about her they all react the same way: "What a wonderful woman!"

She was born into a family of very poor Italian peasants and worked hard from the age of twelve in the house, the fields, the vineyard. Her elder sister, Emilia, was already in France, and Mannolini had only one idea: to save money—"'conomize"—for her passage on the boat to Marseille. Which she took in 1892 at eighteen, without permission from her father, without papers, without knowing how to read or write.

Her sister had found her a place with a Marseille dressmaker, Italian also, who told her: "Don't do as I did. If you want to live here, learn French, learn to read and write. I'll house you, feed you, teach you hatmaking, and I'll pay for your lessons."

Even at eighty, as she read the newspaper or a detective novel (she loved crime stories), my grandmother would bless the memory of Signora Adelina, who had advised her so well.

Of course she never lost her half-Italian, half-Marseillais accent, so pronounced that, like Cyrano with his nose, she was the first to mock it.

On the eve of this century, she married an Italian from Piedmont named Meirone, who had a small moving company and who gave her two children: Margherita, my mother, and Henri. Mannolini wanted them all to become French citizens, but her husband stubbornly fought the idea, saying it wouldn't bring him "fortuna." He was right, for shortly after becoming French he died, leaving my grandmother a widow at forty.

She worked hard to raise her children, with gifted hands that succeeded at anything: hats, dresses, knitwear (I still remember a lavender-blue, nubby wool suit she made for me), sculpture, painting, marvelous gardens wherever she lived. Large, long, beautiful hands—in old age misshapen from work—cool on my forehead when I was ill ("It's nothing, little one, it's nothing"). Mine are their exact copy, but unfortunately without their skill: the only things I can knit are long scarves, which I've made for

Mannolini

(9)

all my friends. She summed it up well: "This little one will never accomplish anything with her two hands."

When I began to give myself manicures, I would do her hands too, which made her giggle. Later she would even ask for "nail polish, please, but colorless." Her hair was crazy, all frizzy and sparkling white, and I spent hours cutting and arranging it.

She was a person of goodness, understanding, broad-mindedness, fantastic modernity. Intelligent, shrewd, wily, generous, lively, intense, she took an interest in everything and everybody. I like to think that if I have any of these qualities, they come from her.

Of course I was her great love too—her passion, her pride. I had all the attributes: I was intelligent (she said), I worked well at school (she believed), I played the piano (it was her idea), and when I started to sing "for real," it was a wonderful bonus. She claimed that this gift came from my Italian side, but I— wanting to be one-hundred-percent French, God knows why— insisted it came from my father. A thousand pardons, Mannolini, but it's true.

He had a beautiful baritone voice, and when I started to sing opera I taught him duets, which we would perform as he stood beside me at the piano. The duet from *Samson et Dalila* gave us a lot of trouble because it's written in canon and he would always take off too soon. Our big hit was the one from *Thaïs*. Because it speaks of fruits and flowers, Mannolini nicknamed it "The Banana Duet."

Through instinct or love, she understood everything. For example, when I fell in love (the expression delighted her) at twenty-three with an orchestra conductor twenty-five years older than I, who left wife, children, and job to be with me—

scandalizing the whole town and greatly distressing my father—Mannolini stood fast. My mother had died three years earlier, and Mannolini told my father: "The little one needs someone more intelligent and cultivated than we are. Leave her alone."

Even if she didn't completely agree, above all because of the age difference, she suffered quietly, only once in a while muttering: "Really! My little one and this old man. It isn't right!" But to me she said, "Follow your heart."

So far as anyone else was concerned, she had a way of glaring at them that made any questions or disapproving comments freeze on their lips.

It's thanks, too, to Mannolini that I love movies. The first time she took me I was barely two years old; films were still silent, and as I was bored silly, according to what she told me much later, I wandered off to the orchestra pit and settled beside the conductor (already!). There I "forgot myself" and, probably because the result annoyed me, removed my underpants and left them beside him. A Freudian analyst would surely see a lot in that gesture.

When the loudspeaker requested that someone fetch the child and her "package," Mannolini was furious. Years later, she would still say about the incident, "Tu m'as fait manquer!" which in Marseille dialect means "You embarrassed me."

Later I went with her to all the operettas she adored: *La Fille de Madame Angot*, *Ciboulette*, *Phi-Phi*, *Dédé*, *Mam'zelle Nitouche*, and others. I was old enough to stay in my seat and listen, but sometimes, carried away by the voices, the orchestra, the dancing, I would join in lustily and the people around us would call out "Shhh!" They had no idea that in a few years they would be paying to hear me, nor did Mannolini and I. We

Mannolini

(1 1)

simply enjoyed ourselves, afterward going over the story for the umpteenth time, singing all the refrains.

Poor Mémé. How she would have loved seeing me in *La Grande-Duchesse de Gérolstein* and hearing my recordings of all those operetta arias. Because to her, opera was a bit serious, a bit longish. Nevertheless, when she saw me on stage she was ecstatic. The first time, at Nîmes in *Otello*, she made a marvelous comment to friends who asked, "Did your granddaughter sing well?"

"I don't know," she told them. "Tonight I could only look at her."

The real triumph for her was my debut in Marseille. All the friends from La Bourdonnière came, and those from Endoume, the section of Marseille where she had a house at the time. And they congratulated *her* afterward, not me!

The poor things had happened on *Boris Godunov,* in which I had only two scenes to sing. They understood nothing, but found me superb in my gown of midnight-blue velvet trimmed with white artificial fur. The thing that impressed them most, though, was the enormous fan of white ostrich feathers my father had given me and which, it seemed, I used wonderfully on stage. So much for my hard work!

Mannolini saw me later in many other roles, when she lived with me in Paris after my father remarried. She followed me to Lyon, Bordeaux, Vichy, Strasbourg, Toulouse, and elsewhere for *Faust, Otello, Lohengrin, Le Nozze di Figaro,* and *Tosca* (in which she particularly loved the scene of the tenor's return from the torture room in the second act, when I threw myself at him crying "Mario! Mario!" "That's a real woman," she would say).

We once even spent two months in Milan, in a superb apartment I had rented. I was engaged at La Scala as understudy for the title role in Strauss's *Die Liebe der Danae,* with the promise of singing the sixth performance. But it was such a success that it was withdrawn after the second, so Mannolini never saw me sing in Italy. That was 1952, and she died the following year.

The year 1951–52 had been full of new things for me. I had been dismissed from the Paris Opéra; had auditioned successfully for the conductor Victor De Sabata at La Scala; had discovered that renowned theater, Callas on stage, the celebrated tenors Giuseppe Di Stefano and Mario Del Monaco, and the great mezzo-soprano Giulietta Simionato; and had worked with Margherita Wallmann in the first opera she directed and with the conductor Clemens Krauss, Richard Strauss's close friend and associate.

Yet the only thing that counted for me was being able to pay from my own earnings for Mannolini to make the trip—in a sleeping car, if you please—to Milan, where she had never been. *Otello* at La Scala, restaurants, Italy rediscovered (and, according to her, in luxury). Maybe I realized she wouldn't always be there.

But she was hale and hearty at eighty, still clambering up the olive and mulberry trees in her garden. She had had a heart murmur since the age of twenty, but that didn't stop her from postperformance midnight meals of sauerkraut in Strasbourg, sausage in Lyon, or cassoulet in Toulouse. In the middle of the night I would find her sitting up in bed looking perturbed.

"My plumbing isn't working too well," she would say.

To her, anyone who didn't like to eat was suspect, as you could read in her eyes when plates with food left on them were carried into the kitchen.

"They'll never set their feet under my table again," she would say. "Ils tchaoutchillent" (They peck). That was drastic.

And yet it was Mannolini who caused my first real grief, my first betrayal.

Mannolini

(1 3)

Certainly I knew François Burignan. But how could I understand at eleven that this man had loved my grandmother for years; that he hadn't been able to marry her because he had a wife in a mental institution; that Mannolini wasn't indifferent to his tall and impeccably dressed figure, to his gifts at each visit? She told me they were her first gifts from a man, and I jealously insisted, "But when I'm rich, *I'll* give you presents." She smiled, full of confidence in me.

She wasn't indifferent, either, to the beautiful house he owned in Marseille, with the lovely garden—half flowers, half vegetables—where she would reign for ten years. So one September evening in our big bed, Mannolini, in tears, announced that this was the last summer we would share the cabin. I had often tumbled out of bed at night, but that night I fell three times, crying in my sleep. And I spent my next several vacations with the two of them.

Poor man, whom I was never able to call Grandpa as he wanted me to so badly. He didn't make me suffer for long. He died four years later, in 1942, his big body unable to survive the hardships of wartime.

He was an individual of extraordinary goodness, who loved my parents as his own children. He had a passion for my grandmother; on this, we were in total agreement.

We went back often to La Bourdonnière, for a day, a visit; it was fiesta! But babyhood had ended for me, and vacations were never the same. I think it was only at twenty-four, at Cavalaire near Saint-Tropez, that I enjoyed a real vacation again.

My Mother

R AYEEN CRESPANG, rue Glangdevess, numéro sannnk."
My name and address, the first things I learned by
heart, which I recited at age four with a heavy Marseille accent. I remember very little about that time or about the
apartment near the square where the opera house stood. I've
been told that I was a well-behaved little girl, solemn, shy, and
neat. I have a dim memory of my father's large easy chair, where
I played "taxi," and of my favorite doll, Julot, who left on a trip
one day—long enough for my grandmother to make him another outfit—and whom I found the next day sitting in front
of the door. I remember shouting, "Julot! Julot came back!"

But my true life—my adolescence, my studies, my first piano
and singing lessons, my first loves, my first sorrows—was in
Nîmes, which I consider my hometown. (Later, each place
would reproach me when I said I came from the other.) My
parents settled there in 1932, when I was five, to open an immense shoe store with seventeen saleswomen. The days glided

by, happy, cozy, dreamlike (I have the impression I was in a trance before I started to sing), until I was almost twelve and made several discoveries.

The first, after the small Catholic class that put rings on my knees from kneeling and then the small and quiet elementary school, was the big and impersonal girls' school, where I felt lost and anonymous. My lifebuoy was Maguy Molinari, my friend ever since. The day of our mutual entrance into the seventh grade, she made her first and last gesture of authority.

"You! Do you go to Mass?"

I breathed a timid "Yes."

"Good. Call for me at eleven o'clock Sunday. We'll go to Saint Perpetua."

But my church was Saint Baudile, so on the next Sunday we went to Mass there. From that day on, I took command of our activities, and she followed like a faithful consort.

Dear Maguy, my pal, my sister, my accomplice, my mother, my daughter, faithful Maguy who for years I had no time to see because she lived in Cannes and I in Paris or elsewhere, whom I would telephone every thirteenth month of the year and who would unresentfully ask, "How *are* you, my Chérinoute?" We would talk for an hour, expressing impatience for retirement and the time to see each other more often, and that would be it until the following year.

It's thanks to her that I discovered opera. Her father, an ardent fan, had given her the bug, and she passed it on to me straightaway. The first time we went to the opera house, when we were thirteen, it was to see *Lohengrin*. I didn't understand much, but I remember perfectly how dazzled I was by the orchestra, the voices, Elsa in a white veil on the balcony in the second act. (Coincidence: I made my debut in that role ten years later).

My next discovery was the war. I was horribly affected by seeing my father, in a hospital bed after a serious car accident, crying because he couldn't leave with his regiment, which probably saved his life. Some time later, I experienced hunger and cold for the first time, before the notorious black market was organized. Then the sensation of physical fear, when a bomb fell on our building. On that day, my parents were in Montpellier and I was alone with Bibi, my mother's Angora cat. Some neighbors had taken me to the shelter in the basement, where I was so frightened that I turned Bibi over to them, leaped up the stairs, and ran through the streets like a wild thing, covered with dust and followed by members of the civil defense squad. I ran all the way to Maguy's house, and she burst out laughing when she saw me. I really did look like an apparition from one of our favorite operas, yet her laughter introduced me to the feeling of ridicule.

But the biggest discovery, the most painful, the one that had an effect on my entire life, that made me turn inward to hide the shame—even Maguy knew nothing about it for more than thirty years—was that my mother drank.

It must seem so childish, so incomprehensible, to have suffered so much over that. So the woman drank; poor thing, she must have had sorrows, problems. Maybe someone could have helped her, made her talk about it.

But at twelve I understood only one thing: that this drunken, staggering woman who could hardly speak, who didn't know what she was doing, was no longer Mama. Mama was the daytime woman: beautiful, intelligent, full of life, amusing, ultra-

My Mother

(1 7)

feminine in one of her many stylish dresses, her big black eyes full of mischief, beautiful dark hair rippling. Mama was the person everyone adored and whom I started to loathe because she had become this nighttime woman: haggard, irrational, pitiful. But I had no pity for her.

I don't know how many times I saw Mannolini on her knees in front of her, crying: "Margo, don't drink anymore. You're going to kill yourself, and me too. You're making us all so unhappy." Finally, exhausted and powerless, my grandmother left to live in Marseille, and I never forgave my mother for driving her away.

How many times I saw my father—weary and crazed by sorrow and anger—go so far as to hit her. How many bottles we threw away before her pleading eyes. How many times, getting home from school at seven-thirty, I would listen for her footsteps to tell me how far along she was.

The evenings when she hadn't been drinking were a miracle. I could timidly kiss her, fearful because I still carried the hurt of the day when I had gone toward her and she had pushed me away, yelling, "They sent you to see if I've been drinking, right?"

I was so hurt by all this that I refused any tenderness—already so rare in my family—until I was thirty and met Lou, my ex-husband. How I wrapped myself in his tender gentleness, his kisses and little hugs ("schloupfles," he called them in Alsatian dialect). He was the first person I could talk to about my mother, ten years after her death.

And yet how I loved Mama, without realizing it. I didn't want to admit it until I began psychotherapy at forty. One day, I was talking about her warmly, praising her qualities, when my analyst, who had let me rhapsodize slowly, suddenly asked in a soft voice, "So, you loved her?"

I stopped short, disconcerted, and didn't answer for a few minutes. Then with a sob I said, "Yes," and cried for the rest of the hour.

That day I remembered that I hadn't cried for her in twenty years, since the day of her death. My father had found her in the morning in her bed; she had had a cerebral hemorrhage during the night. I watched stone-faced, tearless, as people streamed into the house, all her friends crying. I watched the arrival of my distraught grandmother, her son already dead of tuberculosis at thirty-five, and I asked her coldly, "Why are you crying?"

Poor Mannolini. Her daughter dead at forty-nine, and her granddaughter asking such a question.

I remembered that my father, before the coffin was closed, said to me, "All the same, kiss her." But stubborn and hurt, not wanting to give in to this apparent hypocrisy, I answered: "Why? I didn't kiss her when she was alive."

He sadly grabbed me by the neck and forced me to bend over her. And night after night for many months I had a recurring nightmare: that I kissed her corpse and she bit my cheek.

I spent the night of her burial alone in her room, and because I couldn't sleep, opened her wardrobe and found a small pink wooden chest that I still have. Inside were all my letters, mementos of my childhood and adolescence, my photos. And among them, a photo of me on my communion day, at age twelve. On the back, in her large, elegant handwriting, she had written, "Forgive Mama."

And I cried, at last.

My Mother

The Voice Discovered

To put it simply, I became a singer because I brilliantly flunked my college entrance exam.

I had been hopeless at math since the seventh grade, despite all the private tutoring (who said that mathematics and music go well together?), and I sat there stumped behind my white examination paper while Maguy wrote and wrote and paid no attention to my desperate whispered appeals. As I handed in a paper with my signature the only blemish, I knew very well that my academic career had ended.

Collective unconscious? Not really. But somewhere behind all this was the germ of an idea. Why else did I never get around to telling my father that there was a makeup exam in September? I hypocritically entered a state of conspicuous idleness, full of avowed remorse and hidden hopes.

Farewell, pharmacy—my mother's dream. Farewell the shoe store and its bookkeeping—my father's dream. In midsummer, two years after my first voice lesson, I became totally immersed in singing.

When I think back on my high school days, I wonder how I got as far as graduation without repeating a class. I have the feeling that I was a zombie for six years, except for a few compositions marked "Interesting!" when I wove in some musical references, a few honorable mentions for remembering things like the ancient names of China and Japan (Cathay and Cipango), and some good marks in Greek and Latin because we had a wonderful teacher. Always perfect marks in music (not a required subject), even if Madame Jacquot often had to yell, "Not so loud, Crespin!"

In sum, if culture is what remains when everything else is forgotten, then I was very cultivated at eighteen! So much so that, until quite a bit later, my literary references came mostly from opera librettos, which are not exactly known for their literary merit.

(I remember that my first year at Bayreuth, floundering in German, I would often begin my answer to a question from Wieland Wagner—Richard's grandson—with the words "Mich dunkt," which can be compared to saying "It would appear to me that" instead of the simple "I think." The first time I did it, Wieland laughed aloud and said, "You sound like my grandfather."

("*Walküre*, second act," I replied.)

I had taken my first singing lesson at sixteen. My piano teacher found, as she taught me solfeggio, that I had "a pretty little voice," and she gave me some mélodies by Cécile Chaminade and Reynaldo Hahn. I much preferred the songs of

Charles Trenet, but Mother Crespin was tired of hearing the same "nonsense" all the time, and offered to treat me to singing lessons so I could learn something "more intelligent."

Off we went, therefore, one afternoon, to the home of Madame Kossa, a retired opera singer about as tall as three apples, who at seventy-something could still let loose a glass-shattering high C. I sang my little mélodie and I can still see her, seated on the piano bench, peering at me above her eyeglasses and saying: "You want to sing? And with what?"

I answered quickly, "It's not *my* idea; it's my mother's."

After an explanation from the lady herself, Kossa said: "All right. I'll take you on for a three-month trial, but I warn you, you'll never be a singer. You have the chest, but you have no voice. So—next Thursday, four o'clock."

"J'ai traversé les ponts de C; c'est là que tout a commencé . . ." ("I crossed the bridges of C; it's there that everything began . . ."), as Apollinaire wrote in a poem so wonderfully set to music by Poulenc. I didn't cross "les ponts de C," but I set out on the long road of varied, irksome, maddening, and fascinating vocal exercises, which got me more excited and enthused than anything in my life to that point.

I started by singing very high things like *Lakmé* and *Lucia di Lammermoor,* since my voice—"about as big as the head of a pin," according to Kossa—climbed well. At the end of the fateful three months I had lost all my high notes, but my voice was enormous. La Kossa couldn't get over it.

"Where were you hiding all that?" she asked. "My little one, you're a solid mezzo." I didn't know what she was talking about.

After three more months of work, in which my voice developed further, Kossa declared that I would be a big dramatic soprano in five years.

For the moment, I worked on *Faust, Otello,* Salome in *Hérodiade, Thaïs,* Micaëla, Mimi. I was delighted, my parents were too, and Mannolini was walking on air. Of course for them there was no future in any of this. I was simply one more young girl who would embellish evenings at home or the end of her father's business dinners. But Kossa, already envisioning my future and her renown, had begun a serious campaign to undermine the plans for pharmacy, bookkeeping, and even marriage—although I was too timid, without boyfriends, and raised too strictly by my father even to dream about that.

So my blank exam paper gave Kossa a new burst of enthusiasm, because she was obsessed by one idea: that I complete my voice studies at the National Conservatory in Paris. She pondered for a month, telephoned my father for an appointment, and arrived at our house one sunny Sunday morning wearing her dress-up set of false teeth and ready for battle.

My father took her into the living room and closed the door for an hour that seemed an eternity. From their expressions when the door opened, I knew the match was lost. My father looked sterner than ever, and Madame Kossa's stentorian voice filled the house as she left:

"Monsieur Crespin, I hope you realize the consequences of your decision." She might have been Clytemnestra.

I laugh now, but when my father told me that singing and the theater were out of the question, that it was nonnegotiable, and when he turned to my mother and said the maid could serve lunch, I was so shattered I couldn't even cry. My mother, usually a pretty good chatterbox, was speechless too.

The Voice Discovered

(2 3)

The silence continued for a good part of the summer. When I left for Marseille to visit Mannolini, my father—who understood how unhappy I was and who I think was even unhappier than I—sent me a long letter explaining that I was asking for something impossible, that he couldn't lose me like that, that he had sacrificed everything for me, that his life was a long martyrdom, that I should wait and we'd see. In brief, a true blackmail, which almost worked because I adored him and knew he was sincere.

But in the fall, my mother had a brilliant idea (which had to have come from the rascally Kossa). One day at lunch, she gave me a broad wink behind my father's back and said: "Tell me, do you want to sing badly enough to show your father and me how you can do in the *Opéra* magazine competition? Quarter-finals in Nîmes, semifinals in Marseille, finals in Paris. What do you say?"

"Yes, sure, if Papa agrees, I'd like to try," I answered.

With his two women against him, and a slight case of guilt, he finally consented, and it was settled. I hurried to the theater to enroll, then to Kossa's house to start working on the arias from *Hérodiade* and *Sigurd*.

And I was first in Nîmes, first in Marseille, and named a finalist for Paris. Hallelujah!

My mother claimed the right to go with me, but the exultant Mr. Crespin said, "Oh no! I'm the father, after all." My mother and I burst out laughing.

So the two of us "went up" to Paris. I had an adorable pair of pink satin evening slippers from my father's workshop to go with my pink tulle evening dress, but they were so uncomfortable that at the last moment I put on my good old brown crepe soles. Which didn't prevent my winning first prize!

And that really jolted Father Crespin. Nîmes, after all, had been our hometown. Marseille was next door. But Paris!

I went on stage when my name was announced, and when the entire Gaîté-Lyrique theater exploded in applause, I gathered up my skirts and—crepe soles in full view—ran off to tell Papa. As if he hadn't heard; he was already in the wings, yelling, "Go back, go back, they're applauding you. Smile. Smile!"

The applause lasted a good ten minutes, and I think that's what decided him. Everyone ran up to us, shouting:

"Mademoiselle, a photo for *Opéra* magazine."

"Mademoiselle, a photo for my newspaper. Turn this way."

"Monsieur, stand next to your daughter." He didn't need to be asked again.

When we got back to Nîmes there was no fanfare, but there were Kossa excited as a bushel of fleas, Mannolini practically dancing, my mother crying, Maguy and my friends asking a hundred questions at once, the saleswomen prancing, and my father, ignoring all of them, crying out:

"We got them this time. We took those Parisians for a ride."

And we all went to a restaurant for a joyous meal, during which Kossa said to my father, "All right, you didn't believe me, but will you believe Edmond Carrière, the opera's music director?"

Papa agreed.

At seven o'clock the following Saturday evening, we were all ready: my parents, my grandmother, the maid hovering behind the door (which served no purpose, since she was practically deaf), Kossa, and the family doctor, a friend and opera lover my father trusted.

At last a rather short man (in the opera house I had seen only his head and arms as he conducted) arrived: square-jawed, forceful, animated, a permanent smile on his lips. Saying "Later, later" to my mother's offer of a drink, he seated himself at the piano and asked in his deep voice, "So, what are you going to sing for me?" And we began.

He played well, and I—in heaven—sang as well as I could and went through my entire repertoire. At the end, Carrière turned toward my father and said, "What exactly do you expect from me?"

My father stood up and explained seriously, "You understand, my only child . . . in Paris, that den of vice . . . my wife and I. . . ."

Carrière got up in turn, and with a superb gesture interrupted:

"Monsieur, you would be a criminal to stop your daughter from singing, for if she does nothing with a voice like that, it's enough to. . . ." He was surely about to use one of his favorite expressions, "It's enough to make you take them and bite them!" But he finished by saying, "I will take responsibility."

My father solemnly offered his hand. Carrière shook it vigorously. The champagne corks popped. Kossa got drunk. I sang again. And Carrière left.

Poor Papa. He had no idea that he himself had let the wolf into the sheepfold.

So I FOUND MYSELF BACK IN PARIS IN OCTOBER 1947. MY father came to settle me in the apartment of an elderly woman from whom we had rented a small rear bedroom that looked out on a courtyard and was dreary enough to depress a regiment of grasshoppers. The bed was so short that my feet hung over the end (luckily I like to sleep with my feet uncovered). The small armoire couldn't hold half the things that had filled my suitcases: woolens, jackets, pullovers, suits, socks, bed jackets, mufflers, all made by the magical hands of Mannolini, who had been working on them for almost a year. My mother had filled a valise with sugar, chocolates, salami, ham, pâtés, assorted canned goods, crackers, and ration coupons, which were still being used for people under twenty-one. My father had supplied me with boots, shoes, warm slippers, music cases and handbags (with a little persuasion, he would have emptied the store), and above all, numerous and varied recommendations in the form of small notes that I found everywhere, mixed in with those from my mother.

I had chosen this room over other, prettier ones for three reasons: first, it was not far from the Conservatory, and I liked the idea of being able to walk there because the Métro terrified me. Second, because there was a piano in the living room that I could use. And finally, because the owner was as deaf as two posts! The possibility of being able to howl at my leisure thrilled me.

And that's what I did on my first evening, when I had unpacked everything and written to my parents, Mannolini, Maguy, and Kossa. I sang and sang because I didn't want to cry or admit that I was racked with fear. Fear of not passing my entrance audition for the Conservatory, fear of not being "up to snuff," fear of what my father had decreed:

"I give you three years. If you don't succeed, you come back home. Because if it's to sing little roles, or in a chorus in the provinces, out of the question."

He had no idea how much more difficult it is to sing in a little theater than in a huge one, to be a chorister lost in the crowd.

I believe—I *know*—that that year when I was twenty, fear entered my life. And through all my successes, my failures, my joys, my falls, my rebeginnings, it stayed with me.

The end of October arrived quickly, and the entrance auditions too. Dying but steadfast, I began the aria from *Sigurd*, only to hear the fateful bell after ten measures. I left like a whirlwind (I was always good at going offstage quickly), thinking, "Oh, my God! What am I going to tell my father?" when Madame Cesbron-Viseur, the teacher I had applied to, ran after me to whisper: "It's in the bag! I'll see you on Monday."

I didn't even wait for the official announcement, but ran to a telephone to call Nîmes.

My father, joyously: "Bravo, my girl. It's up to you now."

Anxiousness from my mother: "Well done, little daughter! Are you eating enough?"

An explosion from Mannolini: "You're the greatest!"

Strengthened by the praise, I treated myself to a meal at the corner restaurant. But what nerve it took for me to enter alone!

Who would ever believe now, when I enter a restaurant or some other public place like a great ship plowing through the waves, that this haughtiness and scornfulness I've been accused of hides an immense timidity that the years have scarcely diminished.

But it's true. After all the years of performing before a few thousand people, after the hours of standing out there singing, playing, crying, or laughing, I am still timid. t-i-m-i-d.

Madame cesbron-viseur, whom we all called mer-raton (Little Mother), had only girls in her class: she detested boys and didn't want any. She bore a slight resemblance to my grandmother, but despite her angelic smile she was hard, almost nasty. She also preferred girls who were well dressed, so I didn't sit too well with her. In reaction to my ultrafeminine, elegant mother, I paid no attention to clothes, wore no makeup, and let my long hair go any which way. For a while I felt I was in a fashion contest rather than a singing class. All the same, I think I began to dress more smartly little by little to please Merraton. It certainly wasn't for the boys I saw at the canteen, for they scared me silly.

As for work, which I was eager to do, she said that my big voice would succeed on its own, and gave me practically no help or vocal exercises.

When I asked, "Merraton, how exactly do you breathe to sing?" she would glare at me with her pale blue eyes and answer, "Oh, just inhale and sing."

So I would take in air up to my shoulders—an absolute no-no—and strangle right in the middle of my phrases, not know-ing how to control the wretched breathing that gave me night-mares.

In truth, she never explained anything to me. I think that since she was due to retire two years later she had already "dis-connected." So I simply watched the more advanced students, trying desperately to understand, and in the evening, back in

The Voice Discovered

the apartment, I cried with rage and frustration. Demi-teintes, or pianissimi, were my torture because I didn't know how to produce them. When I think that later they became my great specialty!

One of the students was working on *Shéhérazade*, Ravel's beautiful cycle, full of the mysterious pianissimi. I learned it in secret, all alone, and arrived in class one day as proud as could be, my score in hand, and asked if I could try "Asie," the first of the three mélodies. Oh, what a look I got from Merraton!

"But my poor child, you'll never sing that. Sit down and listen to Agnès, who does it so well."

I cried like a baby while Agnès sang.

Several years later I sang *Shéhérazade* on what I believe is one of my best recordings. And still hurt, I sent a copy to Merraton, who had retired long before. She quickly sent me a telegram:

"Mea culpa! Mea culpa! Mea maxima culpa! You're superb. Bravo. Merraton."

I found it deliciously gratifying.

That first year, I was kept very busy with classes in singing, solfeggio, ensemble, music history, makeup, acting, and fencing (which lasted only one day for me because the second day I fell as I got off the bus, my knees having betrayed me). The acting teacher, René Simon, wanted me to lose twenty pounds and become a comic actress. He predicted a superb career for me in the movies.

Years later he came to see me in *Otello* and told me, "You were damn smart not to listen to me!"

The things I most remember about that first year at the Conservatory are the great fits of laughter in the canteen, in the small corner café, in the ensemble class, in the streets, in the stores. We were a notorious team, which included Gabriel Bacquier, who strolled down the street shouting nonsense slogans in his strong southern accent; Michel Sénéchal, who would softly ask silly and risqué questions of department store saleswomen; and Michel Roux, who drove our exasperated ensemble professor, Jules Mazellier, to shout one day, "You, Roux, Roux, what's your name anyway?"

Poor Professor Mazellier. We really drove him crazy. I remember telling a new girl in class, "If you really want to get along with Mazellier, start out by calling him Maestro Jules."

Which she did. And he, with a rolling Toulouse accent, replied, "Oh! I find you very familiar for a new arrival."

Little by little, I progressed. The second year, I was enrolled in the stagecraft class of Paul Cabanel, who was away all the time singing, meaning there were no classes. But the role coach, who saw my potential, said, "Come anyway, and we'll work on some operas."

That's how, when I left the Conservatory two years later, I knew five operas by heart: *Faust, Otello, Le Nozze di Figaro, Tosca,* and *Lohengrin.* There's some good to be had from every bad situation!

That second year, I was going to take part in the competitions for singing and stagecraft. But since a first prize in singing would mean the end of my vocal studies, the school director said he would like me to have only a second prize, because I was still very young and he thought I should stay on for another year. I agreed but said someone would have to explain to my father. And that's what the good man did, by telephone.

The singing competition came first, and I had my prearranged second prize. But for the onstage competitions, in

The Voice Discovered

opera and opéra comique, I won two first prizes, for scenes from *Aida* and *Tosca*.

I returned, therefore, the following year to work with Merraton's replacement, a tenor, Georges Jouatte. And what a pleasure! He was my first great singing teacher. It was he who taught me to breathe, to sing flexibly in the famous pianissimi, to tell the difference between recitatives by Mozart, Gluck, and Verdi. He explained the importance of facial expression, of the tongue, the cheeks, the diaphragm, of the body attitude in general, and made me vocalize at full speed despite my big voice.

He was erudite, musicianly, and interested in a thousand things, and he transmitted his passion for work well done, for research, for curiosity, for books. Through him, because I worked with him for a long time after leaving the Conservatory, I taught and refined myself.

I can't count the number of times, as I've faced my students with their problems, their enigmas, that I've asked myself, "What would Papa Jouatte do?"

F   O   U   R

❧

On the Podium: My First Love

I SPENT my well-earned summer vacation in 1949 with my
father and my grandmother, who had lived with him since
my mother's death. My mother never saw me on stage,
though she had wished so much for it and often said to me, "I
don't know why, but I see 'Crespin' everywhere, 'Crespin' written in giant, blazing letters. . . ."

What a pity.

With my pals from the Conservatory scattered, Maguy away
on vacation, and my tall, dark, and handsome "flirt" from
school captured by a homosexual in the next classroom, I began
to be seriously bored after three or four weeks.

I wandered between the cinema, the music festivals in Orange and Avignon, games of checkers or cards with Mannolini
(a bad sport who spat on the cards when she lost), horse races
with Papa on Sundays, and football matches where I screamed
my head off, "Go, Nîmes!"

I spent my evenings in bed, reading late into the night, listening to the fountain and its illusion of coolness in the square below, hearing the town clock that kept time with my insomnia. I devoured novel after novel, but my heart wasn't in it.

Then came the afternoon when I happened to meet Edmond Carrière, who had a thousand questions about my studies, my work, my future. He kindly offered to help me with my upcoming roles, and I accepted enthusiastically. From then on, I rang his doorbell every evening at six-thirty with my scores under my arm. And so began an extraordinarily fascinating period of my life.

First the work, with this excellent musician and wonderful pianist who deconstructed each piece for me, measure by measure:

—"Attention, here the orchestra is forte, so you need a little more voice."

—"No, there it's better to be well prepared, because the phrase is long and the conductor is surely going to slow down."

—"Here you can save your voice, there's nothing going on in the orchestra."

—"Ah! More expression there, more soul; think of the words."

—"Sing this passage more softly, so when the fortissimo comes it will have more importance."

—"No, no, don't breathe here, see how much more beautiful the phrase is if you don't break its line. Taste it. If you get pleasure from singing it, the public will get pleasure listening to it."

I was thrilled by the endless conversations on music, personalities, ways to approach a role, to understand it, to assimilate it and make it my own. He talked to me also of his passion for

Ravel, whom he helped me understand; of Debussy, Poulenc, Satie, Stravinsky and the other Russians; and of the writers he loved: Giono, Montherlant, Baudelaire, Anna de Noailles, Gide.

How many books I read, thanks to him. How many things I learned; I was a veritable sponge. He spoke well, in a deep, musical voice. He loved to laugh, and he told me a thousand opera-house anecdotes. All in all, I spent my days waiting impatiently for the evenings, and the months flew by.

But the inevitable didn't happen that summer.

I LEFT AT THE END OF THE YEAR FOR MULHOUSE TO PREpare for *Lohengrin*, with some beautiful new costumes and a long, blond wig given to me by my father. Curiously, neither he nor my grandmother came to hear me. Curiously as well, I remember very little of those performances.

Of the work and rehearsals, yes, and I was well prepared for both. I discovered an unknown region of France, the loneliness of the days before and after a performance—painful always, but with the years more easily assimilated—and the joy of singing with an orchestra for the first time.

I do remember one funny incident. Elsa in *Lohengrin*, who is accused of killing her brother, makes her first appearance on-stage with her head bowed and gives no response to the King's four questions except to gesture more and more dejectedly. At the end of the performance, a member of the audience came backstage and asked if I had had stage fright.

"Yes, and how!" I said.

"Ah! I knew you were making your debut, and when I saw

On the Podium: My First Love

you answer only with gestures, I thought you weren't going to be able to sing for the whole first act."

I didn't correct her.

But oh, yes, I sang. And not badly, judging by the reviews and all the offers I received. Glowing from various successes, I returned to Nîmes in October 1950 to sing *Otello* with the great tenor José Luccioni and, on the podium, Carrière.

We had written to each other often while I was away: I about my work, my rehearsals, my discoveries, my progress; he, wonderful letters—refined, amusing, charming—written with a fountain pen (he hated ballpoints). And little by little a bond developed between us, much more tender than we had ever imagined.

Otello! The rehearsals! The Nîmes audience, warm and welcoming to its newly discovered daughter! Mannolini! Kossa! My father, his glasses misty with tears, waving his arms like de Gaulle! Flowers, tons of flowers! The crowd afterward, filling the wings and my dressing room! And finally Carrière, coming to congratulate me, alone. He closed the door, grasped my shoulders, looked at me intensely with his eyes full of tears, and said, "I'm thinking of your mother."

And with that he placed his lips on my forehead and gave me a chaste and tender kiss. He left without another word, but we both knew we would be together again soon, for a long time.

My Father

ENRI CRESPIN, who were you?

When I was little, it seems, I had such a passion for you that Mama was a bit jealous. Didn't she say to you often, sometimes laughingly, sometimes enviously, that you would be the only love of my life?

Analysis and Oedipus aside, it's true! I literally adored you, until the day in March 1955 when you died on my shoulder after three days and nights of suffering. Your large, ravaged body, battling silently and stubbornly, found the strength to slip out of my arms, which ached from holding you down on your bed so many times. Oddly, the first two nights I sensed death in your bedroom but was sure it wouldn't conquer you, not yet. But when the third night came, I knew.

During your illness, I had become your mother, whom you said I so resembled when I tied my hair in a chignon. That last night, you were truly my child as well as my father, my last link with the family unit.

Mama died alone in the night, without calling to anyone. And Mannolini, after her heart attack, facing fear and death far from us, said these wonderful words to the friends she was staying with:

"Anyway, I'm glad Régine isn't here. She's going to have enough grief later."

You and I faced the horror together, alone like a mother with a child about to be born. But you left me, perhaps to be born in another dimension I couldn't reach. Hardly five minutes later, your drawn, pained face became peaceful, handsome again, and I, undone, was momentarily angry with you.

You were truly good-looking, and I wasn't the only one to think so. Your large body was well proportioned, muscled without an ounce of fat, your wrists narrow, your hands beautiful. Dressed in gray, beige, or navy blue, you had a natural elegance. But when you wore the sleeveless undershirt called a *débardeur* (I hated it at the time) which leaves the arms, shoulders, and neck bare, you were superb.

You bequeathed me a long-boned carcass, but the Italian fat from Mannolini took over a bit. And when the whims of my thyroid gland, added to Mannolini's culinary talents, seriously rounded out my figure at twelve, you didn't hesitate to comment to my mother, who defended me as well as she could:

"You married me, and I was just as plump."

And your superb answer:

"Yes, but she's my *daughter!*"

Macho you certainly were, with no compunction. And you wanted your daughter to be beautiful, perfect—more than perfect—in all ways. I didn't provide you with much at first, only my love. And, passion doubtless being catching, you returned it fully. With us, it was "until death," and whatever happened, the other was always right, against everyone else.

But you were strict with me. A simple look from your green eyes, just one of your bushy eyebrows raised, could make me want to crawl into a hole. When my high school friends called for me, they preferred to wait outside after two timid rings at the door, because they were a little afraid of you.

Serious as you were, though, you knew how to laugh, and to swim like a dolphin. (I was more like Mama, a cement block in the water, until the day at age fifteen when I headed into the sea with a policeman's determination, telling myself, "Either you swim or you drown!" Mission accomplished!) You knew how to have a good time, and you danced like a master. Especially when you bought that little place in the outskirts of Nîmes, a small house on a large piece of land full of olive and apricot trees, lilac bushes, boxwood shrubs, cicadas, and birds. You knew all sorts of facts about the earth and you explained them to me, but I was barely interested at the time. I preferred to close myself in my minuscule whitewashed bedroom, the little window open, and read, read, read (even at night, by the light of two candles because there was no electricity), ignoring Mama's pleas and obeying only your growling voice.

For I was a little bored by all your friends and their silly laughter, their singing while they drank pastis, their dancing to the phonograph after a copious lunch. You loved to waltz and Charleston; Mama liked slow fox trots. You adored Charles Trenet; she liked Lys Gauty. But if she listened twice in a row to the song "Le Chaland Qui Passe," which I still know by heart, or if she danced twice with the same friend, your expressive eyebrow would make it clear that that was enough.

My Father

(3 9)

You were jealous and prickly about honor. For you, a promise was the equivalent of a contract. But it seems that you once held a revolver to your Margo, who never so much as looked at another man, because a friend had held her too tightly while they danced. Paradoxically, you weren't at all angry at the friend, but at Mama. For you it was very simple: the man asks and the woman refuses. You could have been Corsican!

But despite your difficult character, your stern eye, the macho selfishness that had you spend your Sundays at the races or soccer matches and frequent nights at poker or elsewhere, you were good, gentle, and kind, with a tenderness you didn't know how to show and that one had to sense. It was so hard for me, whom you took in your arms so rarely and hardly dared touch—even to slap—to get to know your prudish tenderness, your softness, the selfishness that I took for strength and almost admired. Oh, yes, it was selfishness pure and simple that set you against my making a career of singing; you wanted me to stay with you, get married, have children, and always be nearby. Later you looked at me so reproachfully when I held my godson Philippe in my arms that it made me feel guilty for years afterward.

I didn't understand the painful combination of distress, contradictions, and even destructiveness that make up parent-child relationships, the torments that can be passed from parent to child. And I wonder if you realized that, young and unformed, loving you without really knowing you, I was almost maimed for life by you. And all, of course, in the name of love and caring.

For a long time I believed that the hurts from the umbilical cord attaching me to home came from my mother. In fact, it was you who rolled the cord around my neck, almost strangling me.

What strength it took, what courage I needed, to stand up to you that first and only time so I could sing, SING! A necessary step in growing—one eventually has to "kill" one's father—that I didn't understand and that terrified me.

Because until I was twenty you had held me in tow with Draconian severity.

No going out alone, even with Maguy. Only one evening out per week, at the movies or the opera. What a dilemma: *Tosca* or Jean Marais in *L'Eternel Retour.* But thank you, anyway, because to this day I get a curious shiver in a theater waiting for the curtain to open.

No makeup, no eccentric hairdos or other "sluttishness," you insisted.

No boyfriends, of course, because you were so afraid for me. A fear transmitted, which is probably why the arms of a girlfriend at the Conservatory welcomed me for a time, almost traumatizing me permanently. Fortunately my healthy equilibrium understood that the experience could be enriching.

No dancing, either. And when I hesitantly tried a few steps of the lindy one evening at a party for a friend of the family, you told me somberly, "Come sit down. You're not good at it."

Obviously! Dancing with the other girls in high school wasn't a very good way to learn.

Do you know that I never dared go out on a dance floor again until I was thirty-five and spent an evening at Trude Heller's in New York? But I've caught up since; if you saw me now, you wouldn't be displeased.

And our meals: noon and eight o'clock precisely. If I arrived

My Father

(4 1)

a few minutes late for dinner, you didn't say a word, but your eloquent glance at the mantel clock behind you turned me to jelly, even in my twenties. Although that didn't stop me from slipping out after you were asleep to go watch rehearsals at the opera house and see Edmond Carrière. He would bring me back in his car and we would talk at length about the opera he had just rehearsed, about music, about us. What emotion, what fear, as I turned the key in the lock. But when I slipped into bed, I was so happy, from the long conversations and the tenderness that had been so lacking in my life.

I know. In place of Papa Crespin, I had put Papa Carrière.

Today I can explain, thanks to analysis, the attraction that silvery temples have for young girls. I can even tell you about him.

What a happy nature, what vitality, what enthusiasm, what goodness, what good humor that man had!

I had nicknamed him Mi, because it was part of the word *ami* (friend) and the name of the musical note we both loved intensely. Also P'tit Cheval (Pony), because he raced with me like a crazy young thing along the beach at Cavalaire, where he treated me to my first several seashore vacations.

Yes, yes, I know he was twenty-five years older than I, that he was married and had children, a mother, a public career, and that I couldn't keep our relationship secret. You once even said, "At least if he came from another city, like Strasbourg, for instance. . . ."

Well, I finally listened to you, because I married an Alsatian.

But at the time, I was deaf to everything and everybody. You understand, I was in love, with little remorse. I discovered everything at one time: tenderness, intelligence, communication, laughter, books, the sea, games, intimate restaurant dinners, sex. God, it was wonderful.

We never lived together completely, because he never totally left his family; he was still very devoted. But for almost seven years we spent every possible moment together, in Rennes and later in Lyon, where for a long time he was the permanent music director of the orchestra, and in Paris, where he spent the beginning of every week with me.

Oh, Papa, you must have imagined all my good times, even if you said nothing, locked in by your chagrin, your anger, your disgust. You wanted to "go break the bastard's arm," you told Mannolini, who calmed you down but warned me nevertheless. All our dinners were shared in a silence as cold as the wind that descends the Rhône valley, and seated at the table as rigidly as a jackknife I wavered between panic and lionhearted courage. I waited. And one evening, when Mannolini took refuge in her bedroom from the approaching storm, you finally talked about it.

We sat in your bedroom and as calmly as you could, you tried to explain your sorrow at the wounds to your pride and your honesty; you tried to explain your anger, to move me to pity over your difficult childhood, your long "calvary" with a mother who drank, as mine had, being orphaned at fourteen, your loneliness (which you filled the following year by remarrying, albeit unhappily).

I struggled to hold my own, but finally, running out of words that would convince you, I screamed, "But you've been in love once in your life, haven't you?" And you gave me a long look and started to cry.

The only tears I had ever seen in your eyes were tears of joy,

My Father

(4 3)

especially when I sang, and I started to sob in your arms, which you finally had opened to me and then closed tightly around me. You propped me up on your bed and made me promise one thing: to leave him if he hadn't divorced by the time I was thirty. (Be happy; I did). That was the only time in my life that I fell asleep crying on your shoulder, and you cradled me in your arms all night.

You never talked about it again. You let me live my life as I wanted, in a way resigning yourself to accept everything you had fought against: singing, my career, Carrière.

You even made an extraordinary gesture when Mannolini died. When I returned from Vichy where I was singing, you came yourself to meet me at the station, but you had a friend tell me—you couldn't get yourself to do it—that you had informed Carrière and that he was waiting for me at my hotel, because you thought I would need him with me that night. It was a gesture full of love and delicacy, but you know what? Even if you had said nothing, I think I would have preferred consolation from you.

After your death, when all three of you had left me within a span of five years, I didn't fully realize how alone I was in life. And even now, when I hear friends my age say "My father told me such-and-such" or "My mother did this or that," I'm always a little astonished.

Henri Crespin, my gentle tough guy, my handsome silent one, how I wish you were here so I could look deep into those green eyes, put my hands in yours, and say:

"All the same, you can be proud of your daughter."

Paris Opéra: Exile and Return

Great artists have no homeland.

ALFRED DE MUSSET

THE OPÉRA didn't engage me when I left the Conservatory, to my great disappointment and everyone else's surprise. The house preferred a charming young soprano whose uncle played in the orchestra and who eventually devoted herself to operetta.

To show they weren't totally ignoring me, they invited me to a performance, which I asked to watch from the wings. That's how I saw *Tristan und Isolde* with my idol Kirsten Flagstad, from a chair at stage left. I watched her chug in like a machine at 250 pounds, place a bottle under a sofa, and sip from it from time to time. It was fascinating to watch her, in profile, take an enormous breath like an accordion spreading and to see how effortlessly she seemed to sing. At the end, I was introduced to her, and with no idea of what to say I pointed to the bottle and asked, "Water?"

"Water? *Nein.* Cognac!" she answered. She had drunk the whole thing.

So, instead, I cut my teeth in the provinces. And it was in Vichy in 1950 that Madeleine Mathieu, the wife of the Paris Opéra's director, Georges Hirsch, heard me in *Lohengrin* and found it shameful that I wasn't at the Paris house. She promised to speak to her husband, and sure enough, he hired me that October to make my debut at the Opéra the following August in *Lohengrin* and at the Opéra-Comique in *Tosca*, roles that I continued to sing, along with *Le Nozze di Figaro, Cavalleria Rusticana, L'Etranger* by Vincent d'Indy, and one of the eight Valkyries in *Die Walküre.*

(For my debut in *Lohengrin* I had as partners the renowned Canadian tenor Raoul Jobin; Renée Gilly, whom I would succeed twenty-four years later as a teacher at the Conservatory; and the attentive and cheerful André Cluytens on the podium.

(The Paris critics praised me roundly, except for one who wrote, "This young singer, full of talent and with a magnificent voice, is not, however, and never will be a Wagnerian singer." Hah!

(Several years later, at Bayreuth, the same well-known critic wrote in a review of *Die Walküre*: "One cannot imagine a Sieglinde more moving, more beautiful, more beautifully sung. Régine Crespin is the greatest French Wagnerian since Germaine Lubin." Double hah!)

The Opéra even offered me *Otello*. I sang all the rehearsals, but one week before the premiere I was told I wouldn't do Desdemona because Géori Boué, a big star at the time, wanted to make her return in the role. They asked me to be in the hall for the premiere, and it was the first—and last—time that I suffered from professional jealousy. It hurt me so much I promised myself never to let the sensation attack me again.

Contracts ran until the end of September but were renewed at the end of March, so by March 15 (1952) everybody was trembling. Not by so much as a hair on my head did I doubt I would be signed again, for I had done well with everything they gave me and had even begun to study *Aida*. But around March 20, I saw one of our representatives circle around me with an embarrassed expression, and eventually I was told that the new director, Maurice Lehmann, didn't want me in the company. I turned pale. Why? A mystery! No one dared say.

Finally Madeleine Mathieu told me: Lehmann found me too fat! She was furious, grumbling and fuming in the corridors, repeating that this was the sh . . . abbiest thing Lehmann had ever done. I was terribly upset, but I had to admit it was true; I *was* too fat!

While my impresario at the time, Alphonse Cambarrot—Camba, a lovely man who followed my career for ten years—worked hard at finding me engagements around the country, I furiously started dieting, unfortunately with the help of a crazy doctor who made the whole Opéra lose weight with a variety of pills. We all lost pounds with dizzying speed, but some people lost their voices as well. It isn't bad for singers to diet—quite the contrary—but it should be done slowly and without medication.

I cheerfully lost thirty-five pounds in three months, with Mannolini despairingly repeating that I looked like a plucked chicken. But when I started to sing again—*Faust*, in Marseille—I had to use every trick I knew because my voice was so weak and colorless. Mannolini stuffed me with sugar lumps at each intermission, and later she cried, warning that I would lose my voice permanently if I continued. I believed her and started eating normally and without pills. Little by little my voice came back, and I didn't gain an ounce until I met Lou five years later and—happiness helping—ballooned again.

In 1953, Lehmann, who had heard about my slimming, called me to come see him, and when I walked in, dressed in black with a large pink hat, he was stunned. He stood up and said, "Ah, bravo, bravo! You're superb. Now I'll hire you."

Acting aloof, I asked at what fee.

"Well, when you left, you had one hundred thousand francs" (old francs, of course—about $285). "How much do you want?"

"Twice that."

"Out of the question! It's too much."

I got up, said good-bye politely, and left him flabbergasted.

Back to the provinces, where I sang and earned a very good living.

The next year, same scene. I don't remember what I wore, but he said, "All right. I'll give you your two hundred thousand francs. What do you say?"

"The same thing, Mr. Lehmann. Double it."

This time he got angry, calling me insolent and practically ordering me out of his office.

The best part was the following year. Georges Hirsch had become director of the Opéra again, but as Lehmann was to stay in the post until September, he had to sign the contracts with the artists Hirsch wanted to hire, and the first contract Hirsch wanted was mine, at a million (still old francs) per month.

I went back to the director's large office, where Lehmann handed me the contract without a word. I signed it and said with a smile, "Mr. Lehmann, I want to thank you for firing me.

If you hadn't, I never would have sung all the roles I've done in the provinces, and I never would have come back with the red carpet out."

He looked at me skeptically. "All right, I know I made a mistake with you, but don't rub it in. May I kiss you?"

I let him, and he wished me good luck.

I MADE MY "REENTRY" IN GRAND STYLE IN *OTELLO*, again with the tenor José Luccioni and with André Cluytens conducting. The Paris public welcomed me with open arms, and from 1955 to 1958 I had a yearly contract and sang much of my repertoire. My biggest successes, in addition to *Otello*, were *Un Ballo in Maschera* and above all the Marschallin in *Der Rosenkavalier*, often with Suzanne Sarroca, a handsome Octavian and a great pal, and Janine Micheau, one of France's finest singers and an admirable Sophie.

Those years at the Opéra (which frankly was in a lean period) gave me the chance to work in peace and quiet, with a stable troupe and under good if unexciting conductors, who were always on hand to help me with their advice.

Many people have said that the Opéra should have been my longtime mother house. Yes, in Germany or Italy that would have been the case. But I'm not sure I would have found it very satisfying.

Good luck sometimes comes from a bit of bad luck at the start. Mine was being obliged to start out in the provinces, where I got on-the-job training as the Marschallin in Marseille, Tosca in Nancy, Cassandre and Didon in Lyon, Desdemona in Bordeaux, Sieglinde in Nice, Ariadne in Aix-en-Provence. I even sang Donna Anna, though not very well (everyone has the right to a mistake!). I also sang the world premieres of two operas: Henri Tomasi's *Sampiero Corso*, and *Geneviève de Paris* by Marcel Mirouze. My luck was also to figure out that those who go far will be slow and reserved. In those two qualities, I excel.

All those major engagements might have seemed too risky, but I think I unconsciously planned it that way. I know that such passionate singing is always a little suicidal, but the intensive training prepared me much better than if I had begun, as so many do, in smaller roles. After all, an artist has nothing better to vanquish than himself.

Obviously my "wanderings in the desert" left some thirsts: for work, team spirit, teachers, directors. Well, I learned the work almost singlehandedly, understanding little by little that on stage sometimes, an unknown, untamed force and a sort of electricity impossible to describe escape from you and push you to the forefront. The teamwork I found often, in New York, in Buenos Aires, at Glyndebourne, and with teachers like Zinka Milanov and Rudolf Bautz. I also came to understand that our art is nourished by gratitude, by others' love, and I learned very quickly that the public should be respected and honored, and that most of the time it repays you well. I was modest by nature, and I became even more so about my work.

I understood that unlike some singers, I could not bring to life a character I didn't like, that I needed to be sincere, that I couldn't stand apart from the role. Maybe some people can find a subtle and selfish pleasure in that, but it didn't satisfy me. I had to let my subconscious run free and do my calculations later. Isn't surprise the very essence of theater? One constantly learns, and even mistakes can be rich and instructive. Technique is necessary, yes, but it wasn't the most essential element for me. And sometimes you have to take reasoned risks, to learn just how far you can go. There is no talent without a bit of madness; I was happy to have a touch of it. Perhaps the heart isn't the solution to everything, but it turned out to be so for me.

I think what I lacked most were great directors like Luchino Visconti, Giorgio Strehler, Franco Zeffirelli (I narrowly missed him in New York for a reprise of *Cavalleria Rusticana*, which he bowed out of; my help came from the gentle Fabrizio Melano). Patrice Chéreau, another great name, I met only at the lowest point of my "slump"—for the minor role of Giulietta in *Les Contes d'Hoffmann*, a bad-luck opera for me. The first time I sang it, my father died; the last time was during my debacle at the Paris Opéra (more on that later).

My first directors were serious craftsmen like Pierre Deloger in Mulhouse and Vichy and Roger Lallande in Bordeaux. They really taught me the basics, the rules of gestures, of entrances, of the restrictions of music and voice, those two iron corsets that singers try to forget and make the audiences forget. I also had the good luck to work frequently in Lyon with Louis Erlo, a beginner like me. We experimented together—seeking, erring, sometimes finding answers—with the superb *Iphigénie en Tauride* that we took to San Francisco, Buenos Aires, and finally to Paris, and with Spontini's *La Vestale* at Fourvières.

I also "broke in" several directors from the theater or cinema, like Luigi Squarzina for *Fedra* in Milan, Mauro Bolognini for *Tosca* in Rome, André Barsac for a *Tosca* reprise in Paris, and Maurice Jacquemont for the Paris premiere of *Dialogues des Carmélites*.

Paris Opéra: Exile and Return

(5 1)

Squarzina—very intelligent, maybe too much so—was totally lost in his first effort at opera and left me to my fate. Bolognini, from whom I expected great things, simply sat back and extolled my every phrase and gesture: "Che artista!" "Che bella!" (I certainly was not "bella" in the awful costumes he amorously decked me out in.) Barsac, of whom I have a fleeting memory from two afternoons of rehearsal, left happily, declaring that such an artist had no need of him. And Jacquemont, charming and sweet, was totally laissez-faire.

Jean-Laurent Cochet, at Aix for *Ariadne auf Naxos,* despite all his talent was a little intimidated. With Raymond Rouleau, whose Paris reprise of *Carmélites* was a failure, we had to move to the strident sounds of his whistle, which he blew to stop our "racket," he said. I would have liked to work more with him, for although he was strict, demanding, and humorless, he had great lucidity and enormous talent.

The only actor with whom I worked well was Paul-Emile Deiber, on *Werther* at the Metropolitan Opera, although he was so affected by my predecessor as Charlotte, Christa Ludwig, that he married her!

Díos mío! I almost forgot Jean Cocteau for Honegger's *Antigone,* in Paris in 1952. But I was so young, and the role of Ismène was so blah. Even so, I remember he made magic of everything he set his elegant hand to.

The briefest, most surprising work was in Paris with Jean Le Poulain—a theater actor—on *Tannhäuser* (and what on earth he was doing on that project I still don't know). I arrived at the start of what was to be three weeks of rehearsals, and the first day, he asked me to show him what I usually did when Elisabeth appears in the second act. I acted everything out for him, and here is the exact conversation that followed:

"Good! It's perfect. And after that, are you finished?"

"No, there's the prayer in the third act."

"Ah! Is it long?"

"Five or six minutes, plus the exit, which is very important, slow and beautiful."

"Good! How do you do the prayer? On your knees?"

"If you say so."

"And the exit?"

"I can walk upstage, maybe."

"No, you'll be carried on a litter; it's more dramatic."

"All right."

"So, everything is settled?"

"I guess so. See you at the dress rehearsal?"

"Yes, in eighteen days. Take it easy."

And that was that.

I obviously provoked such painful memories for him that whenever we met later he pretended not to know me. Happily, there were the sets and superb costumes by Leonor Fini!

I give mixed reviews to Margherita Wallmann, the first woman director I worked with (the second, for *Les Troyens* in Boston, was Sarah Caldwell, officially a conductor but a genius of a director as well). When I met Wallmann in Milan for that first *Love of Danae*, it was her first directing job (another "breaking-in"!), and she annoyed me by telling the tenor, as he rushed over to greet me, "No, no, she's the stand-in!"

So I wasn't at all displeased, some years later as a "star," to meet her again in Paris for *Un Ballo in Maschera*. But this charming, pretty woman busied herself more with the massed choruses than with the soloists, who in general are unwilling to try anything new. She had pretty much given up on them, I think. Happily, I had beautiful costumes and a voice in great shape.

When she directed me later in *Les Troyens*, the costumes were really awful, but the role of Queen Dido was—modesty aside—exactly to my measure. A pity that Wallmann didn't get me to eradicate some sterotypical gestures, some attitudes a little too "grand opera," because I wasn't intractable and asked only to be surprised and to work well. It's very hard to be one's own director, even with a natural gift; it's a thankless job, with everyone pulling in different directions, trying to outshine everyone else when the only person one should outshine is oneself.

Ultimately, after Wieland Wagner, the two "greats" were Carl Ebert and John Dexter. At Glyndebourne, where I sang the Marschallin in German for the first time (and twenty-six times in two years), I had the luxury of six weeks of rehearsal and of Carl Ebert, a distinguished old man with snow-white hair. He knew how to use an artist's personality without stifling it, giving it its own way within the scenic universe he had conceived. With me, he tried to forget his usual routines and to put Strauss and me in the forefront. It was a true team there, with the brilliant Jani Strasser in charge of rehearsal coaching. (Because he lived in a trailer, which the French call a caravan, we called him Jani von Karavan.)

I have wonderful memories of that time, of the minuscule theater in an old homestead surrounded by fields and cows, and of the "lord of the manor," John Christie, and his delicious humor:

"You can't play the Marschallin!"

"Why ever not?"

"Because you don't have dimples!"

I burst out laughing.

"But I do, when I laugh."

"Well, that's all right then!"

With him one evening, I discovered the drink Pimm's No. 1 and got memorably drunk.

John Dexter, whom I met in New York for *Dialogues of the Carmelites* and who also did the marvelous staging of the play *Equus*, was a skillful man with a good sense of humor, who let everyone work in an atmosphere of joy and calm. A master of "less is more," he talked little but well, provided information galore, and never criticized what one did badly but touched it up here and there like a painter, with great exactingness while seeming to allow everyone great freedom. Working with him was a joy.

But the director with whom I laughed the most, though we worked morning, noon, and night, was Robert Dhéry for *La Grande-Duchesse de Gérolstein* in Toulouse. Behind his appearance of a well-brought-up young man, what subtlety of laughter, detail, and elegant farce. We were a great team: Robert and his assistant Maurice Ducasse, Michel Trempont, Rémy Corazza, Charles Burles, Michel Roux, Michel Plasson, who joined in the fun, and Colette Brosset, Robert's wife, always with a repertoire of anecdotes and jokes.

So I may not have had a mother house, and there were some awful quarter-hours in my crossing of the desert, but what good times nevertheless!

Paris Opéra: Exile and Return

Bayreuth: The Turning Point

THE TURNING point in my career and in my private life
was Bayreuth.

And the reason, or reasons, were four men: Richard
Wagner, his grandson Wieland, the conductor André Cluytens,
and Lou Bruder, my husband.

"And in the beginning, there was . . ." Wagner, and his festival in the Bavarian town of Bayreuth, reopened in 1951 by his
grandsons Wieland and Wolfgang.

André Cluytens was invited there to conduct *Lohengrin* in
1956 and was unanimously praised by the critics. He was Bel-
gian, but his career was made mostly in France and above all
in Paris, so when Wieland wanted to know if there were any
French singers worth engaging at Bayreuth, Cluytens was the
one he asked. (Since the operas presented were all Wagner's, the
only changes the festival could provide were the casts, conductors, and stage directors.) That's how it transpired that, one

summer day in 1957, I received a telegram from André asking if I would be willing to come audition.

In his *Artistic Voyage to Bayreuth*, Alexandre Lavignac wrote, "I would have gone on foot, on horseback, by carriage, by bicycle, by train or even on my knees." As it happened, I went by car.

Bayreuth! I knew, of course, what it represented in the world of music, and in the world itself. A prestigious summer festival, opened in 1876, adored at the beginning, later decried, rehabilitated by Wieland in 1951. The wise Liszt said it well:

"Don't ask questions. You are here to admire."

But when Madame Cluytens led me to the Festspielhaus and I found myself amid the scenery for *Die Meistersinger*, which I was to see that evening, on the famous slanted stage that was so uncomfortable to newcomers, and realized that Wagner himself had stood where I was standing, I started to tremble. My arms, my legs, my hands shook, and I couldn't stop them.

Fortunately my voice didn't waver when, standing as straight as I could in my fiery red dress, I sang Elsa's, Aida's, and Sieglinde's arias, all in French. (I hadn't yet sung in German.)

I don't know how I got off the stage, but the only thing I could say, to a stagehand who happened to be there, was "Peepee, peepee." I must have made myself clear, because he took my hand silently and escorted me to the ladies' room.

When I got back, calmer, I met Madame Cluytens, who had been searching all over for me.

"Wieland wants to see you! Wieland wants to see you!"

The trembling began again and I had to sit down with her on a bench outdoors. I tried to imagine what he was going to

Bayreuth: The Turning Point

offer me. One of the eight Valkyries? A Norn? Elsa, perhaps? Senta? My head was spinning.

Suddenly, there they were in front of me, Cluytens smiling and happy, Wieland with his handsome, expressive face aquiver, examining me carefully up and down as he spoke, while André translated:

"He congratulates you. He says that you have a very beautiful voice, very warm, Italianate. And that you are beautiful also."

My face became as red as my dress.

It turned out that he wanted me to sing in *Parsifal* the following year. If my good upbringing hadn't kept me on my feet, I think I would have fallen back on the bench.

Parsifal! Kundry! At thirty-one? He was crazy, this Wieland. I timidly suggested that perhaps Elsa . . . or Sieglinde . . . ? Categorical refusal.

"Those fools are uninteresting! And I've had enough of these black-voiced Kundrys. I want a sunny, Mediterranean voice like yours, as light as your hair" (I was a platinum blonde at the time).

I stood there gaping as Wieland asked if I could stay over to see his production of *Parsifal,* adding with a smile that it wasn't half bad. He would see me at the end of the performance to find out what I thought of the role. And kissing both my hands, he gave me a big wink and said, "Auf Wiedersehen, die Kundry."

Needless to say, for the next two days I inhabited a rosy cloud and hardly slept. I rushed to buy the score and read it hungrily, dying of nervousness, of fear. If I had realized the full immensity of the role, I think I would have left running. Ah, the ignorance of youth!

Wieland came to see me at each intermission during the performance of *Parsifal*, whispering questions, and I, facing these wonders—the famous Bayreuth direction, the fascinating lighting, the circle on the stage that has been so widely imitated—all I could do was repeat ecstatically:

"Beautiful! Beautiful! Beautiful!"

And he crushed my hands in his as he repeated, "Ach, Kundry. Sie, Kundry."

Finally he suggested that I work on the role, think it over, and give him my answer in January. But in October I received a formal contract: four performances of *Parsifal* in the 1958 festival.

(Several years later, while I was singing in *Tannhäuser* at the Paris Opéra, it fell on me to announce Wieland's death to the audience. And eight months later, in the identical situation, to announce the death of André Cluytens. An odd and moving coincidence.)

I had begun to go through the *Parsifal* score during the summer, without the words, and now the first decision I made was to learn German.

Starting in September I had begun regular sessions with a coach at the Opéra who knew *Parsifal* by heart. I worked with him three times a week all winter and once a week with Germaine Lubin, the great prewar singer. Since she had made her own Bayreuth debut as Kundry and was there when I auditioned, Wieland had asked me to work on interpretation with her. It was very emotional, the following summer, to find myself onstage singing Kundry with Germaine in the hall. Just twenty years—1938/1958—between the only two Frenchwomen ever invited to sing at Bayreuth.

Bayreuth: The Turning Point

I started an urgent hunt for a German teacher, and some friends told me about an extraordinary professor of German literature. When at month's end this rare bird still hadn't responded to my friends' many messages, I decided that if he hadn't telephoned by October first, I would make an appointment with a woman who had also been recommended. But on October first, my very pleased friends announced that the much-awaited Lou Bruder had phoned and would call me that evening. What they didn't tell me was his response to their words about me.

"What? An opera singer? That doesn't interest me at all. She's probably an idiot. Well, all right, I'll go once for your sake, since you say she's not so stupid."

"Veni, vidi . . ."—I don't know who conquered, but he came, he saw, and he stayed!

Three times a week I took my lesson like a good little girl, learning grammar and declensions and translating *Parsifal* with his help. And we chattered like a couple of magpies.

Our five-to-six sessions quickly became five-to-eight, so much did we talk or, in my case, listen. For little by little I found in this attractive man of thirty-four a person of incredible richness, of vast culture, whose conversation could veer from literature to painting (his passion) to theater to movies to politics. As to music, he leaped from Monteverdi or Gesualdo directly to Berg or Boulez, leaving a great gap between.

Opera made him laugh, he said, but I defended it like a warrior, which made our discussions even more intense.

I began to find him more and more attractive, with his wriggly mustache, his bright blue eyes that stared into mine or sneaked looks at "the shadow between my knees," as he told me later.

I was troubled and trapped, but I didn't want to acknowledge it. He told me he was in the midst of divorcing, that he had a girlfriend—later I called her the interregnum—but that he wasn't happy. And I, with the boldness of the timid, told him, "Well, take a third; she'll make everything come out right."

Obviously, I was this third. And it happened not on just any old day, but on New Year's Day.

Since our next appointment fell on that very afternoon, I suggested changing it. He slyly said, "Oh, I never do anything special on New Year's Day. If it's convenient for you, I can come at five o'clock as usual."

"All right," I said. "But I'll chill a bottle of champagne."

I did take my lesson, while we drank the champagne, and talked about how much I disliked the Christmas holidays because I was always alone. We drank a second bottle, and he watched me silently, his gaze filled with meaning, provoking old timid, fearful me into saying:

"I think I want you to kiss me."

He didn't hesitate for a second. And we resurfaced around five o'clock in the morning.

We were practically inseparable for the next twelve years.

THE YEAR 1958 WAS MORE THAN BUSY FOR ME. IN ADDI-tion to German lessons and *Parsifal* sessions, I was singing at the Opéra two or three times a week, in *Der Rosenkavalier*, *Tosca*, *Otello*, and *Un Ballo in Maschera*, which meant other rehearsals and preparations. And I started to make my first record, for Pathé-Marconi. I remember those recording sessions very well, because they often began at eleven in the morning after I had fallen amorously asleep in Lou's arms at dawn. Michel Glotz, who had proposed the record and was producing it, noticed that I yawned a lot and kept plying me with black coffee.

Good Michel, who was responsible for so many recordings that did so much for my career, especially after he became a top impresario. He had an enormous laugh that could wake up an entire restaurant and a devastatingly bad temper that I could never get the better of (especially when he was right) except by crying, which left him speechless. I think he's the only person on whom I've used that most feminine of weapons.

Despite everything, the recording wasn't bad. When I'm in love, I can move mountains!

Then, voilà! In the midst of all these diverse involvements, I became pregnant for the first time in my life. And, sadly, the last.

I was born under the sign of Pisces, which makes me eternally hesitant. But in this case, I had only one idea: to have the baby, which I wanted badly. But—Bayreuth. Would I be invited again? But—Lou and I. Was our relationship solid enough? And because I still saw Mi occasionally, I wasn't completely sure that the baby was Lou's, though my animal instinct said it was.

Finally I decided to talk to both of them. Their reactions were very different. Mi, very upset, told me:

"You can't keep it! What will you [!] do?"

And Lou, his blue eyes even brighter:

"It's mine! It's mine! What should we [!] do? If you want to keep it, I agree. But if you don't want to, I understand, and I'll help you."

I spent a horrible week, with Carrière's selfish attitude reminding me of my father's words. I sought advice from my friends and they were unanimous: Bayreuth first, baby later.

And finally, painfully, the decision was made. In favor of my career. The career with a capital *C* that began to surround me and slowly consume me. The career that became my only child. That gave me so much joy and so many tears, like one's child. I have few regrets overall, but that one still occasionally eats away at me.

I left with a small valise for a clinic in the provinces, all alone, not very bravely, not very proud of myself either, and returned without any apparent psychological scars. I say "apparent" because much later, psychoanalysis revealed a lot of buried pain.

I decided to clarify my life, because I hate lies and being torn and divided. I knew that I loved Lou deeply, totally. But it was so hard to tell Mi, to explain, to see him suffer. Oh, he agreed to everything I said; he recognized that he had never wanted a divorce because of his daughters, his mother; that he was trapped in this neither-here-nor-there situation, selfishly leaving me alone on Sundays, holidays, vacations; that what had happened was inevitable. He even said that in the six years he had loved me, he had asked himself every morning the painful question, "When?"

We cried together. At last I phoned his son, Jean, and asked him to come to Paris to help his father. Without any questions, he arrived the next day, and with a warm smile said simply:

"How old is he?"

Bayreuth: The Turning Point

"Thirty-four."

"Good."

And they left.

We wrote to each other for a long time and even saw each other a few times. And life, cruel as it can sometimes be, continued.

I THREW MYSELF TOTALLY INTO MY WORK. AND ALSO into Lou's arms. Now he really began to run me through the mill as he taught me good German pronunciation. I spent several years in that "mill," enthusiastic, excited, and sometimes furious:

"Enough! I can't take any more! My brain is going to explode."

And though sometimes we had been working for hours, Lou would say calmly, "Just one more time, Tulipette." (The nickname, one of many, was because of my fan-shaped feet.)

I therefore arrived at Bayreuth the following June well able to sing *Parsifal* backwards. But if I thought that was going to be enough, I soon found out otherwise. I had simply fallen into the hands of new torturers.

Mornings I had at least two hours of music rehearsals with one of the two *répétiteurs* who spelled each other like the good cop and bad cop during an interrogation. Walter—a young pianist (later a conductor) full of enthusiasm—seemed to be the good cop. He would turn to Lou when I had sung a passage particularly well and say ecstatically, "Ist das nicht fantastisch?" (Isn't that fantastic?)

But to me: "One more time, please!"

Both *répétiteurs* polished each word, each inflection, each musical meaning, supervised by Lou, who noted down things to work on in the evenings.

Afternoons, I spent several hours in Wieland's hands for stage directions. Then with his wife, a former dancer, for movement. I was learning much about that. Until then, I had always sung on very brightly lighted stages and had made much use of my face to express my characters' feelings. At Bayreuth, and particularly in *Parsifal*, the stage was very dark, so facial expression was almost useless. To express oneself, aside from the voice, of course, one had to count on extremely rapid or immensely slow gestures.

Moreover, there was the famous "cheese" on the stage, an enormous, extremely slanted disc on which one moved about. Wieland explained how to use my feet, which because of the tilted floor could almost never be placed together. I had to learn all the different positions to use, according to what was being expressed. For example, when one leg was behind the other, if the right leg was in front bearing the body's weight, the left arm's value diminished, while the right arm could express emotion, whether aggressive or entreating.

I had to learn a whole set of rules also for walking, turning, facing away from the audience, moving my head, and so forth. The singers who have conquered this disc are easily recognizable by their acting style, which can sometimes seem out of place in another setting.

I began to be aware of the dramatic possibilities of my body, of my gestures. I attached myself to this Kundry, this personality so new to me, both mythic and familiar, savage and gentle, this liar and truth-teller, playactor or sufferer of a thousand deaths, siren from the far reaches of the earth, flower woman

Bayreuth: The Turning Point

(6 5)

from hell, convincing earth mother and humble serving maid, ultimately calm, happy, and in a state of grace. In sum, the entire range of human and superhuman emotions were wrapped into this incredibly complex character.

There was also the vocal side, terribly difficult because of its long tessitura, which went from the earthiest, most visceral low notes to the most extreme high ones, sometimes sweet and cajoling, sometimes aggressive, hysterical, almost bestial shrieks, the cries of a soul stripped bare.

The hardest things for me were the raucous low notes, those barely expressed groans—sounds that should hardly be sung. They gave a lot of trouble to the young sweet-singing performer I was at the time. And I think it finally came together only in the third year. That third year when the extraordinary Hans Knappertsbusch said to me during an intermission:

"Frau Crespin, you are the best Kundry I have ever conducted."

It was one of the most beautiful compliments of my life.

I left the theater around six o'clock every evening dead tired, physically and mentally. And that lasted five weeks, Sundays included! At last, four days before the premiere, a smiling Wieland told me:

"I don't want to see you for the next few days! You can go yodel in peace on your Oschenberg!"

That was the hill where Lou and I had rented an isolated house with a pool about the size of a pocket handkerchief, where we were as happy as the fish of our mutual birth sign.

THE PREMIERE WAS A GIGANTIC SUCCESS, AND I HAD wonderful reviews in newspapers all over the world. But paradoxically, during four consecutive years at Bayreuth, I didn't receive one stroke of applause onstage: according to Richard Wagner's wishes, no applause was allowed for *Parsifal*. It was very strange to leave the stage without a sound, while the audience filed out in the same silence. Of course the public made up for it at the stage door, waiting and applauding and offering flowers, and at the various restaurants in the town, particularly Die Eule (The Owl), whose owner—as wide as she was tall—would announce, "Ach! Die Kundry, Frau Kundry!"

(But the fourth year, when I sang Sieglinde in a new staging of *Die Walküre* by Wolfgang Wagner, Wieland's brother, I think I received four years' worth of applause in a single evening. It was extraordinary!)

One memory of the first *Parsifal* is both horrible and funny. Despite all my preparation, and knowing my role down to my fingertips, I mistook one phrase for another in the second act and blithely skipped four pages of the score. Stage fright? Nervousness? Who can say? All I know is that I saw Knappertsbusch (who conducted from a stool) suddenly leap to his feet, frantically waving his left arm, and I understood what had happened. I stopped for a moment and let the orchestra catch up, but I was really embarrassed, and especially ashamed in front of the great "Kna," as everyone called him. He never said anything, but at every subsequent performance during those four summers, a few bars before that fatal passage he would take an enormous white handkerchief out of his pocket and wave it at me. I never made the mistake again, of course. And as soon as the phrase was completed, he would use his left index finger to give me a mock salute, smiling kindly. The audience was unaware of this little comedy, because at Bayreuth the pit is completely covered and

Bayreuth: The Turning Point

the conductors aren't seen, which allows them to work in shirtsleeves, seated and relaxed—at least seemingly. (It's said that certain conductors refused to work there just because they couldn't be seen. But I won't mention any names!)

Kna became nicer to me each year, though he was known not to be particularly fond of the French—at least until the day when the mayor of Paris, Pierre Devraigne, decorated him with the Legion of Honor at the Bayreuth town hall before a small group of friends, including the local mayor, Hans Walter Wild (who took office in 1958, the year of my Bayreuth debut, and who was always friendly, gracious, and a pleasure to be with). That day I saw the great Kna, usually reserved to the point of aloofness, unable to say a word because he was crying. And the rest of us, too.

I remember another funny moment. Lou and I traveled to Bayreuth by car each summer, but he would send his adored motor scooter by train, and often when we went into town to shop or collect our mail we would ride down on the scooter. One day we were speeding around the lanes near the Festspiel-haus—my very Isadora Duncan–like scarf floating behind me as we rode—when whom did I see sitting on a bench, leaning on his cane, but Kna. As we approached he stood up, looking terrified, raised his hat theatrically, and yelled as we passed him, "Ach Gott! Meine Kundry, auf dem rolle!" (O God! My Kundry, on a motor scooter!)

The next day he stormed into my dressing room like a general, grabbed my earlobe, and made me promise I would never get onto that motorcycle the night before a performance, because it was dangerous for my voice. A promise made, but not kept.

BAYREUTH: LOVE! BAYREUTH: SUCCESS! BAYREUTH: TEN-
derness! Bayreuth: Folly! Bayreuth: Joy!

The summers I spent there were marvelous because I began
to develop in every way. My voice blossomed, and my acting as
well. I was happy with Lou and learning so much from him
about life, love, passion, jealousy (oh yes, I'm jealous, and it can
be very painful); we shared long nights, calm or violent, and
breakfasts when I made the only thing I knew how to, the
gigantic pots of hot chocolate that made me gain seventeen
pounds in three months. Obviously, we spent our free time
between bed and refrigerator! (Why is it so good to snack together after making love?) I regretted the extra pounds, but it
was truly the loveliest time of my life.

In those summers at Bayreuth I got to know so many *sym-
pathique* and celebrated people: the Countess of Paris, for example, whom I would see often at the salon of Alexandre, our
mutual hairdresser; the Begum Aga Khan, with whom I became
friendly; Gabrielle Dorziat, a film actress who adored Wagner
and came to see me every summer; the old Count Gravina, a
fount of knowledge who was the Bayreuth Festival's historian;
Maurice Béjart, another Marseille native, who choreographed
the Venusberg scene in *Tannhäuser;* Pierre Devraigne and his
wife, who became close friends.

For my final season at Bayreuth, Dominique Plessis, who had
a very popular weekly radio show, "A Season of Opera," asked
her listeners to send me a card wishing me good luck for my
first Bayreuth Sieglinde. And she was heeded: I received two
thousand three hundred fourteen cards and letters!

I can still see the face of the Festspielhaus concierge as he
bent over to hand me mailbag after mailbag full to bursting,

each time saying, "Herzlichen Glückwunsch, Frau Crespin" (Happy Birthday, Madame Crespin).

There was also Winifred, Wagner's daughter-in-law and the mother of Wieland and Wolfgang. She invited us many times to her little house and always greeted me or started her little notes to me with "Chère Lionne." It was another nickname Lou had given me, because of my mane of blond hair and my round face. (A journalist, hearing the "Lioness" nickname, asked if I often bit people. "Oh, only my husband," I said. And every year a headline in his newspaper would announce, "The Lioness Who Bites Her Husband Has Returned!")

And then there was Wahnfried, the beautiful residence of the Wagner family, where we attended so many dinners and postperformance parties. A beautiful house, probably too costly to maintain, which is now a museum.

When I attended the Bayreuth Festival in 1982, as much as I adored *The Ring* staged by Patrice Chéreau and conducted by Pierre Boulez with such intelligence, talent, modernism, and imagination, as much as I wept and exclaimed with pleasure at the wonderful singers I heard, as much as I enjoyed seeing Wolfgang, his hair all white; the mayor, his charming wife, and their children—now parents themselves—and the festival staff members who recognized me and treated me so royally, I couldn't bear to go back to certain places, like Wahnfried or the house where I had lived. Those are memories arranged in an interior album, souvenirs I no longer touch but that I cherish in my heart with a profound and joyous serenity.

My Two Mets

"THE MET" is the affectionate diminutive of the Metropolitan Opera, one of the world's most famous theaters. Every important singer dreams—rightly—of performing there, and I was invited regularly for twenty years. It's probably the place where I sang most often, although unlike many of my comrades, I never kept a precise list of my performances (which I now regret).

In fact, there are two Mets. The old one was a building on Broadway and Thirty-ninth Street, inconvenient and too small: during most performances, the sets for the next production could be seen leaning against the rear of the building, and if it rained, the stagehands would race around to move them indoors. The stage was enormous, but the wings, dressing rooms, and stage entrances were pathetically small. Of course there was the famous dressing room Number 10, used by the prima donna (or rather, prime donne). All the top sopranos and mezzos constantly fought over it, to the director's despair.

When the old Met was torn down, everything was sold at auction: tiny pieces of the great red curtain, the sets, the mirrors, the chairs, and so on. I wanted to buy the toilet seat from dressing room Number 10, in memory of all the backsides, small or large but in all cases celebrated, that had sat on it. Alas! I was sixth on the list and missed out on the famous wooden round, which I had intended to decorate with flowers in memory of Rosa Ponselle, Kirsten Flagstad, Lotte Lehmann, and others among my illustrious predecessors.

The hall was immense and warm, rounded in the Italian style, and all around the sections of orchestra seats there were six great velvet ropes that cordoned off the areas for the standees, who could really warm up a performance and influence its success or failure. (All singers adore the standees, who may not have much money but who have a true love of voice and of opera. They brave long waits outdoors in the cold and rain to get into the house or to applaud artists at the stage door after a performance.)

The new Met is situated at Lincoln Center, in the place of honor among the several theaters that make up the complex. It's an immense, modern building, a labyrinth that could keep a Minotaur utterly lost. It takes years to know it well, but it is extremely functional. The stage is gigantic, the wings very spacious, and the dressing rooms—all of them identical to prevent conflict—extremely comfortable, each with a sofa, a shower, and a piano. On each side of the stage, as well as behind and below it, there is a space the same size as the stage where sets for the next scenes can be set up. The whole new set can then slide into place while the existing set slides off to the rear, the side, or below. And the computerized lighting system is one of the most modern to be found.

The hall looks more like a palatial movie theater than an old-time opera house, with almost four thousand seats and a half-dozen enormous chandeliers that rise to the ceiling when the lights go down for the performance. Much disparaged at first by habitués of the old Met, the new theater was quickly adopted, and I have to admit that I love it. Perhaps with the standees dispersed to the rearmost and uppermost regions there's a little less warmth, but they still manage to make themselves heard.

I made my Met debut at the old house, in November 1962 in *Der Rosenkavalier,* conducted by Lorin Maazel. The role of the Marschallin was truly my lucky charm, and luck made it the role I sang in my first appearances at many of the great opera houses: Glyndebourne, Covent Garden in London, the Teatro Colón in Buenos Aires, the Berlin Staatsoper, the San Francisco Opera, and the Staatsoper in Vienna—the Marschallin's own city.

In truth, I had had offers two or three years earlier from the Met's general manager, Rudolf Bing: I had turned down *Faust* because I no longer wanted to sing it and *Le Nozze di Figaro* because it wasn't truly my repertoire. But the real truth was that the thought of such a long plane trip scared me half to death.

My first experience in the air, from Nancy in France to Tunisia, was nightmarish: a horrible storm, lightning striking an engine and leaving the cabin without lights, airsickness, a woman who had recently undergone surgery screaming, the passenger next to me crossing himself every five minutes, and I in the

My Two Mets

middle of all that, perspiring heavily in my first fur coat, which I had bought only recently and kept on because I didn't want to lose it if the plane went down. It was a long time before I was able to see a plane—even in a movie—without getting sick to my stomach!

But when the Teatro Colón invited me in 1961 for ten performances of *Parsifal* and *Rosenkavalier*, with three Marschallins in Mexico en route, I couldn't decently refuse, although I suffered a thousand deaths in the month before I left. And making me even more miserable was the fact that Lou couldn't leave with me, but would join me later in Argentina. I made the whole trip without eating or drinking a thing, as stiff as a broomstick in my seat. I won't even go into my flight from Mexico to Buenos Aires, in a propeller plane with its countless bumps and stops along the way. The only thing that got me through was the thought that if the plane did go down I would see Mannolini again.

So with my South American travels behind me, and despite some remaining fear, I accepted Rudolf Bing's offer of a long series of *Rosenkavalier* with great joy, particularly since Lotte Lehmann, one of the great Marschallins of the century, was staging the production. I was thrilled at the chance to meet her and work with her.

Lou had arranged time off for the three months, and we left hand in hand—or rather, my hand clinging to his.

As it turned out, my United States debut happened unofficially just before my Met appearances, when Renata Tebaldi fell ill and the Lyric Opera of Chicago asked me to replace her in *Tosca,* with Mr. Bing's exceptional permission. It was the first time I sang with the great baritone Tito Gobbi, one of the two best Scarpias (the other being Gabriel Bacquier). Terrified by the city and the opera house, I didn't budge from my hotel during the day, my limited high school English allowing little chance of conversation. (One evening at the hotel I asked loudly for "*Glace! Glace!* A lot, please!" meaning ice cubes, and the poor room-service waiter brought me twenty-four drinking glasses.) Luckily, everyone at the opera house spoke Italian.

The Lyric Opera's director, Carol Fox, was very kind and invited me back many times, for *Tannhäuser, Fidelio, Ariadne auf Naxos,* and another series of *Tosca.* And the critics were very complimentary, which gave me a little more confidence about my Met debut.

The notorious Claudia Cassidy—Santa Claudia, feared for her aggressive pen—even compared me to Sarah Bernhardt and gave me the nickname "French 75," after a celebrated cannon of the First World War and a high-combustion cocktail.

When I arrived in New York, I was welcomed by John Coveney, the director of artists and repertory at EMI, for whom I had just made two records, and Herbert Breslin, my publicity agent (later my manager). Because Herbert spoke French, I pestered him during my entire stay. He had decided against any publicity before the premiere, because he wanted to let the public discover me by itself. It was a splendid idea; the reviews were so unanimously rapturous that I had all the interviews one could want. But that's getting ahead of myself. For the moment, I settled into a tiny apartment in a hotel not far from the Met (although I still kept getting lost because I have no sense of direction).

The first day, Mr. Bing welcomed me and very kindly introduced me to everyone. We would have some stormy moments

My Two Mets

later, but that year he was wonderfully attentive. I remade the acquaintance of Anneliese Rothenberger, the Sophie of my two seasons at Glyndebourne, and Hertha Töpper, whom I had met in Berlin; all three of us were making our Met debuts. But I trembled at the thought of meeting Lotte Lehmann. And discovered a charming elderly woman, white-haired, blue-eyed, and kind and gentle as could be.

The rehearsals went on for three grueling weeks in which I went to the theater three times a day and ran to Lou every two minutes to have him translate Lotte's instructions.

She and I were fairly close in our ideas on how the role should be played, except for the end of the first act, when the Marschallin is seated alone in front of her mirror and gives way to a profound melancholy, realizing that old age is approaching and that her lover, Octavian, will soon leave her. It's a scene I felt in my very soul and could never perform without crying, and since I had performed it many times it was difficult to imagine changing the way I did it.

Lotte Lehmann wanted me to play it a bit differently, not letting myself sink into sadness but rather sitting rigidly erect at the end to make the audience understand that I was still the Marschallin, haughty and proud. But I thought and felt exactly the opposite. This woman has just dismissed everyone so she can be alone, she has looked into her mirror and found herself aging, she sings a monologue etched in sadness and resignation, she tells her young, eager lover that he will leave her soon for a younger and prettier woman—all calmly and resolutely and without histrionics. What does she want at that moment? Only to be alone, to wrap herself around her sorrow, perhaps to verify in her mirror . . . ah, yes, old age is there, lying in wait. Oh, she will surely have other lovers; it's not the absolute end of things. But it is the end of a love affair, which is always sad. So since she's finally alone, why not let her sink into momentary despondency? She will be the great and proud woman again in the third act, sublimely offering her lover to the young Sophie and leaving with the dignity befitting her rank. But at the end of the first act, no!

Moreover, you just have to listen to the exquisite violin solo that follows the Marschallin's last phrase to feel her enormous sadness.

I argued it with Lotte step by step, and at last she made a very fair decision: she agreed to let me do it my way at the dress rehearsal, on condition that I change it if she truly didn't like it. It goes without saying that I sang and acted with my very soul. And at the end, a teary Lotte Lehmann put her arms around me and whispered simply, "Ja, ja, ja." It was a moment of intense emotion.

And the night of the premiere arrived. My God, what stage fright, what terror! I knew the huge risk involved, because New York, the Met, could mean the beginning of a great career in the United States and elsewhere.

In the entire life of an artist, of a singer, there are only a few red-letter evenings—perhaps a dozen in an entire career—when you're in a state of grace, when you can make your voice do everything you want, when you're inside and outside yourself at one time. That night in November 1962 was one of mine. The audience was appreciative of everyone, but I must say that for me, the unknown, the debutante, there was a frenzy of applause.

I cried like a fool, and Lou did too. But my emotions really overflowed when Mr. Bing asked Lehmann to take a solo bow, and she answered:

"I will take a bow only if Crespin is with me, because she is the new Marschallin of my heart."

We walked out alone before the great dark red curtain, I in my panniered costume and white wig, Lotte in an evening dress—I can see her as if it were yesterday—and in an instant the audience was on its feet, everyone yelling, clapping, stomping for Lottchen, Lottie, their beloved Marschallin, and for Crespin, the new arrival, adopted on the spot. I became a veritable fountain and Lotte cried too, for me, for her audience, for *our* audience, for her bygone Marschallin. What emotions she must have lived at that moment, which I understand even better now.

As we stood there, all I could do was squeeze her hand and say, "Je vous aime! Je vous aime!"

And she answered in German, "Ich auch!" (Me too!)

I don't know how many times we left the stage and had to go back on.

Mr. Bing was in heaven; Michel Glotz—the real instigator of my Met debut, who had come from Paris for the occasion—laughed like a madman; Ronald Wilford, my American impresario at the time, kept brushing imaginary specks from his eyes (at later performances he let himself go, but scolded me for putting him in such a state).

I don't really remember how the evening ended. There was a supper at Ronald's house with a crowd of people surrounding me and talking in English at high speed. All I could say was, "Thank you! Thank you!"

But from the middle of this sea of people I saw a bald head emerge, absolutely round, with the cutest little pug nose one could imagine, a heart-shaped mouth, and a pair of twinkly eyes full of mischief and emotion, all of this topping a generous body six feet tall, which threw itself at my feet and shouted in French:

"I knew it! I knew it! Ever since I heard your first Marschallin in French at the Paris Opéra I knew you would come here and that it would be a success!"

It was Terence A. McEwen, at the time an executive of the Decca-London record company and since that day one of my closest friends. Terry! I could devote an entire book to telling about his intelligence, his enormous knowledge of music and voice, his human qualities, his wit, his laughter, his transmittable passion for food, fun, dancing, folly. What memorable evenings we spent together, what discussions, what enthusiasms. Terry, more of a prima donna than all of us, with his black limousine and his faithful chauffeur, Tony, a tall, burly Italian with a gap-toothed but irresistible smile, who could carry even the heaviest of us in his muscular arms from the car to the restaurant door if there was too much snow on the ground. Terry, who ruined I don't know how many of my evening slippers by drinking champagne from them after a premiere. I love him so much, I could talk about him for hours.

I returned to my hotel that night drunk from champagne, from success, from fatigue—and of course I couldn't sleep. Lou and I talked until six o'clock in the morning, when the telephone rang. It was Michel.

"If you're sleeping, too bad. Just listen to this."

They had all stayed up to get the newspapers and were as excited as children on Christmas morning. Ronald, Herbert,

My Two Mets

Michel, and Terry took turns reading the reviews to me, each better than the last, and it was a moment of collective ecstasy by telephone.

Ronald yelled, "How much do you have in the bank in France?"

"I don't know!"

"Well, I guarantee that in two years, it will have quadrupled!"

Herbert, always practical:

"Tomorrow at eleven o'clock for two interviews, OK?"

"No, no, it's too early. After six in the evening, I beg you!"

Terry, businesslike:

"I have a marvelous idea for a recording. *Shéhérazade* and *Nuits d'Eté*. When can we do it?"

I begged them to let me get some sleep, and I needed two full days to recover from the tumult. But what a beautiful memory.

MY RECOLLECTIONS OF THAT FIRST STAY IN NEW YORK are a bit muddled. Although I know it better now and adore it, the enormous city—which can make you feel so welcome or lonelier than a lost dog—scared me terribly. I was too afraid to go out alone, afraid of not understanding when people spoke to me, so I spent most of my time burrowed in at the hotel, learning English little by little from television. Lou, who managed better because of his German, spent his time at bookstores, museums, and delicatessens, bringing me all the things that he found tasty. Aïe! My figure! But I was happy in my little corner because I had Lou, *Der Rosenkavalier*, and a lot of books. And it wasn't very long until I was involved in learning a new role.

Mr. Bing called me to his office one day and asked if I had ever sung Senta in *Der Fliegende Holländer*. I hadn't! He therefore proposed a single performance of the opera, in January, but with neither an orchestra rehearsal nor a dress rehearsal on stage, because the series had already begun. Of course a role coach and a stage director would be available, for as much time as I wanted. I had a month to prepare. I asked for a week to think it over while I worked with the coach, Jan Behr, whose advice I trusted. If he told me I could do it, I would take the plunge. And five days later, I said yes. But what work! It was a true tour de force to learn the role musically and scenically, not to mention the German words, which had Lou putting me through the torture mill again, day and night. But I got through it and had a great success—although no reviews, unfortunately, because all the New York newspapers were on strike.

One very moving memory of that *Holländer.* I went to the Met one evening to see the production, with Senta sung by Leonie Rysanek, a wonderful artist whom I admire enormously. As Lou and I went down the aisle to our seats, I heard people start to clap their hands, and I looked in all directions to see which celebrity was being applauded. An elderly man near me stood up and said with a big smile:

"Madame, it's for you!"

I blushed, very moved, and had to turn left and right to wave in acknowledgment, something I was new at, that kind of honor being rare in Europe. (I learned quickly.)

That, too, is the Met.

I FINISHED MY FIRST SEASON AND WENT HOME TO France with a new offer for the following year: a series of *Lohengrin,* including the first performance and the broadcast. Those two things are very important. Singing the premiere

My Two Mets

guarantees you all the rehearsals and the dress rehearsal, which means you're very well prepared. The broadcast is the famous Saturday afternoon performance transmitted live by radio throughout the United States and Canada, giving you enormous exposure in just a few hours. Everyone fights to sing the broadcast matinee.

So the offer was very tempting. But I hesitated, without any valid reason since I had sung the role many times. My instinct told me that after my huge success with the Marschallin, there was little I could add with Elsa: interesting, certainly, but a little pallid, a role that wouldn't allow me to use much in the way of dramatic resources. Deep down, what I really wanted to sing— the complete opposite of Strauss's subtle, vocally and dramatically refined Marschallin—was Puccini's very flesh-and-blood Tosca. But *Tosca* wasn't on the following year's schedule. Bing insisted, Wilford and Glotz said I couldn't refuse, Breslin was discreet, and Lou said nothing. Swayable Pisces that I am, I let myself be persuaded. And I was wrong. Oh, it wasn't a catastrophe, far from it. But the reviews were mixed, and it was the first time (not the last) that I fought with Ronald, accusing him of giving me bad advice. Poor Ronald. I called him one evening at a restaurant where he was in the middle of an important dinner party, and yelled, cried, and hiccuped over the phone until he became so exasperated (he knew I was right) that he yelled "Merde!" and hung up.

Two hours later he was at my hotel, drunk as a lord and on his knees, asking my pardon. The three of us drank a bottle of champagne and consoled one another as best we could.

The next year the Met offered me a single series of *Der Rosen-kavalier* but nothing else, and again I hesitated, because I didn't want to repeat it, and this time *Tosca* was in the repertoire. Ronald agreed that I should refuse, and I did. And it was thanks to my refusal that Elisabeth Schwarzkopf made her tardy debut at the Met. For obscure political reasons, Mr. Bing had never wanted to invite her—what nonsense to mix politics with art—and in his Machiavellian way he arranged for her to spend the entire first act in the arms of Lisa Della Casa (in the role of Octavian), when he knew full well that the two women didn't speak to each other. He must have rubbed his hands in glee at that and at the idea of setting me against Elisabeth, since we were generally acknowledged to be the two leading Marschallins. (We each recorded the role: Schwarzkopf with Karajan, I with Solti.)

I don't know what happened with the first part of his machinations, but the second was a complete failure, for I've always been very friendly with Madame Schwarzkopf. I admire her, applauded her often, and I think there is mutual respect between us.

She even came to hear me in *Rosenkavalier* in my first Met season. Before the third act that evening, Lou came to my dressing room all excited to tell me that Elisabeth was in the audience. Which made me so nervous that I completely messed up the dreaded pianissimo high B-flat at the beginning of the big trio, which was usually easy for me. (In fact, Lotte Lehmann was kind enough to write that mine was one of the most beautiful she had ever heard.)

But I missed it, and I was furious. Elisabeth came to my dressing room after the performance and very sweetly complimented me, and when I lamented my "accident" she pointed out that it could happen to anyone.

My Two Mets

The following summer I received a telegram from Michel Glotz in Salzburg.

"Rest easy. She missed it too!"

I DIDN'T THEREFORE APPEAR AT THE MET IN THE FALL AND winter of 1964, but I sang *Ariadne auf Naxos* and *Tosca* in Chicago, and gave my first recital in New York, at Hunter College. And Mr. Bing, despite his anger at my *Rosenkavalier* refusal, wanted to mend fences. A great event was to take place in the spring of 1965: Maria Callas's return to the Met, in *Tosca*. There were to be sixteen performances of the opera, starting in the fall, and since Maria would sing only two, in March, Mr. Bing was assailed by every soprano capable of singing the role. Finally he decided to divide the pie several ways, giving performances to Renata Tebaldi, Leonie Rysanek, Dorothy Kirsten, Gabriella Tucci, and "Crespinette." But there was still the scheduled broadcast in April plaguing him, because Callas would be gone by then. To keep the peace, Bing decided that the matinee should go to the newest arrival: that is, me! So I returned to the Met in the role I wanted and sang the first of my eventual three *Tosca* broadcasts.

And believe me, the series was quite a free-for-all, with everyone working hard to sing at her best. The overworked tenors who sang most of the performances—Flaviano Labò, Richard Tucker, and Franco Corelli—were sorely tested among all those sweet-singing, excited, fiery Toscas. As for the Scarpias (mine were George London, Cornell MacNeil, and Robert Merrill), they died repeatedly from a variety of wild stabbings.

One of which threw me into a panic. In the second of my two performances, I realized in that last scene of the second act that the fateful knife wasn't on the table, and I wound up killing my pal Bacquier with a well-aimed fork!

That scene proved a much bigger problem during another performance. It was at the Opéra-Comique and Albert Lance was singing Mario for the first time, so all the critics were in the audience. I picked up the knife as usual and hid it behind my back as Scarpia (René Bianco) approached, and at the moment when Tosca should stab him, all my tugging wouldn't free the knife from the seam of my costume where it was caught.

When Bianco whispered desperately, "Stab me! Go on! It's going to be too late!" all I could do was draw myself up and yell:

"Muori, dannato! Muori! Muori!" as I struck Scarpia—with such a murderous glare that he fell backward and died.

The next day one critic wrote:

"It's the first time I ever saw a Scarpia die of fright!"

I SANG MANY TIMES AT THE MET, OLD AND NEW, UNDER the reign of Sir Rudolf: *Tosca, Un Ballo in Maschera*, Sieglinde in *Die Walküre*.

Mr. Bing, Viennese by birth, had lived in England for a long time and had become more British than the British, with an umbrella and black bowler hat his permanent accessories. He was very tall, very thin, seemingly affable and sweet but with a will of iron and the memory of an elephant, especially when someone said no to him. And I was very stubborn, turning down his proposals of *Don Carlo, La Forza del Destino*, and *Macbeth* (one of his favorite productions).

He was known for his wonderful sense of humor, which I once saw at first hand. Before I sang my first *Lohengrin* I was

My Two Mets

interviewed for an article in a French newspaper, and the reporter asked what I thought of Rudolf Bing.

"Oh, he's my favorite dictator," I said.

During the rehearsals we had a discussion about my first-act costume. I wanted to wear my own, which was brand new; he wanted me to wear the old one from the production. No matter how many reasons I gave, he answered, "I'm not a dictator, but . . ."

I finally realized he had read the article when he sent me two dozen roses the day of the premiere and his permission to wear my own costume, with a card signed:

"With all good wishes (and no hard feelings) from your 'favorite dictator.' "

His book *Five Thousand Nights at the Opera* proved, though, that he could hold a grudge, because he mentioned the name of every singer who had ever appeared under his management, down to the least significant, except mine!

But no hard feelings, Sir Rudolf!

THE OLD MET CLOSED WITH AN EXTRAORDINARY GALA, with all the great former and current singers taking part. It was a fabulous, very moving event. In the first part, all the singers who had retired were seated on the stage while others took turns singing arias. The second part was devoted to famous duets (I sang the one from *La Gioconda*, with Biserka Cvejic), and the third part was trios, quartets, quintets, and choruses. For the third part, I was seated in the hall, in a box beside a renowned soprano. And during the superb trio from *Der Rosenkavalier* she leaned over to ask what it was. When I told her, saying that it was one of my operas, she gave me a commiserating smile and said:

"You sing that? Oh, *poverina.*"

The new house opened its doors in September 1966 with Samuel Barber's *Antony and Cleopatra,* with an all-American cast. (Noblesse oblige!) I sang there for several years: a series of *Fliegende Holländer* (this time with rehearsals, premiere, and broadcast), *Les Contes d'Hoffmann* (my bad-luck opera); another series of *Rosenkavalier* conducted by Karl Böhm, with whom I did not get along at all, and *Werther* with Franco Corelli and later with Alfredo Kraus. I also went on my first Met tour in 1969, singing the Marschallin when the Met took four or five operas, soloists, the full orchestra and chorus, sets, costumes, dressers, makeup people, technicians, stagehands, coaches, and conductors around the country in two huge jets, with a lot of attendant television, radio and press coverage.

But in 1968 began the major crisis of my life, both personal and professional. A major upheaval that eventually kept me far from the Met—and many other things—for two and a half years, until the autumn of 1975 when I returned with a new role, Carmen, another milestone in my career.

My Two Mets

Crisis

BENEATH my brisk exterior, I am slower than slow. Slow in my decisions, in my opinions, in my inner rhythm. I was supposed to be born in early February, but didn't leave my hiding place until the twenty-third of the month, kicking in all directions and not very happy, it seems. It's known that every birth is profoundly traumatic, a physical suffering in which we're attacked by cold, light, noises, slaps, by the air that suddenly fills our lungs. It seems that I gave a great cry of rage as I filled mine and continued yowling for an entire day. And as I was—oh, the irony!—long and thin as a flower stem, the midwife said to my mother:

"She won't be enormous. But she can certainly make herself heard."

I was slow during my childhood, my schooling. My parents said my head was always in the clouds. I know now that I awakened from my somnolence only when I started to sing. And this slowness that seemed my second nature, but which was really my first, kept me from realizing that the crisis that erupted in 1968 had been simmering since 1964.

It has been said that a love relationship shatters at the end of three, seven, or eleven years. True or not, I began to detach myself from Lou without realizing it in our seventh year together and left him completely in the eleventh. And it took all that time to understand that I was no longer happy, no longer in love. It was hard to acknowledge. It had all begun so well. Under the sign of the color red. Red for victory, red for love, red for the bright fur-lined coat I treated myself to that year, which I wore the first time Lou took me out, to the theater to see Jean Vilar in *Henry IV.* I was still under the spell of the play as we walked back to my street afterward. I can see myself puffing up the front of the coat and saying to Lou, "Oh, I would love to be pregnant."

Which I was, without knowing it.

The rejection of that baby, which we wanted so much, eroded our relationship, but surely wasn't the only reason for our failure.

Despite my thirty years, I was like a young girl, without much experience, a little too taken with purity, make-believe, dreams of eternal love. And I thought I had found it all. I believed it so strongly that I often said, "If Lou leaves me, I'll kill myself!"

And I was the one who left.

Our eleven years of joint existence can be summed up in four words: Love, Tenderness, Folly, Suffering.

The first years were blue sky without clouds, or almost. I discovered everything with eagerness, passion, astonishment, with delicious apprehension, sometimes with shocked amaze-

Crisis

(8 9)

ment. This "everything" seemed round as an apple, red as a tomato, and as self-contained as an egg.

The four summers at Bayreuth and the next four on the island of Giens off France's southern coast were happy and relatively calm, Lou's fertile imagination mitigating all his longings, all his specters.

Lou—subtle, clever with words (too many words), full of fascinating secrets—had experienced a lot of living before we met. Everything he *might* have done, he *had* done, always with his taste for going too far, just to see. Above all, he had gone through the war, had been deported as a young Alsatian and forced to wear a German uniform, had known hunger in a concentration camp and such thirst that he resorted to drinking water from a toilet; had seen the Liberation, grandiose and dangerous. And he emerged with a fierce hunger for everything, like a ravenous animal, like a corrida bull who leaps from the shade into the sun-drenched arena.

I was dazzled by so much life, so many lives. Innocent but terribly curious, I made him talk, talk about everything and everybody, about everything he had been or done "before me." And then I was shattered by jealousy and pain, wanting to *know* instead of understanding "the imperious feminine instinct of giving everything, of listening and saying nothing." All those years of singing Elsa, whose curiosity ruins her marriage and kills her, obviously had taught me nothing.

There was the tender Lou, who every morning before leaving for the school where he taught would deposit little notes everywhere—I must have thousands—or who, when his Tulipette was far away, would write beautiful letters of love or eroticism; the calm, Sunday Lou who would ask if I wanted to go to a restaurant, a movie, a play, and to whom I invariably replied: "No. Let's talk."

That Lou talked endlessly to his avid Lioness: of Hölderlin, whom he had translated; Kleist, whose plays he had adapted. He explained the paintings of Bosch and Klimt, jazz—Count Basie, Oscar Peterson, Dizzy Gillespie, Erroll Garner, Satchmo—and patiently went over and over my German librettos with me.

There was also the Lou of cruel games, sadistic words, fiendish suggestions that sometimes tempted me and often tortured me, crucifying my endless need for purity, and his; the Lou with his deeply feminine imagination fighting against his cruel and violent masculine fantasies; the Lou who, like Fellini, had a marvelous obsession with women and could make them beautiful or debase them; the Lou who marched toward death consciously, with an intelligence too encumbering, too lucid, sometimes negative, already self-destructive; the Lou who returned from war alive but who, like Don Giovanni, had started to kill himself in a thousand ways, who because a tyrannical sexual fantasy can end only in extremism, tried, tries, and will always try to draw the woman in his life along with him in his slow, slow descent.

And then there was the Lou suffering in silence from his complexes: complexes of inferiority, of shyness, of a man with a wife who is better known, who earns more money than he does; the complex of always seeming to be "Mr. Crespin."

And that Lou I didn't know how to understand or help, being so preoccupied with myself, my career, a career that practically forces you into selfishness. Shut up in my ivory tower, I saw nothing coming, I had no inkling of the inevitable.

Crisis

(9 1)

Of that Lou I ask forgiveness, from the bottom of my heart.

The only thing I began to realize was that I no longer could or wanted to put up with this sexuality, this frantic eroticism that tortured me beyond endurance, that made me call for mercy. Oh, a gentler love followed, a pure love that rocked me to infinity and made me cry with bliss. And I couldn't understand why I had to submit to that torturous rite to get there.

Malraux wrote, "Eroticism is humiliation of oneself or of the other, perhaps of both."

And Michelet, "To submit, one must be free; to give oneself, one must be oneself."

And I was not sufficiently myself for that. It took many years of analysis to know who and what I really was, and what I wanted or didn't.

What I truly wanted, and Lou also, was a child. I remember touching the belly of every pregnant woman I met, hoping the luck would be catching.

I finally went to see my gynecologist, who examined me and found nothing abnormal (and there was nothing wrong with Lou, who already had a son from his first marriage), but who tried to dissuade me because of my career and my age—thirty-six. Then, seeing my disappointment, he said:

"All right. Make me a test-tube baby, you two, if you want it that much. But this year or never."

My mind was made up; madly happy, I went home and told Lou. But it would mean canceling our trip to Buenos Aires, where I was to sing *Les Troyens* and he was to gratify a whim by staging it. He had already tested the waters with a few plays he had translated: Büchner's *Wozzek,* Kleist's *Little Catherine of Heilbronn,* and others. He was very enthusiastic about *Les Troy-*

ens and I a little hesitant, knowing how difficult it is to control an opera and not really liking this package arrangement. (He actually didn't do badly and was invited back to do *Norma*.)

My enthusiasm flattened like a failed soufflé before Lou's evasiveness. He didn't want to cancel the trip, saying we'd think about a baby for the following year, etcetera.

I can see myself standing at the foot of the bed where he was stretched out, staring at his blue eyes, which kept evading mine, and I know that was the moment when I realized, deep down, that we would never have a child and that we would eventually break up.

We went to Buenos Aires. And that was when I met Victor-José, the man who would later help me leave my husband. But I didn't really notice him that year, being still wrapped up in Lou.

I became more and more involved with my career, which had become international and tyrannical. I was singing everywhere, traveling a lot, learning new roles and mélodies, working enormously to fulfill all my offers. In 1967 I had the honor of taking part in the first Easter Festival in Salzburg, singing the role of Brünnhilde in *Die Walküre* for the first time (and recording it), under Herbert von Karajan's direction.

That autumn I went to New York in late October because the Met was going to present the Salzburg production of *Walküre*, and I was also going to sing a recital at Hunter College. Two days before the recital, I was invited to Carnegie Hall to hear Elena Suliotis make her debut in a concert version of *Norma*. It was a "hot" evening, because two other great Normas were present: Zinka Milanov and Maria Callas. The audience

Crisis

applauded the arrival of every artist, myself included, though I had nothing to do with *Norma*. And at intermission, in the bar, I literally jumped when someone yelled: "Rrrrégine! Rrrrégine! Lou! How are you?" For a moment I thought I was in Buenos Aires, for there was Victor-José, newly bearded. Naturally I invited him to my recital, and accepted his invitation to dinner on the night after it, lonesome already because Lou was leaving that day and wouldn't be back until my *Walküre*.

I had a lot of spare time—I already knew the production, and Birgit Nilsson, who was going to sing Brünnhilde for the premiere, had all the rehearsals—and I spent a lot of it going out with Victor-José, as friends.

He was thirty-five, tall, slender, very handsome, of superior intelligence, in love with art, music, theater. He lived on income from investments his father had left him, and he went out every night. Thanks to his help, because in addition to French, German, Italian, and his native Spanish, he spoke English fluently, I finally dared go to the theater, to concerts, to musical comedies, which I still love. We would have supper afterward and talk for hours about art, opera (which he adored and knew better than I did), about his life, about mine.

I invited him to the gala premiere of *Die Walküre*, a glittery affair for which I wore a beautiful white silk brocade ensemble trimmed in mink. When he called for me his eyes were so full of admiration, which already resembled another sentiment, that it touched my heart. In the theater, sensing my discomfort at seeing Nilsson in my role onstage, he took my hand and kept it in his for the rest of the evening. At Sardi's, where we went later, we talked of this and that, but of nothing special.

I hadn't paid attention to another man in all the time Lou

and I had been together, so my reaction surprised and bothered me. I didn't understand until much later that Victor-José represented the pretext I'd been looking for. After all, what did I need to be able to leave Lou, to find the courage to do it? To fall in love with someone else! And that's what I did, or at least what I believed, because in fact I didn't really love Victor-José until a year later, when I knew him better.

But our flirtation very quickly became something deeper. He confessed that he had been in love with me without fully realizing it since the first time he had seen me in Buenos Aires, an evening when I had had dinner with him and a mutual friend, Carlos Pemberton. I remembered the evening well, going back to my hotel in the car and sensing a weighty presence behind me that made me a little uncomfortable.

In brief, the pieces were in place on the chessboard, but I didn't know how the game would be played out.

When Lou got back to New York his incredible instinct told him something had happened, but he said nothing. We spent the holidays in France, then went back to New York for my *Walküre* performance as Brünnhilde in February and to Salzburg again in April.

In June we were in Venice, where I was singing a cycle of mélodies, *Par le Feu*, that Marius Constant had written for me, set to poems by Lou. We stayed for a few days after the concert to see a bit of the city, and one evening on our way back to the hotel with friends, I saw Lou go a bit far with a young woman in another car, undoubtedly hoping to have me join their little party later on. Once in our room we had another long argument, which became the last straw.

The next morning I was deadly calm. Lou went out to visit

Crisis

museums and we arranged to meet at Harry's Bar. He waited for hours, because I had left for New York. I did phone before boarding my plane, and he—understanding that this time it was serious—made all sorts of promises, swore to leave me in peace if I would just come back. But I had already learned not to believe drunken promises, and I left, without saying where I was going.

I spent a weekend with Victor-José at Terry McEwen's house on Fire Island and flew to London to take refuge with my friends Vera and Edna Lindenberg before confronting Lou.

I knew from Catherine, my housekeeper at the time, that he was in the house, unwashed, drinking from morning to night despite his loathing of alcohol. His misery tortured me. I tried to talk with him, to clarify things, but he wouldn't answer, sometimes crying silently, sometimes yelling and attacking me.

In the most dramatic situations, there is often a ridiculous episode. One day Lou drunkenly cornered me in the bathroom and tried to slap me. I yelled to Catherine, who came running, calmly turned on the cold water in the shower, and aimed it straight at Lou's face. The shock sobered him a little and he fell to his knees, asking me to forgive him and saying to Catherine, "Merci, Maman."

It was grotesque and pitiful, as was the rest of the summer, which we spent at Saint-Tropez in the villa I had rented for the second time from Herbert von Karajan.

I was uneasy, restless, suffering from being without Victor-José, whom I phoned in New York whenever Lou went off—seemingly carefree, maybe even happy—on the maestro's motor scooter.

I listened nonstop to Ray Charles singing:

The sun died,
The sun died with my love
When you left me blue.
The summer died too.

Or I would go barefooted across the lawn of thick, cool Moroccan grass, to stand at the white fence and look at the sea, lost in my thoughts.

"You don't love him anymore. Why?"

"Are you going to leave him? But how? How?"

It seemed insoluble, and I was afraid, superstitiously afraid.

A song by Jacques Brel colored the summer:

Nous étions deux amis et Fanette l'aimait.
La plage est déserte et pleure en juillet.

("We were two friends and Fanette loved him. The beach is deserted and weeps in July.")

Saint-Trop madness, Saint-Trop parties. All too quickly accepted to avoid being alone with Lou, to numb myself with alcohol, cigarettes—new for me, which reminded me of Victor-José and his ever-present Winston longs—and a false sense of freedom.

I remember going home before dawn one morning after one of our many harrowing carousals, a costume party at Eddie Barclay's with Régine—the other one, as we each say—and a whole gang. Pale, windless dawn, the sea calm, the morning dampness

Crisis

(97)

waking the odor of tomatoes, basil, thyme in the kitchen garden. People I didn't know at all were already waiting for us; it seems I had invited them.

The odor of fresh coffee Lou made is still in my mind, too, and of butter melting on hot toast. At one end of the garden, a high voice called out that she didn't like coffee and preferred wine. Young women were scattered about like colorful paper flowers, laughing, falling as they scurried excitedly around the grass carpet. The men began to chat quietly, their hands wrapped around the warm coffee cups. And Lou, happy and excited in the middle of it all, kept giving me conspiratorial winks as he tried to lure the women to the bedrooms.

As I watched him, completely detached from the scene, it was as if a sudden chill wind had come between us, breaking a mirror that foretold seven years of bad luck.

I locked myself in my bedroom, tearless but knowing that everything was said, everything finished.

And slow as always, I waited until the following June.

I spent the 1968–69 season going from San Francisco to the Met, on a concert tour in the United States, back to the Met for Sieglinde, to Los Angeles for *Les Troyens,* and on the Met tour in April and May.

In June I finally broke with Lou and left for Saint-Tropez, where Victor-José joined me. And I discovered that I had left one hell for another even more awful one.

Since Victor-José and I had started seeing each other in New York we had often slept together, but without any real sexual contact. I stupidly thought he felt conscience-stricken about Lou, who was his friend too. Now that I was truly separated, I couldn't understand why he shied away from me, why he took refuge every evening in an entire bottle of whiskey. Ever since meeting him I had seen him drink like a fish and smoke four or five packs of cigarettes a day, and if I had been a little more perceptive, a little less self-absorbed, I would have asked myself why this young man full of human and intellectual qualities was so suicidal. I would have tried to understand the reason for his two suicide attempts, the reason he had abandoned his medical studies in the final year, the reason for his interrupted psycho-analysis. But benevolence wasn't one of my traits at the time.

I didn't understand. I didn't want to understand. And then, I was punishing myself for having left Lou. I had left an encum-bering sexuality to fall into a nonexistent one. And it was tor-ture.

We were together for most of that year and the next. Needless to say, life was chaotic. I was no longer practicing, hardly sleep-ing, singing on willpower alone. My voice and my usually solid health began to be seriously affected.

I needed help, advice, but how could I confide this heavy secret that wasn't mine to reveal?

We left in early September 1970 for San Francisco, where I was going to open the season with *Tosca*. I arrived ill prepared, having had neither the time nor the courage to work since the summer, and with a bad case of the flu. Badly advised by a laryngologist whom the opera's director, Kurt Herbert Adler, had recommended because he didn't want his season opening to be ruined, I sang anyway, which caused a hemorrhage on one of my vocal cords. Another doctor I saw the next day told me he didn't even want to know the name of the charlatan who had allowed me to sing in that condition, and forbade me not only to sing but to speak at all for two weeks. I canceled my

Crisis

other performances, infuriating Adler, and went back to New York, where I was supposed to sing *Tosca* in October and *Parsifal* in late November and December. I shut myself up in the apartment that a friend, Sheila Nadler, had kindly lent me after seeing my pitiful condition. Zinka Milanov—with whom I had often studied and who was touchingly kind to me—lived in the same building, and after my two weeks of silence I began to work a little with her. But the resilience was gone. My body refused all my efforts, my voice did too, and I left my lessons with terrible headaches.

I paced the apartment alone, Victor-José having stayed in San Francisco to leave me in peace, too intelligent and sensitive not to understand, suffering terribly from our mutual pain but avoiding the explanations that I sought, that I demanded.

Even today, I ask myself how I tolerated all that without running away. Some would call it stupid, but I was truly in love, and perhaps unconsciously I wanted to lose myself at the time.

The *Tosca* rehearsals began and I struggled along until the dress rehearsal, which I left smack in the middle on the pretext that the conductor had made a nasty comment, this odious Francesco Molinari-Pradelli, who had already fought with me and many of my colleagues as well. Mr. Bing came to my dressing room and I cried as I told him that I wanted to cancel. He took me by the arm, gave me a long, friendly look, and said:

"Is this really your decision? All right. But Madame Crespin, remember that before being a singer you are a human being. Take care of yourself. And come back in a month for *Parsifal*."

I must have looked really sick.

I stayed shut up in the apartment for several days, telling

myself I had gone crazy, that I would never sing again, thinking that maybe I should end it all. Yes, me—solid, earthy, courageous—I looked at the street one day from my fourteenth floor, fascinated, dangerously attracted, and I was afraid. That day I phoned Milanov to talk. She comforted me as well as she could, thinking like everyone else that it was only my separation from Lou that had put me in such a state. She suggested that I phone Christa Ludwig, who had gone through a bad time after her separation from Walter Berry and who had been helped by a doctor. I called Christa, who gave me the number of a Dr. Lilly Engler. I don't know how much the analyst grasped, but three hours later I was in her office. (She told me later that my voice had been so shaky, she had canceled another appointment to see me.)

And at last, I could talk! She saw me every day, understanding the problem before I did but paying almost no attention, her only goal being to get me to sing my *Parsifal* performances. She guessed that if I didn't sing right away, I probably would never sing again. And we succeeded! And indeed I mean "we," because she didn't leave me for a second, even preventing Victor-José from seeing me at the intermissions because she realized how fragile I was. During all the performances I trembled, perspired, and had terrible headaches, unbearable pains in my arms and hands, and sudden bouts of dizziness.

Several days later, Lilly told me that I was truly in danger, that I should find an analyst in Paris with whom I could speak French and above all talk, talk, talk.

I got back to Paris in mid-December, found a psychotherapist through a friend of Lou's, and began a course of treatment.

Victor-José, meanwhile, went home to Buenos Aires after fi-

Crisis

nally agreeing to go back into analysis. And his doctor, wanting to save two people he thought could form a couple, asked to meet me, to see me with Victor-José.

It was tempting, but I hesitated, because the analyst in New York said that if I went it would be a form of suicide.

Well, I went, and I'm not dead! But what difficulty, after having begun in English, to continue in Spanish! I stayed for a month, spending the worst Christmas holidays of my life. We went three times a week to "talk," but in fact I didn't understand very well and wasn't enlightened enough to get anything out of it. Before I left, Dr. Roblès told me I could write to him, asking all the questions I wanted to, and that he would answer frankly.

At the airport, Victor-José and I stared at each other intensely for a long time. Then I said, "Maybe . . ."

"Yes, maybe . . ."

I went regularly to Patrick Sauvage, my analyst in Paris, little by little finding my true self, my complexes, my problems stemming from childhood, from my mother, the conflict between Crespin and Régine. Crespin who devoured everything, taking all the space from and shattering poor Régine who wanted to live also, freely and without guilt. It took months for the two to be able to live together in harmony, but *Gott sei Dank,* they got there.

Meanwhile, with Patrick's help, I had written to Dr. Roblès, asking three simple questions and leaning strongly toward the first:

"Impotence?"

"Another woman in his life?"

"Homosexuality?"

One morning in June 1971, as I was getting ready to leave for Vienna to finish a recording, Patrick called to say he had received an answer from Buenos Aires and that we would talk about it when I got back. But I insisted, and he read Dr. Roblès's succinct answers to my questions:

"Absolutely not."

"Never."

"Very rarely and with horror."

"Well, at least we know now," I told Patrick briskly. Then I left for the airport, without any apparent reaction.

Oh, Crespin, the snail. It was only the next day that I began to throw up day and night, to empty myself literally of everything I thought I had digested well. Two days later, leaving a vague written excuse for "the Decca boys," I went home, truly sick. I don't know how they managed to piece together the aria from *La Damnation de Faust*, which I had left half done and in bad shape. I can't listen to it without shame and remorse. Bravo, Christopher Raeburn, for your engineering miracle.

I got my bearings back slowly, but it was hard. I spent my vacation alone for the first time, in a house at the sea that I rented from a friend, Michèle Venture; I can see myself sitting alone on the terrace and crying. It's bad enough to cry alone at night; in bright sunlight, it's horrible. Michèle consoled me as much as she could, with her enthusiasm and infectious laugh. I'll never forget the friendship she gave me at a time when I needed it so badly.

I grew stronger, continued my analysis, sang better, and even went to Buenos Aires to give some recitals. But Victor-José was in Caracas, his native city, and I didn't see him. I wrote to him from time to time—"the most beautiful letters in the world,"

Crisis

he said exaggeratedly—but he didn't like to write, or at least not often. It's odd that apart from Lou, none of my men were facile with a pen.

In the fall of 1971 I reopened the Paris Opéra, which had undergone repairs for eight months, as Sieglinde in a *Walküre* originally staged by Wieland Wagner. I can truly say that those twelve performances were triumphal. I was happy again to sing, to live, to buy new dresses—an infallible feminine sign. I had lost weight and was happy with myself.

The following June, there was to be another series of the same *Walküre,* and I waited with healthy impatience. And one fine day—I should say one unhappy day—who should telephone but Victor-José, who was visiting his aunt in Paris. He wanted to see me, of course, but I didn't want it to be at my house or his, so I suggested a meeting on neutral territory, at the Opéra for the premiere of *Turandot.*

Ah! That evening had such repercussions. I arranged to meet him at the ticket counter, but first I went backstage to say good luck to my pal Guy Chauvet, with whom I had sung so many times. To get back to the lobby, I went through the theater and descended the great staircase. Victor-José, at the bottom, turned as if prompted, handsome and elegant as ever. My heart beat a little faster, but I continued my descent—a symbol of another, more serious fall—and kissed him amicably on both cheeks.

As we returned to our seats after the first intermission, he stopped me suddenly with his hand and said, "Crespin, you know that I still love you?"

"Me too," I said, as simply as can be.

After the second act, the audience, or part of it, took after the soprano, who wasn't Birgit Nilsson, to be sure, but who had sung well. I was revolted, and I don't know what got into me, but I couldn't stop myself from shouting, "Idiots! Cowards!" which drew applause from the majority of the audience. It was a real hullabaloo. Victor-José tried to calm me, then said, "You're right. But I think you just signed your death warrant."

His premonition was right. They waited for me patiently, the voices on high, and they got me.

But that evening, I went happily with Victor-José to the Brasserie Lipp after the performance, and we ended the night at the King Club, talking endlessly. We had so much to tell one another. When he took me home I realized I had forgotten my keys—an oversight worthy of analysis—and he suggested that I spend the night at his aunt's house, since she was away in the country.

And it was our first beautiful night of real lovemaking. The last, too, though I didn't know it. I was happy and had wings for the *Walküre* performances. Oh, "they" tried to boo me, but I was in such fantastic shape it was impossible.

Victor-José and I left in September for a cruise aboard the *Renaissance,* during which I was to give a recital. And the old hell began again. I was stronger this time and wanted him to talk to me. I wanted to tell him that I knew about his problem and that I understood. But held back by Dr. Roblès's "professional secrecy," I couldn't be the one to mention it first. And Victor-José, in pain, would answer my questions with, "I don't know what you're talking about."

Unhappy man, fighting with himself, refusing with all his strength the homosexuality he wanted no part of. A banal situation, but difficult and painful. I couldn't understand why he didn't try to accept it, to live with it and be happy. But he

Crisis

didn't want to. He loved me, but he began to escape with alcohol every night. What torture he must have lived through—even worse than mine.

I was going to sing the Schumann cycle *Frauenliebe und Leben,* and since the text translation hadn't arrived, we undertook it ourselves. I can see us as we sat in a corner of the bar one quiet afternoon. As we started to transcribe the final song, in which the woman, after her husband's death, cries, "Nun hast du mir den ersten Schmerz getan" (Now you have caused me pain for the first time), Victor-José raised his head and said through his tears, "I won't ever cause you pain again. I know it."

Back in Paris we had a last blowup, the evening of a recital I gave at the Opéra. That very night I wrote him a letter ending our relationship permanently. But from a last reflex of pity, wanting him to finish his stay in Paris peacefully, I sent the letter to his analyst in Buenos Aires, where he was going to complete—oh, miracle—his medical studies to become an analyst himself, something he had always wanted to do.

And in early January 1973, he died of a heart attack. He was forty-two.

When I sped frantically to the Avenue d'Iéna, he was stretched out on the floor, his handsome face finally peaceful. I remembered his words on the ship and thought, "Yes, my beautiful love, now you've caused me pain for the *last* time."

It took a long time to get over the shock. In one sense I felt, horrible as it is to admit it, relieved, freed of that awful tension. But sorrow took hold. One little thought, the glimpse of a photo, made me cry. I was totally drained of energy. The years of torment in my soul had taken their toll on my body.

I managed to spend a calm vacation in the sun, near the sea, which I need every year, and got back to Paris, where a *Parsifal* series awaited me in November at the Opéra. A stubborn case of the flu kept me from preparing completely. And I was demoralized during the rehearsal period when I started to receive anonymous phone calls. A voice—sometimes a man's, sometimes a woman's—would say only, "We're waiting for you!" Or "We'll get you! See you soon!" It was awful.

I didn't sing badly at the premiere, but in the middle of the second act, during a weighty silence, a voice high up started to boo. It was the first time in my life, and I was petrified. The audience reacted, taking my side, and when I took my bow at the end the weight was against the agitators.

I canceled the second performance because the flu had settled in my throat. My godson Philippe went to the theater to intercept some friends I hadn't been able to tell about the cancellation, and he heard some young people on the opera house steps saying:

"We're not going tonight. She's not singing, so we won't be able to yell."

And one of them added: "You know who I got last night? Fiorenza Cossotto. We really crucified her."

Horrible, no?

The anonymous calls and letters kept coming. One day three pianos were delivered that I had supposedly ordered. Each of the unfortunate dealers had been told it was an emergency and, hearing my name, rushed to help me out. Another time, three catering houses delivered entire dinners. It was awful, and ridiculous.

I sang my other *Parsifal* performances without any demon-

Crisis

strations, but fear began to get the better of me, despite my efforts to conquer it. I went on the radio and on television to defend myself, but I couldn't shake the apprehension.

In October 1974 when I sang *Les Contes d'Hoffmann*, I wasn't myself. My throat was constricted, I was terribly nervous, and I had frequent migraines. I summoned all my willpower to get myself to work, but my voice wouldn't respond, and my body closed up, paralyzed by the constant fear. I was like a show horse stiffening before each hurdle. The premiere wasn't very good. I should have canceled, but I wouldn't let myself. My innate combativeness refused to let me believe I could be heading for destruction. And I was roundly booed! Ah, at times like that, friends are rare! I learned from sad experience, and those who stayed loyal are still very dear to me.

I spent a sleepless night, evaluating. I was in my living room, looking at myself full in the face in a mirror on the wall, and I decided that there weren't thirty-six solutions to my situation: I must either stop singing for good or take myself in hand, and that would mean canceling everything for a few months and starting from scratch. By morning my decision was made. I phoned Rolf Liebermann, the head of the Opéra, and he invited me to lunch at Maxim's. I told him I wanted to cancel, to work on getting myself back in shape, and he kindly let me out of my contract, even giving me the names of several voice teachers in Germany, whom I went to see.

I chose Rudolf Bautz in Cologne and went to work with him three days a week for almost a year. He had a lot of trouble trying to relax me, to restore my confidence. But I was a good pupil, arriving each time with my little briefcase and working like an angel. Little by little my breathing eased; the spasms in my diaphragm disappeared; I was able to vocalize with more supple muscles, with a larynx less constricted, more relaxed. I worked on phrases, on arias. For I finally had a precise and exciting goal: *Carmen* at the Met in October 1975. I knew it would be the final test and that if I didn't pass it I would stop singing forever. And I passed. Oh, yes, I passed.

So there was Crespinette, getting her second wind and starting out on a new career.

CARMEN THE MAGNIFICENT, WHOM I HAD STUPIDLY turned down for years, thinking she wasn't right for my voice and my temperament. But my good friend Alain Lombard, who wanted to record it with me, stubbornly insisted and won me over. He had even offered me a tryout of sorts: two concert performances in March 1972 in Miami, where he led the symphony orchestra, with the promise that if it didn't feel right, he would drop the project. Deal!

Clever Alain! I don't know if I've ever thanked him enough for his intuition and perseverance.

Carmen! I practically knew the opera by heart from having seen and heard it so many times. But when I started to study the role seriously, to my great surprise I slipped into it as if it were an old, familiar outfit shaped to my body. I got an enormous yet delicate pleasure from working it, refining it, taking it over completely, and I left for Miami eagerly. I met up there with my very dear Andrea Guiot, one of the best Micaëlas I've ever heard (she's on the Callas recording), and rehearsals started in the most total joy.

Herbert Breslin came from New York. Several well-intentioned "spies" from the Met joined some faithful fans, my

Crisis

friends Jean Capone and Mary Hanlon, and Terry McEwen, already bursting with excitement.

Olé! What a success. Alain beamed, Herbert was ecstatic, Terry drank more champagne from my shoes, and I agreed to do the recording, in September 1974 in Strasbourg, where Alain was the director of the opera and the Philharmonic Orchestra.

(I'm not completely satisfied with the recording. My Carmen is a little too well behaved, too reserved; I hadn't yet acted the role on stage, and the lack of experience shows. Pity!)

ON A BEAUTIFUL OCTOBER DAY IN 1975 I ARRIVED IN New York to give birth to this new "child" that I already adored—and to fall in love again. Life definitely had more good things to offer.

I threw myself wholeheartedly into the music and staging rehearsals, at first alone, then with Bodo Igesz, the director. We got along wonderfully.

One afternoon I was working on the second-act dance. Hellishly difficult: to dance, beat out a precise rhythm on the castanets, and sing at the same time without losing your breath, while still paying attention to Don José, who straddles a chair and encourages you, and the conductor, watching you from the distance with a considerate baton.

The conductor! In the middle of that afternoon he dashed into the rehearsal hall, nodded without interrupting, and leaned his elbows on the piano to watch for a long moment. And suddenly, hitting the piano with the side of his fist, he exclaimed:

"I've never seen anything as sexy as this woman."

I froze, arms in the air, blushing, facing myself in the mirror.

(I don't usually find that very pleasing, but I wasn't bad in the short costume and the black leg-enhancing stockings.)

From his six feet two inches he gave me an embarrassed smile and said in his enticing bass voice:

"Hi. My name is Henry Lewis. I'm delighted to be conducting your *Carmen*. I'll see you tomorrow for a music rehearsal."

Then, stammering a vague apology for his remark, he left as quickly as he had arrived.

Wow! He was handsome, this maestro. And if he found me sexy, I could return the compliment in full.

But for the moment I had other things to think about. I went back to my castanets and my dance, immersed in my Carmen. I rehearsed morning and evening, with a morale of steel and a will of iron, and at night I slept deeply, exhausted and happy.

I also gave a lot of interviews, and the Sunday *Times* devoted a full page to me, letting me talk about my crisis, the long and patient work on my voice, and the analysis that got me back on my feet. After the article appeared I received many encouraging letters that touched me deeply.

I should say that my work was made easier by Henry's attentive help. He was an extremely meticulous, patient conductor, who loved singers and knew how to make them work. All through those rehearsals, through the quick lunches in the Met cafeteria and the more relaxed dinners, I got to know him better. He was an extremely intelligent, cultivated man who shared my love for long discussions, who could explode into laughter at a good joke or a clever phrase. He was fascinated by psychoanalyis, which each of us was undergoing and which helped us understand each other's problems. My wounds were slowly healing, but his (the separation from his wife, Marilyn Horne) were still raw.

Crisis

For my part, I had Gérard de Botton, my "bone-cruncher" (he's an orthopedic surgeon). Sweet and tender, he was and always will be my best friend. Henry had his daughter, Angela, a marriage ending painfully, and a host of problems about his race and identity. Our mutual attraction swept all that aside for the almost four years we were happy together. But life, our work on different continents, eroded our relationship, which nevertheless remained very affectionate.

Our mutual sense of humor saw us through the separation.

Henry: "Just my luck. I leave one bloody prima donna and fall in love with another one. And French, on top of that."

And I: "You know, resting my head on the telephone at night isn't very comfortable!"

But for a while, he made me happy again. And as Descartes wrote, "When the spirit is joyful, the body feels better." I felt wonderful. Paris seemed far away; I was healed. Forgetfulness is sweet!

BODO IGESZ HELPED ME GREATLY WITH THE ACTING SIDE of Carmen, and we quickly agreed on everything. I knew I wanted to make something more of this woman than a fickle creature in a flouncy dress and gold rings. I knew that my physique wouldn't let me play the usual wiry, excitable gypsy. Carmen is not fickle; she is independent.

"Born of no one, springing from nothing, Carmen remains unique; no one leaves her; she's the one who walks out" (André Tubeuf).

She is free; she loves life, dancing, Manzanilla, sweets, apples, flowers, men, danger. Superstitious but fatalistic, she is a complete woman, exposed to the world.

She is free, yes, she is natural. Free despite the factory, the contraband; she wanders according to her whims, never lingering. She is sharp, lively; with a glance or a flower she expresses everything.

Carmen, like the bull in the arena, doesn't like to be pinned or yoked. In the fourth act, provoked like a bull, "she paces restlessly with the incessant movement of a threatened animal" (André Tubeuf), with the same stubborn courage as a bull. She waits for Don José, facing him—like a bull.

How I hate those stagings that make her try to escape, that have the knife strike her in the back. What a mistake! In the arena, the antagonists don't turn away from each other. They confront one another eye to eye, and only one will survive.

What's more, if she sets her heart on the bullfighter Escamillo, it isn't because he's a celebrity. It's probably because like her, he lives life to the hilt and, like her, could die from it.

She, in any case, has read her death in the cards. She doesn't try to evade it, because she's too proud and, in a way, suicidal. That's the key word: suicidal. In her laughs, her dances, her sarcasms, her bravado—like most people of forced gaiety.

Carmen herself is black and white. And the Met costumes were wonderful: black and white in the first act, black with a touch of red in the second, all black in the third, and spotless white in the fourth.

I loved Bodo's staging, too, his idea that a surge of sexual desire is at play as Carmen—the female mirror image of the eternally unsatisfied Don Juan—provokes Don José to stab her. And I liked my idea not to hurl the ring at him and shriek but rather to extend my arm and let the ring fall with a "Tiens" almost whispered, a disdainful gesture that seals Carmen's fate.

Crisis

(1 1 3)

I was happy to find that the critics, some of them surprised themselves, unanimously praised "my" Carmen. And this new milestone showed me that my own fate had taken a good turn: I could continue to sing and end my career with the dignity it deserved.

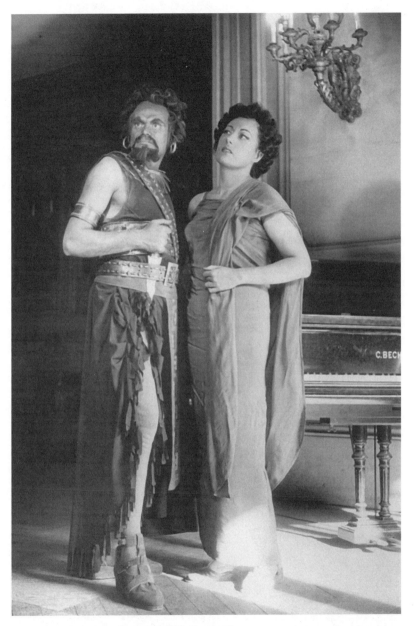

Aida Nile Scene, Conservatory stage competition, 1949

Professional debut:
Elsa in *Lohengrin,*
Mulhouse, January 1950

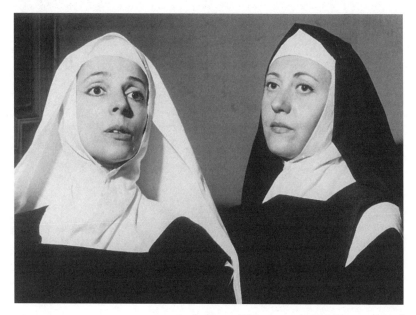

As the Second Prioress in the French premiere of
Dialogues des Carmélites, with Denise Duval, 1957

Three faces of Kundry: Bayreuth debut, *Parsifal*, 1958
(© Festspielleitung Bayreuth)

Wieland Wagner, 1958
(© Festspielleitung
Bayreuth)

With Francis Poulenc
(left), Barcelona, 1959
(photo by Ras)

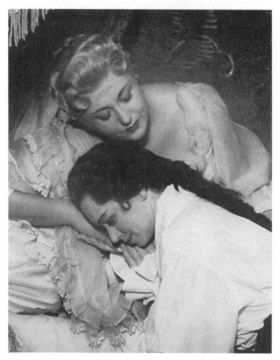

As the Marschallin in
Der Rosenkavalier at
Glyndebourne, with
Elisabeth Söderström,
1959 (photo by Guy
Gravett)

As Cassandre in *Les Troyens,* Buenos Aires, 1964

With André Cluytens,
Paris, 1964 (photo by
Jean-Luce Huré)

With my longtime American accompanist,
John Wustman, mid-1960s

With Cornell MacNeil
(left) and Richard
Tucker after a *Tosca*
performance, Buenos
Aires, 1965
(photo by Alfa)

With Maria Callas,
Paris, 1960s (photo by
Claude Poirier)

As Elisabeth in *Tannhäuser*,
Paris Opéra, late 1960s
(© Photo Pic)

Curtain call with Herbert von
Karajan after *Die Walküre,*
Salzburg, 1967

With Lotte Lehmann, San Francisco, 1968

Sieglinde in *Die Walküre,* with Gene Cox, Paris Opéra, 1971 (photo by Colette Masson)

As Charlotte in *Werther,* Metropolitan Opera, 1971 (photo by Beth Bergman)

Recital during a cruise aboard the
Renaissance, September 1972
(photo by Olivier Roussin)

With Alain Lombard, early 1970s

Carmen, Metropolitan Opera, 1975 (photo by Beth Bergman)

With Mady Mesplé and Michel Plasson, 1976 (photo by Gérard Neuvecelle)

As Santuzza in
Cavalleria Rusticana,
with Plácido
Domingo, San
Francisco Opera,
1976 (photo by
Caroline Crawford)

*La Grande-Duchesse de
Gérolstein,* Toulouse, 1979
(photo by Michel Stuck)

"The Cat Duet"
with Leontyne Price,
San Francisco, 1982

As Madame Flora in
The Medium, Théâtre
du Châtelet, Paris,
1985 (photo by KIPA)

As the Countess in *The Queen of Spades,* San Francisco Opera farewell, 1987 (photo by David Powers)

As Madame de Croissy on her deathbed in *Dialogues des Carmélites,* Marseille, 1988 (photo by Christian Dresse)

Lenox Hill Hospital

On the Mount of Olives, Christ was no longer master.
He knew the fear of death. GEORGES BERNANOS

THAT IS one of the most beautiful, most tender phrases that Francis Poulenc set to music in his opera *Dialogues des Carmélites,* when the Second Prioress confronts Mother Marie's dangerous exaltation with her own serene wisdom.

And that was the first thought I had, one morning in March 1978 at Lenox Hill Hospital in New York, when the doctor told me gently that I had to have an operation for cancer.

I had sung that phrase for years with no other thought than to sing it well, as sweetly and seamlessly as possible, stressing only the words "fear" and "death" as the composer had wanted.

Until the winter of 1977–78, I had always sung the role of the Second Prioress. Francis had even composed the role with my voice in mind, and I had sung it at the Paris premiere in 1957.

Francis. I met him in a funny way. He had been looking everywhere for a Frenchwoman who could sing "an exquisitely pianissimo high A," and our mutual friend Michel Glotz urged a suggestion on him: "Crespin! Crespin! Go to hear her in *Otello* and you'll see!"

And there was Poulenc one night in my dressing room after the performance, all smiles, saying, "That's it! Mother Lidoine is you!"

I opened my eyes wide under my blond wig, not Desdemona anymore but not quite Crespin. He continued:

"Bernanos. *Dialogues des Carmélites.* Do you know it?"

"Oh, yes! I just saw the play. It's glorious!"

"Well, I'm in the middle of making it an opera."

"Oh, no! No music for such a work! It's impossible. Impossible!"

I exploded, as sore as if I'd been rubbed with nettles. Anyone but Francis would have left without another word. But he gave an enormous laugh and invited me to supper with him and his friends. I accepted, embarrassed by my rudeness. How could I—practically unknown—dare act that way with the great Poulenc?

During the entire meal he tried to convince me, sometimes seriously, sometimes playfully. He was in a sparkling mood, declaring that he had found his "exquisitely pianissimo high A." He even told some lewd jokes, and I contributed some of my own. He adored dirty jokes, and later, whenever I arrived for a rehearsal, he would make everyone laugh by calling out, "Crespinette! Have you got a new one?"

For years, I was his purveyor of risqué stories. He liked to say that I sang well, but that I told jokes much better!

I was under his spell that first evening and the next day in his living room, where he cleverly started by playing the prison aria and the final scene, singing "my" part in falsetto. That was the first time I cried at the guillotine scene, but far from the last, because I cried in the wings at the end of every single performance, after dying the tranquil death of the Second Prioress or the fearful death of the First.

Madame de Croissy! First Prioress of the convent at Compiègne during the Revolution. An exemplary woman of high birth, a Carmelite for more than thirty years, Mother Superior for twelve. At the end of her life, sick and old, she dies in the most appalling fear, shouting her anger and dread and even blaspheming God. What a role! What a scene! For years, as I waited offstage for my entrance as the Second Prioress, I watched the First Prioress, fascinated and almost jealous. One day I said to Francis, "The role you wrote for me is very lovely, yes, sweet and strong, but the other: what beauty."

He put his large hand on my shoulder and said, "You'll sing it one day, in fifteen years, you'll see. And you'll be superb."

And I sang it, seventeen years later.

The Metropolitan Opera wanted to do the work and wanted me to be in it. I had a long lunch at Sardi's with John Dexter, the director, James Levine, the music director, and Fabrizio Melano, an old friend. Jimmy Levine thought I would sing my usual role and John saw me as Mother Marie. I wanted neither one.

I lean toward the philosophy that the souls of the dead don't disappear completely; that perhaps they hover around us. And I think Poulenc's soul was near me that day as I made a daring suggestion:

"Why not the First Prioress? It's a little low for me, but I think I can do it. And what a role."

Lenox Hill Hospital

(1 1 7)

Levine jumped at the idea, then the two others, and the conversation heated up, ideas spouting from all sides. I promised a decision as soon as I studied the score, but I already knew deep down that I would do it. And I did! It was a great success, I can say.

If only Poupoune had been there. Michel Glotz, who had known him so well, told me after a performance in New York:

"Francis would be so pleased."

And that made me very happy.

I PLUNGED INTO THE ROLE AS EASILY AS IF I HAD ALWAYS sung it. And I was doing it in English! The Met had rightly decided to do it that way so the audience could better understand the words. And I might add that I, the only non-American in the cast, was the one all the critics said could be best understood.

Usually when I took on a new role, I needed a certain incubation period, time to think about my interpretation, to make the character mine. But I was astonished at how easily I took on the Prioress and her horrible death. John Dexter had devised an admirable production, all simplicity and lighting, and had sketched out for me several gestures, several ideas, leaving me to discover, develop, and settle into the character.

Of course I had already died countless times on stage, deaths of hopelessness, aggression, love. Verdi's Desdemona, a bit spineless, who practically lets herself be choked; Tosca, who leaps to her death; Didon, who throws herself into the fire; Cassandre, who stabs herself; Sieglinde, who dies in childbirth; Marguerite, who dies of madness; Carmen, who kills herself on Don José's knife.

Almost all those deaths were violent, aggressive, almost self-inflicted. But as I began to study the First Prioress's death—just as intense, more than terrifying, which she does not want, cannot accept, rejects with horror—and her long agony (thirty minutes of raging, interrupted by moments of calm), it seemed almost impossible to carry off well. Yet from the first rehearsals on stage, with Dexter, squinty-eyed, watching me, fixing little things here and there, I surprised myself with what I could do, with what I dared to do on that hard, narrow Carmelite bed.

And the final phrase that bursts from Madame de Croissy's tortured face as she falls dead—"Fear . . . fear . . . of death"—is one I might have shouted from my hospital bed that March morning. I had settled in the night before without any particular worry, since the results of my annual checkup had apparently been normal. Some persistent bleeding had made the surgeon want to investigate further, but I had no particular apprehension. I refused all suggestions of help or compassion and checked in almost jauntily. I awoke from the exploratory operation without any bad reaction, asked for my breakfast, and ate it with gusto. If I had known that I wouldn't be able to face so much as a simple boiled potato for the next several weeks, I would have appreciated it even more.

I settled myself as comfortably as possible on the hard, narrow hospital bed that would soon become a closed world of pain, cries, half-sleep, half-dreams, of hope, struggle, stubborn concentration, of quarreling with my body, my soul, my heart. This bed would become almost a cradle where a second (or third) Régine would be born. I savored my tea and toast, listening to the sounds of the immense hospital, looking out sleepily at the bare trees shaken violently by a cutting wind. The spring

Lenox Hill Hospital

weather was late, and thinking I would be going home that day, I wished I had disregarded the hospital's advice and brought my fur coat.

The night before, thinking about going under anesthesia, I had written a new will, lightheartedly, happily distributing whatever belonged to me. I admit that it felt good to give everything away to those I loved.

So I felt delightfully well when Dr. Barber came into my room. But he seemed worn out; his eyes were tired and the lids heavy. He sat down, looked at me in his usual kindly way, and asked, "How do you feel?"

"Fine. Just fine. And you?"

"Mmmm—not so well."

And I, like a fool:

"My God! Are you sick?"

"No, not me. You!"

"Me?"

And he gave me a long, patient explanation of what the tests had revealed: the bleeding was probably from the minuscule beginning of a uterine cancer. A hysterectomy should be performed, and quickly.

The high ceiling of my room seemed to thud onto my head. Dr. Barber must have seen the shock and fright on my face, because he said: "Your godson, your impresario, and his wife are here. Do you want them to come in?"

Like a startled animal whose one thought is to flee, I answered: "No, no. I have to get up, because I'm leaving."

And he, gently:

"To go where? To another hospital? Believe me, you'll be well cared for here. And then, your nightshirt isn't elegant enough for a prima donna."

I managed to laugh and said: "All right. But I'd like to cry first."

"Fine. Go ahead. We're just outside the door. Call us."

And he left quietly.

There were no great sobs. Just some slow tears. I felt as if I had been stopped short in the middle of a leap, forced into stillness, into thought. It was almost the middle of the day. It was the middle of my life as well. And a phrase from a poem by Czeslaw Milosz came into my head:

"Solitude, my mother, repeat my life to me."

I had never been really ill before, never had an operation, and I had often asked myself how I would react to a serious illness, pain, danger. I never really managed to imagine it.

And now, there I was.

Crespin, how are you going to react?

First, fear. Visceral, animal fear.

I had thought I knew fear. Fear of myself, of people, of audiences, of singing, of appearing, of being loved—or not. Fear of failure, of not pleasing, of nothingness, of airplanes, of insects, of snakes, of physical pain, of visits to the dentist. All those fears, I thought I knew.

But in those few minutes or that hour, I'm not sure, I realized what true fear was.

And Gilbert Bécaud was right when he sang that solitude does not exist. It no longer existed when Philippe, Herbert, and Carol came into the room, when Jean and Mary came racing in about ten minutes after my phone call, when Dr. Gould, my

Lenox Hill Hospital

(1 2 1)

laryngologist, and his trusted Cathy arrived. And all the others by telephone, from Paris, London, and elsewhere. Lou, distraught and crying (I had to comfort him); Gérard, who wanted to fly over immediately; my friend Denise Dupleix, who was more terrified than I; her Jean-Philippe Lafont, who tried to be comforting; Isabelle Masset, my almost-daughter, whose stutter came back; Patrick, my analyst, who pretended to be calm; my housekeeper, Jeanette, in a panic.

The only shadow on this chain of love and friendship that linked itself together in a few hours was the man in my life, who couldn't find the time to come see me until seven o'clock that evening. A long time from eleven in the morning. That wound hurt for a long time, although a lot less than the eventual one on my belly. Among other things, I learned to put each pain in its place.

And like Edith Piaf singing, "No, I regret nothing," I could say later that for the first time in my life I was truly proud of myself.

Proud of having cried alone. Proud of holding my head up in front of my friends. Proud of having asked for pills to make me sleep the day before the operation to make sure that my body would be as strong and well rested as possible. Proud later when the surgeon told me I had fought like a soldier. Proud of not having asked for the painkilling injection more often than at its prescribed four-hour intervals. Proud of having gotten through the moment of weakness the fourth day, when my giant of a nurse said, "Reggie, you're going to get up today."

"Oh, no! I can't!"

"Yes you can!"

And I did!

Proud of strolling the hallway the fifth day, the intravenous rack rolling on one side and the catheter pouch on the other. What elegance. Proud of not calling the night nurse to help me turn over in my bed/cage, which took half an hour the first night, then twenty-five minutes, then twenty, then fifteen.

Like a child in a crib, I asked Henry, who finally came to visit every evening, to tell me stories. He did, a little shyly at first, then tenderly, while I lay with my eyes closed remembering Mannolini when I was sick. At night in the dim light I would read my name on the white plastic bracelet around my wrist: Régine Crespin. Thirteen letters. "A good-luck charm," Germaine Lubin had told me when I first met her. "You are lucky and you will bring luck."

Several clairvoyants had told me the same thing. Now I believe it. When I got home to Paris on May first, I glued that bracelet to the inside of a closet in my bathroom. And for a long time, whenever things weren't going right, or I believed they weren't, whenever I felt sad, discouraged, alone, disappointed, whenever I was afraid, I would pull gently on the little thimble case that Mannolini had crocheted for me and that hangs on the door pull of that closet. I would look at my little bracelet and smile, a little egotistically, for this was a matter between me and myself.

Of all the fears I've conquered and all the battles I've won, that one made me proudest. Because it was "my" battle, alone with myself, "for real," as children say.

Régine Crespin, many others have congratulated you in the course of your long career, but this time, I congratulate you myself.

Lenox Hill Hospital

The Art of Singing

My métier and my art are to live. MONTAIGNE

WHAT IS an opera singer? What is singing? What is "technique?"

Without writing another primer on the subject (there are too many already), I'll try to open a little window on the enormous and delicate work involved in the art of singing.

First, it's very obvious that singing is something everyone can do, because we all possess the same organs that allow us to do it:

1. two vocal cords;
2. a larynx, which emits sound;
3. two lungs, which form the bellows, with the diaphragm as baseplate;
4. finally, the resonators, acting as an amplification funnel
   a. in the upper part, the rigid cavities—the hard palate, the nasal passages, the brainpan;
   b. in the lower part, all the flexible hollows with supple

linings—the rhinopharynx, the larynx, the tongue, the soft palate.

This mechanism being the same in every individual, one might easily syllogize:

> Every individual possesses these organs for singing.
> I am an individual.
> Therefore, I sing.

But not so fast! Yes, you can sing—in the shower, for your friends, or for yourself. So go ahead, enjoy yourself.

But as soon as you want to do it in front of, let's say, more than a hundred people, halt! That's where technique comes in. No technique, no singer.

First off, for this "individual" to become "a singer," he or she must possess a number of indispensable characteristics. In optimal conditions, singing depends on

1. the shape, length, and strength of the vocal cords;
2. the size of the pharyngeal, laryngeal, and palatal cavities;
3. the size of the face and the facial and frontal resonators;
4. and let's not forget a good pair of lungs!

They all react according to and depending on the width of the trachea, the power of the lungs, and the diaphragm—the wide, thin muscle attached to the ribs that separates the chest from the abdomen and that should act as the strong and supple base of one's breathing.

So, young woman or young man, you possess all these givens, and you go to a voice teacher to try to develop what God or chance has bestowed on you.

The Art of Singing

And that's when the great odyssey begins, the never-ending pursuit of a fragile, precarious balance—grasped once and lost a hundred times—between you and your hussy of a voice. Like a beautiful woman, it slips away, reappears subdued, then disappears for months, sometimes simple, at times rebellious, never completely under your control, making you chase it like a donkey after a carrot in a frantic, irritating, stimulating race. A race that made even Kirsten Flagstad, at the age of fifty-four after more than thirty years of singing the role, say, "Ah, if I had four or five more years, I believe I would really know how to sing Isolde."

A wonderful comment from the greatest of the century's great Wagnerians. How I admire perfectionism in the extreme. (It was because of Flagstad that I never sang Isolde, a character I had been devoted to since my emergence as a singer and should have sung. But I was terrified by the role, which I identified with the strong, deep, smooth tones of this illustrious elder sister.)

To get back to technique. At sixteen or seventeen (any younger is much too early), you'll find yourself in front of a voice teacher, who will start by teaching you to breathe correctly, since breathing is the foundation of our machine.

But first you must be made to understand that everything you are told, all the explanations, are about things you will never see, never touch; that you will work by feelings, by empiricism. Unlike violinists or pianists, who can see their fingers and their positions, their instruments always available and unchanging, you will always find your instrument elusive, capricious, depending on whether you're in good or bad health, whether you've slept and digested well or badly, whether you're cheerful or sad. And whatever shape it's in, you'll have to work with it and try to control it, even early in the morning when it's not quite awake.

For your instrument is your entire body: living material, not wood or metal, and as such, eminently delicate and fragile, propelled by a thousand often uncontrollable reflexes. You must nourish it with all your sensibilities, your physical and mental fuel, your innermost being, your soul—unashamedly, with constant care, infinite patience, and the courage of a Titan.

Alfred de Musset wrote, "It is only the voice from the heart that reaches the heart." Never forget that.

Ready? Let's go.

Stand up very straight, your head continuing the line of your neck, but not stiffly, arms and hands relaxed. Your first task will be to learn how to breathe. Yes, I know, you think that's something that comes naturally. But in fact, you and most people use only a small part of your lung power. And if someone tells you to breathe deeply, you'll gulp too much air too quickly, lifting your shoulders.

But you must do exactly the opposite. You have to inhale very, very slowly, preferably through your nose. Your stomach will be slowly pushed forward by your diaphragm, your chest will expand outward and upward, the lower ribs on both sides of your waist will expand to the maximum, even your back will seem distended. You should feel like an inflated tire throughout your thorax, stomach, and back. But never, absolutely never, raise your shoulders, because that can obstruct your throat and the vocal folds. Your body must always remain loose and relaxed.

Now for the first hard part: exhale all this breath through

The Art of Singing

your mouth—which should be open only slightly, and slightly rounded—as slowly and steadily as possible, so it vibrates the vocal cords evenly and any sound that emerges is smooth and not abrupt. (In the old days, a frequent experiment was to hold a lighted candle about twelve inches in front of your mouth and exhale fully without making the flame flutter.)

Little by little, you will learn how to conserve your breath, guide it, portion it out in your own time, using all of the diaphragm, the lower abdominal muscles, and finally the back and the muscles of the buttocks. Oh yes, when you sing you use the entire body, keeping it taut but not rigid.

Once you've assimilated this basic breathing technique (which I've greatly simplified), you have to become intimately acquainted with your mouth and your head.

First, you will be asked to yawn and to observe minutely what happens when you do. You will have inhaled more vigorously this time, and you'll feel your larynx shift forward and downward (this is more obvious in men, whose Adam's apple is visible). In this position, your lower jaw is stretched downward, the face muscles are taut, the nostrils dilated, and inside the mouth the soft palate is raised, pressing against the roof of the mouth. All the pharyngeal and laryngeal cavities, the trachea, and the vocal folds are spread wide but not contorted, for this simple yawn is a complete relaxation of the muscles and all the organs of the vocal apparatus. And of course other muscles in the front of the body react too.

This yawn automatically sets up the ideal position and balance between diaphragm, larynx, and resonators.

But you must hold onto only the first phase of this sensation of yawning, when you inhale air, because if you complete the yawn and exhale, everything falls back into its normal place and the ideal position for singing is no longer maintained. It's this first position that you must try to maintain in singing, with, of course, certain modifications according to whether you're going to utter low-, medium-, or high-pitched tones.

Now you'll be taught to place vowels and words on the breath that you exhale, to do vocal exercises. We'll assume that you've learned a bit of solfeggio, that you know your notes—do, re, mi, fa, sol, la, ti—intervals, and so on. If not, you'll be sent to solfeggio class.

This vocalizing will become your daily prayer, every God-given morning until your last breath—as a singer, at least. A voice warms up slowly. A boxer wouldn't dream of going into the ring for a major fight without having jumped rope, run his miles, punished his punching bag. Well, it's the same for singers, who are athletes in a sense. Our vocalizing is the equivalent of a dancer's barre. Dancers work at the barre every day; singers work "the voice."

Accordingly, you will be taught various rhythmic combinations, which gradually become more difficult, to be sung on long or short scales or arpeggios, as vowels alone or as vowels set into words (which I preferred). You'll learn which vowels are round, which pointed, and so forth.

You will learn to use your resonators, to sing "in the mask," or as Félia Litvinne taught, "in the lid and not in the box," the lid being the upper jaw; the box, the lower.

You will be told to place your sounds "behind" the nose and not "in" it, because the nose is a dead end from which sounds do not emerge once they've entered; to lift your uvula before emitting a sound, to open your nasal cavities, to try to feel the

The Art of Singing

sounds in the triangle formed by the point between your eyes, down the sides of your nostrils to your teeth; to place your low notes on the top teeth without forgetting their connection to the sternum; not to yawn too much in the bottom and middle of your voice so you can save a last yawn for the high notes.

Above all, you will learn the importance of the tongue. At least I hope so, for I place great value on it. For the low notes, you must hold the tip of your tongue against the bottom teeth; for middle notes, pull it slightly back and down; for the middle to high notes, place it on the membrane below the bottom teeth, making the tongue a sort of arched ramp to support the sound.

Of course there are exceptions to these rules: the baritone Robert Massard, for example, who sang for more than thirty years, and beautifully, with the tip of his tongue in the air.

If you're not too discouraged, let's go on. For as Don Inigo says in Ravel's *L'Heure Espagnole:*

"This is only the start, a little training exercise."

I've often asked friends to attend classes I've taken or given. And they all leave dazed and fascinated by the difficulties, details, and abstruseness.

Try to understand, for instance, a teacher who says:

—"No, higher on that sound, behind the nose, just there where you snore."

—"Too much in the throat, more in the head."

—"Sing behind your eyes, on a slight smile. Ah, no, not so toothy."

—"Your soft palate isn't raised enough."

—"It's too flat, too white; give me a little color."

—"Too hard; more supple, a lighter sound, and less breath or it will be too fat."

—"Keep your ribs spread until the end of the long phrase, and push your chest forward a bit to use the last bit of breath. And remember to help yourself with your back and your buttocks."

—"Careful! Let your tongue stay relaxed, not taut, or the sound will be taut, too."

—"Don't yawn deeply before the very high notes, but there, yes, open everything, imagine that the sound is going to hit the top of your skull, toward the back, and that it will pass underneath, behind the forehead, the nose, to emerge from the mouth."

—"Project the sound further, against the far wall."

—"Think that a high note often originates in the previous note, so place that one well. If you're having trouble with a high note, it might help to bend your knees deeply just at the start and spread your arms wide."

—"For the top, think low; for the bottom, think high."

I've just touched the surface of this technical gibberish; there are many more examples. Because one uses everything—words, gestures, mimicry—to relax the tense student, make the serious one laugh, get the lazy one going (there are very few of those, to be honest), calm the impatient one, "undress" the overly modest one. The teacher is mother, father, friend, midwife, psychoanalyst, Wise Man, adviser, consoler, and font of all knowledge.

During my seventeen years as a professor at the Conservatoire National Supérieur de la Musique, I would leave after my five or six hours in the classroom almost prostrate with exhaustion. But the next day I would set out eagerly like a good little workhorse, because it's so fascinating to mold these young people, to watch them grow, develop, and understand and apply what they've learned. And one fine day (too rarely, alas), after four or six years, you may see in front of you a singer, ready to leave the nest. I admit that it always moves me to tears to see one of my "children" reach that point. And like all parents, I never like to think of the hundred other obstacles that life has in store for them.

Once you've mastered a bit of technique, interpretation enters the picture. I mean, of course, vocal and musical interpretation of arias and mélodies, not role acting, which will come later with the help of other hands.

Because once you've learned a piece of music by heart, you must interpret it. Oh, that iron corset, the bar measure, where you must count time in silence without seeming to, use the measured silences to rest or to regain your breath—either for expressive purposes or to prepare the next phrase—those silences that you should make your accomplice. I say often to students:

"Never take embarrassed breaths! On the contrary, use them. If the spectators see you take a deep breath, they may become more attentive, more curious about what you're going to say."

A single sound may be bright or gloomy, white, round, soft or strong, delicate or coarse, light or stressed, gay, sad, doleful, aggressive, cajoling, angry, or sensual.

I would sometimes spend days and days thinking about a single sound, hearing it in my head but unable to utter it the way I wanted to, with all its weight and color accurate, but suddenly finding it—sometimes a year later.

Many times I would get up during the night to look at a score, the way one bends over a sleeping baby. Suddenly everything would become clear, obvious. As paradoxical as it may seem, the best work I've done has been silently, in my head, my imagination, my soul, alone at night.

So, my young friends, have you found some of those sounds and colors that you've sought so patiently for such a long time? And assimilated the basic technique that you must now almost forget as you move on to interpretation? I would like to quote the charming response that the great tenor Tito Schipa gave when someone asked him to indicate where he supported his voice:

"On my heart!"

Yes, you must let your heart, your soul, your innards, speak without fear and without reticence.

In singing, as in the theater, reticence does not exist.

You are going to have to express with your voice the rages of Otello, the Machiavellianism of Scarpia or Iago, the loves of Tosca, the felinity of Dalila, the bluntness of Falstaff, the duplicity of Rosina, the lamentations of Elvira, the sorrowful resignation of the Marschallin, the wretched nobility of Wotan, the youthfulness of Pamina, the earthly femininity of Sieglinde, the glibness of Figaro, the thousand facets of Carmen, and more. And all that with your two little vocal cords.

And all the rest, of course.

You must also employ a vocal style. And I mean vocal, not musical, which differs according to whether you're singing a recitative of Mozart, Monteverdi, Gluck, or Rossini, where word and rhythm take priority, while in the aria that follows, your voice will be lighter, more delicate for Mozart or Rossini and a bit wider for Gluck, Wagner, and Verdi.

You will have to learn to color your voice according to what you're singing. And polish it, ceaselessly repeating your arias, your phrases, your roles all your life in accordance with the Ciceronian principle *Docere, delectare, movere* (To instruct, to delight, to stir).

At last, you have made your debut. You have entered the "career," to find that your elders—in more or less good shape—are occupying most of the seats. It's difficult sometimes to make one's mark. To do so, even with an outstanding voice, you will need the courage of a lion, the tenacity of an ant, the organizational ability of a honeybee, the endurance of a camel, the impudence of a puppy, the memory of an elephant, the keenness of an eagle, the flexibility of a cat, the wisdom of an owl, and the hide of a rhinoceros.

You should study Italian, German, French, Russian, and English (and maybe, one day, Chinese).

You will have had to work with a teacher of stagecraft, to learn how to move for your portrayals of a young hero, a jealous father, a cuckolded husband, a woman in love, a young flirt, or a sly chaperone; how to apply different styles of makeup, how to walk properly in costumes and wigs of different eras, how to carry and use a fan or a sword. For operas with spoken dialogue, you must learn to speak clearly and loudly without tiring your voice. You must be as credible as possible on the stage, because unlike actors, who have only the bare words and can dress them up at will, singers cannot always give precedence to the words. The sounds and the silences are imposed on us, not left to our personal inspiration. And after all these obstacles are overcome and technique is gotten out of the way, you have to carry it off by being as natural as you possibly can.

I haven't mentioned the possible imbalance between your voice and your temperament. Are you aware that your voice will not necessarily match your physique or your wishes?

Let's take a moment to explain to the layman that there are three general categories of voice: low, middle, and high.

For men, bass, baritone, tenor. For women, contralto, mezzo-soprano, soprano.

But the subdivisions are many.

Basso-cantante, or singing bass; basso profundo, or deep bass; lyric baritone; Verdi baritone; baritone Martin; heroic tenor; dramatic tenor; lyric tenor; dramatic mezzo; mezzo coloratura; dramatic soprano; Falcon; lirico spinto; lyric soprano; dramatic coloratura; lyric coloratura, and others.

So although you yearn to bring the dramatic Tosca to life, your physical equipment may oblige you to deal with the vocal agility of Lakmé; you may see yourself as Otello in a jealous rage, but have to be content with the charming Almaviva; you may feel yourself the virile Figaro but be stuck with the simpleton of a Don Ottavio; you may be fascinated by the heroic Brünnhilde and have to play the gentle Mimi.

You have to go along with what you received from Mother Nature, who generally arranges things pretty well. What luck that I had to sing a repertoire I adored.

Finally, having at last become a singer, you must now try to become an artist.

Eh, no, they are not the same thing!

Singers have a place just a bit out of the mainstream in the arts, and I believe that with rare exceptions, we are the only ones without a true vocation.

In general, painters, musicians, architects, surgeons, physicists know very early what they want to do in life. But we become performers because we discover at eighteen or twenty or even later that our two vocal cords work well, that we have a tenor or soprano voice. And a beautiful voice is so rare that we are pushed toward a career almost by force. And by a passion for it as well, of course, a passion that becomes consuming. Singing is like a drug: once you've tried it for a while it's hard to do without it. Which is why there are so many unhappy, embittered people claiming to have no luck and hanging on desperately, wanting to be on the stage despite all wise advice to the contrary.

I deeply admire the people who never "make it" but who continue to sing for their own modest pleasure. (I say often that a singing career is thirty percent voice, thirty percent work, thirty percent head and heart, and ten percent luck.)

With the proper vocal equipment, almost anyone can study and work and reach the point of singing Scarpia or Desdemona. But become an artist? Not necessarily. Because at twenty, the dice are already tossed; one is intelligent or not; one has studied or not, received a certain education or not.

But if you have a certain instinct, some intelligence and much humility, reliable taste, if you really want to educate yourself, if you are curious about everything—books, theater, paintings, music in general and not just opera—if you are on the alert at all times, eyes open to everybody and everything, then and only then can you become an artist.

Maybe!

Prima donna! what does it mean? translated directly from Italian: "first lady." According to Webster's dictionary: the principal woman singer in an opera or concert. For the connoisseurs, it's the *article*, the *La: La Stupenda! La Assoluta! La Unica! La Divina! La Diva! La Callas!*

These "first ladies" are adored, idolized, imitated, detested—celestial on stage but with their feet well planted on earth when they discuss their fees, their billing, and their dressing rooms.

For many, La Diva is a goddess, an aloof, mysterious woman who should live in a palace, surrounded by rare flowers and by worshippers to carry her dog or her coat to the long car that sits permanently at her door; a capricious creature who wakes and retires with rosé champagne.

Perhaps in another century it was all of that. But today, what a burden it must be to play the prima donna. Granted, we often have a bullying air, fur coats to prevent colds, dogs to keep us company in our hotel rooms, big hats, gewgaws, and huge rings. Granted, I wear them, but because they suit me, not because I'm trying to look like a diva. (Seriously, can you see me with a teeny hat atop my considerable physique?) If one can be a prima donna on stage, fine. But play the role in real life? No, and no again! I refuse to acknowledge that "the organ creates the function." And if people say I have the air of a diva, well, I don't do it deliberately.

You know what being a prima donna really means? Work, plus work, plus work and still more work. One mustn't forget that this métier we're lucky enough to enjoy is a profession, not an amusement. Many people daydream about us, idealize us, but the reality, the rules, are objective. We must use certain human possibilities better than others, and our endless ques-

The Art of Singing

tioning is like answers to questions that others don't ask. And our nights, our days, even our dreams, are filled with them.

First of all, there are several kinds of days. The emptiest, the shortest, and the longest is the day of a performance, when you can't and don't want to do anything because you are totally preoccupied with thoughts of the evening. After trying out your voice a little, getting it going, you roam around your apartment, with your secretary fending off phone calls and your housekeeper trying to be invisible but helpful. You don't return to normalcy until you're in your dressing room: two hours early if it's an opera performance; if it's a recital, in advance by just the few minutes needed to get into your evening dress.

Of course after the performance, it's often fiesta if everything has gone well. It's hard to go home right away because the decompression is slow and the performance leaves one too stimulated to sleep.

The most agonizing day is the one before the performance, generally a day of rest. You ask yourself a thousand questions, suffer from a thousand doubts and regrets, and fight the desire to run away. Living is crazy enough, but singing! Finally you go to bed early with a good sleeping pill, following the rule "Well-rested body, golden voice."

The most exciting days are the start of rehearsals. Unlike actors, who often rehearse with script in hand, singers already know their roles by heart, having worked on them for months with a coach to "set the voice," as we say. (Those days, alone with the pianist and oneself, are the most self-centered, and they provide a secret pleasure as we seek to marry the words to the awesome alchemy of the music. What bliss we have at times!)

So you go "into rehearsal," becoming a bit detached; everything else becomes secondary. You withdraw into the role, trying to extract the maximum with your voice, your heart, your head. Your partners can help or not, the director can add much or nothing, the conductor can help you or destroy you. And then there are the Tower of Babel days, when the hundred and ten musicians, the eighty choristers, and the supernumeraries arrive and you wander about, sing, discuss, argue, or joke from nervousness, accumulated fatigue, question-racked nights of insomnia. From all those long days, from ten in the morning to midnight, there emerges a well-blended sauce or a fallen soufflé. But when an opera—which contains all the disciplines of music, song, dance, gesture—succeeds, it's a total entertainment that nothing else can equal.

The most tiring days are the fittings: of costumes, wigs, shoes, when you have to battle with the designer about changing a cut, a drape, the color. (Unlike many colleagues, I don't hate green, but, rather, pale blue. And standing exhausts me.)

The craziest days? Those of the pre–dress rehearsal and dress rehearsal, when nervousness and last-minute changes upset everyone. And the evening of the premiere, the director and designers sit in the house almost tranquilly, while for us, everything is merely beginning.

There are, all the same, relaxed days at the hairdresser's, or at the dressmaker's to choose new gowns for concerts. Aside from the pleasure it gives, I place great importance on dressing well, for before you sing a note, the audience watches you enter, and it's reassuring to feel elegant, or at least comfortable, in a color that becomes you. My armoires were always crammed with evening dresses, because if I sang a concert in Paris in February and then a recital in June, it was unthinkable to wear the same gown. And not the following year either. Prima donna oblige!

There are also the secretary days, devoted entirely to the telephone, to letters, to signing photos, to answering invitations—out of town, no time, not free—to accepting or rejecting professional engagements, to airplane tickets, hotel reservations, tax returns (who else can hunt around among my bills, receipts, and pay stubs?), appointments, interviews to arrange, a page-turner to find for the recital—tomorrow. At six o'clock you give up and go on strike.

Then there are the days-of-preparing-a-recital, this art of the infinitesimal, of expression with a light touch, in which—with the pianist's complicity—you must be your own boss, your own stage director, motionless and naked in the curve of the piano, where after having analyzed and digested the music and words, you must justify not yourself but the composer, where you must evoke a universe in which there is no explosion as in the opera but rather an implosion. An enormous and delicate labor, for which I thank those who were my frequent partners: my beloved John Wustman the American, Christian Ivaldi the Frenchman, and the late Geoffrey Parsons the Englishman.

But there are the luxuriant days, of going out to the theater, to the cinema (I could happily see three films in an afternoon), to pleasant dinners with friends. Those are the true rewards.

THERE IS A DOWNSIDE TO THE DIVA'S LIFE THAT YOU discover only as you age, when you realize that all the success, all the adoration, all the bouquets do not keep you warm in your lonely bed, do not take the place of a husband, a friend, or a child who needs comforting.

No one knows the weariness in your back, your nerves, your hands, your skin when you get home after a performance, with no desire to look at your thoughts in the mirror or at the book yawning on your bed. Too tired to arrange your beautiful flowers in vases, you leave them in the bathtub with a bit of water. And who would believe that you sleep little, and badly, because the role has so taken you over that real life is slow to return.

You're erratic, people say. But if your costar is uncooperative or absent from rehearsals, if a journalist asks the same idiotic question for the umpteenth time, if the photographer shoots you from your worst angle, if your fans try to force your door at intermission to steal your fifteen minutes of rest, and get angry if you object, if they boo you when you have a cold or are out of form or sad—well, you have good reason, no?

You are paid a lot of money, but why be ashamed? You've earned it. You've become a little selfish; you've gotten used to all the little gifts and special favors.

You save all your heartbreak, all your pain, to use later onstage. But how can you do otherwise? For you love this drug-profession that consumes you but that you will miss one day. Oh, you prepare yourself little by little, but it's painful, because you've almost always played queens, princesses, heroic figures, and you don't always have the chance, as actors do, to change your repertoire as you age, to portray people less young or more ugly, to take the comic roles for which the public reproaches you because they want to see you perpetually in the roles that brought you glory, keeping your youth and theirs intact.

Do you even have the right, after several decades of good and

The Art of Singing

loyal service to music, to a retirement without scorn? Brigitte Bardot was able to stop making films without being faulted. But as soon as *you* show a sign of fatigue, of weariness, people are quick—too quick—to say, "She's finished!" And that hurts.

You have friends galore when you're on top, ablaze, when your life is spread out in glossy magazines or scandal sheets. And after a lonely death—isn't that right, Maria?—numerous books are perpetrated in your name.

What tenderness, admiration, compassion I have for my sisters. Because the public doesn't realize, doesn't *want* to realize, that each of us is simply a woman.

Buenos Aires, Mis Amores

I remember cities the way one remembers love.
VALÉRY LARBAUD

W HEN THE name Teatro Colón is spoken, I don't
think there's a singer anywhere who doesn't smile
in happy reminiscence. I know I do. I adore this
great theater of more than four thousand seats and superb
acoustics, a copy of the Palais Garnier in Paris.

During the many years I sang there, the work we did was
remarkable: three or four weeks of rehearsal for each production, with the most renowned directors, conductors, and singers. And the operagoers are among the most knowledgeable,
enthusiastic, and loyal in the world. I've known a lot of audiences, but those in Buenos Aires won my heart forever, and
they know it.

Ours is a long love story that began in 1961. I was invited to
sing five performances of *Parsifal* and *Der Rosenkavalier,* and
that first visit was difficult, almost painful. I was alone, I didn't
speak Spanish, and at the time I was pretty unsociable, shy, and
withdrawn. I was staying at a dreary hotel, not yet the apart-

ments at the Edificio Charcas, where all the top singers stayed. Outside the rehearsals I saw no one and suffered from both homesickness and—because he was joining me only a month later—Lou's absence. Time seemed long.

On a sunny Sunday afternoon I took a walk along the river, in a city that seemed deserted. I kept having gloomy visions, imagining that if I were hit by a car I would be taken to a hospital where no one would know who I was, and I would die far from my country, Paris, and Lou.

I worked myself into such a state that I sat down and cried on a bench just opposite a bus stop. One of the drivers, waiting for his "customers," sat down next to me and started to talk in Spanish. I answered in Italian, which I spoke fluently at the time, and it turned out that he was Italian. He understood how I felt, alone and far from home, and asked what I was doing in Buenos Aires. I was sure he would think I was crazy if I answered truthfully, so I invented a job as a housekeeper for an Italian family. With that, the time came for him to leave, and he invited me for a ride along the river in his bus. He sat me down just behind him and explained everything we saw, even making detours over the objections of the other passengers, who were familiar with the normal route. At one point he got up and yelled at them:

"So what! She's my *paisana* and she has the blues. We can at least help her see a little of the city, no?"

Everyone applauded.

I felt bad later at the thought that he might come to the opera, recognize me, and think I had been making fun of him. But it was a unique introduction to a beautiful city and the kindness of its inhabitants.

I sang my two operas with much success and was quickly invited for the following season to do *Tosca* and *Pénélope*, a little-known work by Fauré that the Colón had the courage to mount for me. That season was the start of the delirium, especially after *Tosca*, the much more popular work. The matinee performance, which was always on Sunday at five o'clock, was total madness: the police had to help us leave the theater, and we had to sign three or four hundred photos before people would tear themselves away. And that was the start of what I call my "Mafia," a group of young men and women from sixteen to twenty who were crazy for Crespin and have been my friends ever since. It's very touching to have known them so young and to see them now: doctors, lawyers, businessmen, school principals, psychologists, and the like.

There were about twenty of them, and the "capo" was Barbara, a young girl of German origin, who would wait for hours at my hotel with beautiful flowers. We would communicate by gesture rather than in German—which I spoke badly—or Spanish. The other "elder" was Rodolfo, my *petit amour*, full of sweetness and with a delightful smile. Then came Amalia, Marina, and Rina; Pedro, who also became a very close friend; Adolfo and Eduardo, two brothers, equally charming and handsome as gods; Gustavo the bookseller; Lalla, Antonio, and others. Everyone at the theater soon called them "Crespin's Mafia." They even gave me an engraved medallion that says, "To R.C., her Mafia."

It was that year, after a performance of *Pénélope*, I think, that I invited them all to supper at a little French restaurant and, with the owner playing accordion, astonished them by singing pop songs. As we left, I held Barbara's hand in one of mine and

Rodolfo's in the other, and he swore he wouldn't wash the hand that *she* had held for three days. A promise he kept.

Yes, they love other singers, too. But for them, I am *"Ella!"*

I RETURNED IN MAY 1964 FOR TWO WORKS I HADN'T done before: *Les Troyens* and *Iphigénie en Tauride*.

The *Troyens* was a condensation of the two sections, *La Prise de Troie* and *Les Troyens à Carthage*. I sang the roles of Cassandre and Didon, which gave me the chance to kill myself not once but twice in the same evening! Two superb roles: Cassandre, impassioned, visionary, despairing; Didon, proud queen touched by love, who experiences every womanly emotion before immolating herself after Aeneas's departure. What a scene, Didon's imprecations and death.

Iphigénie was another wonderful character for me, a reserved personage with a beautiful vocal line. Louis Erlo did the superb staging, and we all produced such echoes that the Paris Opéra presented it with the same team, as well as *Les Troyens* some time later, staged by Margherita Wallmann.

The greatest hysteria was in 1965, when I went back to the Colón for five concert performances of *La Damnation de Faust* and five staged performances each of *Werther* and *Tosca*.

When I descended from the plane, all my Mafiosi, who were on the airport terrace, burst into a chorus of "Gloire à Didon" from *Les Troyens*, changing the words to "Gloire à Crespin!" Then, when I entered the terminal a rain of flowers floated down on me. The customs agents waved me through and applauded, without really understanding why.

After I kissed everyone and got into the car with the Colón's director, Juan Montero, and his wife, Elsa, two cars packed with my little ones led the way, proceeding side by side because there was an immense bedsheet stretched between the two, hand-painted with these words: "Vive Crespin! Vive la France!"

Those are things I can't forget.

At my entrance in the first *Damnation* concert, the Mafiosi kept the applause going for a solid ten minutes, making me tremble at the thought that I might not sing well enough to merit it.

I could see almost all of them, seated in the front rows, as I began my first words:

> *Que l'air est étouffant!*
> *J'ai peur comme une enfant. . . .*

My singing wasn't bad that evening, and the chorus was in splendid voice. Beautiful!

Charlotte in *Werther*, all gentleness, tenderness, and restraint, was a very big success, but the crowning glory was *Tosca*. The character is well rounded, a womanly woman who displays everything: love, femininity, tenderness, jealousy, joy, fear, aggressiveness, repulsion; a woman who goes all the way, even to committing murder, to save her lover from Scarpia's clutches. And it's beautiful to sing, although difficult. You can imagine that with the affectionate Argentine public firing me up, I sang my heart out.

Juan Montero called me in one day to ask if I would sing an extra performance with the great Italian tenor Giuseppe Di Stefano—Pippo—who was making his overdue Teatro Colón debut in *Un Ballo in Maschera* but who had decided he would prefer to begin with *Tosca*. A Sunday matinee had been added, but I was doing the final scheduled performance on Saturday night, and singers almost never perform on consecutive days, especially such a vocally and physically grueling role as Tosca. I tried to persuade Juan to replace me at the Saturday performance, but he absolutely refused, arguing that his subscribers would set fire to the theater if I didn't show up. I was worried enough to ask the advice of a famous laryngologist, who told me:

"*Ma belle,* you're going to sing, or I'll kick you in . . . to the theater myself. Come see me Sunday at noon. I'll give you a shot of muscle strengtheners and you can tell me how you feel."

Under the threat of a friendly kick, I obeyed. And I sang even better on Sunday than I had on Saturday! But it was the busiest performance of my life. Poor Di Stefano was at the end of his career and his voice was far from its former velvet and charm. And he realized it, suffering a martyrdom that I shared with him. The audience, knowing his voice well from all his recordings, gave him an ovation at his entrance and applauded his first-act aria, but little by little the voice deteriorated, and the third-act aria wasn't very good. Understanding that this was an artist in trouble, the audience was respectful and polite, and didn't demonstrate at all. But an incident happened at the end.

During the entire performance, I had tried my best to support him and encourage him, and I truly suffered with him and for him.

It's the custom, after the second act, for Scarpia to take a solo bow, since he doesn't appear in the third act, and sometimes the tenor and soprano do the same.

As Di Stefano didn't want to go before the curtain alone, I

didn't go either, because we would have the third act together and I would be able to take my curtain call then.

At the end we went out to bow together, then with the conductor, and in front of the curtain Di Stefano murmured something that propriety prevents me from repeating, but which translates to: "You really had me in the second act. You kept me from taking a solo bow."

My blood boiled! Stunned, truly hurt, I pulled my hand from his and left the stage. Behind the curtain he said more to me, at which I pulled my wig off and refused to go onstage with him again. I ran back to my dressing room in tears.

But the audience, which thought only that Di Stefano had twisted my hand, kept calling for me, and started to yell in cadence:

"Cres-pin! Cres-pin! Cres-pin!"

They were still calling after I had removed my costume. Montero came to beg me to go out again, and I said I would if Di Stefano went too. Poor Montero ran from one dressing room to the other, which took some time, since they were on opposite sides of the stage. When everyone had finally agreed, I put my gown and wig back on and went behind the curtain to join Di Stefano, who was in street clothes. As soon as he saw me he turned around and walked off. I didn't know what to do. And then Juan Montero came up to me and begged me quietly, "They're going to destroy the theater. *Dios mío!*"

So back I went in front of the curtain, pulling Montero along with me. He soon left me alone, and the audience—which didn't know what had happened but thought someone had done something to its darling Crespin—went wild. I don't know how many times I tried to leave and was called back. And eventually the audience invaded the stage and the wings, because the story circulated about what had happened. They were still waiting as I left the theater, and six men had to buffer me from the crowd (poor Pippo managed to leave by a basement door). I succeeded in getting into a friend's car and something really stupefying happened: some of the fans lifted the Peugeot and carried it to the end of the street, shouting:

"Viva Régine! Viva la Diva!"

Several years later I was in the audience when Di Stefano returned to La Scala in *Carmen*. I was very moved by his performance and went to his dressing room to congratulate him. He was surrounded by a large crowd, which he forced his way through to take me in his arms and kiss me. I was very happy with the gesture, and with the end of a silly disagreement.

I WENT BACK TO BUENOS AIRES SEVERAL TIMES: IN 1969 for *Parsifal,* a concert with orchestra, and a recital at the Colón, where I introduced a cycle of mélodies written for me by my dear friend Charlie Pemberton; in 1971 for other recitals; in 1974 for concerts and recitals.

And if you think I've exaggerated about the other events, listen to what happened in 1976.

I was engaged for two concerts with orchestra at the Teatro Coliséo. And a television station invited me to be the guest of honor on an important one-hour interview program. During the interview, someone asked why I wasn't going to be in the *Carmen* that the Teatro Colón was presenting, especially since I had recently had such good reviews for my performances in the opera in New York. I answered truthfully that I hadn't been asked. The host then asked if perhaps I was too expensive for a theater currently undergoing a serious financial crisis, and I said I loved the Colón and its audiences so much, I would be happy to do a performance for nothing.

The next day I was in the middle of an orchestra rehearsal at the Coliséo when someone told me the mayor would like to talk to me. I watched a smiling man approach, and the first thing he said was, "May I take you at your word?"

As I gaped at him he added, "Yes, this *Carmen*, when do you want to sing it?"

I started to laugh, and not wanting to go back on my word, made an appointment to discuss it.

The man who had organized my concerts worked out an agreement with the mayor by which I would sing two performances, the first one to be paid and the second gratis. (In fact, I was paid for neither the *Carmen* nor my two concerts, because the checks bounced!)

The news spread like wildfire and a line formed around the theater for tickets (some people spent a day and a night there). Of course I got tickets to the two performances for my excited Mafiosi. I sang the premiere before a house full of officials, who applauded warmly.

But the second performance, my gift to the public, was one of the most memorable nights of my career. I don't know how many people above the house limit managed to get in; they were stuffed everywhere. The atmosphere was supercharged, and I gave everything I had. When it was over, all was delirium. We took our first bows at midnight, and at one o'clock they were still going on. I don't know how many solo calls I took, ankle-deep in the flowers that had rained down at my first bow (the

Buenos Aires, Mis Amores

Mafiosi confessed that they alone had bought one hundred dozen). I laughed, I cried, I didn't know where I was. And then a tidal wave of shouts began:

"Telón! Telón! Telón!"

I asked backstage what that meant and was told that the audience wanted the curtain to be opened and for me to appear alone in the middle of the empty stage. It was a tribute that had been accorded to only one woman before me: the dancer Maya Plisetskaya. Would I accept?

Would I accept? Oh, yes, with all my heart and soul!

When I found myself alone on that immense, nude stage, with a sea of flowers at my feet, facing an entire audience on its feet, shouting my name, applauding, crying, stamping their feet, I started to sob, overwhelmed and pained by so much love, because for a moment the theater made me think of "mine," the Paris Opéra, where I had been so cruelly treated two years earlier in my own country.

So it's easy to see why Buenos Aires for me is "Mis Amores."

T H I R T E E N

❧

Microphone:
My Friendly Nightmare

To die leaving work behind is to die less.

ROGER MARTIN DU GARD

R ECORDING was always a torture for me, fear to the thousandth degree.

Fear of an audience is healthy; it stimulates you. The people are there in front of you, quiet or sniffling, holding their breath or unwrapping a candy, listening or dozing, but they breathe, they're alive, reacting to good or bad moments. With them there can be mutual lovefests. But how can you fall in love with a microphone?

First of all, a microphone is ugly. It's a cold, steel, impersonal thing, suspended above your head or resting on a pole just in front of your nose. And it defies you, like HAL the computer in Stanley Kubrick's film *2001: A Space Odyssey*, although at least he talked.

No, the microphone waits, unpitying, insensitive and ultra-sensitive at the same time, and when it speaks, it's to repeat everything you've said word for word. The beast; you'd think it would at least be kind enough to correct a note slightly flat or sharp, a missing semiquaver, a German word pronounced incorrectly.

Kind, my foot! It seems rather to be saying:

"I don't smoke, I don't drink, and I don't talk; I imitate! You're on your own. And be careful: if you yowl too loudly, I'll switch off!"

An antipathetic type, no? There were days when I hated it with all my heart.

From fear, of course. Because what it played back seemed, at first, to be someone else's voice, not mine. And I was never satisfied. I always wanted to start over, to improve what I had done.

Instead of thinking about the beauty of the music, of the singing, I concentrated on that piece of steel that would send me into posterity.

I needed a lot of time to be won over, to get used to it and forget about it. To reach the point where I could think, "Let it go to the devil, it and its seeming impassiveness."

I would take an aspirin, and in place of the microphone I would envision a friendly audience or the man I loved.

For my first recording—arias from *William Tell, Il Trovatore, Otello, Tannhäuser,* and *Damnation de Faust*—I hardly noticed the micro, because I was totally unaware of the danger it represented. I was in love, and somnolent.

But when I went to the booth to listen to the takes I thought: "That's my voice? That? Bizarre." Otto Ackermann, the conductor, and Michel Glotz, who produced the record, watched over the poor innocent that I was. And the result wasn't half bad.

The second record, French opera arias, which I made for the

Vega label, was the first nightmare. It seemed to me that the orchestra was too thundering (it was!), so I howled as loudly as I could during all the sessions: it was a battle to the death between me and "it."

When I received the record, I detested it and put it aside for years, until the summer of 1979 when my friend Pedro from Buenos Aires ignored my protests and played the *Reine de Saba* aria twice a day. And every day he quietly added another track until I finally admitted that the record wasn't so bad.

That's why I don't like to listen to my records. Either I hear only the mistakes and wish I could do it over, or I love myself.

The next project, I think, was two records with Georges Prêtre, *The Voice of Wagner* and *Verdi Arias*. Little by little, I began to learn the craft of recording.

I learned when to stand back while still facing front for a high and strong note, to turn my head slightly for a certain effect, to move closer to the microphone to emphasize a breath, to avoid wearing bracelets that would clink against the music stand or a necklace that would move when I breathed.

I learned to adapt to the acoustics of the hall where we were recording: good, flat, or too resonant; to the teams of holy engineers who knew their craft down to their fingertips but who were generally very touchy. You have to learn to know their reactions, to trust them; they know well before you do which take is the best. Finally, it's the technician who's the strongest. If he doesn't like you, if you annoy him, *aïe!*

But they always had a soft spot for me, even if they saw me arrive a little fearfully because the big voices are the most difficult to record faithfully.

The Decca Boys would say: "Brace yourselves! Here comes

Microphone: My Friendly Nightmare

the French cannon!" But they're the ones who "packaged" me best, along with Fan-Fan the funny and Vava the serious at Pathé-Marconi.

I knew, too, that if Michel Glotz of the finely tuned ear said, "That's fine, children," we would be redoing it in a minute. But if he said, "Good! What do we do now?" it was "in the can."

I knew that if Christopher Raeburn of Decca (his first record as a producer was my excerpts from *Der Rosenkavalier*) played with his beard without saying anything, we would have to redo it. But if he said, "It was superb, my deeeeaaar!" all was well.

If Mr. Garcin, at Erato, buried his nearsighted eyes and his Mephistophelean beard in the score, blah! But if he and his sweet, silent wife laughed, it was fine. Although sometimes Jean-Pierre Brossman, the other super ear, would secretly give me a quizzical look, and I would request a retake.

My great love was John Culshaw, who produced so many records for Decca, the last of which was *The Ring* conducted by Georg Solti. John had crinkly eyes, an enormous knowledge of singers, and a very English sense of humor. I found him irresistible. But he only liked snakes.

The people at Deutsche Grammophon were serious as popes—the unfunny ones—but what work they did!

I had to learn also how to do "takes," those tiny bits of recording about five or ten minutes long that are never in the normal order of the score. You can easily begin a session with the end of the third act or the duet from the second. And you have to get into whatever mood is required immediately, like making a movie. Not always easy!

Above all, there's the physical fatigue, the nervous tension,